Pliny's Warning

ANNE MARIA NICHOLSON

Pliny's Warning

HarperCollins*Publishers*

To Peter, Stephen and Eva — my shining stars.

National Library of New Zealand Cataloguing-in-Publication Data
Nicholson, Anne Maria.
Pliny's warning / Anne Maria Nicholson.
ISBN 978-1-86950-773-2
I. Title.
NZ823.3—dc 22

First published 2009
HarperCollins*Publishers (New Zealand) Limited*
P.O. Box 1, Shortland Street, Auckland

ISBN 978 1 86950 773 2

Cover design by Louise McGeachie
Cover images by Shutterstock.com
Typesetting by Springfield West

Printed by Griffin Press, Australia

70gsm Bulky Book Ivory used by HarperCollins*Publishers* is a
natural, recyclable product made from wood grown in sustainable
forests. The manufacturing processes conform to the environmental
regulations in the country of origin, New Zealand.

Acknowledgements

I would like to thank the many people who helped me along my journey of writing *Pliny's Warning*. I thank them for their generous encouragement, knowledge and hospitality.

In particular, I am grateful to Anthea Bulloch, Benedetto de Vivo, Jean-Pierre Brun, Nicola Severino, Giuseppe Rolandi, Pier Paolo Petrone, Giuseppe Mastrolorenzo, Lucia Pappalardo, Grete Stefani, Vittorio Scribano, Robert Bodnar, Katherine Owen, Verica Jokic, Aniela Kos, Catherine De Vrye, David Neilson and Taute Tocker.

In form and shape the column of smoke was like a tremendous pine tree, for at the top of its great height it branched out into several skeins. I assume that a sudden burst of wind had carried it upwards and then dropped it, leaving it motionless, and that its own weight then spread it outwards. It was sometimes white, sometimes heavy and mottled, as it would be if it had lifted up amounts of earth and ashes.

PLINY THE YOUNGER, 79 AD

Pliny the Younger is hailed as the world's first vulcanologist. The Roman poet and scholar was just seventeen when Mt Vesuvius erupted spectacularly in 79 AD, destroying the cities of Pompeii and Herculaneum.

His harrowing and descriptive eyewitness accounts of the three days of devastation, observed from his home in Misenum, across the Bay of Naples from the volcano, are still referred to by scientists today.

His uncle, Pliny the Elder, was the commander of the Imperial Roman Fleet. He perished in the aftermath of one of the eruptions when he sailed away from his home and nephew, across to the settlement of Stabiae to rescue friends in peril.

AUTHOR'S NOTE

Although *Pliny's Warning* is a novel, many of the events it describes in the past happened. The contemporary story contains detailed scientific data based on the latest research undertaken by vulcanologists and archaeologists working in southern Italy.

It is true that Vesuvius remains the world's most dangerous volcano. The threat of an eruption greater than the one that destroyed Pompeii remains very real. Millions of people live around it and would be trapped because of the proliferation of illegal development and congested roads.

It is also true that the people of Naples continue to deal with another threat — the corrupt forces of the Camorra, which controls much of that grand old city's finances.

AMN
2009

CHAPTER ONE

A tiny white patch glowing beneath a bed of sea grass catches Frances Nelson's eye. Her calf muscles tighten as she kicks her flippers hard and dives deeper into the turquoise Mediterranean waters, searching for answers from a lost civilisation to the threatening volcanic cataclysm.

Hovering on the ocean floor, she brushes aside lime green fronds, hunting for the source. Suddenly, she senses a movement close to her face. An eye, like a cat's, gleams, staring straight into her mask. Frances topples back, her air tank banging against a rock behind her. An eel, brown and yellow striped, darts its head out from a bunch of sea lilies.

Her heart pounds, the sound ricocheting into the back of her head; just as fast, the eel retracts. She sucks a mouthful of bitter brine and nearly gags. She spits, forcing the water out of her mouth. Stay calm, whatever you do, stay calm, she tells herself. It's just an eel, not some killer monster from the deep.

Biting hard into her respirator, the bubbles course thickly around her, betraying her rapid breathing as she looks around for Marcello Vattani. Where the hell is he? She can still see the white glow just below and it draws her back, irresistibly, like the Sirens who were said to have lured ancient mariners to their deaths with their beautiful songs, on this very coast. She kicks her flippers again and dives, avoiding the eel's hiding place and heading straight to the bottom.

Sunbeams penetrating the depths shine like torches on a row of tiny white mosaic tiles. She plucks out the seagrass and sweeps away pebbles and stones with her hands. A pattern is forming, black and white, some sort of clover shape, almost medieval in its appearance, but she knows it's much older. A heartachingly minute relic of the Roman empire, it's at least two thousand years old. She touches a fan-shaped rock. It yawns open and the camouflaged clam slams shut, missing her hand by a second.

Frances starts as she feels a tug on her arm. She turns around. Marcello is there, larger than life. There's something about being underwater that magnifies everything and as he smiles, his brown eyes are surreal, enlarged behind his mask. He swims around her, lithe as a dolphin. Raising his hand, he makes a circle with his thumb and finger, asking if she's OK. Yes, she signals back.

She'd love to blurt out her discovery. After all, this is where oratory was once highly prized, the pleasure resort of old Baia, an oasis for the ruling elite escaping Rome's unbearably hot summers. Emperors plotted here as they feasted and the cleverest and most cunning of minds gathered to debate the pressing matters of state.

But in these sunken ruins of once glorious villas there's no longer any scope for words or conversation. Struck dumb, she is reduced to pointing lamely at the mosaics.

Even through his mask, Frances can sense Marcello's excitement. It's the archaeologist in him, buoyed by decades of digging around on land and under the sea, always searching to discover something new from something old. She watches him, his fit body accentuated by his wetsuit, clearing more of the grass.

The pattern runs out. Brown rock bridges a gap to another group of mosaics. They work together, brushing away purple algae clinging to the tiny square stone chips. Gradually the chips form a different pattern in colours of maroon, black, yellow, blue and green, just like the join-the-dots pictures she did as a child. It's broken and much is missing but the picture is clear; a portrait of a woman, hair coiffured and curled around a headband in the fashionable style of ancient Rome, lips full, eyes almond-shaped and crowned with darkly defined eyebrows. Around her throat is a chain of gold. Familiar, but Frances can't quite place her. Is it the face of one of the women who presided here before this house, the Villa Julia, joined the procession of summer palaces and sank into the ocean?

Frances wonders if it is Julia herself, the profligate daughter of Emperor Augustus Caesar. Like a chattel, married off to his friend and loyal general, Marcus Vipsanius Agrippa; then to her stepbrother and father's successor, the brutal Emperor Tiberius Caesar. Even through this veil of water, her face is strong and alluring, a hint of defiance in her smile, as if she knew she would eventually have the last laugh, her immortality finally realized.

Or maybe she's another dutiful daughter of Rome, or a goddess? Heaven knows, Frances has seen plenty of similar images, both Roman and Greek, since she'd arrived in southern Italy to work on the volcanoes project. She wonders if Marcello recognizes the mystery woman.

They scrape around further but the mosaics have petered out. Marcello takes his camera from a bag around his wrist. He shoots and the bright flash pierces the watery gloom.

The two divers leave the portrait behind in a trail of bubbles, gliding together past rows of seaweed-covered foundation stones. Frances pauses to touch one of the ancient building blocks, encrusted with shells and barnacles. It pricks her fingers. In the water, her hand looks green and ghostly and she pulls it away. She swims further, past remnants of walls that tell her little of the opulence and revelries that used to fill this space. There's another wrecked villa ahead and the mortar skeleton of the public baths. All that remains of this jewel of the imperial empire are ghostly souvenirs, sharing the seabed with fish and molluscs, like a Pompeii under the sea.

But Frances is anxious to move on. Old bones and mosaics are interesting, but it's the new seismic threat beneath the waves that really excites her as a vulcanologist. She checks her air monitor. A hundred and fifty. Plenty left. She nudges Marcello and points ahead and they glide on, side by side.

Images of the past continue to plague her as she moves through the ruins. Some of history's most renowned and infamous rulers, the emperors Julius, Augustus, Tiberius, Claudius, Caligula and Nero cavorted here with their rivals and followers, in debauchery and bloody treachery.

She wonders whether they had any idea that not only would they soon perish, but the sea would also consume their coastal paradise? It was as relentless a conquest as their own centurions' marches through the ancient world.

They came here to Campi Flegrei, the land of fire, for the sun and miraculous hot thermal waters that flowed through their magnificent bath houses, never guessing that the source of their pleasure would one day rear up against them.

The ancient Romans believed the craters of the volcanoes around them were gateways to hell and stayed away, but as they expanded their empire, they were oblivious to nature exerting its superior power. Lakes of red hot magma bubbled below them, gradually forcing the land up and then dropping it, a relentless cycle of rising and falling until the cliffs collapsed and the town surrendered to the waves. Once the villas of Baia were the pride of the Mediterranean. Now they are eroding monuments in a sunken ghost town.

Frances swims ahead strongly, more confident than her first dive here with Marcello. For once, she is the leader and he the follower. They slow as they move deeper, skimming above a submerged forest of fronds. Frances pulls her depth gauge and compass from her belt and holds them close to her mask to check. Ten, eleven, twelve metres and heading south towards her target, the ruins of Portus Julius, the harbour built by Agrippa to provide a safe haven for Rome's naval fleet.

She feels her ears pop, pinches her nose and steadies her breathing. As the seabed slopes, two long lines of massive square-shaped pillars appear ahead of them, once part of the port's engineering armoury to protect the shoreline, each one coated with layers of weeds and shells. They zigzag in and out of them like a pair of skiers on a slalom run. At the bottom of the slope the pillars run out. Frances knows they're near and holds up her hand to signal Marcello to stop, pointing to piles of broken stones littering the bottom.

The cracks look fresh, whiter marble showing beneath their weathered exteriors. Must have happened a day or two ago. Large patches of yellow sulphur stain the sea floor and bubbles pop out of holes beneath the sand. Some are tiny specks and others large and fast moving. As Frances moves closer, a sudden surge of hot water smacks her face and throws her backwards, spinning in the water. The force knocks her respirator out of her mouth and hot water floods into her mask, washing over her face. A horrible taste fills her mouth as she chokes on a watery chemical cocktail. She blinks. Her eyes are stinging. She can't see.

Marcello moves swiftly and grabs her, holding her firmly. She feels him push his spare breathing apparatus into her mouth. She clings to him, eyes shut. She breathes slowly from his air tank. In, out, in, out. Keep calm, she tells herself. She starts to regain control, holds onto her mask and blows some air through her nose. It clears away the water trapped in the mask and she can see again. She reaches behind her back to retrieve her own respirator. The tube is tangled up in her tank but she frees it and quickly replaces Marcello's mouthpiece with her own. He's watching her closely and gives her the thumbs up to end the dive. But she doesn't want to, not yet. She still has work to do. She signals to Marcello she's OK to continue and they swim further on, careful now not to get too close to the bottom.

A few metres on a column has fallen and smashed into pieces. Then another and another — a whole line of columns has collapsed. The ground beneath is cracked with gaps as wide as a handspan and the bubbling of water and gas is much stronger.

This is what Frances feared. Back at the observatory she'd seen evidence of seismic tremors that had shaken all of the Campi Flegrei area, on along the deep lake of magma that connected it to Mt Vesuvius in nearby Naples, and further out into the Mediterranean to the ancient volcanoes in the Aeolian Islands. The earthquakes were small but there were dozens of them over two days. The scientific team had spread out to analyse the damage, Frances putting up her hand to inspect the underwater archaeological site.

Marcello is agitated, upset by the damage, darting quickly, photographing smashed pillars that had survived so many other disasters over so many centuries.

Frances fears the destructive volcanic power is back with a vengeance. The rising and falling of the land that doomed ancient Baia has never stopped, and now it's gathering pace, putting the entire coastline at risk.

She has seen this same dramatic volcanism before, pounding another landscape, far away on the other side of the world. Although the water is warm and she's wearing a wetsuit, she shivers, remembering what happened on an island in the Pacific.

No one lived on the island. But here, millions of people lived along the coast, where ancient Roman villas that had been the prizes of the victorious lay ten metres beneath the sea.

As she swims through the hot bubbling mass of water, Frances feels as if time has stopped — she can almost hear the rumblings of the same dangerous forces echo through the millennia.

CHAPTER TWO

Frances accelerates as she reaches a short clear stretch of road leading home to her apartment high on the western hill overlooking the Bay of Naples. The traffic is as impossible as ever and her motorbike is coated in dust after the ride back from Baia. Corso Vittorio Emanuele throbs with vehicles, people on the pavements scurrying in and out, shopping for their evening meal.

The sun is setting and Frances glances towards Mt Vesuvius across the bay, rising sharply above the city. But the metropolis seems to fight its presence, majestic and threatening at the same time, covering it with a smoggy haze. She squints into the light that bounces off the yellow, ochre and white apartment buildings hugging the street, their little balconies festooned with lines of washing.

A horn beeps loudly. She looks in her side mirror and a truck driver waves at her furiously. She pulls over, too timid to stand her ground. The driver, black hair swept back in the latest style, winds down his window and blows her a kiss. 'Bellissima!' he calls out as he cruises past.

Frances laughs at his cheek, glad to be back with the living rather than floating underwater with ghosts. She pulls out again and rides back into the traffic, her fatigue eased by the Italian flirt.

Struggling with the demands of scuba diving seems insignificant compared to the hair-raising antics of wending through Naples traffic. But she's come a long way since her arrival. At first, riding pillion on her roommate Riccardo's motorbike was truly terrifying. She'd clung to him like a child as he wove between trucks and cars or mounted the pavement to get through jams on their way to the observatory. Motorcyclists were the city's anarchists, breaching traffic rules, jumping red lights, anything they could get away with.

As a foreigner, she was reluctant to drive, but as her contract with Progetto Vulcano was for a year, she had figured the options weren't great. Cars were constantly caught up on overcrowded narrow roads, nearly all with a patina of dents and scratches testifying to the wild conditions. And she'd wasted far too many hours waiting for buses and trains that failed to arrive.

Frances navigates her silver Piaggio into a cobble-stoned lane, avoiding a woman laden with plastic shopping bags and a group of laughing teenagers chatting on cellphones. She loves this bike — she'd bought it a month ago as Riccardo and her schedules became increasingly divergent. It was all just a matter of keeping her nerve and keeping moving. And she never forgot one golden rule. Just as holding your breath while scuba diving was a death wish, so was closing your eyes for even a second riding through Naples.

A final burst of speed brings her into the courtyard, riding right up to two young boys, a tangle of arms and legs, pulling and pushing each other. She dismounts, removes her helmet and runs a hand through her shoulder-length fair hair.

'Hey Stefano, Lorenzo, stop that!' The twins are dressed alike in blue jeans with knee patches and red and white checked shirts. She ruffles the heads of the five-year-olds clambering around her trying to grab her helmet. 'How's that baby sister of yours?'

'We don't like her. She poos her nappies,' Stefano smirks. They shriek with laughter. 'Take us for a ride on your bike. Please, Francesca, please!'

'Not now. Maybe another time,' Frances laughs as she extracts herself from their hands. Before she reaches the heavy metal front door of the building, they've forgotten her and are wrestling again.

Above the entry, the large pink bow announcing Luciana's birth, eight weeks earlier, flutters in a soft breeze. She was born the day Frances arrived, but as a stranger, she hadn't known until she heard the unmistakable cries of a newborn some days later. She unlocks the door and climbs the first of the huge grey stone steps that lead up four steep storeys to her apartment, already used to doing without a lift, absent from many old buildings. By Neapolitan standards, though, this is quite new, just one hundred and fifty years or so old, a blip on the city's radar, compared to the eight-centuries-old places crowded into its ancient heart below.

On the second level, she hears the cellist and rests for a moment to listen. The music leaks through the closed door and envelops her on the stairwell, the notes sure and stirring. Bach or Beethoven? She's not sure.

'Ciao, Francesca!' Laura Fogliano emerges from her apartment above on the third floor, looking tired and unusually untidy. Her short black hair is uncombed and her large dark eyes have the drained look of a young mother lacking sleep.

'Ciao, Laura, how's Luciana?'

'You can hear for yourself,' Laura grumbles as the cries of the little girl cascade through the building. 'Sorry, I can't talk now — I've got to get those boys into the bath.' She rushes past to fetch her sons from the courtyard.

The doorway of the family's apartment is wide open and Frances exchanges waves with Laura's mother, Nonna Fabrizia, who is trying to calm her granddaughter. 'Calma, carissima, calma!' she coos, rocking the baby in her arms, her hips swaying.

As Frances opens her own door, she muses how different it all is to her previous two postings; the luxurious Seattle apartment in striking distance of the explosive Mt St Helens, and the quiet house at Lake Taupo nestled below New Zealand's volatile volcanoes. But this was her choice. After the emotional parting from Tori in New Zealand, she didn't want to be isolated.

The beat of so many lives crammed together in one building was a crazy atonal human symphony, offering a strange sort of comfort; the baby's cries blending with the cello, plates clinking in a kitchen over fragments of conversations, a games show blaring on a television.

Her place is dark and empty. She throws open the green shutters on the windows and the doors leading onto a small terrace. Shards of sunlight bounce off the white marble table and red leather sofa and fresh air breathes life back into the room.

Yanking off her worn boots that double for riding and climbing, she then pulls off her leather jacket, shirt, jeans and underwear and leaves them messily on the floor, walking naked into the bathroom. Her green eyes stare back at her from the mirror as she runs her hand again through her dishevelled hair. She wipes a line of dust and sweat coagulated in a crease around her mouth. The combination of the dive and constant congestion on the roads has exhausted her and she's feeling every one of her thirty-eight years.

She luxuriates under the hot shower, a contrast to the hurried wash at the dive shop, where she and Marcello removed their wetsuits and sloshed around on the cold concrete floors.

Looking down her muscular body to her feet she sees sand and pieces of shell collect on the bottom of the bath. The sight pricks a childhood memory; her mother washing her in the tub, wiping off debris trapped in her bathing suit after a rare visit to the British seaside. She makes a mental note to ring her mother. Soon.

A large bruise is forming on her left hip where she fell back hard on rocks under the sea. She rubs the blue purplish spot but doesn't feel any pain.

Lingering under the streaming flow, she considers the hot water and bubbling gas surging out of the seabed at Baia. How might they fit into a new pattern of volcanic activity throughout the Campania region? Seismic tremors are increasing and the seabed is frighteningly active. Early warning systems to predict what might happen are her speciality, but even she has to admit that whether the tremors are symptoms of a major eruption is pure guesswork.

The water runs cold. She adjusts the taps but there is no more hot water. Goose pimples form on her skin and she leaps out.

Frances pulls on a funky denim skirt decorated with Italian bling she'd picked up at the weekend market, a stylish pair of high black boots with Cuban heels and a fitted black T-shirt. Just as she's scooping her work clothes from the floor to her bedroom, she hears a key opening the door and a slam.

Riccardo is standing there, unusually quiet and fidgety. She greets him with a kiss on both cheeks.

'What's up? You look like someone's stolen your dinner.'

He forces a smile that creases his tanned, open face. He's missed a shave or two and black stubble on his chin matches the colour of his thick curls. 'Something odd is going on at the university and the observatory. I don't like the feel of it.'

'What do you mean?'

'I'm picking up some strange vibes. I've tried to talk about the research I've been doing with Marcello on the Avellino eruption of Vesuvius. Professor Corsi and Professor Caterno keep brushing me off. I've bumped into both of them in the last few days and they avoid me. They make me feel like I've got dog shit on my shoes!'

Frances looks fondly at her friend. In his early thirties, Riccardo Cocchia is a large, broad-shouldered, demonstrative man.

'Call me Ricky!' he had said, taking her under his wing when she'd arrived in Naples, offering up his spare room. 'That's what they call me in Australia.'

Other scientists had been less than friendly to her mixed pedigree from America, Britain and New Zealand. As an international vulcan-ologist, she'd experienced resentment before from people rusted onto their jobs, threatened by newcomers. But Riccardo was different, perhaps because he was an outsider himself. He had grown up in Melbourne but was drawn to Italy, his grandparents' homeland on the tumultuous island of Stromboli. He shared her passion for volcanoes and trying to predict their behaviour — it was in his blood.

Frances had often seen him embroiled in loud arguments. He didn't give way easily but he didn't bear grudges. She hated seeing him morose. 'Listen, why don't you clean up and we'll go out to eat. I'll tell you what Marcello and I discovered today. More bad news the venerable professors might not want to hear.'

'OK. And I've got something to show you.' He dangles his backpack in front of her with a mischievous smile that makes him look like a boy again.

The trattoria two streets away is busier than usual but Luca Barra, the proprietor, beams at them and beckons the two regulars inside. 'Ciao! Come in! All the window seats are gone but you can sit there if you like.'

He points to a small corner table at the rear of La Lanterna. The tables are dressed with cream embossed linen tablecloths, candles, fresh flowers, chunky silver cutlery and thick glasses for water and wine. Rich aromas of garlic, onions and herbs waft through the room and although it's just going on eight, many diners are well into their meals. At the largest table, seven people are ploughing into large pizzas, most of them the Neapolitan staple — margherita — topped with tomato, oil, buffalo mozzarella and a basil leaf or two. Another group is eating zuppa di pesce, large bowls of steaming fish soup.

Frances and Riccardo quickly order their favourite dish and wine, a bottle of falanghina from a vineyard near Baia.

'Salute, Frances! You know, it doesn't matter how bad the day is, a good bowl of pasta and a glass of vino always cheers me up.' Riccardo raises his glass to his lips and takes a small sip.

'I've noticed. It's contagious. I'm just as hooked as you now.' She gulps a large mouthful of wine and laughs when she sees Riccardo's surprise.

'You drink too quickly,' he chides her. 'That's what they do in Australia. It's not Italian!'

She grins at him, takes another big sip and tops up her glass.

The waiter delivers two plates, each wrapped in a crown of white crinkly paper. They quickly peel it off to reveal a pile of steaming tomato-coated pasta combining a feast from the sea: mussels, clams, prawns, calamari, octopus and fat chunks of fresh fish.

'Linguine ai frutta di mare! Buon appetito, eat up!' Riccardo urges her.

'This is delicious. It would cheer anyone up.' Frances winds the long strands of pasta around her fork and savours the taste. 'So what do you think is behind your snubbing? Caterno and Corsi set up Progetto Vulcano. Why would they behave like that?'

Riccardo sighs. 'There seems to be some double game. They ask us for information on the risk to the population, but when we come up with the goods, it's as if they don't want to know the bad news. They definitely don't want Marcello involved.'

'Well, he's been essential to my work; I couldn't have done the diving at Baia without him. Is it because Marcellos's an archaeologist? Professional rivalry?'

'Who would know!' Riccardo raises both his hands in frustration. 'But now we're sure of one thing. All of us, scientists and politicians, must change the way we look at Vesuvius. The volcano might be dormant but it is still lethal. All we ever hear about is the 79 AD Pompeii eruption, but the Avellino eruption, three-and-a-half thousand years ago, was much bigger. It destroyed all of the area where Naples now stands. It means the whole city is in danger.'

The restaurant hums with the sounds of sated diners but Frances has suddenly lost her appetite. She leans across the table towards him. 'And today we saw for ourselves how active it is under the seabed. There's been severe damage to the artefacts and it's really bubbling.'

Riccardo reaches under the table and drags out his backpack. 'By the way, this is what I wanted to show you.' He pushes his plate away, pulls out a cloth bundle and unwraps it on the table.

'My God . . . you've got to be kidding! They look human.'

'They are.' He runs a finger over three bones. 'Femur, tibia, skull. Bronze Age woman in her twenties, died 1780 BC. She was killed after the Avellino eruption. We've got plenty more back at the lab, and there are hundreds on the sites Marcello found and documented.'

'That's extraordinary. Can I touch?'

'Sure. She won't feel a thing.'

Frances looks closely at the skull, its mouth open with many teeth intact. She shudders, remembering another one she had found in the crater of Mt Ruapehu in New Zealand. If you dug around volcanoes long enough, bones would always make their way to the surface. 'You just wonder how she died.'

'We think we know. Suffocation. We found her with another skeleton, a male, underneath a metre of pumice. They had their hands over their faces. We could see the instant of their deaths.'

Frances gently touches the skull and tries to imagine what sort of life the woman had and whether she had any notion about the danger of Vesuvius. 'Will you take me to the site where you found her?'

'Sure, if I'm not banned from continuing the work.' He gently rewraps the ancient relics.

'Maybe we'll find out what the resistance is about tomorrow,' Frances muses. 'We've got all the team together so it could be the time to ask questions.'

Over Riccardo's shoulder, Frances sees a young man dining alone across the room. The candlelight picks up the cloudy greenish blue of his eyes.

'Looks like someone's stolen your dinner now, Frances. What is it?'

'It's odd. I've just seen someone who looks very familiar but I can't place him.'

Riccardo twists around and follows her gaze. 'That's Pasquale Mazzone. He's the one you hear playing cello in our building. Come and say hello.'

He has the gentlest of demeanours and his pale complexion is framed by auburn-coloured hair that illuminates his unusual eyes. 'Piacere di conoscerla. Pleased to meet you.' His voice is soft as he clasps her hand. 'I've seen you come and go on your motorbike.'

'And I've enjoyed hearing you play. The cello's a favourite of mine.'

'Then come inside one day and listen properly.'

When he smiles his eyes shine like precious stones. They unsettle her but Frances knows she will accept the invitation. She smiles back at him.

'Thanks. I'd love to.'

CHAPTER THREE

Rows of buzzing and blinking computer monitors fill the hub of the Naples Central Observatory, crowding the walls of the long room from floor to ceiling. The machines are a modern mirror of the innards of the ancient volcanoes of southern Italy.

'Attention, everyone. Before we begin our meeting, I want to show you the new equipment we have just acquired. Hopefully it will make our job a little easier.'

Professor Camilla Corsi stands in the centre of the Progetto Vulcano taskforce, eight scientists, handpicked for the joint project between the observatory and the university, assigned to bring together all the volcanic research in the region. She is slim and stylishly dressed in an expensive tailored black suit and crimson silk shirt, contrasting with the casually attired group she leads. Her thick black hair is brushed back and held with a comb, accentuating her carefully made-up angular face.

'These are the new generation of seismographic machines.' She points to a dozen newly installed computers against one wall. Her voice is deep for a woman's and attests to years of smoking that have made her look older than her forty-four years.

She balances on high-heeled designer shoes, flattering her shapely legs and disguising the fact that she is very short. 'They are twice as sensitive to earth tremors and sounds and will boost our capacity to predict any changes emanating from the magma below Mt Vesuvius, Campi Flegrei, Mt Etna in Sicily and Mt Stromboli in the Aeolian Islands.' She turns to her deputy.

'Professor Caterno, could you give a demonstration?' she gestures imperiously. 'Use the Stromboli example.'

The Professor of Vulcanology, Bartolo Caterno, is a solid, balding man, a good ten years older, and has the technical expertise Camilla lacks. If he resents playing second fiddle, he doesn't show it.

He turns on one of the computers. The screen lights up with a pink and blue hue. 'This is a replay of what happened last March when there was a large night-time explosion in the crater of Stromboli. Here it is captured on the infra-red camera.'

The video pictures of the rocks inside the crater are pink and blurry and remind Frances of the early moon landing images. There's a sudden bang, rocks explode, then the picture stops. He swings around in his chair.

'You see, we had all the equipment, all the seismographs placed all around the island and the flanks of the volcano, but no warning at all of the eruption.'

He turns back to the screen. 'Now watch this.'

Clear views of the crater appear.

'These are live pictures of the interior of the crater. You can see what is happening right now. It's very active with all the smoke and steam. Now keep watching.'

He taps the keyboard and the screen keeps switching to different angles from other cameras. 'So, we have the crater covered. Now look.'

He punches more codes on the next keyboard and the next. 'The wavering lines show what's happening in seismic terms. You can watch the cameras and see how they're reflecting the waves. Then this one here,' he points to a third screen, 'is picking up the sounds.'

'Thank you, Bartolo,' Professor Corsi interrupts. 'So what we are witnessing is a greatly increased sensitivity in the monitoring. We believe this will give us earlier warnings and more accuracy and with your help we will be improving that all the time.'

'But will they make the politicians more responsive to the public danger?' Riccardo's question hangs in the air.

Professor Corsi turns to him sharply. 'Signor Cocchia, maybe you should restrict your remarks to things you know about and not make such careless comments. I would like to remind all of you that we are scientists, not policy-makers. Our job is simple. We must present the best data, within our terms of reference.'

She turns on her heel and calls back over her shoulder. 'Please follow me. Our chancellor, Professor Galbatti, is waiting for us in the conference room and we can continue our meeting there.'

'Whew!' Frances exclaims too loudly before she can stop herself. Others in the group turn to look at her. Riccardo flashes her an amused glance and she crinkles her forehead in response. This is her first experience of Camilla's toughness and she wouldn't want to be in her firing line.

When Frances met her for the first time in her grand office in the university, she had been utterly beguiling. 'Welcome, Signorina Nelson, we're honoured you have come to Naples,' she had said, offering her manicured, red-painted nails. She had exuded charm and courtesy and was quite unlike any vulcanologist Frances had ever met.

'Political operator first. Scientist second. Powerful friends. Don't cross her,' Riccardo had warned.

Now they file behind the professor like schoolchildren, along a long corridor lined with images of Vesuvius, around into a foyer and through to a large meeting room.

'Ah Professor Galbatti, how kind of you to come.' Professor Corsi ushers her team into the room.

Alfonso Galbatti smiles broadly, rises from a padded burgundy leather director's chair at the head of the table and moves towards Camilla. He's a solid, squat man with hardly any neck. He has only to lean slightly to hold her shoulders as they kiss each other, first on one cheek, then the other. She quickly releases herself and turns to the group.

'We are very fortunate that the honourable Alfonso Galbatti, Chancellor of Campania University, has made the time to come here personally. It is entirely thanks to his efforts that we have attracted further government funding for the project.'

Frances watches a two-way river of oozing flattery.

'Come, come, professor, you are underselling yourself. Ladies and gentlemen, if it hadn't been for Professor Corsi, none of this would have happened. Not only is she a gifted scientist, she has a business brain to match. You are in very good hands, I can assure you. And now if you will excuse me, I have some pressing matters to attend to at the university. But I wish you good luck with Progetto Vulcano! Professor, a word before I go?'

His body bends stiffly into a small formal bow. He straightens himself without acknowledging the group further and leaves the room with Professor Corsi.

'A scientist with a business brain! You're in good hands! I think he knows more about her hands than he's letting on,' Riccardo mutters as they take a place around the table.

'It was a superb round of arse-licking,' Frances whispers back.

He laughs but before he can reply, Professor Corsi is back in the room. She has freshened her lipstick and smooths back her hair. Flicking off the lights she walks to a white screen on the wall. 'Professor Caterno has helped me to prepare this PowerPoint plan. Let's begin.'

While Caterno operates the laptop computer, she indicates the images on the screen with a long pointer. The blue and white light dissects her face and body like a Picasso painting.

'You can see we have a programme for the next six months to coordinate our approach in the region. Each of you will have your own area to inspect and talk to other vulcanologists in the different sites. As you know we have too much conflicting information from too many sources and it's the goal of Progetto Vulcano to bring it all together.'

An animated image of Vesuvius erupting fills the screen. A red mass rises like mercury through the centre of the mountain and pours over the top, tumbling in all directions.

'Ah, this is the latest on the projections for Vesuvius if it erupts, though it could be hundreds of years before it does. This shows how the magma would force itself up through the crater. We want to be able to reassure people that we will be able to predict when it will happen and they will be able to get away in plenty of time. This is central to our task.'

'Professor, there's a lot of disagreement about the prediction time. I've heard variations between one day and two weeks. What's the official line going to be?' Frances asks.

'We will have at least a week or two of warning signs, earthquakes and so on. And we will be working hand in hand with the Civil Defence to prepare people to evacuate if it looks like an eruption is imminent.'

'I think that is too optimistic,' Riccardo interrupts. 'We have to consider the worst-case scenario and I think it's as little as twenty-four hours.'

Professor Corsi stares hard at him and pauses very deliberately before replying. 'Signor Cocchia, I think we should agree to disagree at this time. Maybe we can discuss this at a later time. For now, we should move on.'

'But surely . . .' Riccardo stands up and squares his shoulders. 'Surely as scientists we should be talking about those things now. Professor, as you know, I have new evidence of the Avellino eruption that points to a much more dangerous threat from Vesuvius than Civil Defence is currently considering. The heart of Naples is in danger, yet is not included in any emergency plan. There are millions of people at risk and we should be telling them.'

The room is silent, save for the hum of the computer. All eyes are on Professor Corsi. She pauses again and sighs. 'I mentioned before the terms of reference for Progetta Vulcano. At the risk of repeating myself, I believe I have to tell you again that we have certain duties to perform . . . but that does not mean we should all go off on different tangents just because this person or that person says they've made some new discovery. Professor Caterno is a recognized world

27

authority in vulcanology and he has assured the government there will be plenty of time to evacuate. A couple of weeks. Isn't that right, professor?'

Bartolo hesitates and nods his head slowly. 'Yes, I have given that advice. That is not to say I'm not willing to listen to other views.' He shifts uneasily in his chair and refuses to meet her eye.

Professor Corsi narrows her eyes and smiles, her shiny red lips catching the light of the projector. 'Well, of course we all want to listen if there's anything worth hearing.'

She turns towards Riccardo. 'But I have no time for anyone acting recklessly and alarming people. Our mission is clear. This is a vulcanology project. It is not an archaeological or an anthropological project. If we have to listen to everyone who's found a new rock or a bone in southern Italy, we will never move forward. So I ask you again to stick to what you know about.'

Her eyes scan the room and she finishes in a low steady voice. 'That is, if you want to stay on the team and not go back to studying the hills of Australia.'

Riccardo's face is flushed and he shuffles some papers in front of him. No one else speaks.

'Signorina Nelson.' Frances starts as Professor Corsi focuses on her. 'As you are the newest member, I think it would be helpful to us and to yourself if you visited our Stromboli Observatory to see how they're managing with the acoustic monitoring. There have been problems with the system. Riccardo, . . .'

He looks up at her, surprised by her now familiar use of his first name. 'You could accompany her to the Aeolian Islands as that is one place you do know something about. Isn't that so?'

'Stromboli, yes,' Riccardo says quietly. 'Of course I would like to do that. I did most of my training there, not in Melbourne.'

'Good. Now let's move on.'

Frances smiles to herself, admiring Professor Corsi's 'good cop, bad cop' routine. Rule with an iron fist, then throw some lollipops into the crowd. 'Professor,' she interjects, 'I inspected the seabed at

Baia yesterday. There's a lot of volcanic activity and some damage to antiquities and . . .'

'Yes, yes, very good, Frances. Why not put it in a report and I'll have a look at it? Soon we will put all the material together for consideration.'

She firmly brings the briefing to a close and as they leave the room, Professor Corsi turns to Riccardo. 'Signor Cocchia, could you stay behind a moment, please?'

CHAPTER FOUR

Sounds of laughing schoolchildren wake Frances from a recurring dream. She is back in New Zealand and lost on White Island, drifting through steamy mists rising from a boiling lake. Tori's warnings are ringing in her ears, warnings she ignored.

A white cotton curtain blowing in the window brushes her cheek and the sounds of Corso Vittorio Emanuele return her to Naples.

The sight of a pile of dirty clothes in the corner of her room makes her shrug off the dream. Wrapping herself in a sarong, she picks them up and takes them to the terrace, almost tripping on a large pair of women's bloomers lying on the ground. She looks upwards through forests of clothes hanging from balconies above her but can't tell the source of the runaway underpants. She glances at her watch. Just before seven thirty and the warmth of the sun suggests a beautiful day ahead. The children in the courtyard below talk, shout, laugh, grabbing a few precious minutes before they're sucked into the nearby school. Bells ring sounding the start of classes and, abruptly, there is silence.

Riccardo's washing machine is broken so Frances washes her clothes by hand in a large tub on the terrace. After rubbing the dirt spots off some jeans, she swirls some shirts and underwear around and around in the murky water, refills the tub with fresh water and swirls them again, watching the soap suds gather on the top.

After a life of functioning washing machines, dryers and fixed clotheslines, doing laundry southern Italian style had come as a shock. But now she enjoys the routine, keeping in tune with her neighbours and playing a guessing game. The clothes are the clues to the occupants of the apartments. Just below she can see the Fogliano family's profile: baby Luciana's pink jumpsuits and tiny vests and a lacy dress for Sundays; the twins' jeans and T-shirts, and a couple of baseball caps; a striped top she has seen Laura wear; and some large shirts that must belong to her husband, Peppe, who runs the nearby petrol station.

She squeezes out as much of the water as possible from her own clothes and pegs them to a line that dangles over the street below. She fastens each piece carefully, not wanting them to fall on some unsuspecting person's head. Four pairs of black pants and a lacy bra spread across the line. Once she resigned herself to making her lingerie public she had tossed out the old stuff and started again, marvelling at the endless array of sexy Italian designs.

She picks up the damp pair of voluminous white pants and wonders who owns them. Almost on cue, something bumps against her shoulder. A small cane basket hanging on a piece of rope has dropped in front of her. Looking up, she can't see where it has come from but guesses its purpose. She plops the bloomers inside and instantly the rope is pulled up. She follows its course until it disappears onto one of the highest balconies. An old woman's voice calls out. 'Grazie, thank you.'

'Prego, you're welcome,' Frances calls back.

Back inside she unlocks the shutters and glass doors opening onto a tiny balcony with a partial view of Vesuvius. Beyond the lane and across the city, the day is clear and she can see the sparkling bay and one of the flanks of the mountain. Riccardo's revving motorbike breaks the quiet of the day. After the meeting at the observatory, she had completed some research work and returned home alone.

Frances dresses for a day of trekking, hoping the visit to the volcano is still on. Riccardo's keys crunch in the door and when she opens it he looks exhausted. Smiling ruefully at her, he dumps his helmet and backpack heavily onto the floor and thumps around the room.

'That bitch has garrotted me,' he complains.

'Who? What's happened?'

'Camilla Corsi, of course. That stronza! She's scrunched my balls over my last report on Vesuvius. You heard her yesterday talking about being alarmist. That was directed at me.'

'Ah, yes, I was wondering how your quiet word went.'

He smacks a fist into his hand. 'She says I have to pull my head in. And it gets worse. She says the university doesn't want to be associated with the work Marcello and I are doing. Plus she's threatening to withdraw my funding and kick me off Progetto Vulcano.'

'That's outrageous. Surely she can't do that.'

'I think she's doing Alfonso Galbatti's dirty work.'

'But wouldn't the head of the university have to put his name to it?'

'Hah! There'll be nothing in writing, they're too clever for that. It was one of those "pulling me aside for a chat in the corner" numbers. I've got no doubt he's behind it. But I'll fight it. At least Marcello is independent of the university and can say what he likes. Mind you, he needs research money too.'

'Have you talked to Marcello about it?'

'Yes. I stayed over with him last night.' He pauses and grins at her. 'Sorry, I should have let you know I wasn't coming back.'

'Hey, I'm not your mama! I wasn't worried. But I am a bit concerned about your situation. What did Marcello say?'

'Indignant, to say the least. Angry. Pissed off, or incazzato, as the Italians say.'

'You're becoming more Italian than the Italians.'

'Perhaps you're right!' he laughs. 'But only to a degree. I'm not afraid to speak up against the authorities, not like a lot of the locals.'

'I've noticed!'

'Anyway, you can ask Marcello yourself. We're going up Vesuvius today. Do you still want to come?'

'Sure do. When?'

'He's coming by in the four-wheel-drive in half an hour. OK?'

'Suits me. But I'm dying for a coffee. I'm going to head down to the bar.'

'Good. I'll see you there shortly.'

Frances bolts down the steps and nearly bowls over Pasquale carting his cello in its case on a small trolley down the stairs. 'Oops, sorry, Pasquale . . .'

He laughs, and as they walk down together, she notices his eyes again, no less extraordinary in the gloom of the stairwell than in the candlelight.

'It's OK. You must be late like me.'

'No, just hurrying for my coffee. Where are you going?'

'To the Conservatorium of Music; I go every day for lessons.'

They amble along the lane, on to the main street and part company at the local café. She watches him wander down the uneven pavement towards the station, his cello case mounted on a small skateboard following him like a large pet dog.

The café is full of people crowding around the bar. 'A large café latte, please, Massimo,' she calls out.

'Sure, Francesca. Anything to eat?'

She looks at the lines of pastries and sandwiches crowded four levels high inside a glass case on the counter. Cornettos bursting with custard and jam; flaky pastries stuffed with sweet ricotta cheese; fresh bread rolls bursting with prosciutto ham, cheese and eggplant. She points to a round soft roll dotted with ham. 'The Neapolitan panini, please.'

'Giovanni, get that for her.'

It's only a small bar but there are three men working, all dressed formally in black trousers, white shirts and perky navy bow ties: Massimo, the owner, who makes it his business to know all his customers by name; his seventeen-year-old apprentice, Giovanni, with the latest buzz cut and diamond studs in his ears, and, at the till, Roberto, pushing seventy and still working enthusiastically after more than fifty years.

Frances moves to one end of the counter alongside four others eating their breakfast standing.

'Ecco! Here it is.' Massimo pushes the cup towards her and hands her the roll in a piece of paper.

She bites into the fresh roll and sips the foaming coffee, just finishing as Riccardo appears.

'Espresso, please,' he asks Massimo and turns to her. 'You look as if you were born here,' he teases.

'Yeah, I rather like la dolce vita.'

'Well, enjoy. It may not last!'

His tiny cup of coffee arrives. He piles in three spoons of sugar, stirs it quickly and drinks it in a second. When his cellphone rings he walks outside to take the call. Frances picks up the bill for both of them and pays Roberto three euros and fifty cents.

'Marcello's a minute away,' Riccardo calls to her. 'Let's go.'

CHAPTER FIVE

The traffic is gathering momentum as they drive through the narrow roads to reach the tangenziale expressway linking to the road to Vesuvius. Their vehicle is larger than most and Marcello slows on corners to avoid cars and motorbikes banked up on both sides. A bus looms towards them. He swerves sharply into a driveway, barely missing three motorcyclists who have also leapt into the space, to let it pass.

Frances blows at a pile of dust on the dashboard and writes her name on it with her finger.

'Sorry my car is so dirty,' Marcello apologizes. 'There's a lot of dust everywhere. And I must confess I haven't cleaned it since my last holiday. I keep it like this so the thieves are scared off!'

'Naples has a shocking reputation for stealing cars. I remember friends a few years ago leaving theirs for half an hour and finding it gone. Is it still as bad?'

'Who knows? My cousin had his car stolen in Melbourne. Another friend had his car stolen in Torino last month. I think it happens everywhere.'

'Hey, that was probably one of my cousins in Melbourne,' Riccardo calls from the back. 'Sounds like a good excuse not to clean your car!'

'You're on to me!' When Marcello laughs, his whole face lights up and Frances sees how, despite their passion for their research, both men still make the most of each day. She notices his strong hands on the steering wheel, tanned like the rest of him. They're the hands of a working man rather than an academic; testimony to years of excavation, digging on ancient sites throughout Italy and beyond into Tunisia.

They drive for about an hour, inching along as thousands of cars try to squeeze into the lanes.

'Here we go. Finally!'

Marcello turns off at an exit marked Ercolano Portico. Once off the highway, the traffic thins as they follow a narrower road to the Parco Nazionale, the national park of Vesuvius.

'My God, the garbage hasn't improved!' Frances points to huge mounds dumped every hundred metres or so along both sides of the roads. A putrid odour rises from the detritus; abandoned fridges and furniture and hundreds of plastic bags burst open to expose rotting food and clothing.

'It's disgusting,' Riccardo spits. 'And nothing changes.'

'When I first came to Naples I thought there must have been a garbage strike. But what's going on?'

'Il Sistema. The fucking system,' Marcello exclaims.

'What?'

'You've been here long enough to notice that things in southern Italy move slowly or not at all. Il Sistema. Everything is controlled. And garbage — garbage is the new cocaine,' he says bitterly.

'You mean Mafia?'

'Yes, our version. Everyone sees on television the odd shooting on the streets, a corpse found here or there. That's not new, it's the same fighting among the big families, the drugs, cocaine, heroin, pills. But now Il Sistema is much more sophisticated. It has a hold on our economy, the banks, the government, half the shops in Naples and all the services, so if their contractors don't collect the garbage, everyone gets angry and they'll pay more. Extortion!'

'So how long does this stuff stay?' Frances asks as they pass into the national park where the garbage piles are just as large.

'No one will say. No one will act. They say there's nowhere for it to go. You would not believe this but one politician suggested using the crater of Vesuvius as the dumping ground.'

'You're kidding!'

'He's not,' Riccardo replies. 'And it wouldn't be the first time. There are several calderas, old craters, outside of Naples, including one in Campi Flegrei, filled with garbage.'

'That seems impossible. Surely that's against environmental laws.'

'The laws, the laws . . . Il Sistema is the law. I'll tell you something, Frances, the law here can be extremely strict on some things. Yet, if there are people of influence behind the scene, suddenly there is no law. Wheels within wheels — you understand?' asks Marcello.

'You're right about the laws,' Riccardo agrees. 'It is against the law to dump garbage in a seismologically unsound area. And a volcano would have to be the most unstable. Yet, that is what happens.'

'Look, Frances,' Marcello interrupts. 'There's the old observatory, the oldest one in the world. Now it's a museum.'

They've left behind the motley clusters of apartments, modern villas and the occasional restaurant. An elegant nineteenth century classical pink villa stands alone on the pine tree-studded slopes.

'And there's the old 1944 lava flow beyond the trees. Want to stop?'

She nods and he pulls off the road. Halfway up the mountain, the air is still and quiet, disturbed occasionally by a tourist bus careering past.

Frances is eager to see the lava flow. 'Let's go over.'

The three of them scuttle like crabs over rocks and through scrub towards a massive river of solidified lava clinging to the lower flanks of the volcano. The source of the mass of dark grey rock is high up, out of sight. It stretches far below them like fast-flowing rapids that have been snap frozen.

'It's hard to imagine what this was like when it was hot magma. It must have been awesome.' Frances bends to touch the rough surface of the rock which extends for hundreds of metres across.

'All the more so because it happened in the middle of the Second World War. The Allied forces had just taken over Naples from the Germans and the Americans occupied the old observatory back there,' Marcello responds.

'Was it operating?' Frances asks.

'Sort of, there was one vulcanologist from Naples University, Professor Giuseppe Imbo. He's long dead now but he's certainly gone down in our history. The Americans tried to get him to leave but he stood his ground saying the volcano was very active and as he was the only one who could work the seismographs, he should stay.'

'He was a hero. And it's just as well he stayed,' Riccardo continues. 'We have all his records of the eruption over five days. He worked there on his own, going from the observatory up there to the crater and watching the whole thing build up. When the lava flow started, it was one river. On the fifth day this big flow started and then split into three rivers.'

'Frances, come over here.' Marcello is pointing down the valley. 'There are the towns that were destroyed by the lava. Some of them suffered worse than others. Nearly every house in San Sebastiano was destroyed and all the crops.'

'And the people?'

'About 40 people died, mainly old people. Stuck in their houses. It was easy enough for most people to get away.'

Frances peers into the distance, trying to picture this deadly molten flow infiltrating the towns, which are built up so densely they almost roll into one. The fields separating them are cultivated with grapes, olives and fruit trees, concealing the destruction beneath a verdant cover, as though it had never happened.

'It must have been terrifying . . .' she adds, half to herself.

'They were bad times for everyone,' Marcello tells her. 'My grandparents were living there when it happened, just teenagers. My grandfather's still alive. You might want to meet him?'

She nodded. 'I would, very much.'

'I'll take you one day. He's told me lots of stories about that time. One of the rumours was that the Americans started the eruption by dropping all their leftover bombs into the crater after their raids on the Nazi hiding places in the mountains. Certainly the people of Naples started to think they were cursed. First the Germans, then the Allies, then Vesuvius. Nonno, my grandfather, said a group of women stormed into a brothel where the foreign soldiers used to go. They dragged out the naked prostitutes and threw them onto the street, telling them to get down on their knees and do penance for bringing the wrath of the volcano down on the city.'

Riccardo laughs. 'Ah yes, the wrath of God. We heard that a lot in Stromboli too. It's the answer to everything. Of course it's not so easy for us scientists, because we get the blame as well, mainly for not being able to predict what God is going to do next!'

'It's the same with volcanoes the world over,' Frances replies. 'It's natural for people to blame it on the supernatural when they don't have the knowledge to find a scientific explanation.'

As they clamber back towards the car, Frances looks back to the towns below. 'What happens to them if it goes again? How do they get out? What about your grandfather, Marcello?'

'Mio Dio! God help us!'

'It will be disaster on an unprecedented scale,' Riccardo adds. 'Nearly a million people live around Vesuvius and millions more in and around Naples. A lava flow is nothing compared to what would happen if there was a super eruption. Getting them out is the nub of the problem; you know as well as I do, you can't stop the volcano.'

'Yes, but no one believes it will happen to them, least of all my grandfather. They think the saints will protect them!'

'Come on, let's go up the top before it gets too late,' Riccardo says. 'We'll give you a falcon's view from the top and you'll see the scale of the problem for yourself.'

The road snakes up the mountain. Before long they pass above the tree line, overtaking dozens of tourist buses, and pull into a large car park. Riccardo flashes an observatory pass at the attendant who looks at it cursorily and waves their vehicle through. A few people are buying souvenirs from the row of small shops that lead to the gateway to the summit: bottles of Lacryma Cristi, the local white wine made from Vesuvius grapes; curios made from lava — ashtrays, owls, pendants; and the inevitable calendars and tea towels.

They start the ascent, overtaking dawdling tourists puffing up the winding gravel track. Others are returning from the summit, among them two teenage girls in tight jeans, limping in sandals made for the high street rather than a mountain. The air is punctuated with the accents of a dozen or more languages.

Soon they are high enough to see into the vast empty crater. The steamy gas from a few fumaroles drifts over the grey and brown craggy walls that have seen dozens of explosions over thousands of years. Frances looks at the mountain differently to her previous visits, when she helped install some of the new-model acoustic monitors on its flanks to pick up the vibrations of the volcano.

This has the appearance of a sleeper, almost serene, so different to the angry craters she has traversed, spewing boiling water, mud and lava. Yet surely it's a deceiver.

The three of them gaze at the summit of Vesuvius, its peak nesting inside the caldera of the much older Monte Somma, that exploded in 79 AD with such force it blew more than half of the mountain away. It's quiet now but more than any of the visitors around them, they are aware of the time-bomb ticking deep below them, the vast lake of magma stretching some twenty kilometres across to Campi Flegrei.

'Silent and deadly,' Frances utters, leaning against a safety fence and staring into the giant caldera. 'You could fit a lot of garbage in here,' she adds. 'What a preposterous idea!'

Marcello leans so close to her their arms touch. 'You've got a fresh view of this place, Frances. How much warning do you believe we'll have of a big eruption?'

She feels comfortable with him, attracted, and doesn't move away. But his question unsettles her. Everyone asks but few are prepared to answer.

'I agree with the pessimists that it could be as little as a day or two. What do you call it?' she asks Riccardo, on her other side. 'The worst-case scenario?'

'Breve tempo. Soon,' he replies.

'Yes, whatever soon means,' Frances smiles at him. 'I know the official line is one or two weeks and we'd all like to think that was the case. But this reminds me very much of Mt St Helens. When it blew its top in 1980, with no warning, it was catastrophic . . . yet it was very closely watched. That was years before I worked there but the older scientists never got over the enormity and the speed of the eruption. One of their friends was monitoring it kilometres away from the mountain and was killed instantly. And . . . I've had some close calls myself and lost . . .' The last sentence she almost whispers and they don't seem to have heard her.

'Well, you've already seen how our esteemed leader won't hear a bar of it!' Riccardo hisses. 'How do we break through a wall like that?'

'We'll find a way,' Marcello smiles. 'Science will win over politics.' He walks ahead, the breeze ruffling his dark brown hair. 'Come on, hurry up!'

At the top, the vista expands around them; the Bay of Naples sparkles blue below, stretching from Sorrento in the south to Cape Misena and Baia in Campi Flegrei to the north. Beyond, the mystical Ischia, Procida and Capri rise out of the sea, each island blanketed in a ghostly haze. The homes of millions of people are squashed into the metropolis, from the ship-filled harbour, extending in an unbroken sweep, to the villages around the volcano.

'It's the most densely populated city in Europe and those so-called expressways are always clogged or at a standstill. Getting out will be almost impossible if there's an eruption.' Riccardo looks bleak.

'There's Herculaneum, down there towards the water. Everyone there was killed in the same eruption in 79 AD that took out Pompeii. They died first. There were six surges from the volcano. One of them hit the town at one in the morning and the hot gas and ash killed them instantly.'

'Is it right on the water?' Frances asks. 'I can't quite make it out.'

'It used to be but the old town is hemmed in now so it's hard to see from here and the coast has extended a bit beyond it. But we're still finding skeletons there from two thousand years ago.'

'No!' Frances exclaims.

'Oh yes . . . we found hundreds, huddled in boatsheds trying to get out to sea. They died in seconds.' Marcello takes her by the arm and leads her further along the path.

'And there's Pompeii over there,' Marcello points southwards. 'If you look closely you can see the ruins of the old city in the distance. Follow the line of that old road you can see and it will lead you to it.'

As Frances strains to pick out the remnants of the once-thriving Roman city, she can just make out the shapes of the muddy brown ruins shimmering in a green oasis abutting a modern town.

'And, of course, like Herculaneum, it wasn't the lava that killed everyone, it was the ash and the gas. Most people suffocated.' Riccardo's face is set. 'The problem we're facing is that the population believes lava is the threat from Vesuvius and that suits the politicians. They allow development here and turn a blind eye to illegal, abusivismo, development. The real danger is much more lethal; pyroclastic flows and massive falls of ash and gas.'

'How far is Pompeii from here?' Frances asks.

'About ten kilometres. It's hard to believe everyone was killed instantly but the force of the eruption was the same as thousands of the atomic bombs that destroyed Hiroshima. And if you think that's bad, come and take a look at this.'

Riccardo and Marcello guide Frances along the path to face away from the sea.

'That's the city of Nola.' Riccardo points east. 'It's twice as far from Vesuvius as Pompeii but that's where Marcello and I found the oldest skeletons and the remains of Bronze Age villages. They were wiped out by the Avellino eruption fifteen hundred years before Pompeii.'

'Oh yes, Bronze Age woman from the restaurant,' Frances adds. 'When can we go there?'

'Soon, I hope,' Marcello says, and Frances sees him exchange a look with Riccardo.

'What? A problem?'

'We seem to attract problems,' Riccardo replies.

Marcello nods. 'We tried to go back to the excavation site last week and it was locked up. We've been facing resistance from the administrator every time we try to go there. The government is paying top money to some scientists to put a spin on it all and assure people that it's safe. The last thing they want is to scare people and face a revolt. You can see why we're so unpopular as the bearers of bad news. But the reality is that if there's another giant eruption, every town you can see from up here could be obliterated, including Naples.'

The wind picks up and they join a busload of Australian and New Zealand tourists walking back down the path, laughing and chatting, blissfully unaware of any threat. Yet, the scale of the danger is beyond what Frances had imagined when she took on this job. Can an early warning system really do much here? There would be no hope for the hundreds of thousands of people living below, let alone others further away. 'They put so much trust in what we scientists tell them, as if we can control what nature does,' she thinks to herself, then turns to Riccardo. 'What are you going to do about your research?'

'Fight. And then fight harder.'

Marcello puts his hand on her shoulder and squeezes it. 'We do have the law on our side, for what that's worth. We're hoping some of the politicians in Rome who are beyond the reach of Il Sistema might run with this. Under the Italian constitution, scientists have a right to independent research and to publish and discuss their results. So, yes, we will just keep going.'

Finding their car, they follow a procession of buses down the mountain.

'We're going to meet some friends for an aperitivo. Do you want to come?' Marcello asks.

She pauses for a moment. Once she wouldn't have hesitated to accept such an invitation, but this time she pulls back. 'Thanks but I think I'll have an early night. Just drop me at the station and I'll make my own way home.'

CHAPTER SIX

The market leading to the Montesanto station in the heart of the historic centre of Naples has woken up from the siesta. In the twisting cobblestone lanes, afternoon shoppers examine glistening displays of fresh fish and shellfish. Boxes of fruit and vegetables piled on the pavement outside tiny shops vie for attention; shiny purple aubergines, stop-light-red capsicums, jungle-green zucchinis and egg-shaped tomatoes are side by side with bulging bunches of red and white grapes and watermelons, some cut open to reveal their glistening pink interiors.

Frances points to the red grapes and pays for them. She moves along the market and pauses to buy some socks from one of the stallholders.

'Buona sera, signorina,' the Pakistani man greets her.

She smiles at him and passes him a five euro note, enough to buy three pairs of cotton socks.

'Jewellery. From two euro?'

'Another day,' she says perusing a kaleidoscope of trinkets — bangles, beads and brooches — from the sub-continent.

She rides an escalator to the funicular and joins a group of people waiting on the platform to ride to the upper reaches of the city. The modern cable car arrives at the bottom a minute later. Two musicians follow Frances on board and the doors have barely closed when the violinist and the accordion player burst into a tango. Their faces have been kissed by the Naples sun for at least forty summers and the two men play together with a practised and passionate ease.

Frances notices the other passengers escaping momentarily from their daily worries. They're listening closely, tapping feet, nodding and smiling. The mood is contagious and she feels her fear of the volcano lift as the music takes over. A little girl of five or so stands and dances around her seat. Her mother laughs but her older sister, a serious-looking girl of about eight wearing glasses, stares at her lap, embarrassed.

The younger girl doesn't care. She jiggles around, singing and dancing, her face alive with happiness. When the playing stops she sinks laughing onto her seat, prodding her silent sister. The accordion player starts again while the violinist walks up and down the carriage, proffering a cup. Frances drops in a euro coin which jangles with the rest.

When she alights on Corso Vittorio Emanuele, the street has also come alive and she resists an urge to tango along the pavement. On a whim, she buys a pot of crimson cyclamens from a roadside stall and strokes the tiny blooms, so perfect they could be made of silk.

Pasquale is playing when she climbs the stairs and she hesitates, wondering whether to knock, but the exertion of the Vesuvius climb keeps her moving home. She opens the shutters in her apartment, where the light is fading fast. She whisks some eggs and makes a cheese omelette and a green salad, pours a glass of falanghina and flops onto the sofa to eat, relishing her simple meal and the sweet crisp white wine.

Hearing voices in the lane below, she leans outside the window to see who's there. Darkness cloaks their identities. Under a light further on, a street regular, a blonde-wigged transvestite, waits for some evening trade, cigarette glowing like a welcome beacon, and Frances closes the shutters on the Italian night.

Realizing day will have dawned in New Zealand, she turns on her computer and clicks onto the Internet site for White Island. Instantly, photos appear, a chequerboard of images, each slightly different, of swirling white steam covering the rugged brown of the main crater. The images would have been taken just minutes earlier on cameras she had installed herself to record the hydrothermal activity.

Frances fingers the keys nervously, her guts churning, as though this simple action could erase the memory of the time when the island was a raging hellhole. How simple it would be to push delete and pretend it hadn't happened. She taps the keys to see more images. For now, all is quiet.

Frances yawns, glad the apartment is quiet and she can have an early night. She doesn't expect to see Riccardo back for hours, if at all.

But sleep evades her and she thinks of Tori, and for the first time in ages, wishes he was lying there with her. They had found each other when neither was looking, both feeling like the flotsam and jetsam of relationships that had run their course. They had met in New Zealand, while embroiled on different sides of a bitter conflict. She had come from Mt St Helens to Mt Ruapehu to ramp up the early warning monitors. Just as well too, as it was only a matter of months before the volcano emitted a massive lahar of water and mud from the crater lake. Had the system not functioned, there could have been a repeat of the 1950s Tangiwai train disaster that had stolen so many lives, including her baby sister's.

Tori Maddison was the Maori leader who had repelled moves to bulldoze the summit of the mountain. The volcano was sacred to his tribe, he'd said, and was part of its mana, its power. There should be no interference. Against the odds, the wishes of the indigenous people were heard. And against the odds, the two of them, from such different worlds, fell deeply in love. For a time, they floated together in warm harmony. But when they parted she felt they were both treading water, just to stop drowning.

'Frances, don't go to Whakaari, I beg you. It's not right to go there. It's tapu, forbidden to Maori, and it's dangerous for you. Please listen to me.'

His words still ring in her ears, urging her not to go to White Island, known to the Maori as Whakaari. But she hadn't listened. Couldn't. If it was a test to see if she could embrace his world, she had failed miserably. But what were her choices? To turn her back on a life of work and research that meant so much to her? Her expertise gave people a chance to escape from the fury of volcanoes. The life of the baby sister she had never known was taken so cruelly because there had been no warnings of the disaster. But if she'd listened to Tori, would another life have been saved? Would they still be together? Frances turns over and twists the soft white sheets around her. But she finds no comfort.

∽∽

The first sighting of White Island had sent the same tremor of nervous excitement through her that came with each new volcano. Bob Masterton had tapped her shoulder from the back of the helicopter as the island appeared on the horizon, the tip of an enormous cone rising out of the ocean.

'She's pumping today, Frances. We should get some great samples and readings.' She had turned to smile at the man known as Mr Volcanoes. There wasn't a crater in the country Bob didn't know and White Island was no exception. He was a frequent visitor, his tanned face and muscled body evidence of his long involvement with New Zealand's Volcano Watch team.

She had pointed to the bag by her side. 'I've got the new cameras here. They're state of the art so they should give us some fine photos if they survive the heat.'

The previous day there'd been a vigorous earthquake swarm with dozens of tremors caused by magma and gas movements beneath the volcano. One of the cameras that recorded all activity on the island had stopped working, its power supply extinguished. In the wake of the Asian tsunami, fears of a local tsunami activated by landslides on White Island had become a constant worry. It didn't look like it, but this was the biggest volcano in New Zealand, with nearly three quarters of it below the sea.

As the small red helicopter slowly flew through the great blue expanse, drawing closer to the island, Frances had felt like a little bird trapped inside. She had sat in the front with the pilot, Hamish, a confident, tall, black-haired, freckle-faced, twenty-five-year-old who had already been flying this route for three years. Strong winds buffeted the chopper and it had lurched noisily from side to side, narrowing the fifty-kilometre gap eastwards between the mainland and the island. In every direction she'd looked, left, right and down through the window between her feet, all she had seen was the deep blue sea. Only the island ahead interrupted the line. A huge white cloud of steamy gas towered over the island.

'See that cloud?' Bob had said. 'That happens after a lot of heavy rain.'

As they had drawn closer, it had occurred to her that Tori's story about its mythological origins correlated well with the scientists' version. Both agreed this was part of a line of fire stretching across the Pacific, Maori believing it came from Hawaiki, their mythical island home. He'd told her the fire had arrived in answer to a prayer from a powerful tohunga, the high priest Ngatoroirangi. He had been leading Tori's ancestors, who journeyed in canoes in search of new lands. Climbing the high mountains in the middle of the North Island, he had nearly frozen to death. Anguished, he'd cried out to his ancestral spirits to send warmth. 'Ka riro au i te tonga, tukuna mai te ahi! I am seized by the cold wind from the south. Send me fire.'

Frances was always totally drawn in by Tori's dramatic renditions. He was so passionate when he told the old stories; eyes flashing, arms waving and his voice strong and emotional. He'd said the priest's prayers had been answered and the fire roared under the sea, emerging first in White Island, then heading inland to create hot pools and geysers and finally, bursting into flames in the sacred mountains of Ruapehu, Ngauruhoe and Tongariro.

A fresh tail wind soon had them circling the island and Frances had shrugged off Tori's mythology. She had also put out of her mind his anger when she had told him she would be coming here. What lay ahead needed her full concentration.

White surf was crashing against craggy rocks then ricocheting onto colonies of sea gannets nesting above. Two of the birds had taken flight, each plunging into the sea in search of fish. She could see a deserted black beach on the far side of the island where currents of yellow sulphur stained the waves as they lapped in and out of the sand. The mouth of the volcano was dotted with smaller craters belching smoke and steam. Even from the air, she could see its deadly heart, a boiling lake gargling in a seemingly bottomless throat.

'There's the old sulphur mine down there, by Crater Bay,' Hamish's voice had crackled through her headphones as they descended. 'All the miners who lived here were killed overnight in 1914, by a red hot avalanche. Poor bastards! Only their cat survived.'

Frances had peered out of the helicopter window at the frames of old buildings above the beach. There were no other signs of human habitation, just a barren moonscape. No reason on earth to live there.

'Get ready,' Hamish had told them. 'Going down.'

A few minutes later they'd touched down on a clear stretch of rocks, perching like a praying mantis as the engine shut down. Strong wind had blasted them as they opened the doors and stepped into blinding sunshine. Frances had taken one look towards the gaping crater before she had started coughing. The stench of sulphur and other gases was so strong and acrid she had almost vomited.

She'd quickly hoisted her backpack out of the chopper, put navy overalls over her jeans and shirt, swapped her sneakers for long insulated rubber boots and pulled a bright orange mask and headdress over her hair. Bob had dressed identically, covering his own greying cropped hair. She'd then grabbed the bag with cameras.

Hamish had put on a smaller facemask.

'See you in an hour or so. I'll be waiting here.'

The two of them had looked like a pair of beekeepers trekking towards a ring of fumaroles puffing out a heady chemical mix of steam. The walls of the crater rose up around them. A stream of hot muddy water was rushing alongside them and they had to navigate its twists and turns, carefully stepping across the current.

'I must have been here more than twenty times and it's never been the same.' Bob's voice was muffled through the mask. 'There can be hundreds of tonnes of gases pumped out in a day and the heat is tremendous. This stream has taken a new path. Look!' He'd pointed to a boiling mud pond the size of a child's backyard pool. 'That's new. Come up in the last month.'

'It's the closest place to hell I've been!' Frances had edged close to him so she could hear above the wind. 'Are you sure it's a safe time to do the testing?'

'Sure, just watch your footing carefully and keep your mask on. We'll start with the Donald Mount fumaroles and then we'll check the other monitors and I'll help you get those cameras going.'

He strode ahead as she trailed behind, gingerly stepping on the brilliant yellow and white sulphur crystals, red earth and crumbly rock. Steam was pouring out of the ground in dozens of places and from the main crater some three hundred metres ahead. When Frances had bent over to touch the ground, it burnt her hand.

Bob had reached the fumaroles first and quickly assembled the testing kit from his backpack and put on a pair of gloves. 'Stay behind me!' He'd positioned himself close to the mouth of the largest vent, the size of a football. Uphill from him, it was covered in steam when he plunged a thick tube into its hissing and bubbling core.

Frances had waited close below, passing bottles to capture the samples of carbon dioxide, sulphur dioxide and halogen gases to analyse back in their lab.

'I'll bag some of the soil,' she'd told him as he stepped away from the fumaroles.

They'd packed the samples into their bags and backtracked towards the helicopter and across to the ridge overlooking the craters. As they'd passed, she'd noticed that Hamish had wandered down towards the beach.

The air had cleared and they carried their headdresses. It had been a relief to feel the breeze cooling her face. When they'd nearly reached the top, she'd spotted a camera and its support frame lying on the ground. 'Looks like it's been knocked over by a rock. It's also heavily corroded,' she'd said, fingering a clump of crystals on the camera.

Bob had fixed the framework, hammering it into the scoria. Frances unpacked one of the new digital cameras and took a photo. 'Check this out. Pretty good, don't you think?' She'd showed him the image on the tiny screen of the boiling lake that lay below them.

'Extraordinary. Much clearer than the old one. Take one of me and I'll take one of you.'

They'd laughed like a couple of schoolkids on an excursion as Bob raised his hand in a victory sign, or the volcano sign, as he called it. Frances had balanced on her toes in a pose she'd learnt at childhood ballet classes.

'Something to show the office boys and girls who never leave their desks,' he'd joked as they looked at their images. Frances fitted the camera into the framework and fiddled with the radio modem that would relay the photos back to the computers at their headquarters. She cleaned some loose ash off the solar panels powering the cameras and the two of them walked along the ridge to replace the second camera.

'All done?' he'd asked. 'Come and help me clean up the other gear. You do the microphone and I'll tackle the seismograph.'

Bob had led Frances further round the ridge. 'It's so volatile here we've had a lot of problems with ash and rocks knocking out the power,' he'd said.

Frances had quickly cleaned the small microphone that picked up volcanic tremors. As Bob worked on the seismograph, Frances had paused to gaze across the island. She could see Hamish sitting on the sand on one side, his tall gangly body sheltering beneath some scrubby trees near the site of the derelict miners' settlement. The sea was all around and there was no other land in sight.

The interior of the giant crater was completely devoid of vegetation. It was a landscape like no other; a maritime volcano active for hundreds of thousands of years. The potential was there to erupt with such force that it could blow right into the stratosphere and alter the climate for hundreds of kilometres. Frances had reflected on Tori's tale. The origins of this fiery beast were somewhat older than the priest's story that dated back less than a thousand years, but the small error of fact had given her no comfort.

'C'mon, Frances, I want to show you the crater lake before we go.'

They had skidded down loose rocks, put their masks back on and Bob had broken into a quick march towards the lake at the far end of the crater. She'd found it difficult to keep up because the ground was so pocked with hot pools and boiling mud she was afraid she would lose her footing.

Swirling clouds of steam had gathered between them but she could still see the glow of his orange headdress moving further ahead. She'd called out to him to slow down but a loud roar from the crater left her voice in the wind. She'd stopped. Suddenly, she could see nothing at all.

CHAPTER SEVEN

Oone euro, signora.'

Camilla Corsi passes a coin to the newspaper vendor at the kiosk opposite the university and quickly takes her copy of *Il Mattino*. She flicks through it until she sees the photo on page eleven. The image of her is flattering, showing her in the control room of the observatory.

'Naples professor to spearhead volcano inquiry', the accompanying article announces. She nods her head with satisfaction and turns back. 'Another five copies,' she calls to the vendor. She tucks the papers into her alligator skin briefcase and hurries across the road.

The imposing fifteenth-century main building of the university towers over her, its red and grey stone exterior glowing in the last hour of sunshine. As she glances up, the light catches the motto engraved beneath the ornately sculpted pediment. *Ad Scientiarvm Havsvm Et Seminarivm Doctrinarvm* — To the honour of teaching and learning of science.

'There was a time I believed it was that simple,' she thinks, as her heels echo on the decorative mosaic floor of the vestibule leading to the central courtyard near her office. Her secretary has gone for the day, leaving a neat pile of messages and mail on Camilla's green leather-covered desk. She sifts through them, discarding all but one letter. The envelope is cream embossed with gold, her name written in handsome calligraphy. She opens it.

'The Ambassador of the United Kingdom requests the pleasure of the company of Professor Camilla Corsi at a commemorative dinner at the Palazzo Capodimonte to celebrate 300 years of British diplomatic presence in Italy.'

There's a handwritten note below.

'Love you to come, C. Let me know. Will be good to escape Rome for a couple of days. XXX B.'

'Ah, dear man,' she thinks as she draws a large red tick on the invitation and puts it in her out-tray, already pondering whether to dash out to buy the new-season Versace cocktail dress she had spotted in her favourite shop in Via Toledo earlier in the week.

A folder with a stick-on note saying FOR YOUR URGENT ATTENTION is next to her phone. She picks it up, ignoring the flashing message alert button. Inside are the recommendations from the three members of the panel set up to appoint the new Director of the Chemistry Faculty. She smiles when she sees the decision is unanimous: Professor Luigi Paoli. It had certainly been helpful that Luigi didn't share his uncle's surname — that it was well known that his mother was Alfonso Galbatti's sister was of little importance. Sometimes, appearances were everything. 'Madonna,' she thinks, 'where would any of us be without our patron?' There would hardly be a worthwhile position in any Italian university that didn't have a patron behind it. Still, this one had come at great expense, even by her standards.

Transparency and accountability to Parliament were becoming more of an issue now the Left had a bigger say, though they were as much into nepotism as anyone. She'd had to fly in the three professors from different campuses around Italy three times, accommodating each in one of the best hotels on the waterfront at Santa Lucia. Of course, they knew what was expected. They dutifully interviewed the seven short-listed candidates each time before reaching the inevitable conclusion that Luigi Paoli was the best person for the job. The three had all benefited from research grants Alfonso controlled so Camilla was surprised when one of them had confided that he had reservations, and believed the woman from Rome was better qualified. She made a note to herself not to invite him to the next panel.

She remembered when she had her own first major break in the university hierarchy, thanks to Alfonso. But the germination of her rise to the top started long before that. In fact, if she really thought about it, the seed was planted thirty-six years earlier, when she was just eight.

∞o∞

Her father had returned home late for dinner at the family house in their village near the old town of Nola where he ran a small trucking business and had an interest in an olive oil concern. Giuseppe Corsi was proud that his family lived comfortably and his wife, Antonia, could afford to provide a good table. On this night, Camilla, her three brothers and mother had already finished supper when her father arrived. He sank immediately into his favourite armchair and she had leapt onto his lap to hug him. 'Daddy,' she said pulling at his already loosened tie, 'you smell really nice, like sweet roses.' He pushed her aside gently and eased her off his knee. She caught the look exchanged between her parents; his eyes, was it embarrassment, shame, or some other emotion? She couldn't recall.

But she remembered her mother's response. Crushed. An expression like a ripe peach squashed in your hand. She never sat on her father's knee again. The look was one Camilla was to see more and more on the faces of other women. She started to notice other things too. Her father was a popular figure but not in the league of the men who gathered every night in the central bar, their well-cut suits a contrast to the working men who clustered in the other two bars across the piazza. The women, like her mother, the young girl, noticed, were never there in the early morning and evening when the men liked to huddle together. Occasionally she'd see women she didn't know. Their expressions weren't crushed and they were always laughing and drinking and smoking together or sometimes with one or other of the men.

Camilla decided there and then that she would never have a crushed expression. When she was sixteen, she made one mistake. Once she had dropped her guard and allowed someone to get too close, but she had solved the problem and rarely thought of it now.

She excelled at school and when she was accepted into the prestigious University of Campania, she chose vulcanology, partly because she had grown up in the shadow of Vesuvius and knew by heart the stories and legends of the eruptions stemming back thousands of years, and partly because she was a natural scientist. She breezed through her courses, studying hard and eschewing the social life. Camilla knew she was no beauty and could not compete with some of the classically beautiful girls in her year. Boys her age showed no interest in her but she noted early on that older men saw in her immediately a discreet sensual quality that eluded her contemporaries.

Alfonso Galbatti was one such suitor. He had cut a dash as the head of her faculty, but it wasn't until she had earned her doctorate and the university medal that they had any contact. He had held her hand slightly longer than necessary when he handed her the prize and an invitation to coffee to discuss her future followed. Before long, she was offered a junior lectureship. Two years on, a little after her thirty-fourth birthday, there were three more offers on the table. At the age of fifty-nine, one year younger than her father, Professor Galbatti had been elevated to the top job and his life was about to accelerate. Would she like to accompany him to New York to assist him at an international conference? There was an opening in the department for an associate professor. Would she be interested? The third offer wasn't mentioned. They would stay in the Waldorf. Two rooms.

The young associate professor saw little of her hotel room, merely a place to leave her clothes and change. For five nights she shared the chancellor's king-sized bed and from then on became the other woman.

On her return, she was offered a university apartment at a peppercorn rent. It had been used for visiting fellows but, conveniently, was now surplus to needs, or so she was told. Alfonso travelled extensively on day trips to Rome, Florence, Pisa, Milan, Bologna and Palermo. He told his wife, Helena, that it was too exhausting to return after a day's hard work and he needed to overnight in the other cities, but always came back to Camilla and the apartment. She made sure she never crossed paths with Helena. The last thing she needed to see was another crushed expression.

◦−◦

Her telephone rings on her desk. 'Camilla, are you coming?'

'Yes, now.' She hangs up.

She picks up the folder and one of the newspapers and walks down the grand corridor with vaulted ceilings, marble statues of long-dead Neapolitan scholars and gilt-framed portraits of past chancellors towards Alfonso's office.

He rises from his large, elegant seventeenth-century wooden inlay desk and strides across the rich red and blue Persian carpet to greet her. He pulls her close. Not a tall man, with her high shoes she reaches his shoulder. She tilts her face to his and briefly kisses him on the lips. Then she pulls away. 'Evening, Alfonso. Something to sign and something to savour,' she smiles at him.

'Ah, good. Luigi will be very happy. Let me sign that straight away.' He takes the contract with the newspaper to the desk to sign his nephew's appointment. He gazes at the photo and article of Camilla. 'Brava, Camilla, another well-deserved triumph.' He beckons her over and embraces her again, more tightly than before. 'It's been too long, cara,' he whispers in her ear.

She knows what's coming and gives in to his grasp, closing her eyes and thinking instead of her new lover. Once, Alfonso would have taken her on the desk there and then. He'd done it many times before. But since his heart operation, his potency had faded. Their twenty-five-year age gap had widened and, almost overnight, he had insisted on becoming the giver of pleasure rather than the taker.

'Relax, darling, . . .' he coos as he runs his hand up her leg and strokes the soft skin above her stocking. She drapes her arms around his neck and forces herself to surrender. It won't be long now before he's seventy and edged out the door.

His fingers move under her pants and inside her. He's practised, persistent and patient. As her body tenses and she starts to shudder, he fondles her breasts until she relaxes in his embrace. 'Cara, can I stay with you tonight?'

He releases her and she kisses him tenderly. 'No, Alfonso, but soon. I must do some more work on Progetto Vulcano. It really can't wait. And anyway, won't your wife have your dinner ready?' She curls her lip.

'Ah Camilla, you can never resist the final shot, even after all these years. You know I would have married you if I could.'

She blows him a kiss and turns to leave. 'Goodnight, Alfonso.'

One day she might just tell him that marrying him was never on her agenda and now, as he enters his declining years, she can't think of anything worse than sleeping next to him night after night.

She looks at her watch. Nearly eight, she runs in a panic to the bathroom. She sits on the toilet and relieves herself then switches to the bidet and lets the cleansing hot water surge between her legs. She dries herself quickly then checks her reflection in the mirror. Her cheeks are glowing and she buffs them with loose powder. She smooths back her hair and just as she's applying a coat of glossy red lipstick her cellphone rings.

'Where are you?' he asks abruptly.

'Two minutes away.' She hurries to her office, grabs her briefcase and within minutes she's on the street, cursing her heels as they clatter on the hard pavement towards her rendezvous a block away, out of sight of the university.

The late model black Mercedes with tinted windows is parked against the kerb ahead. As she approaches, the back door opens and she slides onto the leather seat next to him. 'You've kept me waiting more than five minutes,' he says without a smile.

'Sorry. An unavoidable delay with the project.'

As his driver accelerates into the night, he pulls her close and plunges his tongue into her waiting mouth.

CHAPTER EIGHT

Just as the early morning light sneaks through the shutters and caresses her eyes, Frances hears a low rumble. Her eyes flicker open and in the semi-gloom of her white-washed room, her body tenses as she feels the vibrations. Disoriented, she sits up, for a few seconds terrified she is caught up in another eruption.

'Stefano, Lorenzo, viene qua. Viene, qua subito!' She hears Laura calling the twins, urging them inside as a wave of thunder heralds a Naples storm.

Frances pushes open the shutters. The curtain buffets her face and a gust of wind whistles through her room, blowing papers from her desk onto the floor. She shivers in her thin white cotton nightdress, brushes her hair from her eyes and looks out, beyond the forest of satellite dishes and television aerials on top of buildings, to the mountain. Although still autumn, Vesuvius is dusted with snow.

'Il plena. If furo viene. Stefano, Lorenzo. Viene!' Frances leans over and below in the courtyard Laura chides the boys and orders them in from the rain.

Lorenzo rushes through the front door of the apartment building. But Stefano defies his mother. 'No, Mama, voglio restare con i miei amici!' He pleads to stay with the gaggle of other small boys dressed almost identically in T-shirts and jeans loitering on the wet cobbled laneway. They ridicule him as he wriggles in her strong arms. She drags him towards the doorway and despatches him inside. For now, the child is no match for the determined Laura.

A streak of lightning strikes a pole across the street and as thunder roars almost simultaneously, the three other little boys scream. Heavy drops of rain pelt their tousled black hair and they scatter.

The rain bites into Frances' face and she quickly pulls the shutters closed. She picks up the pages of a report she had been meaning to read for ages. They have spread around the room and she drops to her knees to retrieve several under her bed. A diagram on one of the pages grabs her attention and she sits on the floor and studies it. In the centre is Mt Vesuvius. Branching out from it are blobs of different colours illustrating the fallout of ash for the eight eruptions during the last twenty-five thousand years. The largest blob by far, drawn in green, shows the vast extent of the Avellino eruption of 1780 BC, the one Riccardo and Marcello have been talking about. A large red blob shows the Pompeii eruption.

Marcello had insisted this report on wind patterns for the Campania region from the Italian military weather stations was vital to their research, though she struggled to see the relevance.

Now she is drawn into what at first appeared to be a very dry report. The red blob covers all of the area southeast of Naples and far out into the sea. She hadn't realized how huge it had been, the ash covering more than three thousand square kilometres.

Blobs in blue, yellow, purple and the big green one show areas far to the east and north of Naples that were covered in ash.

She flicks to a page of graphs. They interpret the wind directions throughout a full year. For the thirty years of the study, the pattern didn't alter. The wind blows in the same way at the same time, year in and year out. Frances stands up and opens the shutters again. The rain has eased but the cold wind fills her night dress with air. She spins around imagining people through the millennia being blown by the same winds in this very place.

Her cellphone rings on her desk. She slams the shutters closed, grabs the phone and flops onto her bed. It's Marcello. 'Glad you're awake, what are you doing?'

'Trying to keep warm.' She pulls her blanket over her, enjoying hearing his warm voice. 'And reading the wind report.'

'I'm impressed. What do you think about it?'

'Not as dull as I thought.'

'Good. There's a reason I wanted you to see it. I've discovered something that will now make a lot of sense to you. Do you have time to come to my laboratory today?'

'Sure. It's an easy day. I feel like walking so I could be there in an hour.'

Frances pulls on her jeans, warmest sweater and leather jacket. She searches in her suitcase for gloves and a woollen beanie she hasn't needed until now. Pasquale is playing the cello as usual as she skips down the stairs. She pauses outside his door — sounds like he's strangling the classics today.

The streets are unusually quiet for a week morning. The rain has stopped but the cool southeasterly is blowing strongly. Frances jogs along Corso Vittorio Emanuele until she reaches a wide stone stairway. Looking across the bay, banks of puffy black clouds have blanketed Mt Vesuvius. She descends quickly, two steps at a time, counting in her head. Once she gets to a hundred she stops and looks back up. She is alone. Everyone else must be taking the funicular to the old city. She jumps as a skinny grey cat meows at her. At the bottom of the stairs a narrow laneway twists between rows of tiny terraced houses until it widens into the market streets.

It's a quiet day for the vendors. The biggest group of shoppers clusters around the fish stall. Frances moves closer to watch. A big swordfish, its large eye staring heavenwards, lies on its side. Too big for the table, its spear stands tall in midair. The fishmonger chops off large pieces of the flesh and slices them up. His wife works alongside him, packing the slices.

'Spada, spada fresca!' she calls continuously, in a high-pitched voice, handing small parcels of the swordfish to customers shouting out their orders. The man cuts further and further up the body of the fish and flings off-cuts of bone and skin into a bucket on the ground. As much as she likes eating fish, Frances turns away, repelled by the smell and the sight.

Further along, she stops outside the bakery, pressing her nose against the window to admire displays of fresh cakes and pastries. She can't resist and goes inside. 'Two pieces of that one. What is it?'

'Ah, caprese! Made this morning.' The young woman cuts two wedges, packs them into a small box and ties it with a pink ribbon. 'Almond and chocolate, molto buono. Very good. Enjoy!'

She dashes across Via Toledo through a sea of cars and bikes and into the gloom of Spaccanapoli. No cars are allowed in this long straight street that splits the heart of the ancient city but she has to dodge between students on motorinis and lovers lingering in doorways. High-walled shops rise up on both sides and she searches for clues to the city's earliest days when its Greek founders called it Neapolis, but realizes all the evidence is below the ground, not above.

An old painting of Vesuvius in the window of a bookshop distracts her; a large and familiar romanticized nineteenth-century image of the mountain, a plume of smoke rising out of the crater, something that disappeared in 1944, when it last erupted. In the middle of the painting is the silvery blue of the Bay of Naples and in the foreground, elegantly suited men and women in long flowing dresses strolling beneath parasols. Frances studies their faces then looks at the people around her. Nothing to worry about then, nothing to worry about now. That seems to be the measure of Neapolitans. She's seen some of their dark side but also the light, and their 'live for the day' philosophy is more and more appealing.

She must have been smiling to herself because suddenly a young man with a wheelbarrow piled high with neatly cut firewood is walking alongside her. 'Sei bellissima!'

She understands he is telling her, very matter of factly, that she is beautiful. He says it with the confidence of a man much older than his twenty or so years. He's so assured he might just as well have been commenting about the state of the weather. His head is shaved and his expression is earnest. They chat together like old friends until they reach a pizzeria where he is delivering the wood for the oven. 'Best pizza in Naples. You must try!'

'Don't worry, I will.'

A few minutes later she spots the marker she uses to find her way to Marcello's laboratory, a marble statue of Nilo, the ancient Egyptian river god. His face looks down on her with a grumpy expression, prompting her to buy some mood-lifting coffee from the café opposite. She balances two espressos as she rings the bell of his building.

'Come up!' Marcello replies on the intercom as he clicks open the door. 'Let me help.'

He descends the stairs and takes the two small plastic cups of coffee and the box of cakes from her. 'Great, I'm starving. I've been here half the night.'

'There's quite a crowd in here, I should have brought more coffee and cake.' Frances reels in mock horror around his laboratory. Three full skeletons stand to attention on plinths. Skulls and other human bones are placed in groups along two walls.

'Yeah, they're great companions, always quiet and cheap to feed. They're from Herculaneum, Pompeii, Stabiae, Nola.'

They drink the coffee quickly and devour the cakes. Then he guides her to a stool. 'Now sit up here because I have something to show you — booty from Pompeii that will bring that dull old wind report to life.'

Dozens of gold, silver and bronze coins are arranged on a long bench. All different sizes, they're worn and misshapen, but the markings on a few are clearly distinctive.

'Wow! How did you get your hands on those?'

'They're all from Pompeii. I've found them on excavations.'

'Finders keepers?'

'No, don't be crazy! Eventually they'll go to the museum. What do you think I am? A grave robber?'

She laughs. 'I don't know you well enough to say.'

He runs his hand along a line of the coins. 'Once you understand the marking on the coins, you can trace the precise date they were made. All of these have the faces of Roman emperors and the honours they were awarded.'

He selects one silver coin. 'This little coin is dynamite. I believe it will change our view of history.'

'That's a big statement. Let me see.' Frances holds it in her hand. The head of a man wearing a laurel crown is on one side and a flying goat on the other. Marcello's eyes are burning with excitement as he watches her turn it over several times. Latin inscriptions border each side and she strains to read them. 'What do they mean?'

'I'll show you.' Marcello places the coin face up. 'This is Titus, who was emperor at the time of the 79 AD eruption. So these letters here,' he traces his finger around the edge of the coin, 'IMP TITVS CAES VESPASIAN AVG PM, are abbreviations for his full name: the Emperor Titus Caesar Vespasian, after his father, Emperor Vespasian; then Augustus, Pontifex Maximus — the highest priest of the ancient Roman religion, a position that went with his crown. Literally it means the greatest bridge maker and today the Pope has the same title. Now look at the other side.'

He flips to the side with the flying goat. 'This is the rest of the inscription: TR P VIIII IMP XV COS VII PP, which is an abbreviation for Tribunicia Potestate VIIII, Imperator XV, Consul VII, Pater Patriae — all his awards and decorations.'

'You've lost me, Marcello. What's the significance?'

'I sympathise, I've studied coins and inscriptions for decades and it's not easy. OK, let me take you through it one step at a time. Tribunicia Potestate VIIII means he was given wide-ranging powers and protections by the senate nine times over. And although Rome was a republic, it gave him the powers of a king. Then, more significantly for us, is Imperator XV, which means Titus had received an imperial acclamation *fifteen* times. I'll explain more about that in a minute. Consul VII means he held the republican office of Consul seven times, and Pater Patriae, that he was the father of the country.

'Now, coming back to the crucial letters . . .' He points to the letters IMP XV. 'This is short for Imperator XV. Imperator is an award a battle commander received from his troops after a victory, and Titus made his reputation as a soldier long before he became emperor. He conquered Jerusalem in 70 AD and destroyed the Great Temple. The only surviving piece is the Wailing Wall, so he made quite a name for himself throughout the empire by defeating the Jews. But it's the XV, or fifteen, that is the most significant, because it means he was acclaimed for *fifteen* war victories and the question for us is when did that happen?'

'No idea.'

'Do you remember the date of the 79 AD eruption?'

'August, I think it was the 24th of August?'

'That's what everyone believes, but when you look at those wind patterns in the military report — and they're right up to date — it doesn't add up. The windspeed in August, when the eruption is supposed to have happened, is low and could never have spread the ash to Pompeii and so far beyond. So for years scientists here have always regarded it as an anomaly. The markings on this coin prove there was no anomaly — the eruption must have happened later in the year.'

Marcello reaches for a folder. 'A number of researchers have been searching for the truth. And now we have it. Look at this.' He pulls out a photograph and two documents and spreads them along the bench. The photograph is of a skeleton lying on a dusty floor. 'I found the coin in a bag wrapped around the waist of this skeleton at Pompeii, a woman who died during the eruption.'

Frances glances around the laboratory at the dangling skeletons. 'Er, she's not with us today, is she?'

'No, she's safely at rest in the museum.'

He points to the documents. 'And these pieces of paper prove beyond doubt that the coin was made after August. In August, Titus had only received his *fourteenth* imperial acclamation. The *fifteenth*, or the IMP XV,' he points again to the initials on the coin, 'came later in the year.' He picks up one of the pages with Latin inscriptions. 'This is a copy of a letter found in a museum in Spain, written by Titus to the rulers of the city of Munigua. And you can see at the top,' he points to some small lettering, 'he describes himself as Imperator XIIII, the *fourteenth* acclamation. The date of the letter is VII idus Septembres, seven days before the ides of September, which is the seventh of September. Now there's no way an emperor is going to deprive himself of an extra honour!'

He puts the paper down and picks up another. 'This is a copy of a document in the British Museum which was found in Egypt. Again, Titus is described as Imperator *Fourteen* and here at the bottom, the date VI idus Septembres, six days before the ides of September, or in other words the eighth of September. There is no way the eruption could have occurred before this date, because this coin wouldn't have existed.'

He places the page back in the folder and pulls out a sheaf of papers. 'And finally, some extracts from the Roman historian, Cassius Dio, writing about the events of 79 AD. He tells us Titus received the Imperator Fifteen — for his victory in Britannia — and that the eruption of Vesuvius occurred in autumn.'

'So what you're saying is that if the eruption happened later in the year, it puts a whole new light on predicting what could happen to people living around Vesuvius if it erupts again!'

'Precisely, Frances. Precisely.'

'But surely the date of the eruption must have been recorded. How could historians get it wrong for so long?'

'The confusion stems back to the letters Pliny the Younger wrote describing the eruption. His was the only eyewitness account. Pliny wrote them on papyrus scrolls which disintegrated, so what we are left with is a handful of copies of the letters made by scholars many centuries later. In fact, the oldest in existence were done in the Middle Ages, fourteen hundred years after Pliny died. The problem is the manuscripts either have different dates for the eruption or no date at all. The most famous and the one that is generally accepted as most accurate is the codex Mediceus in the Laurentianus library in Florence, which puts the eruption at the date you mentioned, the 24th of August. I no longer believe that is the true date.'

Marcello packs the documents back into the folder and turns to Frances with a playful look. 'Are you up for a challenge?'

'Always.'

'I have a clue about the whereabouts of a manuscript which might hold the answer and back up the evidence of the coin. Do you think you could help me?'

'Try to stop me. Where do we start?'

'First you need to see where I found the coin in Pompeii. Then we'll go hunting for the missing manuscript.'

CHAPTER NINE

Frances crouches and strokes one of the large grey stones of a Roman road that dissects the old city of Pompeii. It feels smooth and cold. She scrambles to her feet and steps from one stone to the next, counting them in her head like a child. Her boots clack on the hard surface and she can imagine the soldiers laying them in long, straight lines, more than two thousand years earlier.

The way is hemmed in on either side by pocked and worn brick walls that once supported houses and shops. She peers through doorways leading into hollow buildings without roofs, turns into another street and ahead, through a large archway, sees Vesuvius. The thin morning layer of snow has melted and in the clear afternoon light she thinks how benign the volcano looks from a distance, just as it must have appeared to those who perished in the fury of its terrifying liquid avalanche.

'Over here!'

She hears Marcello calling her from somewhere beyond the arch.

Before her, a patch of grass breaks up a deathly expanse of concrete dotted with broken columns, snapped off like pieces of candy stick. No matter how many times she sees it, the sight of this natural holocaust, with not a single survivor, still shocks her.

Through the opening of another wall she finds Marcello sitting on a marble step in the ruins of a large rectangular building. 'This was Pompeii's seat of power. The Basilica,' he tells her as she sits beside him. Tall columns line one side and, at the far end, the only surviving portion of roof is supported by six smaller ones. In the centre, just the stubs of a once mighty construction system remain.

'All wiped out by the eruption?' she asks.

'Not all. There was a massive earthquake seventeen years earlier, in 62 AD, when much of the city was destroyed, including many of the major buildings. That's when the roof of the Basilica collapsed. So at the time of the eruption, much of Pompeii was still being repaired, saving many lives, because people had moved away.'

'It follows the pattern then. Sooner or later, an eruption follows a major earthquake.'

'Sometimes, but look at what happened in Campi Flegrei with the earthquakes in the eighties. We're still waiting for an eruption from those!'

'I hope we're not here to see it. The eruption that destroyed Pompeii must have been terrifying.'

'Absolutely, and it lasted for twenty-four hours.' Marcello glances at his watch. 'In fact, this is about the time of the first eruption. One o'clock, when people were getting ready for lunch. When it first blew, the debris was blown so far into the stratosphere it blocked out the sun, so it would have been dark here. And before anyone could work out what was going on, tons of pumice and ash starting falling. Going inside didn't help because the roofs collapsed and they were buried.'

'But a lot of people escaped, didn't they?'

'Yes, many ran away, but only temporarily. Most of them returned at night or in the early morning, when they thought the danger was over. But there were further eruptions and surges of hot gas and rocks, the pyroclastic flows that raced down from the mountain. That's what killed the rest, burnt and suffocated them. The whole city was buried. And it stayed that way until it was discovered in the seventeen hundreds. It's a veritable time bubble of an ancient Roman city.'

'And we know it could all happen again any time.'

'Come on, I want to show you where I found the coin.' Marcello takes her hand and squeezes it and Frances relaxes her hand in his. The more time she spends with him, the more comfortable she feels.

They wander through a maze of streets, dodging groups of tourists following guides with tiny flags. Dozens of accents combine to sound as if a modern-day tower of Babel has risen in their midst. A rangy black and white dog squatting on a busted pedestal outside the ruins of a house barks a warning at them as though it's only a matter of time before its master will return.

'Here's our street . . .' Marcello points to a sign on a brick wall, *Insula Occidentalis*. One minute later he stops outside a plain brick building, taller than those nearby. A metal gate blocks the doorway but views of the sea are clear through the shattered remains of the three-storey villa.

'Welcome to the House of the Golden Bracelet.' He removes some keys from his pocket, unlocks a padlock on the gate and ushers her inside. 'Or as I've renamed it, the House of Clues. It's closed to the public because we're doing more digging and restoration work, but I can show you around.'

Frances steps into what must have once been a grand foyer. Mosaics still decorate the floors and brightly coloured frescoes adorn the walls. But everything is cracked and broken, as if a cyclone has recently passed through.

'Watch your step,' Marcello cautions as she almost falls into a tiled square recess in the middle of the floor. 'That was for collecting rainwater. There used to be a hole in the roof to funnel it down. That's when there was a proper roof!'

Frances looks up to makeshift steel roofing that extends throughout the villa. They reach a rough concrete staircase and walk down. The lower level is dusty with loose rubble in piles around half walls.

'This is where I found the coin, with the bodies.' He points to a spot on the bare earth at the bottom. 'We were excavating and found the skeleton of a woman. She was wearing a beautiful gold bracelet around her wrist, which is how the house was named. It was in the shape of a double-headed serpent clasping a tiny portrait medallion, and she had a bag of coins around her waist. The coin with the head of Titus Fifteen was among them.'

'Why do you think she was here?'

'She must have been trying to escape with the family's valuables but the building collapsed on her. She probably died after the first eruption because she was buried beneath piles of tiny pumice stones.'

Frances shifts uncomfortably. Standing where this woman died so violently unsettles her. Although fresh air is blowing through the gaps in the walls, she feels as if she's suffocating in a tomb. Turning away she moves through a series of rooms connected by archways, each more decorative than the last, the remnants of rich black and red frescoes splashed around the walls.

'This was a dining room,' Marcello says of a room more intact than the others. 'Look at those pictures, it must have been their idea of paradise.' Lush images of a beautiful garden bursting with fruit and flowers, exotic birds dipping their bills into fountains and wild animals roaming fill the room on all sides and extend into a curved ceiling. On the floor a large black mosaic is mostly intact with images of an array of fish, octopus, squid and lobsters swimming in an inky sea.

'We found some of the food they were eating, probably for that day's lunch.'

'That seems impossible after so long.'

'Not with the DNA testing we have today. Just small dried up pieces but the same food the very first archaeologists who dug here nearly three hundred years ago found. There have been suspicions for some time that the date of the eruption was wrong, that it wasn't in summer but later in the year, because all the food they found was from the autumn harvest — pomegranates, figs, chestnuts, walnuts and fresh olives. We've also found scraps of carpets and fireplaces that had been burning, and all the victims were wearing heavy clothes. The Romans lived with the seasons and they wouldn't be burning fires in the height of summer. It's the same way we Italians live today. Like clockwork, with the seasons.'

In the next room, daylight floods through an opening in the wall. As Frances looks out to a clear view across the Bay of Naples, Marcello comes up behind her and places his hand on her shoulder. Without thinking, she puts her hand on his, welcoming his closeness.

'We have the opposite view to the one Pliny the Younger had of the eruption. Right across there is Misenum. He was staying there with his uncle, Pliny the Elder, who was commander of the Roman navy. His uncle sailed off with a fleet to rescue survivors and never came back. His nephew recorded very accurately how the eruption unfolded. 'And there,' he says, pointing towards Naples to a densely built area that melds with the coastline, 'you can see Herculaneum.'

'It's much closer to the mountain than here,' Frances comments.

'And much closer to Naples. Everyone there died in the first pyroclastic flow. You can imagine the devastation if the wind took a surge from Vesuvius into the centre of the city.'

'Is that possible?'

'Of course, and that's why we need to understand how the wind patterns affect the impact of an eruption, so we can have the safest evacuation plans.'

Frances looks down to a garden beneath the house. 'Can we go down there?'

'Yes, but I have to warn you, this is where we found more bodies. And we've made casts of them.' He smiles at her. 'I think you vulcanologists are a little more sensitive than we archaeologists. I'm so used to keeping company with the dead, it doesn't bother me.'

Frances takes a deep breath and follows Marcello down a dark narrower staircase. The clomping of their feet is the only sound.

'Oh my God!' Frances exclaims. On the bottom steps is a man's body, sprawled face down with his head on the second step. His legs are spread and one arm is on the third step and the other resting by his side. 'The last moment of his life?'

'Yes, captured forever.'

Just beyond she sees another. A naked woman curled on the ground in a foetal position, her hands holding her head. Next to her, a young boy, sitting hugging his knees, the terror of the instant of death imprinted permanently on his face. Closer up they look more like grey zombies, yet the graceful curves of their bodies define them as unmistakably human. She bends down next to the child's cast and looks up at Marcello. 'What a terrible way to die. What happened to them?'

'We think this family returned to the house at night thinking the eruption was over and were caught by the second surge early the next morning. That's when most of the people of Pompeii were killed. After they came back, thinking it was safe.'

'How is it possible that the shape of their bodies is so intact?'

'The gas was so hot it moulded the ash to their skin and clothes and then hardened, like a glove, over their bodies. The bodies were then buried beneath piles of ash and stones and eventually they decomposed. But the bones survived, and the cavities formed by the decomposing flesh. So when archaeologists found skeletons they realized what had happened and filled these cavities with plaster. When this set, they chipped away the volcanic debris on the outside and here you have it — perfect copies.'

Marcello sees the look of horror on Frances' face. 'We always like to think they died instantly. But you can never be sure.' His voice trails away as Frances leans closer to the child.

The hands are clasped together against his forehead, his eyelids are clearly visible and he seems to be crying. Frances is deeply shocked. She touches the boy's shoulder as if she could reach back through the millennia and offer comfort. The images of her own sister drowning in the volcanic lahar in New Zealand fill her mind, the helplessness of another innocent sucked up in nature's fury. She looks at the casts of the two adults, probably the boy's parents. An entire family extinguished in seconds. She feels the return of an almost unbearable sorrow that was once a constant travelling companion. 'They knew . . . you can see their agony,' she whispers. She feels dizzy and as she almost topples, Marcello pulls her to her feet.

'I'm sorry if this is upsetting. I forget . . .'

'Forgive me, I must look like a wimp, but my only sister died when she was just eighteen months old, before I was born. But I still feel the loss, even though I didn't know her. Seeing these poor people . . .'

He strokes her head and she feels his strength calming her. 'That's

73

what it means to be human. We'd all be reduced to plaster casts if we didn't feel pain and love and joy.'

'But this brings it home, doesn't it? Dust to dust, ashes to ashes — is that what we're all reduced to in the end?'

'Maybe our bodies, but not our souls.'

Frances looks deeply into the eyes of this man who handled skeletons as comfortably as a baker tossed around loaves of bread. He returns her gaze, more intimately than she'd seen before. It takes her by surprise and she feels uncertain. She brushes his cheek with her fingers. 'You seem so sure. You really do care about these people.'

'You mean for a scientist who usually demands evidence,' he laughs. 'But you feel it too. Why else would you be so moved by this? And your sister? I think she is with you still, in some way.'

It had been a long time since Frances had stood by the river where Valerie had been drowned in the train wreck, another victim of a volcano that would not be tamed. She had finally found the courage with Tori to let go of her sister, so her spirit could be free and the living could go on living.

He smiles at her. 'Enough of this sadness. I have some surprises for you.'

The gloom of the house dissolves as Frances follows him outside and blinks in the glare. Despite being buried under metres of ash for centuries, the garden still possesses a charm and beauty. New plantings replicate the trees and shrubs of old. In one corner of the courtyard a tall and graceful pomegranate tree spreads its branches, rays of sunshine spotlighting the plump ruby fruit.

Marcello goes to the tree and picks one of the pomegranates. 'For you, melograno, the fruit of abundance.' He places it in her hand. 'It's late autumn and you can see the tree is at its peak. This is the time of year I believe the eruption occurred.'

Frances smells the apple sweetness of the pomegranate. The skin is shiny and variegated in shades from deep red to pale pink.

'Would you like to try it?' She nods and Marcello takes a pen knife from his pocket and, setting the fruit on the top of a stone fence, he scores the skin and pulls it apart. Clusters of bright red seeds burst out from the creamy white pulp.

'It looks like a heart that's been broken,' she murmers.

'Or one that's bursting with life and passion!' he laughs, passing one half to her and crunching into the other. Frances bites into the fruit, wincing when her teeth break several seeds at once. 'Bitter!'

'Keep eating,' Marcello laughs. 'You'll get used to it.'

She eats another mouthful. The seeds explode in her mouth, releasing a watery liquid, sometimes sour, sometimes sweet. 'Enough. That's enough passion and abundance for me.' She hands him back the fruit and wipes her chin.

'Mm. I hope not.' His eyes are shining and Frances feels her face redden. But he looks away before she can reply and casually tosses the remains of the fruit under the tree. 'Not quite ripe.' He smiles. 'Maybe a few more weeks.'

The lower level of the villa features a row of outdoor rooms supported by high brick archways. Dozens of ancient amphoras are stacked inside one room, the elongated pottery wine vessels forlorn relics of bygone feasting. Vivid paintings decorate another. A giant mural of a verdant garden is studded with miniature painted masks of men and women with strangely haunted expressions, as if possessed by the secrets of some sinister underworld.

'We have to cross to another street.' Marcello unlocks the garden gate leading to a side alley. Frances is compelled to glance back at the mural. Were they the faces of the dead lying inside? Did they eat and drink in this alfresco dining room, blissfully unaware of what was to come?

CHAPTER TEN

As they slip into the lane alongside the Villa of the Golden Bracelet, heavy drops of rain bounce off their heads. Their footsteps echo on the hard stones as they hurry through the deserted streets of Pompeii, through tourists escaping from the weather to waiting buses. Frances breaks into a run to keep up with Marcello. They pass the old dog cowering beneath the portal of the ruined house, no longer interested enough in them to bark.

He rounds a corner and she follows. But the lane splits into three, each heading in a different direction, and she can no longer see him. She stops, the rain now pelting down, soaking her hair and face.

'Got you!' Marcello jumps out from a doorway and grabs her. They shriek with laughter and he takes her hand. 'C'mon, I don't want you to get lost.'

She glimpses signposts on walls, Via Terme, Via della Fortuna, Via Stabiana, as he guides her quickly through the ancient streets. 'Not far now.'

They turn right into Via dell'Abbondanza, a much wider road stretching out of sight. Some of the large paving stones are missing and the holes are filling with water. They splash through the puddles. They're both puffing and dripping wet when he stops suddenly and pulls her into a doorway. 'This is it.'

'Another House of Clues?' She looks into the ruins, where splashes of red, gold and cobalt blue stain the brick walls. The room ahead is without a roof and the tiled water collector recessed in the ground is full of rainwater. Beyond lie a covered courtyard and a garden.

'You'll have to wait and see,' he teases her. 'Let's make a dash for it.'

She follows him through the rain to the shelter of a large portico supported by fluted columns, the greyish white limestone worn at their bases. The garden is surprisingly formal; box hedges frame small paths and manicured lawns planted with sculpted fig trees. She pokes her head into dark alcoves decorated with remnants of old frescoes and scans the recesses of the courtyard.

Marcello is standing looking at a large mural. She sees on his face an expression she has come to know; the look of satisfaction when he has made some discovery. She goes to him and what she sees truly surprises her. 'It's her! The woman under the sea!'

The painting is of a naked woman reclining in a large shell-like boat. A small angel is riding a dolphin in the water on one side of her and another is peering over the edge of the boat on the other.

'The goddess of love, Venus. That's our mystery woman, without her clothes.'

'She's beautiful.' Frances looks closer. The woman is wearing gold jewellery on her wrist and ankles and the same gold necklace.

'Did you realize it was her when we saw the face under the water?'

'I wasn't sure until I came back to check, but I had a good idea it was the same image. Venus is painted in hundreds of different ways, depending on the fashion of the day. And this one here,' he points at the mural, 'is unique to this part of the world. The Pompeiians and the Romans who went to Baia worshipped Venus and built temples dedicated to her.'

'Look at her hair, it's so curly. It's the same style as the mosaic.'

'Who knows, it could have been the same model. Women then used hot irons to curl their hair.'

'And make-up?'

'Of course, influenced by the Egyptians. We've found brushes, mirrors and little jars, still with traces of minerals in them that were used for colour.'

'Colour?'

'Yes, look at her eyes and her lips. They used vermilion to paint their lips and cheeks and painted their eyes with green and blue shadow made from crushed malachite and azurite.'

'Nothing much has changed then, we'll still do anything for fashion. No pubic hair either — maybe she had a Brazilian.'

Marcello laughs. 'Yes, pubic hair didn't figure in classical art.'

'She has quite a virginal look about her for the goddess of love, don't you think?'

'Ah, that could be deliberate. The mythology has it that Venus was born of the sea and her virginity was perpetually renewed. But I prefer to think she has a worldly expression.' He steps away to look at the sky. 'Still raining. But if you like I'll show you another version that's quite different.'

They run out of the crumbling villa, across two more lanes and into the doorway of another. As Frances wipes the rain from her face on her sleeve, Marcello takes a handkerchief from his pocket and dabs her cheeks dry. His own dark hair is matted to his head and dripping. She takes the handkerchief from him and mops up the water.

He's staring at her hard, his brown eyes glistening. She raises her face to his and their lips meet. It's the gentlest of kisses. Frances feels so drawn to him but something holds them both back.

'Frances . . .'

She smiles at him and presses her forefinger onto his lips. 'I think you're already attached?'

'I was.'

'Not now?'

He looks away and answers her question with his own. 'And you?'

'I was too — maybe I still am. I was very involved with a man in New Zealand but we've drifted apart. Now, I'm not sure.'

He grins at her. 'Ah, complications. You'll be pleased to learn that such love trysts are as old as, well, as old as Venus.'

She follows him inside the ancient villa and through a series of rooms. On the wall in front of them is another fresco of a couple. 'Venus and Mars.' Marcello turns to see her reaction.

Mars is standing behind Venus and reaching around to touch her breast. Venus looks very surprised. Frances bursts out laughing.

'I think the artist was being kind to her. Cheating . . . that's something Venus knew all about.' Marcello smiles wickedly. 'She was the wife of Vulcan, God of Fire and Volcanoes, but she betrayed him and fell in love with Mars, God of War.'

He walks into the next room where there is a line of fading frescoes in different panels of the wall. 'These paintings are based on Homer's story of the betrayal in the Odyssey. There's Vulcan on the right, sitting on his throne and thoroughly pissed off. And there, on the left, is Venus and Mars going for it in bed.'

They stand together in front of the next panel.

'There you see Vulcan, who was a blacksmith, making a net of chains that can never be broken. And here,' he says moving along, 'the lovers are trapped beneath the net. In the next panel there's Vulcan with Apollo, the God of the Sun, looking at his guilty prisoners.'

'And the moral of the story?'

'It's an old story, isn't it — a tale of betrayal but also a tale of when love dies. When I was younger, those things were black and white, but the moral of the story today? I don't really know.'

He moves into the next room and crouches beside another painting, of a scroll, an inkstand and a quill. Some Latin lines are on the scroll but many words have worn away. He looks up at her. 'It's a fragment of a poem about Venus, but I think it is still very beautiful. Can you understand the words?'

'No. My knowledge of Latin is pretty basic. *Amo, amas, amat, amamus, amatis, amant,*' she recites.

'Well, you're on the right track, it's about love.'

She leans over and follows his fingers along the words as he translates.

'*I don't think a Venus made of marble would be as favourable to me as . . .*'

'That's it?'

79

'Yes. So everyone can finish it off as they like.'

'And how would you finish it?'

He stands and pauses for a moment. Then he looks at her and says: 'I don't think a Venus made of marble would be as favourable to me as one without adornment but as natural and beautiful as thee.'

Before she can reply, he pulls her close. Now they kiss slowly and deliberately, Frances enjoying the sensual feelings he induces. 'Quite the poet,' she responds at last.

A loud roaring interrupts them. 'The rain must have stopped. That sounds like chainsaws. They must be cutting down the trees.'

The noisy interference breaks the mood. 'Unlike the gods, we mere mortals can't live on love alone.' Marcello laughed. 'If we hurry we might be in time for lunch.'

The streets of Pompeii have started to fill with people again as they return to the entrance to the old city. They step aside as large groups of tourists spread out across the paths. The surface is wet and slippery and Frances can smell the fresh aftermath of the rain. She feels she is in a beautiful yet ominous dream and can imagine the way the town used to look before the destruction; a town throbbing with life, its people living and loving as if there was no tomorrow, no one suspecting for a moment that for them, there would be no tomorrow.

'Scandalous,' Marcello mutters.

'What is?'

'The trees.' He points to a hillside just inside the walls of the city. 'We had to take out two of those big trees for the excavations. They're right over a major villa we're working on and there was no choice. That's where the noise is coming from.'

A small group of men in yellow overalls is cutting branches off a large tree with a chainsaw.

'What's the problem?' she asks.

'The cost. Eighty thousand euro to remove the trees.'

'You're joking!'

'No. That's the price. Whenever you want a job done anywhere, the contract has to go out to certain people and the price comes back. You have no choice.'

'Surely that's illegal! Don't people have to tender for the work?'

'In theory, yes. In practice, no. It's Il Sistema. Pay up or else!'

'Who pays?'

'The government pays. We all lose.'

Frances shakes her head. 'It's something I can't come to grips with.'

'Nor me, nor most people in this city — it's another reason we often feel powerless.'

They reach the car park and climb into Marcello's four-wheel-drive. The modern town of Pompeii is just a few minutes drive away. Jockeying between lurching tour buses, they soon arrive outside a trattoria, in a small lane off the main street. The tables are occupied but two women who have finished their meals are leaving one near the window.

'Benvenuto! Welcome!' The patrone ushers them to the table and a waiter appears immediately to reset it.

'Do you want some antipasto?' Marcello asks. 'They do a good buffet here.'

They walk over to a long table covered with platters and bowls.

Frances looks at the platters of squid, octopus and fish, bowls of grapes, lemons, olives and pomegranates. 'It's the same food we saw in all the old paintings, the same food people ate here two thousand years ago.'

'Hard to improve on perfection,' he laughs. 'Here, try some of these fresh anchovies.' He piles them onto two plates and they return to the table.

Frances feels warm and comfortable with Marcello, but wonders where it will lead. Is she being foolish? After all, she'd seen so many office romances turn into disasters.

'Are you OK? Your green eyes tell me you're far away.'

'No, I'm right here with you.' And she means it. So attractive, so attentive, so clever.

'Nothing to worry about with me,' he smiles. 'There's no pressure.'

At that moment, a woman with a pram bumps into Frances' chair. 'Mi scusi,' she apologizes, 'so sorry.'

Frances stands to let her pass and glimpses the chubby round face of a baby girl beneath a lacy shawl. A little boy and his father follow them out of the restaurant.

'Grazie, signorina,' the man says as they close the door.

'And the same faces,' she whispers.

'Pardon?'

'The people. The food looks the same and so do the people. That family, their faces could be those on the walls of old Pompeii.' Frances stops eating and looks out the window at the family walking on the other side of the street, unaware of danger, just the same as their ancestors.

'Cheer up,' Marcello snaps his fingers. 'We still have to eat and the food is delicious. What's wrong?'

'I can't help thinking of the dead people we saw in the villa.'

He takes both her hands. 'It's always a shock the first time. But they're a powerful reminder of why we have to make sure people here can escape if Vesuvius erupts again.'

'And if people can't rely on us scientists,' she muses, 'they may have to start relying on the gods again.'

'Or the saints.' Marcellos smiles. 'That's where my grandfather is pinning his hopes.'

CHAPTER ELEVEN

The silhouette of the old man curves like a puppet on the horizon as he bends over the vines and pulls the grapes. He tugs hard and falls back slightly as a bunch of the rich scarlet fruit comes loose in his hand.

'Nonno!' Marcello calls out.

He turns towards them and waves, the breeze ruffling the thin grey hair that has receded from a prominent forehead. 'I'm coming!' He picks up the bucket at his feet, drops in the fresh bunch, then steps gingerly over a trench of soil alongside the green and yellow vines that stretch over a rise and out of sight.

As he moves slowly but assuredly down the hill swinging the bucket, Frances is surprised to see he is wearing a three-piece dark suit and tie and polished black shoes.

'Dressed in his Sunday best to meet you. He's had that suit for as long as I can remember. Cuts a fine figure for an octogenarian, don't you think?'

'Pure style!'

The sun is beating down on the fields and the rows of houses in the village behind. She squints into the sunlight. The purplish brown peak of Vesuvius rises above. The remnants of the river of lava that scorched this landscape in the forties appear stuck to the mountain like strips of silvery grey papier-mâché.

'Marcello! How are you? It's been too long.'

The two men stretch their arms out and hug tightly. As they embrace, Frances sees the old man is as tall as his grandson. Marcello takes his hand and brings him to her. 'Grandfather, Frances Nelson. Frances, this is Raphaele Vattani.'

'Pleased to meet you and welcome to my home.' He puts his hand on his heart and then grips hers firmly. 'Marcello, you forgot to tell me how beautiful she is.' His smile lights up his lined face and dark eyes.

'Thank you for inviting me. I've been looking forward to hearing some of your stories,' she smiles back.

'Plenty of time for that. Come and try some of my wine first.' His warmth makes her feel instantly at ease and when he takes her arm, she happily walks with him. They leave the fields through a gateway and cross the road to a small white-washed cottage with tiny windows. Raphaele beckons them into the cool of the house.

He puts the bucket of grapes down next to a sink in the small combined lounge and kitchen, crammed with old furniture. The floor is covered in blue and white tiles that are clean but worn. Framed photographs hang haphazardly on the walls and a faded lace curtain covers the doorway to what seems to be the only other room. Marcello urges her to join him on a wooden bench at an oblong wooden table in the centre of the room.

'This is where my father and his brothers and sisters were born and I used to come here all the time when I was a boy.' He taps the wood. 'We had lots of family feasts at this table.'

'Where did they all sleep?'

'Anywhere they could find a spot,' Raphaele interrupts with a laugh. He comes towards them with a pewter tray holding a bottle of wine and three glasses.

'It wasn't unusual for people to have as many as fifteen children in those days. Marcello's grandmother and I were lucky. We had only six. We slept through there,' he indicates through the doorway, 'and the kids slept on bunks. Sometimes the little ones were three to a bed. I always remember seeing small feet dangling out. We all managed, they were hard days but happy days.'

As he pours the wine, the daylight picks up the shiny red hue in the glasses. He passes one to each of them. 'Salute!' he shouts.

'Cheers!' Frances replies. She sips the wine that tastes mellow and dry. The two men are watching her expression closely. 'Very good, I like it a lot. Did you make it?'

Raphaele grunts. 'I used to in the old days. Now all my grapes go to a cooperative in the village and they are pressed there and made into wine. It's much quicker and I think it's still good. Like everything today, a lot easier.'

A black and white wedding photo of a young Raphaele and his dark-haired bride hangs next to a tiny shrine with a statue of Mary. The woman is wearing a small lace veil and her lipstick accentuates a wide smile that reminds Frances of Marcello. 'That's Teresa, my wonderful wife. Nearly ten years now since she died.' As he shakes his head, a small tear appears in his right eye.

'Come on, Nonno, no time for crying today.' Marcello pats his shoulder. 'Frances wants to hear your stories about Vesuvius.'

As he clears his throat Frances takes a green cotton handkerchief from her bag and passes it to him. 'Thank you. Of course. I'm sorry. I'm a silly old man.'

'No,' she presses his large hand that is tanned and heavily veined. 'It's natural. Your wife looks beautiful.'

As she sits with him, his emotion quickly taps into her own. She notices the cuffs on his suit jacket are starting to fray. The collar of his pressed white shirt is a trifle tight, pressing onto his neck but his royal blue tie is perfectly knotted. She glances back to the photo to Teresa and she chokes back her own tears, remembering her losses.

Raphaele tops up each of the glasses and sighs. 'We met when we were fourteen. She lived in the next village,' he begins. 'It was just a year or two before Vesuvius erupted. We children took part in processions at the different churches. It was a bit of a competition between the parishes to see who put on the best show. One day all the kids came from the next town, curious to see what we were doing. That's when I saw Teresa for the first time. She was so beautiful I was in awe of her, wearing a white dress and a little veil, like a bride. And like all the other girls, she carried a small basket with rose petals they scattered through the church. She was with her parents and I was too scared to talk to her, but I plucked up the courage after the mass.'

'He's always been good at talking to the girls, as you can see Frances.

I don't think you were that scared, Nonno!' Marcello nudges him.

Raphaele grins. 'I was so keen I walked all the way to her village and back again, just so I could talk to her.'

'Were they all walking?'

'Everyone walked! Everyone went on foot. There were no buses or trains or cars like today. You know, people would walk for hours with huge heavy baskets of fruit on their heads to sell them at the market in Naples. We thought nothing of it.'

'So were you together when Vesuvius erupted?'

'Not at first. I was with my friends here. But later, on the last day we watched it together.'

'What do you remember?'

'Everything, it was springtime, the eighteenth of March. It was my mother's birthday, so I never forgot. They were terrible days. It was wartime and the Germans had been bombing us. The night before the eruption they bombed the middle of the city and hundreds of people were killed.

'The first thing we saw was this red-hot lava pouring down the slopes. We thought at first it was the bombing and that the crater had been blown up. The lava flowed down the mountain and into our towns. On the third day we heard lots of explosions and at night the sky was lit up with burning cinders and we had to keep running away because there were showers of ash. A huge tree-shaped cloud filled the sky. The lava flowed for five days. Many houses were destroyed and all the crops but we were luckier than most. In those days I lived around the corner, with my parents, on the second floor of an apartment. We escaped damage but we lost our grapes and olives and the local church. Most of the houses, including this one, were rebuilt afterwards.'

'How shocking for you.'

Raphaele laughs. 'It should have been but I was just a teenager. Me and my friends, we thought it was exciting. We were running everywhere, having fun watching the lava hit buildings and destroy them. We didn't really understand the terrible blow for the people who lost everything. We were innocents.'

He shrugs his shoulders and looks at her. 'It was only when I was older I realized what grief it had caused. There were dozens of people killed, mainly old people. Like me now, I suppose.' He dabs his eye with the handkerchief. 'They must have been trapped in their houses and suffocated by the gases.'

Marcello stands. 'Nonno, let's show Frances what's left of the church.'

The old man looks at his watch and nods. 'Yes, why not? It's still early.'

The sun is high in the sky as they walk along the dusty street and pass a row of small shops busy with people shopping for lunch. At the town square, a group of men is gathered outside the central café sipping coffee. A woman selling newspapers calls out. 'Buon giorno, Signor Vattani!' He waves at her.

They cross the square and Marcello takes Raphaele's arm as they climb a steep path lined with houses. Soon they reach the ruins of the old church. Clumps of spindly vegetation poke out from cracks in the grey granite and a flock of small birds flies in and out of the once glorious house of worship.

Raphaele stares at it in silence. He runs his fingers down one of the walls. 'I remember this church well,' he says at last. "The Church of the Assumption of the Virgin Mary, the protector of our town.'

They follow the old man as he wanders around the outside of the building. The entry is barricaded shut. He turns to Frances. 'I haven't been here for years. It brings back so many memories — the processions, the laughter. This is where I met Teresa.'

He peers inside through a gap in the mortar and pulls back when a bird suddenly flies close to his head.

'We watched the lava coming from over there.' He points to an apartment building on a street higher up. 'The building wasn't there then. It was just a hill. But the lava moved quite slowly so you could find a place to get a good view. The lava flowed straight into the church and smashed it. Everything inside was lost. After it was wrecked, the American and British soldiers were here guarding it.

They wouldn't let us in. Probably too dangerous but we didn't know it then. We really believed in the power of the Virgin Mary and the saints.'

'And do you still?'

'I have to admit it was dented on that day. But yes, without doubt. Don't you?'

'I wasn't brought up in the Catholic faith, so I don't have those beliefs.'

'Come on, you two,' Marcello says, 'let's finish our philosophical discussions back at the house.'

As they walk back across the square, a truck loaded with gas tanks is blocking the road. A line of cars builds up quickly behind it. The drivers sit waiting, faces set with resignation. Two women get out of their cars and chat on cellphones.

'You see how difficult it is here to pass through? Just a single small truck can hold everything up. It would be impossible to escape quickly if the volcano erupts,' Marcello says.

They stand a moment and watch the truck driver remove three tanks and take them into a hardware shop. A second line of cars has built up in the other direction and nothing can move. The driver returns to his truck, waves sheepishly at the cars and moves on. Gradually, the cars disperse.

'You know, Nonno, we might all have to walk if the mountain goes. That might be the best way out if you have half a million people on the move.'

Frances locks arms with Raphaele as they walk. 'Are you afraid of the volcano?'

'Absolutely not! Nor is anyone else around here. I know Marcello doesn't agree. He's always on at me to make plans to leave. But at my age, what's the point? There's nowhere else I want to go. Anyway, I think it will be many decades before anything happens. These phenomena come in cycles every one or two hundred years and it hasn't been a hundred years since the last one. The people here are not afraid physically because the lava is slow and takes more than a day to move just one kilometre. It's hot and destroys everything in its path but there's time to get out of the way. People who haven't seen it like me, hear from their father or their grandfather. They're only worried about losing their houses and property. And we have faith. We believe God will look after us.'

'Faith! Really, Nonno, I've told you before that the danger is much greater than the lava flows of 1944 — don't forget Pompeii. That's much further away than here. These villages could be wiped out by a pyroclastic flow. Everyone would be killed.'

'That's why we're relying on you scientists with your good educations!' Raphaele snorts. 'You will have to give everyone time to leave. We know about the danger of gas and ash that killed everyone at Pompeii, but I don't believe the same thing could happen again from one moment to the next. Let's say the people here are fatalistic and don't really believe in the danger.'

When they reach his house, Raphaele invites them back inside. 'Frances, I want to show you something before you go.'

She and Marcello return to the table, where Raphaele removes three bunches of the grapes from the bucket and puts them into a paper bag. 'Here, look at these. Smell them. Taste them.'

Frances bites into a grape. It is sweet and juicy.

'You ask me if I am afraid of the volcano. These grapes are Aglianico, the oldest in all of Italy. They grow because of the fertility of the mountain. The Greeks and the Romans made wine with them and we have eaten them for more than two thousand years.'

He chuckles. 'We have a saying here — carpe diem — seize the day. It's how people who stay near the volcano live their lives. We make the most of every day.' He hands the bag to Frances. 'Take these home. And remember what I told you when you eat them.'

Marcello and the old man embrace once more.

Then he kisses Frances on both cheeks. He takes a step back, still holding on to her shoulders. His face is weathered but his skin is shiny and strong and his eyes twinkle. 'What on earth is there for me to be afraid of? Teresa is waiting for me.'

CHAPTER TWELVE

As she rides into the centre of the old Roman town of Pozzuoli, Frances can see the tips of three ancient columns rising from the ruins. The day is hot and still and the rows of yachts anchored just off the seafront are barely moving. She edges her motorbike into a spot between two cars parked in the street and looks around. 'Safe enough,' she thinks, and with her helmet tucked under one arm and her day pack over the other she walks towards the park leading to the ruins. The second she does, she hears a voice behind her.

'Prego, signorina . . .'

A man of sixty or so is at her elbow. His face is burnished from the sun and seems to blend with his old but well-pressed brown suit. 'One euro. For your motorbike,' he says proffering his hand.

'You'll look after it?'

'Of course, signorina. And your helmet.' He smiles broadly, revealing a dazzling set of white dentures. She passes the coin to the unofficial parking guard and threads the helmet strap over the handlebars, sensing there is no option, and anyway, it's a safe investment. 'Grazie.'

'Thanks. I'll be back soon,' she replies.

Terraced rows of pink, yellow and white apartments overlook the park on three sides. She strolls across the soft green grass towards a huge sign.

Macellum of Pozzuoli
This is the site of the ancient covered marketplace built by the Romans in 200 AD. It was destroyed by the volcanic phenomenon of bradyseism, from the Greek: bradi = slow

and seimos = tremor. Bradyseism occurs when pressure exerted by a deep mass of magma below the earth's crust causes deformation of the rocks above. This leads to the ground rising and then falling. This site is a snapshot of 1500 years of bradyseism in the Campi Flegrei region where the ground has moved many metres up and down and hundreds of buildings have been lost to the sea. When the ground rises quickly, it can indicate an imminent eruption. This occurred in 1538 when the ground rose nearby by five metres and formed Europe's youngest volcano, Monte Nuovo. More recent movements occurred in the early 1980s, followed by a massive earthquake that destroyed much of this town of Pozzuoli and left 30,000 people here homeless.

Frances scrambles down a flight of marble steps into the old market-place. Immediately she can see how far the earth has slumped below the new town. The three tall pillars and a large circular grouping of smaller ones tell more of the past. Each is pockmarked with wide bands of holes from the base upwards. She walks to the tallest pillar and pokes her fingers into the holes. They're rough and sharp and it's clear from the markings that they've been home to marine life, probably mussels. She looks up. The same markings are high above her. All of this must have been below sea level and has risen again. The ground is muddied from recent rain and she bends over to rub away the dirt and uncovers patches of a mosaic floor. The same black and white pattern of mosaics she saw underwater in the sunken villa at Baia emerges. That was kilometres away. The extent of the destruction of the coastline is far worse than she imagined.

She scans the apartment buildings around the site, guessing they were built in the last hundred years or so and must have survived the recent earthquakes. As she's trying to estimate the distance the ground has dropped, her phone rings.

'Where are you? I'm waiting at Solfatara for you.' It is Riccardo.

'Sorry, I'm on my way. I'm in Pozzuoli looking at the old Roman marketplace. I've been meaning to come here for weeks. It's extraordinary.'

'It certainly reveals the extent of bradyseism and what we're up against. Did you realize that Pozzuoli is almost at the centre of the old caldera of the eruption of thirty-five thousand years ago?'

'The Campanian Ignimbrite?'

'Exactly, Frances.'

'It's hard to imagine the whole place erupting here.'

'You won't feel like that when you come to where I'm standing. It feels as if it could go at any time. How long will you be? It's really hot here.'

'Fifteen minutes.'

'I'll be down by the testing equipment in the crater. Follow Viale delle Ginestre and you'll find me.'

Frances races up the steps two at a time then stops, pausing to look at the apartment buildings again. How vulnerable they look.

She walks back to her bike and the parking man is waiting as though he has never moved from the spot. He insists on helping remove her helmet from the handle bars and passes it to her. 'Were you here when the earthquake hit?'

'Si, it was terrible. Many people lost their homes — so many.'

'Did you?'

'No. My family was spared. But our building was badly damaged. Over there.' He points to the apartments near the ruins.

Frances climbs onto her bike and turns to him. 'Do you worry about it happening again?'

He screws up his face and laughs, raising his weathered hands. 'No. What's the point? What can I do about it? Life, it goes on. Buon viaggio, safe journey, signorina.'

Following the road northwest, away from the old port, rows of modern apartment buildings mark the new town boundaries. She accelerates as the road rises sharply, then dips again, and steam floats high into the air.

Soft umbrella pine trees form a shady canopy over the entry to the Solfatara volcanic park, where Riccardo's motorbike rests against one of the trunks. She parks next to it and as soon as she takes off her helmet the smell of sulphur fills her senses. A breeze rustles through the trees and a short way ahead, swirling steam rises and blends into the blue of the sky. A sign marks the path to the crater and she walks quickly towards it, brushing against broom bushes covered in yellow flowers that crowd the edges.

The path opens abruptly into a vast emptiness. Columns of smoke escape from unseen holes and the air is thick with fumes. The size of the crater amazes her — a massive field of stone, denuded of vegetation, stretches in an almost rectanglar shape until it disappears beneath scrubland that rises up the walls. High above, silhouettes of apartment buildings crowd the ridge on one side and spindly pines on the other.

She scans the barren landscape for Riccardo but can't see him as her footsteps echo on the hot ground. The tip of a satellite dish rises out of the steam.

'Frances, up here!'

Following the voice, she sees him examining the dish behind a crude enclosure of chicken wire, the rusty fence contrasting with its bright whiteness. She finds the gate and watches him cleaning a control panel beneath the dish.

He stops and walks towards her, arms held out. 'Welcome to the home of Vulcan, God of Fire and Volcanoes. This is the place he called Hades,' he says as he hugs her. 'I think you can see why.'

'I wonder what Vulcan would make of all of this gear. And us. Are we the modern guardians of the underworld?'

'The sentinels? Yes, I think so. Come over and look at the dish. This picks up the readings from the reflectors planted around the crater and then transmits the data to a space satellite. From there it's relayed to our observatory, part of the national network assessing seismic risk. The data we capture here can be downloaded by observatories and Civil Defence agencies throughout Europe.'

A loud explosion echoes around the crater. 'It's coming from the Bocca Grande.' Riccardo points to a huge spraying geyser in the centre of the crater. 'Let's go over.'

Frances notices the likenesses to White Island, the boiling mud pools and furious steaming fumaroles, spewing out yellow sulphuric fumes. And yet Solfatara is also very different, so much part of old Europe. She glances up at the apartment buildings and wonders how many thousands of people live near the rim.

'This crater was formed maybe five thousand years ago,' Riccardo explains. 'There hasn't been an eruption at Solfatara since the eleven hundreds and in the wider area since the one in the fifteen hundreds which formed Monte Nuovo. But we believe all of Campi Flegrei is getting more active. You saw it for yourself when you went diving at Baia.'

'Do you think it's as dangerous as Vesuvius?'

'Campi Flegrei is linked by the magna lake about twelve kilometres below us that stretches all the way to Vesuvius. While a massive eruption there would be a catastrophe for Naples, there's plenty to worry about here too. This is earthquake central.'

'The big one that wrecked Pozzuoli in the 1980s — what happened in the lead-up?'

'They monitored more than fifteen thousand quakes in the two years prior. It must have been extraordinary, shakes all day and all night.'

As they walk, their feet sound as if they're beating a drum. Riccardo picks up a rock the size of a football and heaves it into the air. It booms as it hits the ground. 'There're a lot of holes underneath from all the rainwater gathered there. That's why it sounds hollow . . . My God, look up there!' Riccardo is pointing above the apartments. 'I don't believe it. Those lying bastards!'

'What's the matter?'

'Look, the cranes. They're building more blocks of apartments. They're crazy!'

'Surely it's no longer legal to build there?'

'Not if you have the right connections. The authorities know how dangerous it is. And they promised not to after . . .'

Riccardo is silent and staring into the distance.

'What? After what?'

'After the deaths.' Riccardo strides on leaving Frances standing alone, feeling left out of the loop. It's a sensation she often has in Italy — as a foreigner you're told half the truth, always left with a feeling that something else is going on. Another agenda.

He calls back to her over his shoulder. 'You want to know why people are afraid? Come, I'll show you.'

She can feel her heart racing as she follows Riccardo towards the lip of the geyser. Hot water is spurting high into the air. It plops onto the gritty ground and trickles into a bubbling pond.

Riccardo stands there, banging his fist into his hand. 'Nothing here ever really changes. This is a place of execution. In the third century the Romans brought prominent Christians here to kill them. They chopped off the heads of Gennaro, who became the patron saint of Naples, and Proculus, the patron saint of Pozzuoli. Some say you can see the devils of hell dancing here — now I'm beginning to see them too.'

'That sounds like hocus-pocus. And it was a long time ago.'

Riccardo turns to her. 'Yes and no. But there is something I haven't told you.' His face is strained and he turns away and looks at his feet.

'What is it?'

'A year ago it happened again.' He turns back. 'Two men were murdered, scientists who stood up to Il Sistema over plans for development here and around Vesuvius. They spoke out and complained to the government, through the newspapers, even on television. Then they disappeared. We found their bodies here.'

'What happened to them?'

'Beheaded. Modern-day martyrs. Killed and dumped in the boiling pool like dead dogs.' He crosses himself.

'No!' Frances feels a chill rush through her. 'That's barbaric. I can't believe anyone could do that.'

'It's part of the war. You see all the stories on TV about boy soldiers in Africa and the Middle East — well, there are boy soldiers here too, part of Il Sistema. They're desensitised young guys high on power and money and probably drugs who do what they're told. Human life means nothing, they kill to order, even their own relatives. Worst of all, they know one day it will be them and they simply don't care.'

'Did you know the scientists?'

'Not well. I met them a couple of times at the observatory in Stromboli. They came from the north, from Pisa. Both were in their thirties, with young families. They thought they could get away with bucking the Naples way of doing business and they paid for that mistake with their lives. But the government promised the development wouldn't go ahead and we believed them. And now . . .'

They walk slowly past the boiling pool. The water is bubbling and murky and it's impossible to see the bottom. It flows into another pond of mud boiling like hot fudge, hundreds of little bubbles popping and sinking into the mire.

'So, you and I, and Marcello — if we speak out, if we tell the truth, are we in danger too?'

Riccardo doesn't reply. 'Come on. Let's leave this place.' He links his arm in hers and their footsteps crunch on the rough ground, filling the silence between them. Soon they are away from the crater and sheltered by the avenue of trees. He lets go of her arm and at last finds the words. 'The ancient Greeks believed that only true heroes could cross these lands, the fields of fire. Everyone was terrified by this place. This was hell, the underworld. You've heard of Hercules?'

'The strong man?'

'Yes! He was the first to dare to cross here. Hercules, the strong man who fought evil, was the only one who could withstand the flames, the rumbling ground, boiling water and fire. Now thousands of years later, the evil is just as prevalent. It just has a different name. Maybe that's what we need — some more heroes like Hercules.'

Frances can still hear the hissing geysers behind them and the smell of sulphur tailing them as if it was the rancorous breath of the underworld, and wants desperately to wash it from every pore in her body.

'Are you a hero?' She looks directly into his eyes.

He turns away and sighs. 'I don't know. I hope I don't have to find that out.'

CHAPTER THIRTEEN

Corso Vittorio Emanuele is bustling in the late afternoon when Frances rides home. Shutters are thrown open and she glimpses an old woman, face pale and drawn, sitting behind a window. She stares out at the street as if waiting for someone who went out years before and never returned. Propped on the pavements outside the greengrocers, wooden crates full of new-season capsicums glow, an almost fluorescent rainbow of red, orange, yellow, green and purple.

Frances pulls off the street into the petrol station where her neighbour, Peppe Fogliano, works.

They've spoken only in passing on the stairs when she's been talking to his wife, Laura, but he greets her like an old friend. 'Fill her up, Francesca?'

'Yes please, Peppe.'

She climbs off the bike and stretches her legs while she watches him fill it with fuel, his finely contoured face accentuated by sleek black hair. The blue overalls she's seen hanging on the line fit his stocky body as if they were tailor-made. It never ceases to amaze her how smart Italians appear in the simplest of work clothes. Peppe replaces the petrol pump and she hands him her credit card. He returns from the tiny cubicle that serves as an office with her receipt, a bucket of water and a thick yellow chamois. 'I'll just clean some of that dust off,' he says kindly, 'it's a bit of a mess. Where've you been?'

'Out to Campi Flegrei and off the road a bit. Thanks.'

Although she guesses he's younger than her, he speaks to her like he's speaking to one of his twin boys. 'Be careful when you're riding alone in the country,' he cautions. 'Best to go with others.'

She's tempted to ask him the dozens of questions that are crowding her mind but something tells her not to. She wonders what he knows about Il Sistema.

They live just a few streets above the Spanish Quarter, a tangle of dark narrow lanes and crowded tenement buildings notorious for its clan crime. She's heard whispers about rackets and standover tactics, sometimes wondering about the quiet conversations in corners of shops she frequents. Instinctively, she's always quickened her step along these streets. Until now it hasn't really bothered her, but she can't get images of headless bodies thrown into the boiling pools out of her mind. Where were the heads, for God's sake? Floating alongside?

'There you go. You can even see in the mirror now.' Two more motorbikes pull up behind her, then a car, beeping its horn. 'OK, OK!' Peppe calls. 'Madonna, some people are so impatient!'

'Busy time?'

'Yeah. Everyone's in a hurry to go somewhere.'

Laura sometimes complains that she hardly sees him. He's here six and a half days a week till all hours. As if he's read her mind, he tells her they're closing earlier. 'If you see Laura, tell her I'll be home soon. We're shutting up shop early.'

As Frances rides past the last line of shops leading home, she notices the small shrine to the Madonna mounted on the wall of the lane is overflowing with fresh crimson roses, almost hiding the statue of Mary and artificial candles behind.

Stefano and Lorenzo are playing chase with several other small boys in the courtyard. They flock around her, begging for a ride, but tonight she's not in the mood to play and tries to shrug it off, feeling sick to her stomach. 'Ciao, ragazzi! Hello, boys! Out of the way now.'

They let her pass and continue chasing each other, their voices shrieking with the thrill of the game.

As soon as Frances climbs the stairs she hears the cello, a lilting sound that seems to be calling to her like a voice. She pauses outside Pasquale's door where music soars, rich and mellow. She listens for several minutes until it ends. Then she knocks.

The door opens slightly. The woman's shoulder-length platinum blonde hair is curled in an almost old-fashioned Hollywood style. Her eyes are startlingly blue, and ringed with black kohl. 'Si?' She looks surprised to see a visitor.

'Hi, I'm Frances, I was wondering . . .'

'Frances, come in, come in. It's OK, Poppaea, she's a friend,' she hears Pasquale call.

The woman smiles and opens the door wide. The room where Pasquale is sitting with his cello mirrors the shape of her own lounge but furnished in an old Italian style. Half-drawn heavy curtains block most of the light from the balcony. An upright piano is against one wall, beside a glass-doored cabinet packed with books.

Pasquale leaps up from the old chaise longue and props the cello against it. 'Welcome.' He extends his hand. 'You've come at a good time. We're stopping for coffee. This is my sister, Poppaea.'

As Poppaea shakes Frances' hand, a loud clatter sounds from the kitchen. 'Merda!'

'Hey, Satore, what are you doing? Trying to smash everything?' Pasquale calls. 'Bring an extra cup if there's any left. We have company.'

A young man with short hair, gelled upright, and a line of silver rings in one ear totters into the room balancing a tray. 'Sorry, I just lost a plate. It was an old one.'

Pasquale laughs. 'Don't worry. I picked them up at a junk market.'

He places the tray on a green metallic coffee table that is at odds with the faded elegance of the room. 'Ciao, I'm Salvatore but you can call me Satore. And you might have guessed this ugly table is another of Pasquale's finds!' His voice is deep, like crushed gravel, in contrast to his friend's soft melodic one, and when he shakes Frances' hand she feels the calluses that mark his long manicured fingers. 'You like espresso?'

She nods and he pours a steaming brew from the coffee maker into four small cups. He piles three spoons of sugar into his own and gestures at the others to help themselves.

'What was that beautiful piece you were playing?' Frances asks.

'It's "The Swan" from *The Carnival of the Animals* by Camille Saint-Saëns. You like it?'

'It's very moving . . . and very sad.'

'Pasquale is practising for an important audition,' Poppaea explains. 'Satore's accompanying him on the piano. I'm here for moral support so you can join me here if you like.' Frances sits beside Poppaea on a green velvet sofa opposite Pasquale.

Satore drains his coffee and sits at the piano. 'I prefer the violin but anything for a friend, eh? OK. Let's go.' He rubs his hands together, turns and signals Pasquale then starts to play, his fingers moving easily through four bars.

Pasquale raises his bow and the music flows from him. The long instrument melds with his body, its spike planted in front of him like a tiny third foot. His face almost touches the neck and moves with the music. Frances is captivated by his cloudy green-blue eyes that follow his fingers as he depresses each string. When he closes them, it's as if a light has been turned off but he keeps the same pace, his fingers moving automatically up and down the strings as he draws the bow backwards and forwards.

Frances closes her eyes and can picture a swan swimming, the water flowing over its thick white feathers. But the music suggests danger; she imagines the bird is threatened, turning this way and that, trembling and afraid. The swan slows and seems sick, ready to die. She opens her eyes again and glances across to Poppaea. She sits motionless, as if in a trance. Pasquale finishes the last lingering cello notes, lowers the bow and rests his hands on his lap. He almost seems to have stopped breathing. Satore's shoulders bend over the piano and he plays the final bars.

No one moves and for a few moments the last notes hover in the room.

'That was wonderful,' Frances breathes.

'It could be better.' Pasquale wearily creases his brow. 'It looks good but this cello is a pretty average instrument — laminated wood, spruce and maple, very possibly artificial.' He taps the side. 'It was probably made in China, like nearly everything else seems to be these days. I'm saving to buy the real thing, something older and Italian. I've got my eye on one in a music shop near the conservatorium. But I haven't got quite enough money yet. I just hope it doesn't sell in the meantime and I can get it in time for the audition next month.'

'What are you auditioning for?'

'A place in the Naples orchestra — it's my dream to play at the Teatro San Carlo.'

'You'd better get back to busking then,' Satore interrupts. 'It's a big night for the tourists at Santa Lucia. I'll come tonight if you like.'

'We have to go to the meeting first, remember,' Pasquale says.

'The meeting?' Frances asks.

'About the rubbish strike. The students are organizing a big protest rally. We're sick of the junk piled up all over Naples and Campania.'

'I've seen it. Right up to Vesuvius. Diabolical!'

'We're being drowned in trash. It's coming in from everywhere in Italy and from other countries. And our own rubbish sits here because there's no more landfill to put it in. Now there's a move to build a giant incinerator.' Pasquale is pacing the room, his usual gentleness swamped by anger. 'We are already the dumping place for toxic waste. And now they want to poison the very air that we breathe!'

Satore nods his agreement. 'That's right, Frances, we are known as the arse end of Italy. Tuscany is the beautiful heart. All the tourists love Tuscany — so eco, so green! But where do you think all their rubbish goes? Here, all around Naples. We're drowning in millions of tons of shit. The industry up north pays people in Il Sistema to bury it here and around Caserta, where we all grew up.'

'How long has this been going on?'

Pasquale grimaced. 'For as long as I can remember. The waste is mixed up with compost and used as fertilizer so we eat the shit. It's in cement and we grow up in apartments made from poison, so our homes are full of the shit. And when we shop, the supermarkets are built from it too, there's no escape.'

'So everyone turns a blind eye?'

'No, not everyone. The people here try but always they hit brick walls. There are government inquiries, which reveal the corruption and a few people end up in jail. A year later, they're out and the dumping goes on . . .' Pasquale starts to cough.

'Calm down,' Poppaea interrupts. 'Focus on the music for now. We have another half an hour. Play one of the Bach suites again.'

She turns to Frances. 'He has to master all the six Bach cello suites for the audition. They'll ask him to play two but he won't know which ones. And there's no accompaniment, so it's very tough. "The Swan" is, how do you say, his signature piece. Easier to play technically but it really shows the feeling of the musician.'

'Ah Poppaea, always the mother.' Pasquale grabs her shoulders and kisses her with a loud smacking noise.

'Someone has to keep you on track.'

'Our mother died young,' Pasquale explains. 'So my big sister has always looked after me.'

A baby's cry pierces the room and Frances stands. 'You have some competition from Luciana! I've had a long day so I have to go. Thank you for letting me listen to you play.'

'Come back again,' Pasquale calls after her.

As Frances climbs the stairs, the cello seems to echo her footsteps. The music is sombre and familiar, a piece she's heard Pasquale play time and time again.

'Watch out! Excuse me, Frances.' Peppe rushes past her, breathing heavily.

'Finished already?'

'Yes,' he calls over his shoulder. 'A good night to be home early and off the streets — there could be some trouble in Naples tonight. I'd stay put if I were you. Good night.'

She passes him as he disappears into his apartment and she climbs the final flight to hers.

Frances throws her jacket onto the floor and falls onto her bed too exhausted to undress. Her legs feel like lead weights but she makes herself lift them up one at a time and pulls off her boots. She curls into a ball and tries to block out the thoughts of the murdered scientists.

Her mind drifts back to White Island as it does so frequently when she feels troubled and she rubs the little scars that mark the top of one foot, a permanent reminder of that hellhole.

CHAPTER FOURTEEN

Umberto Dragorra releases her. 'Hungry for love or dinner, Camilla?'

'Both,' she tells him as she passes her fingers over his crotch and feels him harden. She likes the smell of his expensive aftershave, the feel of his impeccably cut suit, made of the finest wool. And she loves the thrill of her power over one who could snuff her out, but won't, because she offers everything he needs.

'Well, I'm starving,' he laughs at her, pushing her hand away. 'Love will have to take second place. Let's eat.'

He taps the driver's shoulder. 'Mario, take us to Santa Lucia.'

The car edges through the dark narrow streets of the university precinct and slips into a sea of traffic moving at walking pace along Via Cristoforo Colombo.

Camilla cranes to look beyond Mario's shaved head, across the wide boulevard to the harbour, where hulking white ships are warming up to sail to Sicily and the Aeolian Islands, their funnels exhaling small smoky clouds into the night.

'Can't we go any faster than this?!' Umberto shouts, his voice as rough as sandpaper.

Mario turns around and shrugs apologetically.

Camilla soothes him and strokes his hand. She's been on the receiving end of his temper and is in no mood for an argument. 'Here, let's look at the report while we're driving. There's plenty of time.'

He flicks on a small light. Although she smiles at Umberto she doesn't really like what she sees. He is just shy of sixty and has dyed his thin hair a carroty hue in a vain attempt to recreate the dark ginger-red locks of his youth. His face has been smoothed by a daily visit to the barber who still sharpens razors on a strip of leather. But his cheeks have drooped and his jowls have spread, giving him the look of a puffed toad, one that would spray her in poison if she stood in the way of what he wanted. For all that, he excites her. She likes the sensation of brushing up against someone who could transform her fortunes and finally push her into the big league. How fortuitous he was now the chair of the university. As the government media release described him after he was appointed:

Umberto Dragorra is one of the city's most respected and prominent businessmen. It is vital that our university is able to face the challenges of the new millennium and to cultivate graduates to succeed in the new market economy. Signor Dragorra will bring his experience and energy to academia for the great benefit of all.

Ah, so often it was the ugly ones who became the most powerful, with enough of the Neapolitan *furbo*, the cunning, to succeed at any cost.

'It's just a first draft,' Camilla explains as she opens her briefcase.

'Clever woman. I picked you straight away.'

The car is barely moving but Umberto is calmer now and Camilla wonders if he even realizes it was she who picked him. He puts on a pair of gold-rimmed glasses and opens the folder.

He flicks through it, quickly at first, his beady brown eyes flitting from page to page. He returns to the introduction: 'The threat posed to local populations of an eruption of Mt Vesuvius.'

He reads slowly, and turns to a page with two maps, one labelled 'The Existing Red Zone', the other, 'Recommended Changes to the Red Zone'. His stubby forefinger traces over the towns circling the volcano: Torre de Greco, San Sebastiano, Herculaneum, Pompeii, eighteen in all.

He runs his finger along lines, blue marking the boundaries of each municipality, yellow marking safe areas to build, and red excluding all construction. His eyes dart back and forth between the two maps.

Camilla puts her hand on his and places his finger on the map.

'There, I think that's what you're looking for. Your land, or should I say your wife's.'

His finger lingers on the spot where she knows one of his construction companies recently bought large tracts of wasteland south of the mountain. On the first map this is part of the Red Zone. On the second map, the boundary has moved to include it in the Yellow Zone.

'Brilliant!' he mutters under his breath. He turns to the last page and reads a summary. At the bottom of the page is a signature in well-rounded handwriting:

Professor Camilla Corsi.

As he puts the report down, his breath forms into a long slow whistle. 'Well, you've exceeded yourself.' Umberto squeezes her hand hard. 'If this goes through we can have the land rezoned and build the shopping centre and school.'

Camilla pulls her hand away gently and sinks back into the seat. 'As I said, it's a first draft. There are still many people who will comment, and don't expect them all to agree. But in the end, the chancellor, Alfonso Galbatti, will have the final say and then it goes to the government.'

'Perfect! In that case I think we can move our plans ahead with confidence.' He picks up the report again and continues to study the maps. Camilla can almost hear his brain calculating the profits he will make from the land he 'persuaded' a family who had held it for generations to sell to him cheaply before they moved north to Milan.

Mario beeps the horn at a group of motorcyclists stopped on the road in front of them. They scatter and he accelerates. Soon they are skirting around the grey stone walls of Castel Nuovo. The massive castle blocks her view of the bay and seems to stop the city of Naples from falling into the sea. They drive around it only to stop again a few seconds later behind a line of cars. Two blue police cars on the piazza in front of the castle push their way into the traffic. She can see the faces of the young carabinieri enjoying a joke through one of the windscreens.

Seconds later an African man emerges from shadows on the square. His gaze follows the police cars disappearing around a bend. He raises his hand and four or five others, all tall, black and rake thin, appear carrying suitcases. Just a few metres from their car, they spread blankets onto the footpath and tip dozens of fake designer handbags onto them. Camilla watches the men carefully arranging the bags into colours and styles, occasionally glancing about like nervous gazelles. She recognizes copies of new designs for Prada, Gucci, Chanel, Dolce et Gabbana and Fendi she's seen in Naples' most expensive boutiques.

'A hard way to make a living,' Camilla muses, 'constantly dodging the carabinieri.'

Umberto's mood has lifted. 'The Sengelese? They're all part of our economy those men, the clandestini. Always having to hide, yet an important link in the chain — I'm probably making a euro commission from each of their sales,' he laughs. 'We all have to support our families. Would you like one of the bags, cara?'

'Of course not!'

'Just the real thing for you, Camilla? Like me?' He pulls her towards him again and kisses her hard on the lips. 'I should divorce my wife and marry you.'

Camilla pulls back, her voice cold. 'Over her dead body, I should think.'

'Now, now. Let's not speak badly of the living.'

'Finally!' Mario calls over his shoulder. 'We're moving. I'll have you at the restaurant in no time, boss.'

Already small groups of tourists are gathering around the handbags as they leave the castle behind them. They drive along Via Nasario Sauro towards Santa Lucia and she can see the illuminated tips of giant yachts berthed in the marina near the restaurants, swaying gently back and forth.

Mario pulls up at the kerb behind a line of expensive cars.

'Wait here,' Umberto tells him. 'We'll be an hour.'

As they walk along a jetty towards Borgo Marinato where the

restaurants are clustered, she reaches into her handbag for a cigarette and lights it.

'There's no time for that.'

'Indulge me. I'm not allowed to smoke in the restaurant. Give me a minute.'

She inhales deeply and then blows the smoke into the air.

'Filthy habit,' Umberto mutters, striding ahead.

Camilla trails behind. The silhouette of Castello Dell'Ovo rises in front of her like a small island. It occurs to her that Naples has expended a lot of energy over the centuries building fortresses in a vain attempt to repel its enemies. The enemies were often the victors, and they in turn clung to power until the next wave of marauders came calling. The Greeks, the Romans, the Normans, the French Angevins, the Spanish Aragonese, the French Bourbons — a never-ending roll call of foreign rulers followed by a procession of Italians. These days it was impossible to pick who was friend and who was foe, as the gates keeping out strangers had been well and truly left open. Camilla smiled ruefully, knowing the enemy was usually within.

Beyond the castle, across the sea, the slopes of Mt Vesuvius glimmer under a full moon, eternally indifferent to the power play of mortals. Camilla shivers and drapes her red silk pashmina tightly around her shoulders.

Violin music fills the night air and she hears a better than usual rendition of her favourite folksong. She sings the words of 'Santa Lucia' quietly to herself. 'O dolce Napoli, o suol beato, ove sorridere, volle il Creato, tu sei l'impero, di armonia! Santa Lucia! Santa Lucia!'

On a night like this — boats swaying, moonlight on the rippling sea; she imagines it must have been on a night just like this, so long ago, that the composer of 'Santa Lucia' stood here, moved by the magic of Naples at its most beautiful. He must have been inspired by a real boatman enticing passersby to board his boat to admire the city, the place of holy soil, smiled upon by the Creator, the empire of harmony.

My God, harmony! Where did that disappear to? The only

harmony she knows is in music. She spots the busker, tall, wearing a long black coat and woollen beanie. His face is in shadow but she can see his hands clearly, the right lightly gripping the bow, the left around the neck of the violin. She lingers a few more seconds, not wanting to leave, absorbing the passion and longing in the music.

'Bravo,' she says quietly. She drops a twenty euro note into his open violin case. He doesn't look up but nods his thanks and plays on.

She hurries to catch up with Umberto, then pauses, taking a final puff and stubbing her cigarette out on the ground with her shoe. As the sound of the violinist fades, she hears another one ahead. A second busker, shorter with gelled hair, picks up the melody. The music has lifted her spirits, allowed her to escape for a few precious moments.

'Hurry up, Camilla!' Umberto is just ahead, waiting at the front of the restaurant where a line has formed. She drops a coin into the second player's case and joins him. He guides her to the front where the patrone spots them immediately.

'Your usual table, Signor Dragorra?' The patrone lowers his head respectfully and ushers them inside.

'Yes. The usual table, the best wine and your best food,' Umberto booms as they head towards the prime spot overlooking the water. They are barely seated when a waiter in black pants and waistcoat, gleaming white shirt and a peculiarly old-fashioned waxed moustache offers them the menu.

Umberto waves it away. 'A bottle of Fiano de Avellino, cameriere, and show me today's catch.'

The waiter reappears with the wine and as he pours it the white liquid sparkles in the light from the flickering candles in the centre of their table.

Umberto drinks a large mouthful while Camilla sips hers tentatively. She feels uncomfortably on show. Their public appearances have been rare and always with the excuse that they are meeting on university business.

All of the tables around them are full and she notices a few of the diners glancing furtively their way. Is it fear or recognition on their faces? She can't tell. Umberto ignores them and, unusually for him, smiles so broadly that in the candlelight he looks vaguely handsome.

'I feel like celebrating. We will eat well tonight, you and I.'

The waiter returns with a large pewter platter of glistening raw fish.

'The sardines look good. Those, and the calamari to start, lightly done in a little oil and garlic.' Umberto points to the pile of tiny shining silver fish lined up like sentries and the curly white mounds of squid.

'And then?' The waiter flexes his arms and holds the dish closer.

'Pesce spada, for both of us.' He points at thick cutlets of swordfish. 'Grilled.'

Camilla learnt early that when keeping Umberto's company her choices counted for nothing. It didn't even occur to him that she might prefer to eat something different. It was a small price to pay for his patronage. If she felt like veal tonight, so what? Swordfish would be fine.

'Hey, Fabio, come over here!' Umberto is waving across the restaurant.

A broad-shouldered man with wavy brown hair salutes him from the entrance to the restaurant and makes his way around the other tables towards them. 'My son. It's time you met,' he says quietly.

Camilla twists the white serviette on her lap and squeezes it tight between her fingers. Meeting her lovers' families is something she'd rather avoid.

'Fabio, this is the professor from the university I was telling you about. Camilla Corsi. She's very helpful to our business interests.'

He's slightly taller than his father, dressed in a black leather bomber jacket and the latest blue jeans, fashionably worn. She smiles at him and proffers her hand, staring into hard jet-black eyes that tell her nothing. She recognizes that penetrating gaze — he is trying as hard as she is to gauge her measure, the possibility of a threat. He shakes her hand quickly then steps back, bowing slightly in what seems to her a mocking gesture.

'Charmed, I'm sure, professor.' He leans over to Umberto. 'Father, I was hoping to find you here. Can I have a word?'

'Sit, sit.' He gestures to a seat next to him and turns his back to her as the two speak quietly together. Camilla strains to listen but can barely hear a word. She recognizes the odd phrase but they speak in a dialect peculiar to their village north of Vesuvius.

Fabio is agitated, his face strained and humourless and he looks older than a man not yet thirty. He taps one of his highly polished boots nervously on the floor as he talks. His hands are thick like his father's and he wears an identical gold signet ring with an eagle's head on the middle finger of his right hand. There are other family likenesses: an aquiline nose and the same unusual red streaking his hair, perhaps a legacy of the ancient Norman Viking ancestry shared by many Neapolitans. As she muses that his eyes must come from his mother's side, the waiter arrives. He places a metal tray in front of them with the cooked sardines and calamari arranged on a bed of spinach and sliced lemons and stands to one side. The delicious aroma drifts into her nostrils.

Fabio stands. 'Your meal is here, I'll leave you.'

'Call me later tonight. Let me know how it goes.'

'Buon appetito!' He nods at his father then walks swiftly away.

The waiter steps back to the table and, with a steady hand, uses two spoons to lift pieces of the fish onto their plates. He pours more wine into Umberto's empty glass then discreetly disappears.

'A smart boy, that one; he runs our garbage disposal operation. A very tough negotiator.'

Camilla resists the urge to complain about the mountains of garbage blocking the streets. 'And good looking, like his father,' she says instead.

Umberto laughs. 'No wonder I find you irresistible!'

Fabio's visit has made Camilla lose her appetite. But she doesn't want to lose Umberto's attention so she tries to look enthusiastic as she nibbles on a sardine and picks at a piece of calamari while he hungrily empties his plate and refills it again. The waiter replaces the plates with two clean ones. He returns with a hot plate sizzling with swordfish and lifts a piece onto each plate. The flesh of the fish falls apart easily as Camilla scoops some up with her fork. It is so fresh and tender that in spite of herself, she eats a large piece in no time.

Concentrating on his meal, Umberto is silent until he is finished. He drinks the rest of his glass of wine and refills it. Only then does he speak. 'So when will the report go to the government?'

'Soon. Maybe a couple of months.'

'I hope it's no longer. We want to give out contracts for the buildings. The school plans are ready to go and one of Europe's largest furniture retailers wants to open a showroom. A major deal.'

'Does your wife know her name is on the sales contract for the land?'

'Rosanna's no fool. We will all prosper from this deal. You included.'

Camilla glances up at the mountain but it has disappeared. A cloud covers the moon and she can see only darkness. She sips her wine and frowns. 'Do you worry at all about the safety of building there? What might happen if Vesuvius erupts?'

Umberto laughs. Then he leans over and whispers in her ear. 'Don't say you are losing your nerve, cara. You said yourself — it may not erupt for two hundred years. We will all be dead and gone. It won't be our problem.'

CHAPTER FIFTEEN

Although still early, the pizzeria near the university is already humming with the evening crowd when Pasquale arrives with Poppaea and Satore. He presses through to the counter where the customers are calling out their orders.

'Two margheritas and a Napoletana, please, Francesco,' Pasquale says to the man serving, 'and half a litre of the house red.'

Behind him, the pizzaiola is kneading piles of dough with the practised ease of a masseuse working on a line of knotted muscles. His chubby young assistant has switched from stacking firewood to spreading spoonfuls of bright red tomato purée onto the finished rounds.

Pasquale savours the smell of pizzas already cooking in the hot wood oven and realizes he hasn't eaten since breakfast. He often skips meals when he's practising and feeling anxious. Without thinking, he puts his hand under his T-shirt and pinches his stomach, feeling how skinny he's become.

Poppaea and Satore sit at a bench by the window. He props himself up on a stool next to them and places his violin alongside Satore's. Poppaea puts her hand on his shoulder. 'You're playing well, don't look so worried.'

Pasquale sees his sister's concern etched on her face, an expression she's been wearing ever since he can remember — putting him first, standing in for their mother. Sometimes he stares at the faded photos of their mother taken a few months before the car crash, but it's as though he's looking at a stranger. It was always Poppaea looking after him, encouraging his music, going without to buy him clothes and pay for lessons and always protecting him from their father, who wanted his son to follow him into the cement business.

He remembers his father well — his hands worn and stained from a life of concreting, his face lined and mournful. Most of all, he remembers his disappointment, worn as often as his navy overalls. How different they were. Pasquale knew he was never the son his father wanted. He glances down at his own hands. Calluses on the fingers of his left hand from years of playing the cello and violin but otherwise, soft and unmarked.

He leans over and kisses Poppaea on the cheek. 'Another month. Will I be able to master the Bach suites in time? Sometimes I curse the man for writing them.'

'Sure you will,' Satore interrupts. 'But we can have a rest from the German tonight. We have the delights of our own wonderful songs of Napoli!'

Pasquale groans. 'Sometimes I think "O Sole Mio" is the accompaniment of my worst nightmares!'

'Don't knock it. It will help pay for that cello!'

The chubby assistant turned waiter places three wine glasses and a carafe of red in front of them. 'Pizzas won't be long.'

Pasquale looks back towards the oven and sees the pizzaiola sliding out a fresh batch with his long-handled peel, the ferocious heat reflecting on his glowing face. As he lines a dozen or so pizzas along a bench, the steam rises and fills the room with their aroma.

'Ecco!' A minute later the waiter delivers their order.

'The Napoletana is mine,' Pasquale reaches for the plate.

'No cheese?' Poppaea looks at his pizza with its simple topping of tomato, oil, garlic and a sprinkling of fresh oregano.

'No, it gives me a stomach ache.' Pasquale bites into the puffy lip of his pizza. After hungrily eating the rest, he drinks his wine. 'Maybe it's my nerves but I'm getting a lot of indigestion these days.'

'I'm glad I've got a strong constitution,' Satore replies, globs of melted mozzarella dribbling down his chin.

'We're going to need one tonight,' Poppaea says. 'I think the meeting will test us all.'

Church bells playing 'Ave Maria' herald the evening mass as the three of them stroll through a large piazza in the historic centre. A small crowd is milling by the vast walls of the cathedral of Gesù Nuovo when a hearse pulls up outside. Four black-suited men remove a white coffin covered with pink roses.

Pasquale realizes the faces of the mourners look familiar. 'I think that's the body of the girl who was shot in the street last week. I recognize her family from the television news. She was only sixteen, out walking with her friends. They were caught between the crossfire when two men shot at each other.'

'Another wasted life,' Poppaea hisses. 'When will it end?'

'As long as Il Sistema runs our city, never!' Satore says angrily.

Pasquale sighs. He has seen it all before. He watches the men carry the coffin into the cathedral followed by the sad procession of weeping relatives. He'd grown up with death. Everyone from the villages around Caserta did. Violence lurked in every neighbourhood and pervaded all business, and anyone who stood in the way of the powerbrokers knew they were risking everything.

He remembers when his father was killed, eight years earlier. An accident, they were told. He was crushed beneath one of his own trucks on the building site where he was working, when the truck reversed into him. He and Poppaea heard the rumours — the driver was new and had previously worked for their father's main rival, one of the big operators from the next town, attached to the growing Dragorra empire. An inquest cleared the driver of any blame and declared the death accidental.

Less than a month after the funeral, the Mazzone family company was swallowed by its rival. The driver was appointed the new manager. Pasquale and his sister were left with nothing — their father's lawyer said there was no will and the company debts outweighed any assets. They had packed up the possessions of the apartment their family had rented for three generations and moved to Naples to start new lives.

'C'mon,' Pasquale says. 'We'll be late.'

The ornately decorated lecture theatre on the upper level of the university is nearly full as they squeeze past the knees of those already seated in a row near the front and fall into empty seats in the middle. Pasquale sees his neighbour, Riccardo Cocchia, huddled with a group near the podium. He recognizes many students and lecturers in the room but is drawn by one of the men next to Riccardo. Middle-aged, his muscular build and sun-beaten face mark him as someone who has worked his life outdoors. Pasquale nudges Poppaea. 'Who does he remind you of?'

She follows his gaze. 'Dad?' she asks.

'You see it too?'

She nods. The man's profile reminds him keenly of his father, although the back of his head is quite different. Is it the nose? The shape of his eyes? It's an odd thing. His father had been dead now for eight years, and they were never close, yet watching the man in the front row with Riccardo, Pasquale feels an unexpected rush of loss.

'Good evening, thank you for coming. I'm Doctor Fabbiana Masina.' A tall red-haired woman at the microphone interrupts his musing.

'We are here to organize a protest rally against the scandalous state of garbage disposal in Campania. Not only are the streets of Naples and the towns full of rotting garbage, but also the land. I'm an oncologist, and I know first-hand how our cancer rates are soaring, and I strongly believe they're linked to the illegal dumping of toxic waste, which is polluting our farmlands. It is time to speak out and demand action from our government. The health of our people and our environment is at stake.'

Speaker after speaker complain of pollution and corruption, with officials taking bribes to turn a blind eye. As the audience applauds, the doctor beckons the man in the front row. 'And now I want to introduce to you a very courageous man who is prepared to give evidence of criminal activities. He was a farmer but his livelihood has been destroyed by toxic waste.'

Pasquale can feel the man's discomfort as he walks to the

microphone and nervously clears his throat. 'I'm sorry,' he begins, his voice tremulous. 'I am not used to speaking to so many.' He pauses and looks down on the sea of faces. Pasquale can sense the power of his raw dignity. Over many centuries, this theatre had rung with the voices of thousands of great orators but now it falls silent to listen to the message of a man who has never spoken publicly in his life.

'My name is Paolo. For all my life I have been a farmer, just outside Caserta. I have worked the land of my father, and his father and his father. Now I have been forced to walk away from it.'

Paolo goes on to tell them how he was offered a free trial of a new fertilizer by a salesman two years earlier. If he was satisfied with the product, he could buy more, at a cheap rate. Next day, a large truck delivered a load of black mulch, which he spread on his wheat and vegetable crops.

'After the first heavy rain, my ponds went black. Then the fish died. They were floating upside down.' His voice is now steady. 'My sheep, they got sick. And the wheat and the corn — they didn't grow.'

His voice falters again and a film of perspiration melts on his forehead. He takes a handkerchief from his trouser pocket and wipes it. 'I'm sorry,' he repeats, 'this is difficult for me.'

When the doctor gives him with a glass of water, he holds it up to the light. 'I hope this is not poison!' he laughs nervously. 'I am an ordinary man who used to trust people. Now . . . I think twice.' He drinks the water quickly and hands the glass back. 'The fertilizer was poison. It killed my land. Everything died and now the authorities have seized it. My family farmed it for more than a hundred years. Now I have nothing.'

He walks away from the microphone, his neck extended forward in a posture of defeat and Pasquale realizes the man has no physical likeness to his father at all. It's his expression, the same baked-on look of resignation, exhaustion and disillusion.

'Thank you, Paolo. We appreciate your honesty and courage.' The doctor is back on the podium. 'His farm was covered in waste containing heavy metals, including dioxin. Tons of it are trucked here illegally from industries up north. His soil is full of it, the milk from Paolo's sheep was contaminated and his animals have all been destroyed. The farm will be unusable for decades, maybe longer. And he's not the only one. There are many more.'

The doctor closes the meeting and calls for volunteers to organize the protest. Pasquale and the others clamber to offer their help.

'Hey! Good to see you here!' Riccardo calls him over. 'Come and meet Paolo.'

Pasquale shakes the farmer's hand, which is hard and coarse. 'Pasquale Mazzone. I'm sorry about your farm, I grew up in the same area.'

'I know your family name,' Paolo replies.

'Did you know my father, Stefano Mazzone?'

'No, I don't think so.'

'He ran a construction company. He was killed in a truck accident.'

Paolo's face flickers as if he is reminded of something. But he looks away. 'No. I didn't know him. Sorry, but I have to go now.'

He collects his bag from his seat and puts on his coat, a puffy green ski jacket in a style that went out of fashion twenty years earlier. As he walks towards the door Pasquale is reminded again of his father, his reticence, which he now surmises may have been suppressed anger stoked by powerlessness in a society where brutality ruled.

Riccardo taps him on the shoulder. 'This is my colleague, Marcello Vattani. He works with Frances Nelson as well.'

'I saw her tonight. She didn't seem to know about the meeting. Did you ask her to come?'

'No,' Riccardo says. 'We had a big day working at Campi Flegrei and I thought she might be better staying out of all this local trouble.'

'Good idea,' Marcello agrees. 'Frances wouldn't be able to help herself. She'd want to be part of the protest. She'll have enough on her hands dealing with all the developments planned around Vesuvius. There'll be a lot of heat from that.'

'Il Sistema again?'

'Always,' Riccardo says.

'It's appalling that money means more to them than the people's health. Do we have any real hope of taking them on?' Pasquale asks.

'They have money, power and violence. We just have people, people like Paolo. And never forget, we have the truth.'

'You forgot faith, Riccardo.' Marcello grins. 'As my grandfather says, we have to keep our faith.'

Poppaea takes Pasquale's arm. 'Sorry, gentlemen. We have to leave. It's time my brother sang for his supper.'

CHAPTER SIXTEEN

Pasquale kisses his sister goodnight on Via Toledo and he and Satore squeeze onto the back of a crowded bus bound for Santa Lucia. They shuffle around people laden with shopping bags to the middle.

'May as well try our luck,' Satore says. 'How about "L'Inverno"? I feel like some Vivaldi.'

'Let's do it!' Pasquale says. They take out their violins and cue each other with their eyes as they have done hundreds of times before.

From the first notes in F minor of the 'Winter Concerto' from the *Four Seasons*, they have captured the ears of the late-night commuters. Pasquale never tires of the impact of their music. As they play, he can see expressions around him gradually change. Passengers lost in their own worlds suddenly engage with life on the bus. Smiles appear on lips, lines soften on foreheads and heads move in time with the swelling violins. But both musicians know just the moment to maximize the effect. As Pasquale's fingers move to the high strings to play lines of silvery staccato notes, Satore fades out of the concerto. There's only half a minute or so to go. He moves quickly through the bus with a plastic cup he keeps in his coat pocket. Clink, clink, clink. He takes around ten euro before the vehicle lurches to a halt.

Pasquale is almost thrown. He steadies himself and stands aside as people push past to leave and a new group climbs aboard.

'Primavera!' Satore calls. They start playing together again, this time the 'Spring Concerto' in E major. They have managed to abridge the movements to such an extent, they can time their parts almost perfectly to suit the bus route, especially in peak hour when the journey is slow. Two stops later they move into G minor to play the 'Summer Concerto'. For the last leg of the journey, they slide into F major for the 'Autumn Concerto'.

They leap off the bus at the seafront on Via Partenope. 'Brilliant! Forty euro already!' Satore laughs. 'The bus concerto's a winner.'

Pasquale finds Satore's cheerful spirit contagious. He was disturbed by Paolo's story and the man's resemblance to his father; too often these days he feels distracted, just when he's edging closer to achieving his dream.

The moonlight has brought the promenaders out in droves. A young mother and father stroll behind their two children, who are licking enormous ice creams; an elderly couple cling to each other for support as they walk slowly along the lungomare; and a pair of lovers kiss against a lamppost, their bodies blending. The distant lights of the Isle of Capri twinkle to the east, while Vesuvius is silhouetted by the moon to the west.

Pasquale doesn't resist Satore when he links arms with him. The two have been friends since high school where they were both misfits, preferring music to soccer. While their peers were the town's tough boys, experimenting with drugs, alcohol and sex, they kept their distance from the constant spectrum of violence that overshadowed their generation. Instead, they sought each other's company, shared their passion for the classics and practised together for hours at a time.

After Pasquale's father died, they drifted apart. Satore travelled north to study in Rome. It wasn't until they reunited in Naples that Satore revealed his sexual feelings for him and Pasquale told him he could never reciprocate. Still, their friendship endured.

Pasquale had met several of Satore's lovers, usually other musicians, though he once had a strong crush on a young architect. Pasquale had dated many girls. He liked them all but sooner or later the relationships fizzled. They would tire of each other. He often asked himself what it would feel like to be in love, doubting he had ever been. While it was an emotion he wished for, it wasn't a craving. Music and friendship was enough, at least for now.

A line of Mercedes is parked along the roadway by the entry to the Borgo Marinato. Another one pulls up and its chauffeur hurries around to open the door for an expensively dressed couple. They drift arm in arm towards the restaurants.

'I'll stop here. You play up ahead towards Castello Dell'Ovo,' Pasquale says to Satore.

He spreads his violin case on the ground and puts a few coins and notes inside. He discovered when he first started busking that an empty case stays empty. Although clear, the night air is cool and Pasquale puts his beanie on his head.

He raises his violin and bursts into a lively version of 'Funiculi, Funicula'. The first coins arrive quickly — it's a busy night and a constant stream of diners trail past, at least one in three putting their hands in their pockets to find a coin or two.

Three times through 'Funiculi, Funicula' and he's ready for the next staple. A few tourists dawdle past on their way towards the marina to ogle the yachts. When they hear the first notes of 'O Sole Mio' they turn back and listen to the end. They're Americans and want to chat.

'Every time I hear that I think of Caruso,' an elderly woman in the group says to him.

'Ah yes,' Pasquale answers patiently. 'Enrico Caruso was from Naples.'

'Is that so? I thought he was American. He sang at the Met in New York for years.'

He'd had this conversation over and over again. But she meant well. 'That's right,' he says. 'He also sang at La Scala in Milan and Covent Garden in London. But this was home.'

'I was sure he was born in America.'

'No, that was Mario Lanza. He had Italian parents but was born in the States. They both sang "O Sole Mio".'

'Well, God bless you,' she says, dropping a dollar note into his case.

Staple number three, Pasquale says to himself. He raises his bow and starts to play 'Santa Lucia'. For all his cynicism, the barcarole sweeps him up every time. It is his favourite, especially played here on a magical night like this. He sways his body in time to the six/eight metre, the same rhythm as a boatman rowing.

His thoughts are interrupted by the loud footsteps of a well-dressed man with reddish hair who strides by without pausing. He continues playing and with the yachts bobbing in the gentle swell of the harbour, silently mouths the words: 'O dolce Napoli, o suol beato, ove sorridere, volle il Creato, tu sei l'impero, di armonia! Santa Lucia! Santa Lucia!'

He's aware that someone has stopped to listen. Out of the corner of his eye he sees a woman standing alone, smoking. Dark haired and wrapped in a red shawl, he senses she's watching him closely. He tries harder than usual to inject as much emotion as possible into the song.

'Bravo,' the woman says quietly. He sees her drop a twenty euro note into his case and he nods his thanks. The unexpected generosity and something familiar in her voice, maybe the intonation, makes him turn to watch her hurry away, her stilettos clicking on the ground.

Diners continue to file past, well-heeled high-flyers, so different to the people he mixes with at the conservatorium. A revving motorbike stops nearby, drowning out his violin. As he rests his violin on the ground and stretches, a tall stocky figure in a leather jacket almost bowls him over. 'Out of the way!' he yells in an accent that reminds Pasquale of the bully boys from his home town. Before he has time to reply, the man jumps onto the back of the motorbike and has ridden away.

Pasquale yawns. His fingers are feeling stiff and he shivers in the cooling air, despite wearing his thickest winter coat. He packs his violin away, pockets a handful of coins and saunters towards Satore. 'Let's call it a night. I'm exhausted.'

Satore stops playing 'Santa Lucia'.

'Do you get sick of those songs?' Pasquale asks.

'No, because they are accompanied by the best tune of all — those coins and notes playing doh ray mi in our cases!'

'I worry that I'm relying on Il Sistema for donations. Did you see that lot coming here tonight? Talk about the godfathers!'

'Sure. But you're a good cause. Let's count the loot.'

Pasquale counts eighty-five euro and three American dollars. Satore has seventy euro.

'Better than usual — thank you, Mr Moon, for helping everyone open their wallets!' Satore exclaims, glancing up to the dark sky. 'With the money from the bus that's nearly two hundred euro. Here, you keep half of mine towards your cello.'

'No, I can't.'

'You must.' He pushes the money into Pasquale's coat pockets. 'I'll just waste it on beer and boyfriends.'

'Oh, in that case, yes, I can,' he laughs, then breaks into a coughing fit.

Satore taps him on his back. 'C'mon. You'd better get out of the cold. That cough is getting worse.'

'It's just the change in the weather, it always affects me.'

They walk back to the promenade and Satore runs to catch a bus heading in the direction of his apartment.

Pasquale waits at the bus stop alone. Thick clouds obscure the moon but there's light on the seafront. The marble arches of an elaborate baroque fountain illuminated by spotlights steal his eyes. He's drawn to the sculptured sea creatures cavorting beneath, holding aloft a large carved chalice gushing torrents of water. Flyaway droplets shimmer like shards of diamonds in the blackness of the night.

The line of expensive cars is starting to leave. He notices the dark-haired woman who had stopped to hear him play, climb into one and depart. There's no sign of his bus and he can't stop shivering. He sets out on foot, knowing exactly where he will go.

Soon he can see the brightly lit Piazza del Plebiscito. He crosses the road and walks towards the enormous square. Save for a few cyclists, it's almost empty and his feet echo on the cobblestones as he walks past the thick stone walls of the sprawling royal palace. Not far now. At the end of the square, small groups are clustering around the Café Gambrinus. The outdoor tables of the coffee house are empty but he can see people inside through the windows. Turning the corner, he collides with the post-concert crowd, milling in the street, elegant in tuxedos and evening gowns, and he knows why he is being drawn here. A minute later, he stands in front of the Teatro San Carlo as he has done so often before. He walks up the steps to the front doors but they are already locked. He goes back down and looks up towards the roof, seeking solace from the statue of a beautiful woman holding out a crown in her hand. She has given him hope in the past.

Two stragglers from the orchestra, one with a cello case, the other a trombone, are chatting and smoking beneath the grey granite arches. He feels alone, an outsider, excluded from the music that is his very essence. He likes to imagine the sculpted woman is his guardian angel, beckoning him in and nourishing his dreams, but tonight she shuns him and shows her true nature — a cold marble statue.

He hates it when this mood descends to stifle his spirit, sneaking up on him without warning. Tomorrow he will return to the cello and summon the muse to lift him again. He will sit there and master the Bach suites, if it's the last thing he does!

Turning away from the theatre he walks back past the café to Via Toledo. The boulevard is shutting down. Displays of up-to-the-minute clothes, shoes and bags dazzle in the windows of shops that have already closed. A few bars are buzzing and outside one, Pasquale sees a young group gathered on their motorinos. They're uniformly dressed in short leather jackets and jeans that look as though they've been sprayed on their taut bodies. The girls all have long flowing hair and they flick it this way and that, flirting with the boys revving their scooters and smoking. He slips by unnoticed.

At first the road ahead is quiet enough with only some late night traffic and a few people promenading. He hears it first, a hubbub just off the main street. When he reaches the turnoff, he sees a small crowd hovering around a massive rubbish pile. Two large metal skips have been upended, their foul contents spread across the pavement and onto the street. A fire is burning, the smoke spreading a disgusting odour. Several people are shouting at once and he can't tell whether they are arguing with each other or agreeing.

When he is closer, he surmises they all live in the surrounding streets that mark the start of the Spanish Quarter and are enraged about the garbage. Half an hour earlier, a gang of darkly clad youths had descended on motorbikes and thrown the rubbish far and wide.

'It's the clan, payback because some of the activists around here are shopping them to the authorities,' a woman whispers to Pasquale. 'Naming names and there have been some arrests.'

Pasquale is sickened but feels helpless. His exhaustion weighs heavily on him and he walks away towards the funicular that will take him home. He has barely rounded the next corner when he hears a motorbike loudly accelerating and leaps aside as it flies past. He hears a shot. Screaming. Two more shots. Doors slam. Shutters bang. A minute or so later he hears the motorbike disappearing. He presses against a wall, paralysed. He hears footsteps and a man runs past with a gun in his hand, so close, he could reach out and touch him. He's very short and doesn't notice Pasquale in the shadows.

Pasquale hears another loud thumping. He realizes it's his heart, drumming in double time. He clings to the wall until he feels he is going to faint. He wants to keep going but he knows he has to turn back.

His feet feel as if they're made of lead as he drags himself back around the corner. The crowd has disappeared and at first he thinks everyone has gone. Then he sees the legs. Two pairs crumpled on the road near the skips, the upper bodies obscured by mounds of rubbish. He edges closer and what he sees makes him want to vomit. The unmistakable green parka is oozing blood. He sees the face of its wearer, the farmer, Paolo, his eyes staring wide-eyed in horror into the night, a cross slashed into his lips. Next to him, another man, one he had seen shouting just minutes earlier. His lips are cut too, the blood pooling around his mouth. Pasquale recognizes the symbolism. Il Sistema has sealed their mouths closed, forever.

Pasquale knows this scenario. He saw death early. In the town where he lived, every child had seen at least one dead body, a victim of violence, punished by the clan for some indiscretion or defiance or betrayal. The face of his father flashes in his mind. You too, Papa, you too.

Loud sirens explode in the night and Pasquale staggers away. He flounders through the narrow lanes, welcoming the darkness. His left leg is cramping and he still wants to vomit. He jumps when a motorbike hoots close behind him.

'Pasquale! Pasquale! Hop on!' He scarcely knows the voice but as the rider pulls alongside him he sees his neighbour.

'Quickly, get on!'

Pasquale climbs on and holds on to Riccardo tightly as he lurches off. As the night swallows them and he rests his head against Riccardo's back like a child, he smells blood. A few seconds later, he hears two more gunshots.

CHAPTER SEVENTEEN

Frances relived that moment on White Island when she lost sight of Bob Masterton over and over again. She had stood there for what seemed like an hour but was less than a minute. She'd strained to see a touch of his orange helmet in the mist, desperate for that tiny beacon to guide her through this steaming firehole. Her breathing was heavy and she was sweating under the heavy mask. She'd cried out again but when she listened for a response, all she heard was the roaring wind. Move forward, or go back for Hamish?

She'd looked at her feet and could barely make out her boots, the steam was so thick. She had edged forward, half a step at a time, pointing her toe and feeling the ground before she put her foot down. A gust of wind spun her halfway around and she'd recoiled when she saw what looked like a huge stone face of a Maori warrior. She'd screamed, remembering Tori's warning about what could happen to those who came to the island and broke the tapu — that to breach the ancient law was to risk everything: your life, your strength, your power. 'Ko te tapu te mana o nga atua,' Tori had said. 'Tapu is the mana of the spiritual powers.'

The craggy rock was part of the crater wall and seemed to be advancing towards her. You don't believe this stuff, she'd told herself. It's just a rock. Get a grip.

'Bob! Bob!' she'd called and listened again. Nothing but the roaring of the crater. She'd continue to creep forward and the ground seemed to be vibrating. Even the stone face had been subsumed by the steam and she still couldn't see her feet.

She screamed again, this time in pain. Something hot was scorching her leg. She'd lifted it up and seen mud covering her boot and dripping over the top onto her clothes. Frances leapt backwards.

The steam had subsided and she could see where her foot had broken through a thin crust of earth covering a bubbling blackness.

Panic was something Frances had often overcome. Years of rigorous training climbing volcanoes in adverse conditions, hot and ice cold, scuba diving, and dealing with eruptions at close quarters had made her resilient and clear thinking. But at that moment, Frances felt overwhelmed and out of control. She couldn't see ahead and it was too dangerous to move, she didn't know where Bob was or if he was safe. Crouching behind a rock she trembled like a frightened child, a dull pain in her leg she tried to ignore.

'Frances!' She heard the voice not far behind. 'Bob! Frances!' A silhouette appeared through the steam. By the time Hamish spotted her, she was standing, shaking. The burn on her leg was aching but she'd put it to the back of her mind.

'Careful! The ground's unstable.' Her voice sounded croaky and broken and sweat was pouring down her face inside the hot mask, stinging her eyes.

They'd walked towards each other and she pointed to the mask he was still carrying. 'Put it on, the gas is really strong.' By now the swirling steam was lifting but she still couldn't see ahead to the crater lake.

'Are you OK? What's happened to your leg?' Hamish had gestured to her mud-sodden clothing. Grateful to see him and fighting back tears, she was terrified and wanted to leave as soon as possible.

'That's nothing, I'm fine. But I don't know where Bob's gone. I was following him to the lake but the steam thickened and I couldn't see a thing. Come with me, just watch your step.'

She let Hamish lead. He knew the island, and moved with the fearlessness of a young man who believed he was invincible. They'd walked on slowly, around the fresh mud pool that had appeared in the middle of the track. The ground kept changing as they'd continued deeper into the crater. One moment it was slippery, the next crunchy and all the while there were vibrations and an incessant roar.

Frances glanced towards the stone face that had menaced her. It seemed to have sunk back and was once more a part of the crater wall, the features that had almost spoken to her barely distinguishable.

As they'd neared the heart of the crater, they could hear the sound of boiling water. Bob was nowhere to be seen. They'd both called out but there was no sound that was human.

The steam was thicker ahead and they could only see through it when a gust of wind blew it away. 'Stop!' Hamish was a few metres ahead, close to the rim. 'It's given way!' he called over his shoulder.

Frances caught him up where the ground slid away and they cautiously moved closer and looked over.

A seemingly bottomless lake of green water bubbled below, disappearing and reappearing as clouds of gas were thrown up in front of them. Around them, smaller angry yellow ponds and gaping vents belched out poisonous fumes she could smell in spite of the mask.

Hamish was yelling. Even the fury of this hellish cauldron couldn't drown him out. 'There he is!'

CHAPTER EIGHTEEN

A loud bang wakes Frances. Then there's another. She sits up on her bed, confused in the darkness. There's a third bang. She remembers she's in Naples. Her back is aching and she realizes she'd fallen asleep with her clothes on. She listens but can hear nothing. The whole building seems to be sleeping, or holding its breath. As she fumbles for the light switch, her cellphone rings.

'Pronto! Frances, where are you?' Riccardo is talking softly but with an urgency she hasn't heard before.

'I'm home. Are you OK? I've heard some explosions.'

'I'm fine. But there've been some shootings. Just checking you're safe. Stay where you are. I'm down in the old city. I'll be back soon.'

'What happened?'

He doesn't reply. Frances punches his number on her phone. It rings several times then drops out. She tries again but there is no answer. Two more shots ring out.

She sits on the edge of her bed, unsure of what to do. A sudden cry makes her jump. But it's only baby Luciana below.

Frances opens the door of her apartment and creeps down the stairs. She knocks on the Foglianos' door. She hears Luciana cry again but no one answers. She knocks again.

'Who is it?'

'Peppe, it's me, Frances.'

He opens the door slightly so she can just see his face. His brow is wrinkled and his dark eyes anxious.

'Is everything all right?'

'Ricky just rang. There's been a shooting.'

He pokes his head out of the door and looks around before inviting her in. Laura is pacing the floor in the dimly lit lounge, holding the baby. She looks exhausted.

'Sit down,' she smiles at Frances, indicating the couch.

'Peppe, you warned there might be trouble tonight. What's happening? Did you hear the shots?'

He looks away for a moment. She sees him exchange glances with his wife. 'I heard something,' he says at last. 'Is Riccardo OK?'

'I don't know, the phone went dead.'

'Papa, I'm thirsty.' Stefano has woken and stands before them in blue pyjamas rubbing his eyes.

'Here, take the baby.' Laura hands Luciana to Frances. 'I'll get it.'

Frances has had little experience with babies and feels stupidly inadequate holding her. She rocks her in her arms and strokes her head. Luciana smiles up at her for a few seconds then changes her mind and starts to howl and writhe. Stefano is delighted by the distraction and looks very pleased to be out of bed. He squeezes closely next to Frances. The baby continues crying and Frances looks up helplessly at Peppe.

'Here, I'll take her,' Laura says rushing back in with a glass of water. 'Stefano, bed!' She hands him the water and takes the little girl.

'So, what do you think's happened?' Frances presses Peppe.

'Unfortunately shootings are common in Naples. The big families of the clans fight among themselves, sometimes kill each other. And sometimes others get in the way,' he says, more animated now and gesticulating. 'You understand me, Frances?'

'But you seemed to have some advance warning tonight. Did you know?'

Peppe's brow creases more and he hesitates. 'The word gets around. At the petrol station, you hear things — whispers, rumours. I listen and make sure we're not out there.'

'Have you ever been threatened?'

Laura laughs, bitterly. Registering the tension, Luciana starts crying again and both Stefano and his brother sneak into the room to try to sit with Frances.

'Boys, back to bed,' Peppe orders and they scamper away.

'Sshhh. Calma.' Laura comforts the baby and her cries stop.

Peppe walks over to a polished wooden cabinet and takes out a bottle and three small glasses. 'Grappa?'

'Why not? Yes, please.'

He pours the golden liquid into the glasses and hands her one. 'Salute!' They toast each other. The local brandy is stronger than she expects and burns her throat. Frances hates the taste but resists the urge to screw up her nose. 'Buona, eh? From my uncle's vineyard,' Peppe says.

'Yes, very good.' Frances notes Laura has left her glass untouched.

'So have you? Have you been threatened?' Frances persists.

He looks at her as if weighing up whether he can trust her.

'Yes. And no. When you grow up here, you learn very young how to stay out of trouble. Our families, mine and Laura's, we're not part of any clan. But the mere fact that you live here means you can't escape their influence, so you try not to take any sides. Try to be even with all the families and not look like a threat to them or their businesses.'

Frances sees Laura is listening closely but saying nothing.

'And the petrol station? Is there a problem running the business? Do you have to pay protection money?'

Peppe laughs. 'You know more than you let on,' he says. 'Or maybe you've seen too many Hollywood movies.'

'Well, I've seen an awful lot of people around here who look like they've walked off the set of a Mafia film, especially some of the young ones hooning around on their Vespas!' she exclaims.

Laura and Peppe both laugh.

'Of course, you're right,' she says. 'The films glamorize the clan. I can't tell you the number of copycats in Naples for Al Pacino's Scarface gangster and Marlon Brando's Godfather.'

'And Tarantino's films. And Scorcese's,' Peppe adds. 'Lots of young tough kids here act out the movies.' The smile dies on his lips. 'The trouble is they believe that's the way to behave. But to answer your question. I don't own the petrol station, I only manage it. If money is changing hands, I don't know about it.'

'And he doesn't ask questions like yours,' Laura sighs.

A revving motorbike resonates from below.

Frances jumps up and looks through the shutters to the courtyard. 'It's Ricky! Thank God. I'd better go.'

Peppe lets her out and she turns back.

'And thanks for the grappa.'

'You're welcome. Plenty more for next time,' he smiles.

She runs down the flights of stairs and unlocks the front door.

'Here, let me help you.' She hears a voice and is surprised to find Pasquale parking the motorbike while Riccardo stands rubbing his shoulder. She recoils when the street light reveals his jacket and hands are bloodied.

'You're hurt!' She reaches out to help him remove his helmet. 'Are you OK? Shall I get a doctor?'

'No, no, it's not my blood.' He is limping and she puts her arm around him to help him up the stairs.

'Come with us,' she urges Pasquale.

Riccardo flops onto the sofa. Frances takes his jacket to the bathroom and returns with a bowl of warm water and a towel, then gently washes his hands and face. His eyes are puffy, his clothes are dirty and a combination of sweat and blood oozes from him.

Frances thinks of Peppe's grappa and remembers she has a bottle of cognac. She finds it in a kitchen cupboard and pours a glass for each of them, which are both quickly skulled.

'Two dead,' Pasquale says first. His voice is soft and shaky, his normally bright eyes dulled in shock.

Riccardo nods lamely. 'I was there. After the university meeting about the garbage crisis, a few people got excited about taking action. I know some of them and I went back to their neighbourhood. When we got there we walked straight into trouble. Some gang had arrived and was tipping up the garbage skips and setting them alight. They were just young guys, probably following orders. We tried to stop them. That's when I got whacked around the legs with a pole and a fist in my face.' He rubs his swollen and red cheek. Then they jumped on their bikes and left.'

'That's when I arrived,' Pasquale says. 'I'd been busking at Santa Lucia and heard the racket. I didn't see you, Riccardo.'

'I was upstairs in my friend's apartment when the shooting began. But a lot of locals poured onto the street, furious about the garbage. No one expected they'd come back. By the time I got down, the two of them were dead. I bent down to check their pulses and . . . they were mutilated. Those bastards cut their lips with a knife.' He throws up his hands, still streaked with their blood.

Frances strokes his shoulder. 'Who were they?' She looks from Riccardo to Pasquale but neither man answers.

They both seem to be stuck in time. Frances is reeling, still coming to terms with the murders of the scientists — and now, more killings. The violence is coming closer.

'I recognized Paolo,' Pasquale says at last. 'A farmer who spoke up after his land was poisoned. I met him earlier at the meeting.'

'And Leonardo,' Riccardo adds. 'He's been agitating against Il Sistema, calling for the government to stop the flow of toxic waste into Campania. Now they've both been silenced.' He rubs at the blood on one of his hands, trying to get rid of a red stain ingrained in a wrinkle on his palm. He looks up and exclaims. 'That's my life line. Maybe it means my time will be cut short too!'

'Shssh! You're OK. It's just the shock.' Frances looks at them both. 'Did you call the police?'

They both shake their heads. Riccardo speaks slowly, as if explaining something to a child. 'You may not understand this, Frances, but we both got out of there as quickly as possible.'

'But didn't you see who did it?'

'No,' Riccardo says. 'I saw the young thugs but not the killers. The others told me they were two men who stormed in on a motorbike and did their dirty work.'

'Nor did I,' Pasquale says. 'A motorbike flew past me just before the shootings and …' He hesitates and shakes his head. I did see someone later,' he says slowly. 'But not on the bike.'

They look at him closely.

'A very short man, almost a dwarf. He ran past me after the shootings. He was carrying a gun and running very fast in the opposite direction.'

'That's odd,' Riccardo says, 'Neither of the killers was a dwarf. People would have noticed.'

'I'm so exhausted I'm starting to wonder if I dreamt it.' Pasquale stands and heads for the door. 'I'm sorry but I have to go home. I'm totally drained.'

Frances locks the door after him then pours another brandy for herself and Riccardo.

He sips it and lies back on the sofa. Soon he is sleeping.

Frances sits opposite, watching him. Is she dreaming it all too; caught up in someone else's nightmare? Decapitated vulcanologists, people gunned down in cold blood — no exploding volcanoes, however dangerous, had prepared her for the eruptions of southern Italy.

CHAPTER NINETEEN

The ringing assaults her ears. Her room is black and she accidentally knocks the phone to the floor, missing the call. When she climbs out of bed and flings open the shutters, harsh daylight floods into her room and she's surprised to see the sun is already high in the sky. She glances at her watch. Eleven o'clock. Oh God, she's overslept! She finds the phone where it landed, on a pile of dirty clothes under her bed, and flicks it on. Four missed calls, all from Marcello.

She wanders out to the lounge where Ricky is still asleep on the sofa, cocooned in the blanket she found for him the night before. In the bathroom she finds some painkillers and takes out two of the white tablets, then gets a glass of water and nestles next to him. She strokes his forehead until he stirs.

He slowly opens his eyes and groans. 'Hey, don't sound so pleased to see me,' she says in as cheerful a tone as she can manage. 'Here, take these.' She helps him sit up. 'I think you might need them.'

Riccardo swallows the tablets obediently, like a schoolboy home on a sick day. 'I feel like I've died and been to hell and back,' he mutters. 'Ouch, my fucking leg!' he yells as he tries to stand.

'Hey, take it easy. I'll help you up. Have a hot shower and see how you feel.'

When Frances hears the running water, she quickly rings Marcello to tell him about Riccardo's misadventure, but he's already heard about the shootings.

'It's all over the news,' he says. 'I met the two men who were murdered at the meeting. I'm glad you were well away from it all. This city is lurching out of control.'

'I can feel it in the air,' she says. 'I can almost taste the violence —

it's unlike anything I've ever known. But I'm trying to stay focused on our task — the bigger picture of protecting millions of people.' Frances reminds him the three of them were planning to visit the excavations of the Bronze Age settlements that day. 'Is it too late?'

'No. I have another couple of hours' work to do in the lab. Why don't I pick you up in the city around two?'

'Perfect. I don't know if Ricky will be up for it.'

'Call me later and we can confirm the meeting place,' he says. 'By the way, Frances . . .' His voice trails away.

'Yes?'

'I've thought a lot about you in the last few days.' His voice is tender. It triggers a release of the horror and fear she had felt washing through her veins.

'I've thought a lot about you too,' she tells him.

Frances turns on the television and switches until she finds a news channel. It's not long before the story about the shooting appears. Shots of carabinieri at the scene, the bodies, covered with sheets, being loaded into ambulances, interviews with witnesses. There are photos of the victims and some file video of the activist, Leonardo, who had previously addressed public rallies against the dumping of toxic waste.

Photos of suspects flash on the screen, one named as Fabio Dragorra. He had come to police attention previously through an investigation of the cartels controlling waste disposal in the metropolis. His father, Umberto Dragorra, is interviewed. He says his son is innocent and was not in Naples the previous night, but in the north on business. Frances does a double take when she hears that among his other roles, Dragorra is chair of the university.

She hears a knock at the door and Pasquale calling to her. She opens the door wide and points to the television screen. Pasquale pales as the reporter recaps details about the murders, wincing when a shot of Paolo's body is replayed in slow motion.

They both watch a second story about another shooting in the city, shortly after the first. A gang member was shot dead inside a bar. He had been drinking with his sister when a lone gunman burst in and killed him.

'The police wish to interview a man who was seen near the scene of the crime,' the reporter says. 'His name is Basso Mezzanotte, believed to be a member of a rival gang.' A photo of a man with a tangle of gold hair, a large nose and a red complexion fills the screen.'

'That's him! The dwarf!' Pasquale exclaims. 'I wasn't dreaming after all. Basso Mezzanotte — Shorty Midnight.'

Riccardo limps out of the bathroom wrapped in a towel, dripping wet. 'Morning,' he nods to Pasquale. 'Have you recovered from our late-night drama?'

'Better than the other two,' he says soberly. 'We just saw the news coverage. Looks like the short man I saw used the opportunity to pay a revenge call on another matter.'

Riccardo shrugs his shoulders. 'Man, this city is falling apart.'

'Marcello just said the same thing,' Frances replies. 'He rang about our expedition to the Bronze Age sites.'

She rustles in the cupboard for a coffee grinder and the apartment fills with its droning roar and the aroma of freshly crushed beans. She spoons the coffee into the espresso maker and tries to light the gas top. 'Damn!' It refuses to spark.

'Here, let me.' Pasquale takes the box of matches from her and fiddles with the control until a blue flame burns brightly.

'I'm not going anywhere today, sorry, I feel like shit,' Riccardo calls back from his room. 'I'm going to try to sleep it off.'

'You do that,' she says. 'I'll see you at dinner.'

Frances removes the whistling machine from the stove and pours two coffees. As she passes a cup to Pasquale she notices his hands are trembling. She puts a hand on his shoulder.

'You're still in shock. Do you want to see a doctor?'

'N-n-no,' he stammers, then steadies himself. 'No. I'll be all right.' He sips the coffee loudly and apologizes. 'I was going to do some serious practice but I don't feel in the mood. So I'm going to busk some more today. I'll take the cello instead of the violin so at least my hands can limber up.'

'How much money do you need for the new cello?'

'Twenty thousand euro. I'm more than halfway there and I might be able to get a loan. But I'm running out of time. And Saturday's a big day for tourists, especially around Maschio Angionino.'

'Where's that?'

'Down town. It's also called Castel Nuovo, the new castle, because it was only built seven hundred years ago. Quite new for here!'

'Why don't I come with you? I've got some time.'

He smiles at her gratefully. 'I'd like that.'

They jump on a bus, Pasquale struggling to squeeze himself and the unwieldy cello case between a crush of passengers. Wearing a black trilby and his trademark long coat, Pasquale towers above the seated passengers. Frances is holding a small foldaway stool and props herself against the other side of the case to balance them as they bounce down the winding road towards the castle. The day is clear and from the bus, between buildings, she catches glimpses of Vesuvius and patches of the sea shining like chips of blue glass.

'Nearly there.' Pasquale pushes the button for the next stop. They press through to the door and emerge into the brightness of the Piazza Municipio. Three tourist buses are parked nearby and groups are meandering to and fro, from the castle to the brotherhood of African bag merchants plying a brisk trade on the pavement, to a mobile gelato van.

'Room for me somewhere in this mix,' Pasquale says. He positions himself near a tree where people pause to rest, removes the cello from its case, puts the trilby upside down on the case and drops in some coins.

As soon as he strikes up the first notes of one of his Bach suites, Frances notices heads turning towards him, but no one comes near. He finishes the piece and turns to Frances. 'Sadly that response is normal,' he laughs. 'Now watch this.'

He launches into 'Santa Lucia', the deep velvet notes of the cello bestowing a richness and complexity on the song. Instantly, a woman wanders over and drops several coins, their noise muffled by the felt hat. More tourists follow and by the time he has played the song through a few times, the hat is half full. A group of elderly Americans gathers to listen. Pasquale breaks into 'Funiculi, Funicula' and again the coins tumble into his hat.

Frances watches their faces, captivated by Pasquale's performance. She senses the music has lifted his mood too, and the brutality of the night before is forgotten, at least for a moment.

'Can you play "That's Amore"?' a man calls out in a New York Brooklyn accent.

Pasquale grins. 'I'll try. But only if you sing!'

'Hey, go, Rocco!' his friends cry out.

'You're on!'

Pasquale raises his bow and plays the first notes. The man steps forward and starts to sing. He's bald and seventy-five if he's a day, but moves like a much younger man. His voice is clear and tuneful and when Frances closes her eyes she can imagine him in a slick cabaret suit rather than the polyester walking pants and checked shirt he's wearing.

'Hey, you're nearly as good as Dean Martin,' one of his friends jokes.

Encouraged, he sings louder, his hand on his heart and swaying to his own beat. The mood is infectious. The rest of the group is singing. Several start dancing. As Frances claps, another of the men grabs her arm and swings her into a crazy version of a waltz. As the group bursts into applause, Frances scoops up the hat and passes it around.

'Help him buy a new cello!' she encourages them.

One by one they drop coins and notes into the hat as Pasquale stands to make a mock bow with the singer. They turn to bow to each other. The singer then fishes his wallet out of his pocket and takes out a one hundred dollar bill. 'That was the most fun I've had since I've been here,' he says handing the note to Pasquale. 'Beats the hell out of old castles!'

The horn of one of their large tour buses beeps and they trail away.

Pasquale quickly counts the money. 'You should come more often — only half an hour and there's one hundred euro and one hundred and fifty dollars.'

'Keep playing. But your sidekick has to go,' she says. 'I've been meaning to check out the castle, even if your fan thinks it is boring!'

Pasquale starts to play 'The Swan' and the haunting notes accompany her as she strolls across the square towards the looming stone walls. Hard charcoal cobblestones lead her up the path to the entrance guarded by menacing brick towers, stained chocolate by the urban pollution.

She walks across a bridge spanning a wide moat, through a sculptured white marble archway into a vast sloping courtyard open to the sky, overlooked by three storeys.

A couple of guards are playing cards beneath a colonnade and barely register her presence when she passes. An ancient chapel lies ahead which she peruses quickly then climbs as high as she can towards the top of the castle.

The stairs are steep and irregular and pass long galleries full of paintings. A vivid flash of red catches her eye. She pauses when she sees it's an old image of Vesuvius labelled 'Eruption 1632'. In the centre of the painting, the mountain spews a fiery mass which shoots into the sky and blows down into Naples. People are fleeing streets piled with the dead, and trying to board boats in the bay. Frances shudders.

She continues climbing. A rush of cold air blasts her as she opens a door leading to the battlements where a young couple kiss passionately against one wall. The long-haired girl and her dark-skinned lover ignore her, locked in their own world. She gazes out across the bay to the twin peaks of Vesuvius, so benign today. She spins around and, as far as her eye can see, the city of Naples spreads in all directions.

The wind is picking up and her leather jacket does nothing to protect her from the cold, although she notices the couple, dressed in skimpy clothes, remain oblivious to the weather.

She runs down the stairs, two steps at a time. At the bottom, a sign outside a large, wood-panelled room says 'Sala dei baroni'. She pokes her head inside. Rows of burgundy upholstered chairs give the stark chamber the air of an inquisition. She's looking up at the ribbed vaulted ceiling when a guide walks over.

'This is where the barons were executed,' he says matter-of-factly.

'The barons?'

'Yes.' He straightens his tie, clearly delighted to have an audience. 'They were plotting against the King, back in medieval times. King Ferrante. So when he found out, he invited his enemies here for a feast. When they were all eating, he told his soldiers to lock the doors. They were all slaughtered.'

'That was some last supper!' Frances says.

'The price of betrayal and treachery is always high.' He stares into her eyes, unsettling her.

She starts to leave but he calls her back. 'You should visit the basement,' he says, a tad conspiratorially. 'Lots of skeletons — most people like that.'

Frances is tempted to keep going but knows she will take the bait. Where there are skeletons, there is always a story. She turns back and he sweeps his right hand out like a traffic warden, gesturing to more stairs behind him.

She walks down two flights of sandstone steps which narrow at each level. Electric lights styled as medieval torches mounted on the walls throw barely enough light to show the way. She avoids dark corners and crevices that whisper to her of a bloody past. Below it is empty and claustrophobic. A row of lights reflects on the ground ahead. Sheets of thick glass have replaced the paving stones and when she stands on them she can see deep into the bowels of the fortress. She recoils sharply. Resting on the rock are the glowing bones of a skeleton. Then she sees another and another, sometimes one on its own, then two together. There are no labels and no clues to their identity. She wanders further and jumps when something brushes against her leg. Meow! A marmalade cat lets her know she's trespassing. She ignores it and passes into another room.

More glass floors reveal the foundations of the castle. She kneels and peers down for a closer view. There are no more skeletons but large rocks and . . . It can't be . . . and yet . . . Frances rubs the glass to try to focus more closely, looks again and can't believe what she is seeing. She crawls to the next section of glass and the next. It is. She's sure it is. Sitting back on her heels she lets out a long, slow whistle then bounds back up the stairs, her heart racing.

The guide is standing outside the barons' room and looks up when he hears her footsteps. She slows down and collects her thoughts. As casually as she can, she walks over to him. 'Thank you for telling me about the basement. It's most interesting.'

'You're welcome, the skeletons are always popular.'

She smiles at him. 'I can see why.' She pauses. 'Actually, I'm also very interested in the foundations. I'm an archaeologist and I was wondering if it's possible to go beneath the glass and touch the stones.'

The guide looks at her closely. He's shorter than her and his stomach betrays his fondness for large bowls of pasta. 'No. It's not allowed.' He turns to go.

'But . . .' Frances pulls out her university identity card. 'Look. You can see I'm an academic.' She puts the card into his hand.

He peers at the photo and back at her.

'Please. I would be very appreciative. I am writing a paper on the foundations of old buildings of Naples.'

'But you have to get permission from the superintendent. In writing,' he adds.

'I will. But if I could have a quick look now then I can apply formally to make a larger study.'

He looks around him. The two security guards are still playing cards in the distance. There are no other tourists to be seen. 'OK. Come on then.'

She follows him down the stairs and can't believe her luck when he leads her to a steel grated door in one corner of the room. He takes out a large set of keys from his pocket and opens it. 'This takes us there. These are the remains of an old Roman villa built long before the castle, maybe two thousand years ago.'

There are only a dozen steps or so before they are on the basement floor and looking at a maze of masonry. 'Over there.' Frances points to a lighted area beneath the glass.

They walk in file, feet crunching on the stones. Frances sinks to her knees and reaches down into a hole beneath the foundation stones. She scoops up a handful of small white oval stones and smells them. She reaches down for more. They're distinctively honey-combed, light and powdery. She runs her hand up and down the layer of loose stones, maybe a metre deep. Her hunch was right. Here below the castle is an ancient layer of volcanic pumice and ash. And if the ruins are Roman, then this happened long before the Pompeii eruption.

She breathes faster, coming to grips with the consequences of the discovery. This is the evidence Marcello's been looking for . . . proof that the winds have previously carried an eruption right into the heart of Naples. If it happened again today, there would be no survivors. She runs her hand down the layer, so deep it would have been lethal. Details of other eruptions flood her mind and she remembers Mt Pelée in Martinique. Everyone who was killed lay under just eight inches of debris, much less than this. And if it has happened here before . . .

'Signorina,' the guide interrupts. Lost in her thoughts, she starts when she hears his voice. 'We must go now.' He taps her shoulder. 'You really shouldn't be here without permission.'

CHAPTER TWENTY

Outside the castle, the sea breeze ruffles her hair as she rings Marcello.

'Ah, Frances. I've finished at the lab. Are you ready?'

She resists the temptation to blurt out the discovery. 'Yes. I'm at the Castel Nuovo. Can you park your car and meet me at the entrance? There's something you need to see there before we go to Nola.'

'Sure. Is Riccardo coming?'

'No, he's sleeping.'

More African traders have set up shop on the path in front of her. One of them sees her and begins to spruik. 'A watch, signorina? New design.' Tall and slender, he opens his jacket to show an array of twenty or more. She smiles at him, holds up her wrist to show her own watch and keeps walking.

The cello music drifts around the piazza and a new audience of tourists has spilled off a red double-decker bus, surrounding Pasquale. Hundreds of people mill around the square, happy faces oblivious to any danger. None of them is included in any emergency evacuation plan. Naples is simply not on the authorities' radar.

Marcello approaches her, walking quickly. He kisses her on both cheeks then lightly on the lips. 'A third for luck,' he smiles.

She takes his arm. 'My turn to show you something.'

The guide does a double-take when he spots her. 'Just showing my colleague.'

He waves her past. 'Don't forget to write for the permission, signorina.'

'What is he talking about?'

'Patience, Marcello, patience.' She leads him to the glass flooring in the basement. 'There, what do you think?'

Marcello peers into the gloom of the foundations. He glances at her, frowning, then kneels to look closer. She's amused to see him repeat her own movements. Crawling from one area to another, rubbing his eyes as if he can't quite believe what he is seeing. 'Pumice? Here in the middle of the city?'

She nods. 'I persuaded the guide to take me down to touch it. Definitely pumice.'

Marcello clutches his forehead. 'My God, Frances. This is what I feared. This is the proof that the Avellino eruption was much bigger than anyone imagined. It covered the city and it could easily happen again.'

She takes his arm. 'Look at the skeletons. Were they part of it?'

'No, much later,' he says dismissively. 'I can tell they're more recent and they're lying several layers above the pumice.' Marcello is agitated. 'I'd like to get down there and have a proper look. But the day is disappearing. Do you still want to go to Nola?'

'Yes, very much. And the guard is insisting we get permission before he lets us down there again.'

They drive north of Naples along the expressway, then skirt east around Vesuvius. Heavy trucks hogging all the lanes slow them but soon they turn off into a dusty road far beyond the metropolis.

'There are two Bronze Age village sites,' Marcello tells her. 'The smaller one is just ahead.'

They pull off the road and park near what looks like a construction site. Earthmoving equipment is lined up like a military armoury but there's no sign of any workers.

'They're itching to get in here and destroy it,' he mutters. 'We're fighting to save the excavations from the bulldozers. They want to build a supermarket here.'

He retrieves two safety helmets fitted with lights, puts one on and hands the other to her. 'No lights there. We'll need these.'

She follows Marcello over a low timber fence to a dug-out area the size of a small football field. They peer over the edge into a labyrinth of holes lined with scaffolding. He beckons her and they switch on their lights and carefully descend a ladder. The smell of the brown earth is almost overwhelming. Going underground has always made her feel trapped but she keeps going down until she reaches a point where the layer of earth changes to pumice.

Marcello is waiting on a platform and grabs her hand. As her eyes acclimatize, she can make out odd horseshoe-shaped structures. 'What you're looking at is the remains of a village that flourished until it was buried by the eruption of 1780 BC.'

She struggles in the poor light but can see half-formed rooms and doorways.

'We've removed most of the objects. The skeletons you've seen, also bones of animals: goats, pigs, sheep, cattle and dogs.'

'Like a primitive Pompeii,' she says.

He nods. 'None of the artwork, but cooking pots, plates and fossils of food, nuts, grains and olives.'

Marcello lowers himself into a trench up to his shoulders. His headlamp shines a ghostly light inside one of the rooms. 'Come down and have a closer look,' he urges her. 'I'll help you.'

'No. I can see enough from here.' Frances shivers. The pit of her stomach is churning and her head is spinning.

Marcello moves to a doorway across the trench, where his light rests on a rough piece of furniture. 'A table. It was set for a meal, but no one stayed to eat it. They must have heard the volcano erupting and fled.'

Frances sits down and puts her head in her hands. The cold stones and earth press into her bottom. 'Marcello, can we go up, please? I feel faint.'

He heaves himself out of the trench, grasps her arm and helps her back to the ladder. She breathes deeply to combat her nausea and climbs steadily out of the hole. When she reaches the top she flops onto her back on the ground.

'Hey, are you all right?'

'I will be in a minute, I just need a bit of air. I hate being underground, it makes me feel as if I've been buried alive.'

He sits next to her and puts his arm around her.

'I saw a horror film once,' she says, breathing more lightly. 'It was about being buried alive. The girl was kidnapped at a service station by a psycho and drugged. When she woke up she was in a coffin and was scraping the lid with her fingers to get out but she was trapped underground. And that was the end of the story.'

'That's gruesome!'

'One of those movies I wish I'd never seen; it gave me nightmares for years.'

'Well, the nightmare of these people was all too real. And I've no doubt they saw what was coming. They would have heard the huge explosion, then there would have been the downpours of hot rocks and pumice. Then darkness. It was an apocalypse. In just twenty-four hours this fertile valley turned into a desert. After that no one could live here for at least three hundred years.' He strokes her forehead.

'I know what you're thinking,' she says.

'Try me.'

'You're thinking it's a blueprint of what could happen again.'

'Partly,' he says teasingly. 'I was also worrying about this fallen vulcanologist I have to look after,' he laughs. 'But yes, you're right. I think everyone is in denial about the extent of the danger. We are way outside the Red Zone here and so is the centre of Naples. Yet there is no escape plan.'

Frances sits up and looks around.

'Are you feeling better?'

She yawns deeply, sucking in the air. 'Yes. Dizzy spell gone.'

Marcello helps her to her feet.

A bluish hue envelops the mountain in the late afternoon. She hasn't seen the volcano from this angle before and tries to envisage what the people who inhabited the Campanian plain four thousand years earlier had seen. The peak would have looked completely different; Vesuvius hadn't yet formed. It was Mt Somma that overshadowed the villagers until it exploded and the younger volcano grew into its own. In the distance, olive groves carpet purple low-lying hills and the tiled roofs of tightly clustered villages dot the horizon. Smoke drifts skyward from a farm bonfire nearby but, save for a barking dog, there is no sign of life.

Marcello has wandered beyond the excavations and is bending down, looking closely at something. He raises his arm and calls her over. On the ground around Marcello, dozens of footprints are etched into the hard brown surface.

'We've found thousands of these preserved in the volcanic ash.' He traces one of them with a finger. 'People from the buried villages.'

Frances pulls off one of her boots and a sock before stepping into one of the footprints. 'I would have been a giant,' she laughs as her foot overlaps the embedded print. 'One-seventy-seven centimetres with size nine feet.'

'An exotic blonde Amazon! You certainly would have stood out.'

Frances steps into one print after another, looking in the direction they were headed, towards the hills. 'Maybe they got it right,' she says. 'Running away on foot may be the smartest thing to do if you consider the chaos on the roads.'

'Only if you know which way to run — these people were running east, hoping to shelter in the forests,' he says, pointing to the hills. 'It was a path to death, straight into the fallout zone. They would have been caught in a pyroclastic flow and asphyxiated under piles of hot pumice.'

She bends down to touch the footprints, such a tangible and human link to a lost civilisation. Male or female? She couldn't tell.

As Frances puts her boot back on, she tries to picture the panic as the eruption continued day and night, the giant plume rising above the volcano, far out of sight into the stratosphere.

A faint droning startles her. High above, a jetstream from an airliner paints two straight lines like shooting arrows across the sky. 'Three times higher than that plane,' she says. 'It's hard to believe, but that's how high the eruption would have gone.'

He is walking away across the barren fields when he stops and turns to her. 'That's why I'm so certain we must understand the winds and where they will blow all the debris if there's another eruption.' He gestures wildly, his hands puncturing the air. 'These poor primitives knew nothing.' He points to the prints. 'They didn't have a chance, just like the people of Pompeii who rushed back to their homes after the first explosion and were incinerated. We have the luxury of the best scientific knowledge at our disposal, yet we will have to run just like these poor wretches. And we'll have to run through another minefield as well, of politics and corruption.'

He turns back and she follows him to another stretch of hard ground, knotty weeds brushing her legs. More footprints mark the rock as clearly as feet pressing into a soft sandy beach. 'These are heading in the opposite direction, north and northwest. If they kept running that way, these people might have escaped.'

Frances nodded. 'You're right. The burning column would have hovered in the stratosphere for hours, maybe a day or two. But when it collapsed into the pyroclastic flows, their survival would have depended on where they had chosen to flee.'

He looks grim. 'And now we know the winds carried the surges right into Naples as well as the entire area to the northeast of Vesuvius, nearly twice as far as allowed for in the current evacuation plans.'

The plane has disappeared and its jetstream is already evaporating when the roar of a second jet breaks the silence.

Frances looks up. 'No chance of escaping that way either. Aeroplanes can't fly where there's ash.'

'How on earth can we get that message out? You've heard how everyone dismisses the threat, even my own grandfather. They think this all happened so long ago. Well, it might be a long time in human years, but it's seconds in volcanic time.'

They walk to the top of a rise but there are no more footprints.

'There's another bigger excavation over there.' Marcello points across a dusty landscape intersected here and there with rows of vines and vegetable patches and a smattering of farmhouses. 'A much bigger prehistoric settlement. Would you like to see it?'

'Sure, but this time I might just stay at the top and look down.'

They drive a few more kilometres then pull over where the road divides into three. Marcello accelerates over a kerb and into a rubbish-strewn wasteland. He looks puzzled and suddenly hits the brakes. Leaping out of the car he slams the door behind him and runs, stopping just ahead by a sea of orange plastic. 'Those bastards!'

Frances has caught him up. His eyes burn black with anger. 'This was one of Europe's biggest and oldest Bronze Age archaeological sites. Now it is a garbage dump!'

He stamps around the periphery of a giant pit filled with thousands of rubbish bags. Pieces of broken fences litter the ground. He kicks a broken padlock lying in the dust then picks up a signboard and holds it up: 'Preserved Bronze Age Village'.

'What a fucking joke!' He throws it down hard.

'When did this happen?'

'It must have been recently — we were here two or three weeks ago.' He bends down to touch one of the orange bags. 'They haven't been here long.'

Frances sniffs. A chemical stench fills her nostrils. She steps back quickly. 'Let's get out of here. I think they're poisonous!'

On the drive back to Naples, neither of them speaks. The rattling of the car is the only sound before Frances turns on the radio. A news bulletin reports more details of the street murders. Fabio Dragorra has been questioned by police but released after he supplied two alibis confirming he was nowhere near the scene of the crime the previous night.

A government minister is interviewed and pays tribute to the two campaigners who had been killed. He promises the inquiry into illegal waste disposal will continue and denied any suggestion that the rubbish situation was out of control.

'Liars!' Marcello splutters. 'They're all liars. That dumping back there — do you think they will do anything? Of course not. They're all in it together — Il Sistema, the politicians. The terrible truth is that they care more about money than the health of their own children. They're poisoning our land and they don't care.'

CHAPTER TWENTY-ONE

The weeks leading up to the mass street protest had been full of frustration for Frances, who was beginning to feel suffocated. Everyone she spoke to was distracted. She was getting the brush-off from the university and no one was showing interest in her research, especially the ever-busy Professor Corsi. Marcello and Riccardo had shifted their passion about the volcano to the garbage crisis, at least momentarily, and with less than a month to Christmas, all of Naples seemed hell-bent on preparing for a celebration and a holiday. No one wanted to hear bad news about a volcano.

The protest would be held in a few days' time and as far as she was concerned, the sooner it was over the better and they could all get back to the job that had brought her here.

Thank heavens for Pasquale! She had welcomed an invitation to accompany him that night to a British diplomatic dinner at the Palazzo Capodimonte. Along with Satore, he had been selected to perform in the the conservatorium's string quartet and was allowed to bring a guest. Ever since the shootings, Pasquale had struggled to sleep and she knew he was a nervous wreck, with his major audition just a week away. A night out with a bit of glitz would do them both some good.

The invitation stated cocktail wear, but after sifting through her wardrobe, Frances realized there was little there except mountain-climbing gear, casual clothes and one sharp suit for the rare times she needed to shed the nerdy scientist image for something more corporate.

A quick jaunt along Via Toledo quickly changed that. Italian fashion was irresistible! The more bling, the better, more sequins and sparkles than she'd seen in her life. Even the new woollen sweaters were covered in glittery finishes. She had moved from one shop to another in search of a dress. Taller and broader than most Italian women, Frances found the dresses either too short or too tight.

In a small boutique in a lane off the main street, she found a rack of silk beaded dresses. They looked perfect. She'd slipped into one and the emerald green had perfectly complemented her eyes and fair complexion. She'd spun around, thinking no, too bright. She'd felt like a Christmas tree and didn't want to be that conspicuous. She'd tried on a black one in the same style — much better. It was more discreet, the hem just above her knee, with a scooped neckline and, as the shop assistant assured her, the latest design from Milan. She'd checked the price tag. Ouch! Oh well, she'd felt like lashing out so handed over her credit card and made the dress her own.

Around six she is almost ready to go. Silky black stockings, a new pair of stilettos and a black pashmina set off the dress perfectly. For once, she takes the time to apply make-up and style her hair. Brushing her blonde tresses back she scoops them into a French roll, securing it with an elaborately patterned clip she'd bought from the Pakistani at the market. Just as she's putting on a pair of delicate drop zircon earrings, Riccardo thumps through the door.

At first, he doesn't notice her standing in front of a mirror on the far side of the room. He looks world weary as he tosses his bike helmet onto the sofa and lets out a huge sigh.

'Madonna!' he exclaims when he catches sight of her. 'Is that you, Frances? Bellissima!'

She laughs when he whistles and insists she twirls around.

'Where are you going all dressed up and looking to die for?' he teases. 'And how come I'm not invited?'

'Pasquale asked me to go with him to a formal function where he's performing. At Capodimonte, the palace.'

'You look like a princess, and you deserve a change from crawling around in the dirt with us. And don't worry about me, I have plenty to do here working out my speech for the protest. Dealing with all the shit!' He adopts a hang-dog look and starts to whine like a puppy.

She slaps him lightly on the shoulder. 'Don't worry, I'll be back to help in the morning, that is if I don't turn into a pumpkin!'

She totters down the stairs, her stilettos loudly clicking, hearing the blare of the television and Laura berating the twins as she passes the Foglianos' apartment. The door to Pasquale's place is open and she calls out to him.

'Ah Frances, good, now we can go.' He shuffles his cello case outside.

'Don't you look the maestro!'

Pasquale is dressed in a tuxedo. His white pleated shirt is pressed immaculately and he wears a black silk bowtie. His reddish black hair falls boyishly around his face. He blushes and smiles broadly. 'All borrowed finery from one of the professional musicians in the orchestra. I have to look the part.'

He steps back to stare at her and whistles.

'Not borrowed,' she laughs.

'Well, let's go. I've called a taxi. We need to be there early so I can set up.'

'That's a relief. I couldn't face the bus tonight.'

Pasquale laughs. 'Just as well, looking like that you'd cause a riot!'

The cab is waiting by the kerb and Frances sits in the front while Pasquale squeezes himself and the cello into the back.

Men from the neighbourhood are congregating in their usual spots around the local square as the taxi drops down into Via Salvator Rosa and past rows of furniture repair shops. At the bottom of the hill, they hit a jam of traffic navigating around the National Museum. Veering left they weave in and out of a line of buses and head up a steep winding road.

Frances glances over her shoulder. Pasquale is peering closely at his left hand. It trembles slightly and she can sense his mood has changed. 'Nervous?'

'No, not at all.' He pauses. 'Well, a little. There will be many important people there tonight so I must play well. We're playing a new work and I'm also playing a solo and . . .' He breaks off.

'What's wrong?'

'Nothing. It is really such a small thing.' He holds up his hand and she notices a bruise near his wrist.

'I knocked it and it's a little sore. But it will be all right.'

She leans over and pats his knee. 'You'll be fine. Don't worry.'

Guards in crisp black military uniforms belted tightly at the waist stop them at the tall iron gates. One of them scrutinizes the invitation Pasquale hands him, fingering it with his white gloves. He stares hard, eyes suspicious, at Pasquale, then Frances and the driver, and reluctantly opens the gate just wide enough for the taxi to enter.

Lines of red, white and blue lanterns illuminate the driveway. They alight outside huge grey stone archways in front of the royal palace. The walls of the renaissance building are spotlighted, showing off their handsome colouring in the signature red of Pompeii. The grounds are in darkness, relieved only by a trickle of small lights along a path that disappears into the night.

'If I didn't have this wretched instrument, I could take your arm,' Pasquale says as they follow an usher along a red carpet through the courtyard and into the grand doors of the palace. No other guests appear to have arrived and they follow the carpet up a wide staircase alone and through a bank of glass security doors.

'The palace is stuffed full of expensive art. Look, there are cameras everywhere.' He indicates closed-circuit television cameras propped in the corners of the gilt-edged ceilings.

They pass into a long ornate gallery, portraits of severe red-capped cardinals and haughty Italian nobles staring disapprovingly from the richly wood-panelled walls. Massive chandeliers light up rows of tables set for a large formal dinner. The red, white and blue British theme prevails; starched white tablecloths and silver settings with placemats and serviettes alternatively red and blue.

'Hey Pasquale, Frances, over here!' Satore calls from the middle of the gallery where he's perched on a small stage with two other musicians. Leaping off gracefully, he prances towards them. Sleekly tuxedoed, his hair is so gelled that it defies gravity and one ear glistens with a row of shining studs. 'Dashing in black and white!' He embraces Pasquale. 'And wow! You could make me change my preferences,' he teases Frances. 'Are they real, darling?' He flicks her earrings.

'Real zircons. Yours?'

'Two diamonds and two fakes. Bet you can't tell which is which.'

She peers closely. 'No. They all look real. Or false.'

Pasquale interrupts them. 'I need to tune up,' he says quietly moving towards the stage.

Satore stares after him. 'What's wrong with him?'

'Nervous.'

'The sooner that audition is out of the way the better,' he mutters, leading her to a table at the back of the room. 'All the musos here together. Plus you.'

Frances can see her name on a placecard.

'We will have to come and go to sing for our supper. But you can stay sitting. No one will be here for another half hour. Why don't you have a look around? See if you can spot the famous flagellation,' he adds mysteriously.

Waiters are hovering around the tables, straightening cutlery and distributing wine glasses.

'Signorina?' One of them arrives with a tray of champagne flutes. She takes one.

'You can go through to the exhibition,' he says nodding to the next set of doors where a banner at the entrance declares: 'British Masterpieces — to celebrate 300 years of diplomatic relations with Italy'.

The walls are covered with an odd mixture of old and new art. She's drawn immediately to the middle of three large oil paintings encased in thick gold frames. Vesuvius is in mid-eruption. A label at the base reveals Joseph Mallord William Turner painted it in 1817, and the artist has portrayed Naples bathed in brilliant orange, the sky above the volcano swirling white and gold, the sea reflecting the turbulence, and in the foreground, Castel Nuovo, where she discovered the pumice, floundering boats and terrified fishermen. She looks more closely but can't tell when this eruption occurred. There were six or so in the preceding century but none that year.

She moves to the next painting, also by Turner. By contrast, Venice's Grand Canal is calm and peaceful, a gondolier paddling across the still water, a blue sky above. In the third, she sees a swirling seascape, the icy crashing waves so realistic she feels cold. Pulling her pashmina closer, she takes a sip of champagne.

More large paintings of the English countryside by John Constable occupy another wall, a cathedral, haymakers and a mill. Opposite, corpulent nudes by Lucien Freud cavort across the canvases.

Flickering lights draw her to the end. A vividly coloured circle covered in butterflies by Damien Hirst spins around and around, making her dizzy when she stares at it for too long. Alongside, streaks of fluoro lights in shocking pink and royal blue. The name of the artist, Tracey Emin, is written on the wall next to them.

She pushes through more doors into the next gallery where subdued lighting changes the mood dramatically. Menacing images taunt her from the walls — scenes of bloody battles, torture and suffering.

A white figure glows in the distance. Frances moves closer and sees the painting is labelled 'Flagellation of Christ' by Michelangelo Merisi da Caravaggio. Ah, that's what Satore was on about. Christ is dressed in a loincloth, his skin pale and fleshy. Three sadistic tormenters surround him, cruelly binding him. At first it looks as though Jesus is bowing in submission, but then she sees the torturer on the right is kicking the back of his knee while the man to his left holds his hair tightly in his fist. She swallows hard. The beauty and the horror are staggering.

Nearby, another scene of torture and she recognizes the painter's name, given to the street in her neighbourhood: Salvator Rosa. He's portrayed a Roman general, Marcus Attilius Regulus, lying in the hands of his enemies, the Carthaginians. His head is sticking out of a nail-studded barrel and his eyelids are cut off to expose his eyes to the heat of the sun.

All around, men and women are baying for his blood. Once she would have dismissed this barbarism as historic, lost in time. But the terrible images of the beheaded scientists at Solfatara haunt her once more.

'Signorina Nelson!' She feels a hand on her shoulder and spins around, dropping her glass. As it smashes to the floor she comes face to face with the chancellor of the university, Alfonso Galbatti, and another man.

'Sorry to startle you, my dear. You are enjoying the art? Personally, I find the modern works quite worrying. My preference is strongly in favour of our great classical artists.'

Although she is a good deal taller than both of the men, at this moment she feels less than a metre high. 'Good evening,' she stammers, noting the champagne is trickling across the polished floor onto a carpet.

'Don't worry about that,' Alfonso waves his hand dismissively. 'I'd like to introduce you to the chair of our university, Signor Umberto Dragorra. He's taken a strong interest in Progetto Vulcano. I'll be back shortly.'

'Charmed!' Umberto holds out a chubby manicured hand and grasps hers firmly. 'I've heard all about you from my good friend, Professor Corsi.'

He barely comes to her shoulder and he's almost as broad as he is tall but there is an aggression in his handshake that makes her go weak at the knees. She withdraws her hand and forces a smile, struggling for something to say until he prompts her.

'And how is the research going?'

Her face lightens. 'Very well. We've made good progress on studying the wind patterns around Vesuvius and what might happen if there's another eruption. Of course, the news is not all good. We believe the Red Zone should be extended and . . .'

A waiter has returned with Alfonso and deftly sweeps up the glass and dabs the carpet with a wet sponge.

Umberto holds up his arm to Alfonso and brings him into the conversation. 'Signorina Nelson was just bringing me up to date with the research.' He smiles with his lips but his eyes do not move. 'You're new to Naples, aren't you? You know, sometimes it's better not to move too quickly. You really have to be very sure of your ground, isn't that right, Alfonso?'

The chancellor nods.

Dragorra continues. 'Change for change's sake. Isn't that what you English say? Well, change is not always appreciated here.'

Two elegantly dressed women walk towards them. 'Ah, our wives,' he says moving away. 'Come, Alfonso, I think we've been missed. A pleasure, Signorina Nelson, a real pleasure.'

Frances feels her face is flushed, runs her hand across her brow then slowly and deliberately returns to the dining room. By now the gallery pulsates with the chatter of hundreds of people. She finds her seat and wishes Pasquale and Satore could join her but sees they are tuning up ready to play.

A tall man with a row of small medals on his lapel taps the microphone on the stage. 'Good evening, ladies and gentlemen. As Her Majesty's Ambassador for the United Kingdom in Italy, I am delighted to welcome you all tonight. Please take your places and remain upstanding for our national anthems, played tonight by musicians from the Naples Conservatorium of Music.'

Frances accepts another glass of champagne from a waiter and quickly drains half before rising to her feet. The rest of her table is empty, reserved for the musicians, and she starts to regret agreeing to come. The first strains of 'God Save the Queen' fill the room and there's an immediate rustling of dresses and clearing of throats as all stand to attention. This was one song she had never heard Pasquale practising but she watches as he, Satore, their second violinist and a violist perform it effortlessly.

The room applauds and seconds later the quartet bursts into an upbeat version of 'Il Canto degli Italiani'. A couple of men start to sing and soon all the Italians in the room join in, some with hands on their hearts. 'Fratelli d'Italia, l'Italia s'è desta . . .'

Their voices rise in unison and at the end of the anthem they cry out a loud 'Si!'

She's relieved when the musicians put down their instruments and Pasquale and Satore head towards her. The waiters are pouring wine into glasses and placing the first course, layers of smoked salmon resting on a green avocado mousse and a bed of watercress.

'Needs trumpets!' Satore says as he noisily sits opposite her.

'Pardon?'

'Our national anthem, it needs trumpets!'

Frances laughs but stops abruptly when she glimpses someone familiar coming through the entrance. It's the green emerald dress that first takes her eye, then she recognizes its wearer.

CHAPTER TWENTY-TWO

Camilla gazes at her reflection and doesn't like what she sees. Why is it that this dress looked so good in the fitting room yet now looks like a sack? She twirls around to check her rear view in the mirror. No better, although she likes the slimming effect of the strappy stilettos. She tears the dress off and tosses it impatiently onto the floor. Hanging inside her wardrobe she sees a group of clothes hidden beneath plastic. Umberto had handed them to her the previous week and she hadn't bothered to look. She peels the covers off and spreads them on her bed. Two suits, one cream, one red, and an emerald green silk beaded dress. Ah, he does have his uses. Of course, they could be counterfeit from some Naples sweatshop but equally likely to be so-called 'excess stock'. They certainly look the same as the latest offerings from the catwalks of Milan.

She slides into the dress and zips it up. Not bad. It sits just above her knee and shows off her waist and cleavage. Of course he knows her size and figure well. Ruffling through her make-up bag she dabs green shadow onto her lids and brushes mascara on her lashes. Camilla steps back from the mirror. Her smoky grey eyes are accentuated by the green dress. She stares for several seconds without blinking and for a moment scarcely recognizes herself, remembering the hours she had spent staring at herself as a teenager, hoping that by looking long enough a miracle would occur and she would become as attractive as the beauties in her class. That didn't happen but there has been a change. Those eyes once so full of hope — now there's a hardness. She starts as the doorbell rings.

'Alfonso . . .' she says opening the door.

'Signora Corsi?'

She's surprised to see a woman there with a bouquet of roses.

'There's a card.' She hands them to her and walks back towards the lift. 'Buona notte.'

Camilla sets the flowers down on her dining table and removes the card.

'Dearest Camilla, Duty demands that I accompany my wife to the dinner tonight. My deepest apologies. I will see you there. Yours always, Alfonso.'

'Bastardo!' Camilla hisses. She wants to fling the roses into the garbage but they are so rich and red she puts them into a crystal vase instead.

Anyway, she consoles herself, tonight it will be better to arrive alone at the British ambassador's dinner. It will make it easier to spend time alone with him. It had been a while since they'd seen each other, when Brian had promised her a trip to London. They had met at a diplomatic reception in Rome, where he had hung back, making a play for her. He said he was separating from his wife, not that that mattered to her. And indeed, when he had phoned her the following week suggesting dinner while he was in Naples, she happily spent the evening with him at a restaurant. It felt only natural to burn off the calories afterwards in his hotel suite.

Damn them all! If they want to play a double game, then I will outdo them with my own quickstep.

Camilla is about to telephone for a university chauffeur but changes her mind. Yes, this is a night to be herself on her own terms. She finds her mink in the wardrobe. This was Umberto's first significant gift, acquired, he told her, from one of his Russian business associates in return for a favour. She had a feeling he might have been an arms dealer but this was information she really did not need to know. Stroking the soft black fur that feels like liquid silk, she snuggles it to her face and can't help herself. Purrr! She adores the sexiness of it, as do more than one of her lovers. Thank heavens the smarter European fashion houses were using it again, in spite of the vitriol of those boring animal liberationists. Most of them wore leather shoes anyway. Hypocrites!

Draping it over her shoulders, she checks her face one more time in the large oval mirror near the doorway and double locks her apartment. The old lift slowly creaks down to the cobbled courtyard. She climbs into her silver Smart car and drives into the street where the dinner crowds are spilling from the pavements onto the streets. She beeps at them and they scatter like pigeons.

Turning into Via Toledo she heads north past the National Museum, navigates up the hill along Corso Amedeo di Savoia Duca D'Aosta and accelerates hard up the winding road to Capodimonte.

She stops outside the gates of the palace and opens the driver's window. The cool air bathes her face as she passes her invitation to one of the military guards. He looks at it cursorily and passes it back to her, deliberately skimming his hand along her fur-covered arm. 'Have a good evening, signora.' He winks as he waves her through to the driveway.

Camilla grits her teeth. Signora! Not long ago the men called her signorina. The area closest to the entrance is already full but her car is so small she can park it sideways in a gap between two others. She looks at her face in the front mirror. Pursing her lips, she touches a new wrinkle. Signora indeed! Quickly she applies a thick new coat of shiny lipstick.

Two ushers guide her through the arches and up the stairs into the palace. She hears the national anthem and glancing at her watch realizes she is late. 'Check this for me please,' she snaps at one of the ushers, and hands him her fur coat. Straightening her dress and fixing a smile, she walks straight-shouldered into the gallery.

Chandeliers shining from above and candelabra glowing on the tables below dazzle her. She brushes aside a waiter offering champagne. The dinner has already started and there's a symphony of clattering cutlery, clinking crystal and clipped conversations as she surveys the room.

'Camilla!' Brian walks towards her, elegant as ever in his diplomatic finery. As he kisses her on each cheek and whispers, 'You look good enough to eat', she can smell the faint hint of whisky on his breath.

'That sounds more fun than dinner, caro,' she whispers back and willingly takes his arm as he leads her to the official table in the centre of the room. The other guests look up as Brian places her in the chair next to his. The four other men at the table shuffle to their feet and she's amused to see they include two of her lovers, Alfonso Galbatti and Umberto Dragorra. Three out of five seated together. 'If only they knew,' she thinks as she proffers her hand to each of them. 'How pathetic they are! Pretending to be merely work colleagues, for the sake of their wives!'

It's a rare night out for Signora Galbatti, pale and piquish in lilac lace, and Signora Dragorra, flushed and fulsome in saffron silk. They greet her begrudgingly, having all crossed paths before and finding little in common. 'Oh, how little they suspect of the common ground we share,' Camilla thinks gleefully to herself. She doesn't know the other two couples and doesn't care that they pay her scant regard.

Another woman is sitting on the other side of Brian, blonde bobbed hair and a flawless English rose complexion.

'Camilla, I don't believe you've met my wife? Natalie, darling, this is Professor Camilla Corsi. An expert on volcanoes and a genuine fiery academic!' He chuckles at his own joke.

'Delighted, I'm sure,' his wife says. 'So when do you think Vesuvius might erupt again?'

Camilla glances from Brian to his wife and back again, furious at his deception and her ambush. 'Unpredictable. Like the weather.' She's aware that all at the table are listening. 'Or marriages,' she adds, managing a smile.

'You can say that again. I'm Brian's third,' his wife laughs.

'Saved the best till last,' he laughs. 'Eat up, Camilla. The salmon's fresh, flown in from Scotland this morning!'

Alfonso is on her other side and she feels his leg pressing against her. 'Did you receive the roses, cara?' he says out of earshot of his wife, who is seated across the table, next to Umberto.

She resists the urge to snarl at him. 'Beautiful. Thank you, Alfonso.'

'Did you see the so-called modern art in there?' he whispers. 'What a load of rubbish!'

'Your tastes are conservative, Umberto. They're all fine painters.'

He's still grumbling as he eats his meal.

Camilla nibbles at the salmon and chews on a piece of watercress, but her appetite has deserted her.

Umberto has turned away from Alfonso's wife, who drums her fingers on the table. His voice is rising as he regales the other two men about government over-regulation and how it is limiting commercial development.

'We agree, Umberto, on the need for free markets we agree. But we are always under pressure. Vesuvius is a major issue, not to mention Campi Flegrei,' one of them says.

She looks more closely and recognizes them as senior government ministers. 'Professor! Professor Corsi.' For a moment she doesn't register that Umberto is addressing her. 'Tell them your views on the Red Zone. Is it reasonable that all development should stop because of the tiny chance of an eruption? Surely people still need decent places to live and shop.'

Camilla breathes in deeply. 'Signor Dragorra, I am flattered that you value my opinion so highly. But tonight is for celebrating, not for such serious discussion. We can talk about this another time.'

He glares at her pointedly, throwing his hands up in exasperation, his creased neck reminding her now more of a lizard than a toad. He is about to say something else but she taps Brian on the back and starts talking to him before he has the chance.

The waiters clear away the plates and Brian springs to his feet. 'Back soon. Talk among yourselves.'

'You don't seem yourself tonight, Camilla. Is everything all right?'

'Yes, Alfonso, I'm fine, I'm just a little tired. I've been working overtime on the Progetto Vulcano report.'

'Well, don't overdo it. And don't let Umberto get the better of you.'

She's about to reply when Brian taps the microphone. 'Ladies and gentlemen, signore et signori. A special treat tonight from our orchestra, which will perform the work of a British composer, Edward Elgar. He's famous for our alternative national anthem, 'Land of Hope and Glory', but I thought that might not be so appropriate tonight. We still have a lot of hope but not so much glory these days.'

The room titters politely at his attempted humour. Camilla has her back to the stage and strains to see the musicians, who are holding their instruments behind Brian. 'Instead, a rarely performed piece, Elgar's String Quartet in E Minor.'

As the mellow sounds of the strings fill the gallery, Brian returns to the table and asks everyone to swap places. 'So we can all learn a little more about each other.'

Camilla finds herself next to Umberto and for once she is pleased his wife is close by. He leans towards her and, uncharacteristically, speaks in hushed tones. 'The dress suits you.'

'Thank you, Umberto.'

'But you know I am worried about you, your attitude.'

'Why would that be?'

'I didn't like the way you humiliated me in front of the others.'

'No, no, caro, you misunderstand,' she says soothingly. 'I was trying to protect you. Discretion is always the best path and I don't think tonight is . . .'

'Don't bullshit me. I'm starting to get impatient about that report, we have contracts waiting. And your foreign researcher — what's her name? Frances? She's here tonight and she was babbling about expanding the Red Zone. You're going to have to rein her in.'

Camilla squirms in her seat. The music's tempo is increasing and the violinists play faster and faster, like bees swarming in the hot sunshine. 'Don't worry. It's all in hand. Where did you say Frances Nelson is sitting?'

'I didn't. I saw her walking around before dinner. She dropped her drink on the floor like a stupid schoolgirl.'

The orchestra is slowing, the last movement nostalgic and sad. Camilla glances around the room but can't see Frances. The last notes fade as the room explodes in applause.

The waiters return, placing large plates of food in front of them.

'A traditional British feast.' Brian is standing again. 'The best rare roast of Angus beef, crispy baked potatoes, Brussels sprouts and, of course, Yorkshire pudding and horseradish sauce. He picks up a glass of red wine. 'But the wine . . . luckily for you, not British.' Everyone at the table is laughing. 'We know you Italians beat us on that score. So fill your glasses with this beautiful 1990 Vino Nobile di Montepulciano. I selected it myself. And enjoy!'

'Buon apettito, professor.'

She turns to see the man on her other side, the government minister, holding up his glass to her. 'Antonio Pane. Salute!' She raises her glass to him and takes a large sip. The soft red is a rich antidote to the friction she's feeling.

'You're right, this is a night to celebrate,' he says. 'Not for politics. But our friend Umberto is not a patient man.' He's a smooth-looking man in his fifties, silvering hair swept back off his tanned face. She can sense him trying to draw her out and for once, she has lost interest in the game. She merely raises her eyebrows and smiles.

She drinks more then eats some of the beef. It's tender and delicious. She pokes the small mound of cooked dough Brian called Yorkshire pudding, pushes it to one side and eats the potato instead. She tastes the green balls of vegetable and dispatches them to the side of the plate. 'I need to powder my nose,' she tells Umberto. He waves her away with his hand.

She walks to the far end of the gallery and turns into a hallway. As she rounds a corner near the toilets, she collides with someone.

'Professor Corsi, sorry.' Frances Nelson steps back and grins. 'Snap! I like your taste in evening wear!'

Camilla is horrified. Her subordinate is wearing the same dress in black. So much for Umberto's exclusive designs! 'Yes, quite. What brings you here tonight? I didn't know you knew the British Ambassador.'

'I don't. I'm here with the hired help. I'm with the band.'

'They're very good. Well, if you'll excuse me.' She starts to walk away then turns back again. 'Frances. The volcano research we're doing. You do realize it's confidential, don't you?' Frances stammers something but she doesn't wait to hear it.

The night has not evolved as expected. Brian is clearly occupied, but she's relieved that Umberto and Alfonso are as well. At least they won't hound her. She washes her hands and carefully applies a fresh layer of powder. When she returns to the dining room, Frances is standing by the doorway looking towards the stage.

'My friend is playing his solo.'

Camilla stands with her as she recognizes the first notes of her favourite song filling the air: 'O mio babbino caro, mi piace è bello, bello.'

The cellist captures the intimacy of the human voice. It is achingly beautiful and Camilla whispers the words of the Puccini aria that was a part of her childhood. The memories of her village flood back and the man who changed her life. It nearly ripped her apart. 'O my dearest daddy, He pleases me, and is handsome, handsome.'

The tall musician is performing it with a passion she has never heard before. Yet he looks familiar and so is his music, which seems to flow out of him like water from a spring. With his extraordinary playing, he conjures up memories she has buried for decades. The ending of her love, the feuding, jealousies and double-dealing. And the loss.

'Mi struggo e mi tormento! O Dio, vorrei morir! I am aching, I am tortured! Oh God, I'd like to die!'

As the musician builds to the climax she recognizes the busker from Santa Lucia.

'Babbo, pietà, pietà! Babbo, pietà, pietà! Father, have pity, have pity! Father, have pity, have pity!'

The cellist stands and bows to a wave of applause. Brushing his soft hair back off his face, he looks across to where they're standing and smiles at Frances. Camilla gasps as she sees his eyes, those unmistakable cloudy green-blue eyes.

'Are you OK, professor? Would you like some water?'

She looks down and realizes she is gripping Frances' arm and quickly drops it. 'No. I'll be OK, I'm just a little overcome by the music. Who is the cellist?'

'Pasquale, my neighbour. Would you like to meet him?'

'Yes, please. That would be charming.'

They reach the table at the same time as Pasquale. 'Fantastic playing,' Frances says kissing him. 'This is Professor Camilla Corsi. She wants to meet you.'

Camilla extends her hand and he shakes it gently. She doesn't want to let it go. She feels as if everything is moving in slow motion and she has to call on every ounce of strength to stay standing.

'Have we met before?' His eyes gently engage hers.

'I've heard you playing at Santa Lucia. You're an exceptional busker.'

He laughs. The laugh too is familiar. 'Helps pay the bills, professor.'

'Well, tonight you were brilliant. That song means a lot to me.'

'I'm glad. It's one of my favourites.'

Camilla says goodnight and walks back to her own table. Brian and his wife are sitting alone and she sees the others mingling around the room. She puts her hand on his shoulder. 'I have to go, Brian. I'm not feeling very well. Thank you for a wonderful evening.'

'I'm sorry to hear it, Camilla — can I arrange an embassy car for you?'

'I'm fine.'

Stumbling through the entrance she beckons the usher. 'My coat, please, the mink.' Camilla leans against the wall until he returns and helps her put it on, then walks carefully down the stairs, clinging to the banisters. Outside, the cold air cuts her face. She walks across the driveway to the grass, slips off her shoes and starts to run.

She doesn't stop until she reaches the woods deep inside the park and feels the evening dew soaking into her stockings. It is completely dark. Collapsing on the ground, Camilla lets out a howl like an animal. Then, for the first time in years, she weeps.

CHAPTER TWENTY-THREE

Wake up, princess. Wake up!'
Frances opens her eyes and at the same time she hears Riccardo calling her she feels her head thumping. She clamps her hand to her forehead. How did she get home? She remembers drinking far too much, first at the dinner and then later at a bar with Pasquale and Satore. One of those trendy bars up the hill at Vomero. She reaches for the glass of water next to her bed. Empty. She pulls on a robe, notes crossly that she has tossed her new dress on the floor, and thumps out to the bathroom.

'Uh oh,' Riccardo says. 'Where did you come from? Where did that beautiful princess go?'

'Ha bloody ha!'

She closes the door firmly, grimaces when she catches the reflection of her unwashed face blotched with eye make-up, and puts the shower taps on full. Today, full is a trickle, and she shivers in the lukewarm water as she splashes herself clean.

Camilla. Of course. Her cryptic comment set her off drinking too much, that and the creepy threat from the chairman. And having to sit on her own for much of the night. Really it was all quite justifiable. Yeah, right!

The water runs down her face and clears her head. She remembers taking a cab to the club and another one home around three in the morning, squashed in the back with Pasquale and his cello. That must explain the bruise at the top of her arm.

She dries herself hurriedly and retreats to the sofa.

'Café?' Riccardo calls from the kitchen.

'How did you guess? With lots of milk.'

A few minutes later Riccardo appears with the coffee and a

plate with two chocolate biscuits. 'Tim Tams! My favourites from home — I thought you might need sustenance.'

She crunches into one, the double layers of chocolate and cream and an odd spicy flavour fill her mouth. 'This is the craziest hangover cure I've ever tried. What is it?'

'From my personal stash of Australian goodies; these ones are chilli flavour. What do you think?' His voice is muffled as he bites into the other biscuit.

'Mmm. Seems to be working. And the coffee's great, thanks.'

'So how was it?'

'Wonderful until I met the strongman and la stronza.'

'What?'

'Umberto Dragorra. He told me to lay off the Red Zone. Then later on our esteemed professor tells me I should keep all our research confidential. By coincidence, they were sitting at the same table.'

'Merda! Were they threatening you?'

'Not in so many words. They just made me uncomfortable and drove me to drink.'

'By the way, Marcello's been trying to call you. He says your phone's not working.'

'Damn. I turned it off while Pasquale was playing. He was amazing, by the way. Even the stronza was impressed. Would you do me a favour and find my handbag?'

He falls to his knees clutching his chest. 'Yes, princess, anything else?'

She throws a cushion at him and he collapses on the floor in mock pain.

'Well, I'm glad to see you've recovered from your injuries.' She fishes her phone out of the bag and switches it on. Immediately it beeps with messages and missed calls. Three from Marcello and one from an international number she doesn't recognize.

She listens to the messages. Marcello asks her to call him back. The next voice is one she hasn't heard since she arrived in Italy. It's Olivia, her work friend from Mt St Helens, telling her excitedly she may have some research work in the Aeolian Islands. She can't help smiling when she hears her sign-off. 'Hope you're kicking arse there, Frankie. Or at least getting some!'

The phone rings and it's Marcello again. He's free of his other work. Would she come with him in search of the Pliny manuscripts? He has a strong lead about their whereabouts. Her head has ceased throbbing and the idea of a drive and a treasure hunt with Marcello is very appealing.

'I'll be ready in a half an hour,' she tells him.

'So what are you and Marcello up to?' Riccardo sits on the chair opposite, drinking his coffee and looking at her cagily.

'Pursuing our investigations on wind patterns around Vesuvius.'

He laughs. 'You manage to make that sound quite boring. It must be the company that makes the task so interesting.'

'Maybe you're right. You've known Marcello a long time. Is that wise?'

'Wise? Probably not, but that never stopped anyone.'

'Has he been involved with anyone else lately?'

'I don't follow him around. He's been separated for a couple of years and there's never a shortage of interested women, as far as I can tell.' He leans closer to her. 'But if you're asking if he's single, the answer is yes.' He pauses as if trying to read her mind. 'The question is, are you?'

Frances shrugs her shoulders. She still hasn't let go of Tori but maybe it's time. Her uncertainty hovers in the air and she says nothing.

'Ah, a woman who doesn't know her own mind.' Riccardo stands and reaches for his helmet. 'Remember, a little amore doesn't hurt anybody. Now I'm off to the laboratory. Have a good expedition, and make sure you tell Marcello about last night. We have to take any threat seriously.'

She waits on the street for Marcello, knowing another tortuous drive through the city traffic lies ahead. But she's looking forward to seeing him and her spirits lift when his four-wheel-drive spins around the corner. He peers over his sunglasses at her as she climbs in and she's conscious of the bags under her eyes. 'Big night on the town?'

'In more ways than one.' She leans over to kiss him lightly on the lips and enjoys his warm response. 'Tell you all about it later. I need to recover a bit first.'

He reaches over and buckles her seat belt. 'We're heading north, to a convent in the hills. You can catch up on some sleep.'

Frances dozes on and off as Marcello stops and starts, pushing through the congestion. Two hours later, she's fully awake and aware she's been sleeping with her head on his shoulder. 'Not far now,' he says as they exit the Rome freeway.

The day is sunny and cool and they leave behind patches of morning fog that cling to the road like balls of cotton wool. They skirt around a village and are soon driving up a long, winding road. Thick pine forests crowd them on both sides and Frances winds down the window to drink the fresh mountain air.

Marcello refers to a scrap of paper on the dashboard with handwritten directions. 'It's at the top of this road. I've told the nuns to expect us.'

'The nuns? Have you been here before?'

'No. I've been trying to visit for years and they've only just agreed. They have a renowned collection of manuscripts from the Middle Ages but they're not keen on sharing them. But I got lucky. One of my cousins knows the Mother Superior so she helped pave the way.'

The trees thin and give way to green and yellow pastures. A stone wall hugs the roadside. It's broken in places and some spindly sheep have escaped through a large gap to graze on the other side of the road. Marcello beeps the horn loudly as one wanders in front of them. It hurriedly retreats.

They follow the wall up a hill where it is intersected by a tall stone archway. Marcello brakes suddenly and swerves through. The vehicle crunches onto a gravel driveway. Rows of grapevines race up a rise, tended by two nuns in long black habits. They look up briefly as Frances and Marcello drive past, then continue with their work. Below them a large vegetable garden glows in the sunshine.

A cluster of buildings lies ahead. They pull up outside the biggest, a church made of the same grey stones as the wall with a cross on top of it, next to a bell tower.

The slamming of the doors and the scraping of their feet on the gravel shatter what seems to be complete silence. They stand together for a moment, unsure of where to go, when suddenly they hear the voices of a women's choir, coming from the direction of the church. They climb a dozen or so steps to the heavy metal doors, but when Marcello tries to open them they won't budge.

Salve regina, mater misericordiae.

The Gregorian chant trickles out of the church as pure as a stream of crystal-clear water. Marcello pulls her sleeve and gestures her to follow.

A long two-storey brown brick building extends from the church and seems to encase it in a square. They find the entry, a discreet recess with a pair of wooden doors. A closed-circuit camera is positioned above them. Marcello rings a bell. No one answers so he rings it again. Thirty seconds or so later, they hear someone sliding open a small partition in the wall.

'Si?' The woman's voice is young. They can see her silhouette through a lattice screen.

'Marcello Vattani and Frances Nelson — we're from the university. We have an appointment with Mother Superior.'

The bolts securing the doors are noisily released and an African nun, her dark face gleaming beneath a white wimple and black veil, beckons them inside.

They follow, her long habit rustling as she walks, across a cobblestoned courtyard to another set of doors. She unlocks the doors and they find themselves in a long corridor lined with lush green pot plants. Their shoes squeak on the highly polished floor and when they reach a staircase, the nun turns to speak to them for the first time.

'Mother Superior has been called away,' she apologizes, 'but Sister Scholastica is expecting you. She runs the library.'

At the top of the stairs, she leads them into a darkened chapel where they pause. A bank of candles near the altar throws enough light on the walls for them to see remnants of old frescoes, a holy man and woman ascending into the arms of angels in heaven while beneath them, snarling devil figures burn in hell.

'Our patron saints. In the fifteenth century,' the nun whispers.

'Recognize hell?' Marcello says under his breath to Frances.

She peers closer. The shape of Vesuvius with the satanic figures wallowing in agony in the fiery crater is unmistakable.

'The church convinced everyone that the volcano was hell. Made their job of keeping everyone in line a bit easier,' Marcello tells her.

A bout of coughing comes from a seat at the back of the chapel. Their eyes have adjusted to the light and they can see a gnarled old nun wrapped in a shawl. She ignores them and seems interested only in the book she is reading.

They pass through to another much narrower corridor. The young sister points to a door ahead. 'I'll leave you here. That's where you go.' She turns back abruptly and they are left alone.

'I feel like I'm back in the Middle Ages,' Frances giggles nervously.

'It's a closed order,' he whispers. 'Probably very little has changed here for the last five hundred years. They're even wearing the same clothes!'

Frances taps lightly on the door and hears a shuffling. The door is opened by a tiny nun holding a walking frame. She has a gold crucifix attached to the front of her habit and smiles at them sweetly. 'Welcome.' Her voice is girl-like. 'I'm Sister Scholastica. Come in.'

Sister Scholastica is barely 150 cm tall. They follow her into the room where she takes several minutes to limp to her desk in the middle of the long wood-panelled room. With great difficulty, the sister eases herself onto her chair, richly inlaid with mosaics. Behind her against the wall are glass-doored cabinets full of books. They sit opposite her in two upright chairs and as the nun peers at them over the desk, Frances feels as if she is back at school.

'Tell me what you want to know.'

While Marcello explains their search for the Pliny manuscripts, Frances gazes at her face. She has perfect, unlined skin, like a child's, and her lips are unusually red, yet her gait suggests she is not a young woman. Her face is slightly contorted and Frances guesses she may have suffered a stroke. Whether or not she is in pain, she cannot tell.

'Yes, the Pliny manuscripts. We have a codex, a book of them.'

Marcello slaps his leg. 'You hear that, Frances? We have come to the right place.'

Sister Scholastica beams. 'As you know, Pliny the Younger wrote about the Pompeii eruption and the death of his uncle Pliny the Elder, who was killed in the aftermath, in a series of letters to his friend Tacitus, a renowned Roman historian. Like all scholars, he wrote on papyrus scrolls, which in our moist Italian conditions would only have survived for a century or two — indeed, some were lost forever. Fortunately, after the conversion to Christianity, many were copied, included Pliny's. Then copied again, and again, many times over the centuries — ours is one of the oldest in existence.'

Although physically frail, it is evident Sister Scholastica is intellectually razor sharp and fully cognisant of the immense historical and academic value of the convent's collection of medieval books, manuscripts and codices.

She turns in her seat and points towards one of the cupboards. 'I had one of the sisters take it down earlier, from up there. Would you mind fetching it? It's over on that shelf.'

Marcello nearly leaps out of his chair.

'Wait!' She passes him a pair of white gloves. 'You must wear these.'

He slides on the gloves and quickly returns with a large book, placing it gently on the desk. 'May I?' His eyes are shining with excitement.

She nods and he picks up the book, carefully turning it over and over in his hands. He traces his finger over the title: 'Epistulae I–VIIII'.

'These are volumes one to nine of letters he wrote to various people. There is a tenth correspondence written much later when he was an important official of Rome, between himself and the Emperor Trajan. The one you have has 247 letters, including the ones about Vesuvius.'

Marcello strokes the book like a baby kitten. 'I can't believe I have this in my hands!'

Embossed with gold Latin text and finely etched drawings of saints and scholars, the green leather cover is in remarkably good condition.

The old woman smiles. 'It's more than five hundred years old and written on the finest vellum, parchment made of goatskin.'

'May I?' Frances points at another pair of gloves on the desk next to the nun. She smiles and passes them to her, and Frances is immediately engrossed. 'The artwork is so fine.'

Sister Scholastica looks pleased. 'All done by our sisters,' she says proudly. 'Our order is one of the oldest and while the monks usually get the credit for these things, many nuns came from educated backgrounds and were highly literate.'

'How long have you been a nun, sister?'

'I went to university first. My parents were very wealthy. Alas, they're long dead now. I found my vocation when I was twenty-three and wanted to join a contemplative order so I could spend my days praying to the Lord.' She touches a gold ring on her wedding finger as she speaks. 'I've been here fifty-five years.'

Frances is stunned. She is nearly eighty years old. More than half a century behind these walls!

'But . . .'

'I know what you're thinking. Most people can't understand us. If you want to know whether or not I ever leave here, the answer is no — there is no reason to leave. I am content. Mother Superior travels when necessary to represent us.'

'How many sisters are here?'

'We are less than twenty. You met Sister Benedetta from Nigeria. That's where the vocations are coming from now. Without young women like her, this convent will not survive after we have gone.'

She shuffles to her feet and grips the walking frame. 'I'll leave you alone to study the manuscripts. I've put a marker in the codex so you can find the Vesuvius letters. I'll be in the chapel praying if you need me.'

Marcello stands to help her.

She raises one hand. 'No need,' she says. 'I have all the time in the world.'

Frances sits side by side with Marcello at the desk as he turns the first page. The parchment is stiff but in excellent condition. The calligraphy is exquisite and each page has finely painted borders and rich illustrations in a palette of red, blue, green and gold. Marcello carefully turns to the middle where a bookmark is placed.

Frances grins when she sees it features a small image of Saint Scholastica, the nun's namesake.

'Here!' Marcello points to a page. 'The letters to Tacitus from Gaius Plinius Caecilius Secundus — Pliny's full name.'

Frances looks closely at the Latin text. 'I don't understand much.'

'Don't worry. I studied Latin all through university and it's one of the tools of my trade. Besides, this is one story I know backwards.' He points to a line of text. 'This is from letter sixteen. Pliny is describing his view of the eruption from the navy port at Misenum, across the bay.'

Marcello translates it as he reads, his voice halting but clear. *'In form and shape the column of smoke was like an enormous pine tree, for at the top of its great height it branched out into several skeins. I assume that a sudden burst of wind had carried it upwards and then dropped it, leaving it motionless, and that its own weight then spread it outwards. It was sometimes white, sometimes heavy and mottled, as it would be if it had lifted up amounts of earth and ashes.'*

He turns to Frances. 'Amazing! Pliny was only seventeen when he wrote that. His way of describing the scorching column of gas, rock and ash that blasted out of the volcano into the stratosphere and then sat there until it dropped and formed the pyroclastic flows is so vivid.'

'Well, he described it pretty accurately — the world's first vulcanologist.'

'So true — now listen to how he describes what happened after his uncle left Misenum with a fleet of naval ships to try to rescue people from the coastline near Pompeii. *Ash was already falling, hotter and thicker as the ships drew near, followed by pumice and blackened stones, charred and cracked by the flames. Interim e Vesuvio monte pluribus locis latissimae flammae altaque incendia relucebant, quorum fulgor et claritas tenebris noctis excitabatur —*'

'Hold up, Marcello,' Frances nudges him. 'I love your Latin pronunciation but you're losing me.'

'Sorry, I forgot to translate. Where was I?' He runs his finger back a few lines and reads again. '*Meanwhile on Mount Vesuvius broad sheets of fire blazed at several points, their bright glare emphasized by the darkness of night. But they could not land because the shore was blocked by volcanic debris, so they sailed south and landed at Stabiae.*'

'Isn't that where Pliny the Elder died? At Stabiae?'

'Yes. He went into his friend's house and rested but the eruption continued so everyone went outside and down to the beach, because they thought it would be safer. That's where he died. He was only fifty-six but in those days that was regarded as old, and he was overweight. It's not clear whether he suffocated as a result of the toxic gases or had a heart attack, because many of his companions survived.'

He turns the page. 'This is how Pliny described it from stories he was told later. *They debated whether to stay inside or take their chance outside. The buildings were shaking violently, swaying to and fro as if they were torn from their foundations. Outside showers of hot ash and stones were raining down. To protect themselves, they tied pillows around their heads. It was now day everywhere else, but a deeper darkness prevailed than in the thickest night.*

'He then describes how they persuaded Pliny the Elder to leave the house because it was filling up with pumice. They carried him to the beach to see if they could escape to sea but the waves were too high so they laid him down on a sail cloth. *The flames and smell of sulphur drove the others to take flight and roused him to stand up with the help of two servants. Suddenly he collapsed, I imagine because the noxious fumes choked him. His body was found intact and uninjured, still fully clothed and looking more like a man asleep than dead.*'

'Can I have a look?'

Frances touches the pages of the codex gently, a tangible link with the past. 'The story is still incredibly moving.'

'It is. Now, let's see,' Marcello turns back a few pages. 'I must concentrate on what we really need to know — the date.'

He puts his index finger on the top line and reads to himself. 'This is it, exactly what I had hoped for. *Nonum kalends novembres.*'

'November. The ninth of November?'

'The Roman calendar was different. The Romans counted backwards from the following month from three fixed points — the *kalends*, the first day of the month; the *nones*, the day of the half moon; and the *ides*, the full moon. So *nonum kalends* means nine days before the beginning of November. That makes it the twenty-fourth of October in today's calendar. The manuscript in Florence said *nonum kalends septembres*, which is the date generally accepted, the twenty-fourth of August. Others have just said *nonum kalends* with no mention of a month.'

Marcello smiles broadly at Frances. 'You realize what this means — this date backs up all the other findings — the seasonal food, the silver coin and, most importantly for us, the wind patterns. The Pompeii eruption definitely happened later in the year, and that has consequences for all of us. If Vesuvius erupts again, at the same time of year in a period with the same wind patterns, people will have to be ready to leave their homes immediately. Otherwise they could perish in the pyroclastic flows.'

Frances looks over Marcello's shoulders as he turns over more pages. 'There's the word Baiae. Is that the same place as Baia? What does it mean?'

Marcello looks at the text closely. 'Baiae is the original Latin spelling, although sometimes it's written as Baios, after the Greek helmsman of Ulysses, who journeyed all along the coast. Now let me see. This is all new to me.' Marcello, brow furrowed, silently reads the text several times.

'Remarkable,' he says at last. 'Listen to this. *Baiae, to me, is a place of great beauty, a paradise of earthly pleasures. That our mighty emperors choose to build their summer mansions on the limestone cliffs above the dappled turquoise waters is no surprise. It is also a source of joy for me to engage in the pleasures this jewel has to offer we Romans. The harbour is a safe haven for our great ships. It provides us with a magnificent feast of fish for our tables. The vines are healthy, giving up fat harvests of grapes that produce the finest of wines. The miraculous thermal waters feed the glorious bathhouses of Venus, Mercury and Diana and restore our tired bodies. But take heed! Do not spoil or take for granted this gift from the gods. The earth moves more violently than before. Sulphur bursts in great waves from the bowels of Hades. Building more and more houses on the cliffs, more places of commerce on the watermark is not wise. For Neptune is waiting to swallow us up if we anger him.'*

'It's Pliny's warning!' Frances exclaims. 'He recognized the dangers of volcanism, and he was right. He's describing the houses we saw under the sea!'

Frances runs her hand down the book. They are so absorbed, they don't even notice Sister Scholastica is back in the room.

'Have you found what you wanted?'

Marcello stands up and reaches over her walking frame to hug her, and the little nun laughs in delighted surprise.

'Better than we could have imagined! Have a look, sister.'

Frances watches them, both clearly excited. Marcello picks up the book and points to the crucial words describing the date: *Nonum kalends novembres*. Sister Scholastica can't stop smiling. Frances detects she has even allowed herself a bit of pride. Proud the codex has survived and proud of the members of her order who created it.

Frances pictures the sisters who so painstakingly copied one of the greatest stories handed down from antiquity, possibly in this very room. Could they ever have imagined that centuries later, they would be part of a vital chain of evidence that could save the lives of millions?

CHAPTER TWENTY-FOUR

Riccardo is staring at a large computer in the laboratory, mesmerized by rows of dancing blue and pink lines snaking across the screen when Frances taps him on the shoulder. 'What's up?'

'Stromboli,' he murmers. 'This is coming in live from one of the seismograph cameras inside the crater. He's going crazy again.' He turns to her. 'Nothing out of the ordinary though. Just like to keep my eye on the old boy. This volcano is like family.'

'Can't wait to meet him. Any other strange relations I should know about?'

'Lots, but I wouldn't want to spoil the surprise.' He laughs. 'You'll have to wait until you come to the island.' Riccardo stands, serious again, and beckons Frances to follow him to his office. He closes the door behind them and opens the laptop computer on his desk. 'We must move quickly. I've heard a few whispers that there's a move to scuttle Progetto Vulcano.'

'What?! We're nowhere near finishing. And we . . .'

'And we are just getting to the pointy end of the problem.' Riccardo finishes the sentence for her. 'That's exactly why they'll disband us. They don't want the truth to come out.'

Riccardo turns the computer towards her. 'I'm racing to compile all the facts to date. Marcello has sent me his notes. How about you? We have to get our report out as soon as we can.'

'All here, Ricky.' Frances removes a memory stick from around her neck and hands it to him.

'Great!' He slides the stick into the computer and clicks onto her files. 'Perfect. I'll merge all of this now into one document.'

Frances watches Riccardo tapping the keyboard, his face contorted in concentration. She feels a knot in her guts, the sick feeling of being deceived. She had never thought for a moment she would be used as part of a political window dressing exercise and still doesn't want to believe it. How could people be so twisted that they would put their own greed ahead of the safety of their own community, their own families?

The printer behind Riccardo comes to life, pouring out page after page. Riccardo scoops them up, making four piles. He puts one in an envelope and hands it to Frances. 'Sorry to put you on the spot, but would you be the bearer of bad news and give this to Professor Corsi?'

'Has she got a gun? I don't want her to shoot the messenger.'

'Hate to say this, but she probably has, though it would be a designer model,' he laughs. 'But if anyone is safe, you are — you're not Italian and you have a career outside of her influence. I just think it's vital this goes out today, before they have a chance to dismiss us all. For the moment, we're all insiders, part of the team. And if this is out there, at least we have a chance to keep on going.'

'Who are the other copies for?'

'Insurance. I'm going to do a bit of selective leaking to a politician from the national parliament in Rome, who's not embroiled in local politics, and a journalist who has been trying to expose the development scandals around Vesuvius. I'll keep the other one up my sleeve.'

Frances slides the envelope into her backpack. She had barely arrived at the observatory and had planned to spend the day checking readings from the microphones she had placed on the flanks of Vesuvius and on key spots around Campi Flegrei. Riccardo must have read her frustration. 'Sorry to do this to you.'

She opens the door to leave, then turns back to him. 'Don't be. We're all on the same side — I'm as passionate about this as you are. I'll take this to her now.'

Frances rides back through the dusty streets of Naples' outskirts towards the old city. Crazy images of messengers on horseback slain for bearing bad news flash through her brain as she rides through a sea of cars and motorbikes. Part of her thinks, 'What nonsense, this is the twenty-first century.' Then the television images of the protesters' corpses lying on the roadside and the floating bodies of the scientists in the hot pools crowd her mind. She can't dismiss them so easily.

As she pulls into a labyrinth of lanes near the university, slows then draws up sharply, the whiff of coffee stalls her mission. Parking her bike outside the café, Frances removes her helmet and gratefully shakes her hair free. It feels clammy after the ride and she quickly runs a comb through it.

'Café macchiato,' she tells the young barista.

A minute later, he places a small glass of espresso with a dab of milky froth shaped in a heart in front of her. 'Anything else, signorina?'

'No, grazie.' She lifts the glass and savours the first foamy sip.

'Rum baba?' He shows her a plate of perfectly formed mushroom-shaped cakes oozing chocolate custard. 'Just cooked. Buonissimo!'

Frances changes her mind. She bites into the sugary dough, tasting the rum and custard together, a helping of sweet courage for the task ahead.

A few students carrying instrument cases linger at the counter and when she leaves she realizes she is close to the Conservatorium of Music. She rides along Via Maria Constantinopolis, keeping an eye out, and is rewarded when she spots the unmistakable form of Pasquale Mazzone towing his cello in a side street off the boulevard. She turns left and buzzes right up to him.

He looks downcast.

'Is everything OK?'

'I've just been paying an instalment on my cello, but there's still a long way to go.'

Frances sees a musical instrument shop behind him. 'Is it in there?'

'No, it's in the piazza at the end of the street near the university. Would you like to see it?'

Although she is anxious to keep going, Frances can see how eager Pasquale is to show her. She follows him to the square and parks her bike. Together they stand in front of a shop window, where rows of string instruments are lined up; violins in the front, violas next, cellos and two double basses at the rear. Each is burnished and buffed, vying for attention.

'Which one is yours?'

'I wish it was mine. That's the object of my desire, that one there, on the right. It's a Gagliano. Made here in Naples in the eighteenth century.'

The cello's glossy red varnish finish shines through the window.

'It's beautiful,' Frances agrees.

'It's not the best, not first rank. It wasn't made by Alessandro Gagliano, the master cello maker — that would cost a fortune. But he had a large family of disciples and it was made by one of them. I love it.'

'Have you played it?'

'Of course — you wouldn't want to buy a cello without knowing it suits you. That would be like an arranged marriage. Best to try before you buy.'

They both laugh, and a man inside the shop waves to them.

'That's the owner, Benedetto. He's very kind, simpatico. He lets me play it now and again if I annoy him enough. I've been dropping in to see it for more than a year now and it's more than half mine!'

Frances smiles at him. 'I'm sure it won't be long before it's yours.'

She leaves him gazing in the window and is about to climb on her bike when she hears her name.

'Frances!'

She looks up to see Professor Corsi leaving a café and walking towards her. Frances feels like a child caught with her hand in the cookie jar and instinctively squeezes her backpack, checking for the envelope. It crackles to her touch.

'Professor Corsi. What a coincidence. I was just coming to see you.'

She appears distracted and not to have heard her. 'Isn't that the musician from the Capodimonte dinner?' Camilla asks, pulling her fur-trimmed jacket closer.

'Yes. Pasquale. He's in love,' Frances says as lightly as she can.

Camilla takes a step back and shakes her head. 'What do you mean, in love? Who with?'

'Not who — what. He's ogling a cello. He's been paying it off by instalments.'

Camilla looks oddly relieved and starts to walk away.

'Professor Corsi, please wait!' Frances unzips her bag. 'This is a progress report from Riccardo and me with input from the archaeologist Marcello Vattani. We believe we have made some significant discoveries that give a much more accurate picture of the volcanic threat.'

Camilla stares at Frances and silently takes the envelope in her red-gloved hand. 'I don't remember asking for another progress report. This is most unexpected, and highly irregular.'

She turns and strides away, her long high-heeled boots tapping on the cobblestones, her hand clutching the envelope.

CHAPTER TWENTY-FIVE

Camilla bangs the desk hard with her fist. The report is spread in front of her and its message is unmistakable. Millions of lives are at threat unless people can be evacuated quickly from around the volcano. The authorities must expand the Red Zone around Vesuvius, banning all new development; demolish illegal buildings to allow road widening; ban all new development along the coast of Campi Flegrei. Diagrams of pyroclastic flows subsuming large slabs of Naples and surrounding towns paint the grimmest of pictures.

Camilla picks it up again and winces at the closing comments. *The Italian Constitution guarantees that scientific research must be free of constraint and political interference. Academic freedom must be respected and scientists have a right to publish and discuss their findings.*

'Interfering bastards!' she yells.

'Is everything all right, professor?' Her secretary pokes her head through the door of Camilla's office. She doesn't reply and dismisses her with her hand, then checks her watch. One hour before Umberto's driver is fetching her for lunch. A business lunch, he called it.

Camilla feels the room closing in. The rich green embossed walls meet the woven golden carpet, threatening to suffocate her. The usually soft glow of the chandelier is suddenly blinding. She puts her hands on her head, closes her eyes and massages her temples.

'Professor.' The secretary is back.

'What is it, Maria? Can't I have a moment's peace?'

'I'm so sorry, it's the Chancellor, Professor Galbatti. He would like to see you.'

Camilla stands and walks over to the wooden credenza against one wall of her office. She strokes the carved garland of fruit on the front of the renaissance cabinet — her first possession of any worth.

The silky feel of the polished walnut is comforting. Opening one of the drawers she pulls out a photo and her own young face stares back, all smiles — graduation day, when she was still a girl with her life at her feet. She sighs and puts it back. You can handle this. You can handle anything, she tells herself.

She walks down the corridor towards Alfonso's office then stops, remembering the explosive report on her desk. She hesitates then keeps walking. No, let that sit there, for now.

'Ah Camilla, come in!' Alfonso doesn't get up from his desk but beckons her over. She goes with as much grace as she can muster and as she leans over him to exchange kisses, she notices a pile of contracts on his desk. 'Sit down, cara,' he says before she has a chance to read them.

'I have something important to tell you, something I want you to be the first to know.' She sits opposite, in a lower seat, forcing her to look up to him. His pallor gives him a cadaverous look and she sees a weariness in his eyes she couldn't have imagined just a year or two ago. She smiles at him but says nothing, waiting for him to speak.

'As you know, I turn seventy next year, so I have decided to retire. I will be announcing it in a week or so.'

So soon. Camilla feels her heart starting to race. Her goal is suddenly that much closer. 'You will be greatly missed. You have achieved so much here,' she hears herself say.

'But will you miss me, that is the question?'

'Of course, Alfonso. But surely we will still see each other?'

'I hope so,' he nods. 'But as the French say, Le Roi est mort, vive le Roi! The king is dead, long live the king. And that brings me to my successor.'

Alfonso stands up and walks around the desk to her. 'Camilla, I am recommending Professor Luigi Paoli for the job.'

'What! Your nephew?' Camilla is so stunned that for a moment she loses control of her emotions. 'But Alfonso, you promised you would support me! Luigi has barely arrived!'

Alfonso props himself on the edge of his desk and takes one of

Camilla's hands. 'It's true that once I did hope you could step into my shoes. But I don't think it can happen. I don't think you would get the support of the board. Whereas Luigi, he's not only a fine academic, he has worked in business as well and these days . . .'

Camilla shakes off his hand. 'You mean he's a man and he's a relative and you're keeping it all in the family,' she spits.

'Camilla. I'm disappointed. I was really thinking of you in all of this. My position is very stressful and I wouldn't like to see you having to deal with the burden of it all.'

Alfonso returns to his seat and shuffles the papers on his desk. 'Besides, I have already drawn up a contract for Professor Paoli.' He waves the paper. 'You already have an important position here at the university and I'm confident you will work well with Luigi.'

Camilla bites her lip and stares beyond him to the window with a view over the bay. From her seat she can see the tip of Vesuvius on the horizon. She can sense Alfonso's discomfort but knows he will not change his mind. 'By the way, how is the volcano project progressing?' he presses her. 'When can I expect the final report? I've had an enquiry from the minister and the newspapers are always asking. It would be good to see it before we break for Christmas.'

Camilla's mind is racing but she steels herself. 'No. Nothing further yet.' She stands and walks to the door. 'I'll have a word to the team and ask them to hurry things along. I'll certainly try to get it to you before Christmas.'

Her face is burning as she returns to her office and slumps into her chair. Treacherous pig! He duped me into bending the rules to get his nephew here and now he drops me. If he thinks he's going to get away with this, he's mistaken! She goes to the cabinet and reaches inside for a silver hip flask and a tiny glass. Pouring a shot of cognac, she throws it back. It burns her throat but instantly calms her.

Her mobile phone rings. Umberto tells her he's five minutes away and to be waiting at the usual place.

She puts on her coat then scoops up the report and jams it into her briefcase. Colliding with hundreds of students crowding the corridors between lectures, she pushes through and welcomes the cool wind blowing outside the university. For a moment, she leans against the wall breathing deeply, then turns the corner just in time to see the black shiny car pull over to the kerb.

Mario jumps out and opens the back door for her. As she slides in, she's surprised to see Umberto is sitting in the front seat.

He turns around to her, beaming. 'Good afternoon, professor. Everything is looking great for our developments. Right on track. I've just come from a meeting with the minister and he's on side. He agrees it's in Campania's interest.'

Camilla smiles at him but says nothing, her briefcase gripped tightly to her side.

As Mario drives towards the harbour and follows the road to Santa Lucia, Umberto chortles. 'Just as well really, as I've handed out all the contracts to the cement and construction companies.'

'Umberto, changing the Red Zone might not be quite so simple. Some of the scientists . . .'

He cuts her off. 'The scientists are irrelevant try-hards. I don't care what they say.'

'Well, the final report may not be as favourable as we'd hoped.'

'Hoped? Camilla, I'm relying on you to produce a report that gives the green light.'

They drive past Santa Lucia, further around the seafront to Chaia, and stop outside a line of restaurants. A gust of wind almost knocks Camilla over as she leaves the car. Above her, seagulls fly haphazardly as the stiff breeze blows them off course. The masts of dozens of yachts moored in a marina tinkle and the sails of one offshore flap wildly like a cracking whip.

Umberto takes Camilla's arm and guides her into one of the restaurants. The waiter seats them immediately, fluttering around with menus and serviettes.

'Just some pasta for me,' she says quickly. 'Penne arrabiata.'

'Spaghetti marinara.' Umberto adds, 'No wine today, I need a very clear head.'

Camilla sits back in her chair and gazes out across the bay. The hazy shape of Capri sits on the horizon and thick cloud crowns Mt Vesuvius, like a ghostly party hat. She lights a cigarette and draws in deeply. Then she stubs it out irritably when she spots the waiter pointing to a 'No smoking' sign.

'You look worried.'

It is more of a statement than a question.

'Yes, I am. I'm worried for you.'

'You don't need to worry about me!' Umberto scoffs.

'It's Alfonso. He's pushing me to release the volcano report. And the latest information is not good. It's especially bad for you because it would rule out your development completely. I'm trying to calm Alfonso down but he seems very determined.'

Now she has Umberto's full attention. He leans towards her and grasps her hand. 'What is the problem? What?'

She reaches under the table for her briefcase and pulls out the report. 'Here. You can read it for yourself.'

The waiter places the steaming plates of pasta in front of them. Umberto has suddenly lost his appetite and his sense of humour. He pushes his plate aside and reads the report. Camilla relaxes. She tastes the pasta. It's perfectly cooked and the spicy tomato flavour lingers. She takes a second mouthful and a third. Umberto continues to read, paying close attention to the maps of the proposed Red Zone.

'Merda!' he yells, and people at adjoining tables stare at him.

Camilla puts her hand on his. 'Calm down. I'll try to help you.'

He points to the names at the bottom of the report. 'Frances Nelson. Isn't this the foreign woman who was at the dinner?'

She nods.

'Too clever for her own good. She clearly doesn't understand how we do business here. And who are they?'

'Riccardo Cocchia, an Australian-Italian, and another member of the team. Marcello Vattani is a troublemaking archaeologist.'

'When did you get this?' His eyes are narrow and angry.

'A few days ago. I've been trying to bury it but Alfonso . . .'

'Fuck Alfonso! You must make sure this doesn't see the light of day.'

Camilla smiles at him. 'It's not that simple.'

He raises an eyebrow questioningly.

'I would be risking everything. In particular, my position at the university and my reputation as a scientist.'

Umberto raises his hands in a gesture of exasperation. He pulls his plate towards him and starts to eat, quickly ploughing the spaghetti and seafood into his mouth.

Camilla waits until he rests his fork on the plate. 'But there might be a way. Alfonso is retiring soon and he is grooming his nephew, Luigi Paoli, to take over. Paoli is of the same mind.'

'What are you getting at?'

She holds up the report. 'Alfonso doesn't have a copy of this and I can keep it to myself for a time, certainly until the appointment of his replacement. And I will be putting myself forward to take over from Alfonso. The decision will rest with the board and you are the chairman . . .'

Umberto laughs, his face lighting up, his eyes now amused. 'So this is your price?'

She doesn't reply but coolly meets his gaze.

The waiter clears away their plates and they order coffee.

'And what do you propose to do to shut your scientists up?' Umberto continues.

Camilla shrugs. 'I can muzzle them and disband the team.'

The coffee arrives, two espressos. Umberto stirs three spoons of sugar in his and sips it. 'You take care of Alfonso, and I will take care of you, my dear,' he says. 'And if the scientists don't listen to you, they can answer to me.'

'Just let me do it my way. They might be creating waves but I don't want them harmed.'

He shrugs and raises his hands, palms facing up.

'I mean it,' she says.

As Mario drives her back to the university, she asks him to stop a few blocks away. 'I have to do some shopping,' she tells Umberto who sits in the back with her, his hand on her knee.

'Can I visit you tonight?'

'Of course. I'll look forward to it.'

She walks briskly now, crossing a busy street and heading for the small square. The door of the music shop is locked. She steps back and peers through the window at the rows of instruments, then hears footsteps behind her.

'Good afternoon,' the proprietor greets her as he opens up after his lunch break.

Camilla glances over her shoulder then follows him inside.

CHAPTER TWENTY-SIX

The day of the civil protest against the garbage crisis starts like most others for Pasquale: three hours of solid practice of the Bach suites, an hour's break and another three punishing hours.

Pasquale puts his cello aside, stands up and stretches his fingers, in and out, in and out. His left hand throbs and his shoulders and back don't feel much better. He checks his watch and remembers he has to meet the others in less than an hour.

The hot shower soothes his body and for a moment he wants to fill the bath, sink into it and forget the protest altogether. But the gruesome sight of the mutilated bodies of the farmer Paolo and the campaigner Leonardo, lying like discarded dogs on the street, haunts him. He remembers Paolo's wounded eyes at the meeting as he described the destruction of his land and his life by toxic waste, recalling that same defeated expression on his father's face, just before he was killed.

Scumbags! Pasquale dries himself roughly, cursing the corruption that still seeps through his childhood village and continues to sap the city.

A text message beeps on his mobile phone. *'Waiting at the bar. Satore.'*

Pasquale throws on his clothes and runs up the two flights of stairs to Frances and Riccardo's apartment. He knocks loudly but there is no answer, and when he comes downstairs to the courtyard, both motorbikes are gone. A cold wind sweeps him along Corso Vittorio Emanuele. The platform of the station is packed and when the funicular pulls up, people flow onto it like a wave. He finds a place to stand and in a few minutes is whisked down to the city.

The bar is crowded. He orders a beer and takes a large sip. He hasn't eaten all day and orders two arancini, one filled with aubergine and the other with spinach and ham. The pyramid-shaped rice savouries arrive quickly and he devours them.

'Over here!' Satore calls out to him from a table in the far corner. Riccardo and Poppaea are with him, and a pale young man with red hair, sitting close to Satore.

'This is Rufus. He's on exchange from Ireland,' Satore says jumping up to greet him. 'He's an amazing bass player and an equally amazing blogger.'

Pasquale shakes his hand. His grip is surprisingly strong, defying a rather fragile appearance. 'Good to meet you, I'm sorry I couldn't get here earlier to help.'

'You're exempt. You have to keep up the practice,' Poppaea says. 'Are you OK? You look tired.'

'Too much Bach.' He squeezes in next to his sister.

'I sympathise,' Rufus says in a soft brogue. 'I prefer jazz to classical, there's more room to improvise.'

Satore puts his arm around his shoulders and Pasquale realizes he's the newest boyfriend.

'We've had a big day getting the banners ready and we've all been blogging furiously to try to get a crowd,' Poppaea tells him.

Riccardo is on his other side, unusually quiet and edgy. Since the murders, Pasquale has felt a bond with his neighbour, cemented by their ride through the night, away from the horror on the streets. He nudges him. 'Everything all right?'

'A bit nervous. I'm addressing the rally about the threat from the volcano and I'm right out of my comfort zone,' he confesses. He brightens suddenly. 'Ah good, they're here.'

He waves to Frances and Marcello. As they cross the bar to join them, Pasquale sees the strain etched on their faces. 'Ricky, we're not convinced you should do this,' Frances says, as soon as she reaches his side. 'What happened to the journalist? Did you give him the report?'

'Of course, but there's a massive cover-up. The journalist wrote the story but the newspaper wouldn't publish it.'

'What do you expect?' Marcello shrugs. 'We don't have a free press in Italy. The mass media is controlled by a handful of powerful men and they muzzle journalists.'

Satore nods. 'We couldn't get the newspapers or television to report on the rally either so we've bypassed them. We've got a huge blog site and people are responding by the thousands. This is the new politics. We will force the politicians to listen or make them irrelevant.'

'And I'm so angry I'm prepared to speak up,' Riccardo says.

'Bravo! Bravo!' the others say.

Pasquale notices that Frances and Marcello are quiet. 'You have to be careful,' he hears her says. 'Remember Solfatara.'

Satore stands. 'Time to go,' he says.

The crowds are gathering by the time they reach the huge open square of Piazza del Plebiscito. Remnants of a winter sunset illuminate the massive dome of the Church of Saint Francis on the far side. They push through large groups alongside the walls of the Royal Palace to a stage set up in the centre.

'We can collect signatures for the petitions here beneath the galloping Bourbon King,' Satore says, leading them to a row of tables beneath a statue of a massive equestrian.

More and more people are flowing into the square. Some carry huge colourful banners condemning the building of a massive incinerator outside of Naples. Others have caricatures of government ministers, their heads poking out of mounds of stinking garbage. Posters portraying Paolo and Leonardo dressed as medieval martyrs adorn the stage.

Poppaea hugs Pasquale. 'It's working. The blogging is reaching people.'

'I hope so. I'm so disillusioned with our democracy,' he replies. 'When you lose faith in your own government, it's like finding out your father has been cheating on your mother. You can't believe the betrayal.'

'Mmm. I don't think that happened. Do you?'

Pasquale sees his father's image sharply. But he struggles to remember his mother, even the fuzzy photos of her holding him as a child before her accident.

'Probably not.' He leans down to kiss her forehead. 'But we'll never know, will we?'

Riccardo is in a huddle with Frances and Marcello. He breaks away and comes over to Pasquale. 'Hey, can you mind this for me?' He passes him his backpack. 'I don't want to have it on the stage.'

'Of course.' He tucks it next to his own bag behind the table and reassures him. 'You're doing the right thing.'

'I hope you're right.' Riccardo climbs onto the stage and sits with the other speakers.

By now the crowd has grown to such an extent they are totally hemmed in. The piazza is almost full, from the grand church on one side to the palace on the other.

'Buona sera. Good evening and welcome!' The voice of Doctor Fabbiana Masina fills the square, slightly distorted by the radio microphone. 'On my way here I passed kilometre after kilometre of rotting garbage filling our streets. I saw rats, flies and other vermin that pose a serious health hazard to all of us.'

The wind gusts through the piazza, blowing her scarf as she speaks. It does nothing to distract the crowd, quiet, listening to every word.

'Perhaps more seriously, we have new evidence that the dumping of toxic waste throughout Catania has already taken a huge toll. Cancer rates have soared by five hundred per cent; brain tumours, leukaemia and a host of other diseases.

'Heavy metals and poisonous chemicals are polluting the groundwater, farmland and the food chain. Farmers have had to destroy thousands of sheep when it was discovered their milk was full of dioxin. We are here today to demand that our government acts. And we also call on the central government in Rome to make sure it intervenes if our local government fails to act. What we don't want is an enormous incinerator pumping more carcinogens into the air we breathe.

'But importantly, all of you must increase the pressure on the authorities. Please sign the petitions and maintain the anger. We are fighting criminal corruption. We don't want heroes like Paolo and Leonardo to have died in vain. We have the truth on our side.'

Roars of approval rumble across the square and people surge towards the tables to sign the petitions.

Riccardo rises to speak.

'He looks nervous,' Frances whispers to Pasquale.

Riccardo clears his throat too loudly and it reverberates around the square. He struggles to win the crowd's attention as people chat and have started to drift away.

'I have come here today to warn you of an apocalypse,' he says loudly. 'Please listen. Our garbage crisis is a scandal. But there is an even greater danger to our wellbeing.'

The crowd is silent again.

'You know about the destruction of Pompeii, but do you know that the people of Naples and all the towns around Vesuvius face an even greater threat? Millions of lives are at risk. We have scientific evidence that Vesuvius is active again and the next eruption could well be a super eruption. And . . .'

Suddenly, the sound cuts out. Riccardo continues speaking, not realizing that nobody can hear him.

'We've got to help him.' Frances turns to Pasquale, who suggests they check the sound. At the far side of the stage they pull aside a black panel concealing the audio booth. There's no one there. Pasquale picks up a bunch of electrical leads, wrenched out of the sound deck.

'Look!' Frances yells. Two policemen are escorting Riccardo off the stage.

Some booing and hissing starts up near the front. Others join in, crying out to let him speak. But the police ignore the protesters and as they disappear with Riccardo, the crowd loses interest and starts to disperse.

'C'mon! We've got to get to Ricky.' Pasquale follows Frances but it is impossible to penetrate the wall of people between them and the steps off the stage where he was taken.

'Satore!' Pasquale cries out over the heads of the crowd. But his voice doesn't carry and his friend doesn't see him waving for help. They push through arm in arm. When they finally reach the steps there is no sign of Riccardo or the policemen.

Pasquale sees Marcello a little way ahead and calls out to him. 'Where has he gone?'

Marcello shrugs his shoulders. 'I'll go to the police station,' he yells back. 'I'll phone you when I have news.'

Pasquale sees Frances is pale and teary. 'Riccardo hasn't broken any laws. I'm sure he'll be fine,' he tells her, his voice betraying his own doubt, his knowledge that Naples' law is a law unto itself.

'Should we go to the police station too?'

'No. Leave it to Marcello, at least for now.'

Lines of people are signing the petitions and Pasquale joins the others behind the tables. 'I'll help out here a bit longer. Best for you to go home, Frances. Could you take Riccardo's backpack? I'll come and see you when I get home.' He watches her walk away, her usual optimism in retreat.

Yet few of the onlookers seem aware of Riccardo's abrupt disappearance. Pasquale senses the rally has buoyed the spirits of his fellow citizens queueing to express their anger against their weak government and officials. For a moment at least, they can taste a modicum of the empowerment they had all but lost to the bullies of Il Sistema. But all of his friends are on edge, their euphoria dampened by concern for their colleague.

The day has all but disappeared and as night falls, the crowd tails away. Noisy chatter fills the piazza as Pasquale and the others pack up the tables, concealing a new sound. The buzz of motorbikes surprises them. Around a dozen riders circle them, acceleration cracking the air. As Pasquale looks up, a white spray smacks his face. He hears Poppaea scream. Each rider has a pillion passenger holding a fire extinguisher who all spray bursts of chemical foam onto the volunteers.

'Vaffanculo! Get fucked!' The riders yell abuse. 'Mind your business or the next time we'll spray you with bullets,' one of them shouts as they circle one more time then roar away across the cobblestones.

The foam stings Pasquale's eyes and he desperately wipes it away with his sleeve. Poppaea has dropped to the ground and is clawing at her face so he seizes one of the banners and goes to her. Gently he wipes away the foam. He pours water from a bottle in his bag and washes her eyes.

'At least it's not acid,' he says helping her to her feet. 'You'll be fine.'

'Where are the carabinieri when you need them?' Satore asks bitterly. He and Rufus are covered in the white foam, along with a dozen or so other volunteers. When a van pulls up they quickly load the tables and banners.

'We're going to a club. We need a beer after all this,' Satore says. 'Coming, Pasquale?'

'No, I'm going to check on Riccardo and then I'm going home.'

'Tell us when you hear and let us know if there's anything we can do.'

Pasquale takes Poppaea's arm and walks her to a bus stop. He relishes being able to protect the sister whose life has revolved around him. Sweet Poppaea. Her eyes are red and sore but she forces a smile. 'Be careful,' she warns, before climbing on the bus.

Pasquale's hot breath streaks the cold air as he cuts through back streets. He passes the university and as if his legs were on automatic, he finds himself walking to the music shop. He crosses the little square to gaze through the security bars that guard the window at night.

The instruments still stand to attention, a soft light reflecting on each. His eyes go immediately to the cello on the right. At first he thinks the spray has affected his vision. The cello looks different. He rubs his eyes hard. He looks again. Disbelief spreads through him. It's gone. The cello he has craved for so many months has disappeared. The replacement is an ugly imposter.

Pasquale turns away, his stomach sinking. It's just a couple of blocks to the main police station yet exhaustion stalks his every step. Soon the white headquarters of the carabinieri tower over him. As he nears the entrance of the brightly lit building, the familiar figure of Marcello is coming down the steps. Even from here he can sense there is something wrong.

He calls out and, as Marcello turns, he sees he is talking on his mobile phone. 'They claim they never saw him,' Pasquale hears him say, his voice agitated.

He finishes his call and embraces Pasquale. 'You heard? I was just telling Frances. The police say they didn't arrest Riccardo. They don't seem interested and are not trying to help.' Marcello trembles, a dark duet of frustration and fear playing in his veins. 'Pasquale, I don't know what to do!'

They sit together on the steps, Marcello resting his head on his knees. Pasquale rings Riccardo's number, never expecting a reply.

'Si?' The voice of a child answers.

'Who is this?' Pasquale stammers.

'Carmine.'

'Where did you get this phone, Carmine?'

'I didn't take it. I found it. Promise.'

'Where?'

'In the gutter. Near my house.'

'How old are you?'

'Eight-and-a-half.'

'Can I talk to your parents?'

'Am I in trouble?'

'No. You're not in trouble. It's just that this phone belongs to my friend. And we've lost him. So we need to get the phone back. Carmine? Carmine?'

She doesn't answer. Pasquale's eyes lock with Marcello's but they daren't speak.

'Si?' He hears a man's voice.

Pasquale explains the phone is lost and he needs it urgently.

'No problem. My daughter says she found it a short time ago. You can come and collect it now.'

They hail a taxi and drive ten minutes to the upper reaches of the Spanish Quarter.

'Here. Stop here!' Marcello says. They pull up outside a line of dingy terraces and he hands the fare to the driver. There is nothing to distinguish number 260 from its neighbours, the same unpainted walls and crumbling masonry. They climb three levels and ring a buzzer.

'Si?' Pasquale recognizes the father's voice. The door is opened by a man of thirty or so. A young girl with saucer-brown eyes and long black hair stands beside him. 'Go on. Give it to them,' the father urges her.

The girl hands Pasquale the phone. Marcello glances at it quickly. 'Definitely Riccardo's. Thank you very much, Carmine. This is very important to us.'

He turns to the father. 'Could you let her show us where she found it?'

The man nods and takes his daughter's hand. He locks the door behind him and together they descend the stairs to the street. They walk to an intersection with a wider street.

'There,' she points to the gutter. 'Right there. That's where I found it.'

Marcello pulls a twenty euro note from his pocket and hands it to her father. 'That's for Carmine.'

The man tries to give it back. 'That's not necessary. We teach our children to be honest. They don't need to be rewarded for doing what is right.'

'Please. This means a lot to us,' Pasquale says. 'We want to thank her.'

The father shrugs and Carmine giggles as they turn back to their apartment.

The two men pace up and down the street, looking for more clues, the sign of a struggle. But they see nothing. Marcello checks the phone, looking for any calls Riccardo might have made. He clicks onto the message menu. 'There's something here!' He holds the phone up to Pasquale. 'Riccardo's tried to write a message. *Not police.*'

'He obviously wasn't able to send it. Maybe he threw the phone out of a car?' Pasquale says. 'Where do we start to look for him?'

'I don't know. I just don't know.'

The light of a bar burns onto the street above. Marcello gestures to Pasquale and he follows him up a small rise and opens the door. The barman and a cluster of men sitting at the tables inside the single room look at them curiously when they enter.

'Grappa. Two please.' Marcello orders.

The barman places the glasses in front of them and they both drink.

Pasquale appreciates the strong warm liquor. He gauges the atmosphere in the bar has relaxed, their intrusion dismissed as harmless.

The door opens again and the girl's father walks in. He greets them warmly and offers to buy them a drink. They shake their heads. 'But maybe you could help us,' Marcello says quietly. 'We are very worried about our friend. He was taken away from the garbage protest by two men dressed as carabinieri, but we don't think they were police. They may have driven past here where Carmine found his phone.'

'No problem. These are my friends,' the man says. In a loud voice he retells the story, embellishing all the details and asking if anyone had seen two policemen in the street just after sunset.

Laughter punctuates the air. 'The real police are too scared to come up here unless they bring a battalion,' one says.

'I saw something.' A deep voice comes from a small table in one corner of the bar.

'What did you see, Bruno?' asks the father.

'Police, and maybe some others, driving a Mercedes. That's why I noticed. I've never seen that before. It sped up the hill here.'

'Did you notice a number? Anything else?'

'No. It was a dark-coloured car, very expensive. That's all I saw.'

Pasquale and Marcello thank the men and leave the bar.

Marcello shakes his head. 'I'm feeling helpless. But I'm going to go home and get the car and start driving around the streets. Just in case. Pasquale, why don't you go home and see Frances? She's worried sick and it would be good if you kept her company.'

The two men go their own way. But the same darkness of spirit, matching the blackness of the Naples night, follows them.

CHAPTER TWENTY-SEVEN

Frances wakes to the sound of sirens below and for a moment wonders if Riccardo's disappearance was just a bad dream. She has fallen asleep on the sofa but when she sits up and sees Pasquale slumped in the chair next to her, she remembers the hours of waiting through the night for news, any news at all that might stymie their worst fears.

She goes to the window and throws open the shutters. Two paramedics are lifting an elderly woman on a stretcher into the back of an ambulance parked in the street.

'What is it?' Pasquale is awake.

'An ambulance, but not for Ricky,' Frances says. 'A woman. I don't know her.'

Pasquale is beside her, putting on his coat. 'I'm sorry. I didn't mean to stay here all night.'

'I'm glad you did. It's not a good time for either of us to be on our own.'

Frances opens the door for him. 'I'll let you know if I hear anything from Marcello.'

He walks down a couple of steps and returns. 'Frances, I know this sounds trivial with Riccardo missing . . .'

'What is it?'

'The cello. The one I've been saving to buy. It's gone from the shop.'

'What happened to it?'

'I don't know. I passed by last night and it's not in the window.' He looks like a lost child, his striking eyes still reddened from the spray attack.

Frances smiles at him. 'Maybe the shopkeeper just moved the

instruments around. Don't worry, you've been paying instalments so he won't have sold it to anyone else.'

She closes the door and checks her watch. It's still early. She rings Marcello's phone but there's no answer. Riccardo's backpack is propped against one wall. She unzips the front. A half-full packet of his precious chocolate biscuits falls out and crunches as she picks it up. She feels sick to the stomach, remembering his laughter and praying she'll hear it again. Where on earth is he? She bites her lip hard then tries Marcello's number again. Still no answer. She hears the ambulance leaving. Hospitals — they must check all the hospitals and all the other police stations. She throws on her leather jacket and hurries downstairs. Her bike stands alone and she remembers his bike must still be in the city.

The café is empty and Massimo starts making her café latte before she has even ordered it. 'Buon giorno, Francesca. Anything to eat with your coffee?'

'No thanks, I've lost my appetite.'

'Must be serious,' he teases her.

She's about to tell him about Riccardo when her phone rings.

'I've found him,' Marcello says.

'Is he —'

'He's OK. A bit knocked about, but OK. I'm bringing him home.'

Relief and joy, the emotions are so strong she must have looked overwhelmed.

'Everything OK?' Massimo asks.

'Yes, couldn't be better.' She quickly rings Pasquale. 'He's safe!'

'Thank God. Where is he?'

'Marcello's bringing him home. Can you tell the others?'

Frances drinks her coffee slowly, her mind racing. Brutal images of the murdered scientists force their way back and she inhales sharply. That was her deepest fear — first Riccardo, then Marcello, then her.

She pays for her coffee, then waits on the pavement, where scores of schoolchildren jostle together, heading for another day in the classroom. The shutters are pulled up and the small shops are trading, women with shopping baskets are buying food for lunch. The day is so deliciously ordinary. Ricky is alive.

But still, her stomach lurches as Marcello's four-wheel-drive approaches. She waves him over and climbs into the back seat. Riccardo sits in front but doesn't speak. Marcello smiles at her over his shoulder, weariness lining his face.

Frances drapes her arms around Riccardo's neck. 'I'm so pleased you're safe.'

He lets out a sound like a sob. She rubs his shoulders and says nothing more.

When Marcello parks in the courtyard and jumps out to help Riccardo, Frances pulls him aside. 'Shouldn't we take him to hospital? He's in shock.'

'I tried to but he stopped me. He doesn't want to go.'

Together they half carry Riccardo up the flights of stairs to the apartment, where they peel off his coat, jeans and shoes. Frances smells a bitter cocktail of urine and the streets as they lay him on his bed. His face is stained with dirt and blood, one of his eyes is blackened and there are cuts on his hands and bruises on his legs.

Doing her best to conceal her shock, Frances strokes his forehead. When Marcello returns with a basin of hot water to wash his face and hands, she makes a pot of strong tea. He manages a smile and they gently raise him to sip the steaming brew. He acknowledges them with his good eye but seems incapable of speech. Soon he closes both eyes and drifts into sleep. Frances covers him with a blanket and removes the fouled clothing.

Marcello pulls her towards the lounge and holds her close.

She clings to him, breathing in concert. 'What happened?' she whispers.

'I drove around for hours before I found him dumped in an alley. He's lucky to be alive. They've let him off with a warning, and a message to all of us.' He releases her and pulls a piece of paper from his pocket, a coarse charcoal drawing of a decapitated man, his head lying at his feet. 'This could be the future for you and your friends' is scrawled beneath it. 'This was pinned to his coat.'

Frances gasps. 'Il Sistema?'

'Must be, posing as carabinieri. What amazes me is that they didn't murder him.'

'What stopped them?'

'I don't know.'

Marcello holds her again and she wants to collapse in his arms. She leads him to her bed and they lie together, their limbs tangled, as they drift into a deep and troubled sleep.

A loud groaning wakes them — Riccardo calling from his room. Frances checks her watch. They've been asleep for three hours.

He's trying to sit up in his bed. 'Ricky, careful now.' She sits next to him and takes his hand.

'Thank you,' he murmers as Marcello joins them. 'I thought I was going to die.'

'Not yet, as my Nonno would say, the saints aren't ready for you.'

Riccardo laughs then clasps his ribs. 'Ouch! They really did me over.'

'Can you tell us what happened? We saw you disappear off the stage with the police, then we couldn't find you.'

'Well, they fooled me at first. But when they bundled me in the back of an unmarked Mercedes I realized they weren't carabinieri.'

Marcello holds up his mobile phone with the message. 'We figured that!'

Riccardo holds out his hand to take it. 'Madonna! A miracle! I started to write a message on my phone but I was interrupted when one of them got into the back and pointed a gun at me. When he opened the window to throw his cigarette away I managed to toss the phone out. I never imagined it would bounce back so fast.'

'What did they do to you?' Frances asks.

'There were three of them, the driver and the two goons. They took me to some warehouse, full of clothes. I don't know where it was. They gagged me and started punching and kicking me, warning me not to spread rumours about Vesuvius that would stop development. Then they drove me around again and dropped me in the alley where you found me. But first . . .'

He starts to cough. 'But first they tipped bags of rubbish over me then one of them pissed on me. They finished me off with a few more kicks and I don't know whether I passed out or not, but I know I was lying there for a long time.'

Frances scans his face and body, fearful of his injuries, not just physical but to his indomitable spirit. 'I think we should get a doctor.'

Riccardo shakes his head. 'No, nothing is broken.'

'Well, how about a good hot bath? You don't exactly smell like a rose garden.'

While he is soaking, the doorbell rings. A courier hands Frances an envelope embossed with the university's logo and addressed to Riccardo.

'Who was that?' Marcello has helped dress Riccardo and is leading him to the sofa.

Frances hesitates by the door. 'For you, Ricky.' She hands him the envelope and he tears it open so clumsily the letter falls out. His left eye is so swollen and black he squints to read it, then spits and throws it on the floor.

Frances scoops it up and reads it out loud.

Dear Signor Cocchia, I am under instructions to inform you that your contract with Progetto Vulcano has been terminated. In spite of previous warnings from the director, you have continued to breach the terms of your contract that require you to keep the research findings confidential until they have been substantiated and released officially by the university. It has come to our attention that you have addressed a public rally about the project without permission and in further breach of your contract. Regrettably, this amounts to professional misconduct and cannot be tolerated. Your termination is immediate.

Professor Bartolo Caterno.

Frances sits down next to him, caught in a cross-fire of emotions, struggling to find anything that might console him. 'Would you like me to talk to Professor Corsi? Ask her to reconsider?'

He shakes his head. 'I wouldn't waste your time.'

Marcello paces the floor. 'They've done a Galileo on you.'

'What do you mean?'

'When Galileo declared the earth revolved around the sun, he was condemned by the Church. He was forced to recant and spent the last eight years of his life under house arrest.'

Riccardo grunts. 'Nothing much has changed in four hundred years!'

'We could try the media. Get your story out,' Frances suggests.

'Another waste of time.' Riccardo smiles grimly. 'No, I think I will go to Stromboli. I don't like to run away but I need to get my strength back. I'll go there for Christmas and put myself under house arrest.'

The doorbell rings again. Frances opens the door and is taken aback when another courier gives her an envelope from the university, this time addressed to her.

She walks slowly back into the room and holds it up, wondering if she's about to become another Galileo. Opening the envelope carefully she reads the letter, raises her eyebrows and reads it through a second time, more slowly. She puts it down and turns to her friends.

'Looks like I'm going to Stromboli too.'

CHAPTER TWENTY-EIGHT

The shelves in the small shop bulge with hundreds of painted figurines, Christian icons side by side with pagan symbols. Frances picks up a small pink angel and turns it over in her hands.

'What's it made of?'

'Cork, moss and bark,' the shop assistant replies. 'They're traditional, the presepe artists make them by hand. Would you like it?'

Frances nods and hands it to her. Perfect for baby Luciana. She reaches to a higher shelf and removes a plump reindeer with a bulbous nose for Stefano. And for Lorenzo? She scans the shelves and picks up a shepherd. He looks a little too real for comfort, with a five o'clock shadow and arthritic fingers. She puts it back and settles for a younger shepherd holding a dog on a leash. The shop assistant carefully wraps each piece in tissue paper and places them in Frances' basket.

She steps into a dense crowd of Christmas Eve shoppers milling around the crèche shops each side of the narrow thoroughfare of Via San Gregorio Armeno in the heart of the old city. The shops try to outdo each other with their nativity scenes. Some would fit into a shoebox, while others are so large they would fill the room of a house. Motorized angels fly through the air, the three kings dance like a clownish chorus in the background and complete casts of moving shepherds and animals watch over a myriad of representations of Mary, Joseph and baby Jesus in the manger.

A crowd of people laughing outside one tiny shopfront attracts her attention. Frances stands on tip-toes to peer over a scrum of shoulders. A cast of life-sized wooden figures is arranged in a stable. The intricately carved faces resemble ministers of the government. She starts as she recognizes the image of the politician she met at the British Embassy dinner. He is a severed head, neatly sitting on a silver platter.

She shivers and walks away. A sweet smoky smell drifts down the street. An old man is leaning over a charcoal burner roasting chestnuts. 'Castagne, castagne,' he utters, voice frail and teeth missing. Frances hands him some coins and he gives her a brown paper cone filled with the nuts. They're steaming and she gratefully warms her hands on them. She bites into one, tasting its floury nutty centre.

Ahead of her a line of food shops overflows with Christmas fare; supersized packets of pasta in a rainbow of colours, rich chocolates and fine olive oils. Bottles of liqueurs dangle temptingly in the doorways and she walks into one to buy a bottle of bright yellow limoncello.

The crowds continue to grow and press against her. Suddenly she is pushed hard. Men are shouting and she's squeezed as the mass of people around her compress and panic in the confusion.

Close by, a short man pushes through, holding a gun above his head. She's so near, every feature of his face is visible, including a deformed ear. It's grotesque, a remnant of an ear, hacked or chewed off. His face seems familiar and those around her shrink back to let him through. Frances clings motionless to the wall beside her. A gun fires and she hears screaming and loud footsteps. Then, nothing. The tension is choking. No one talks. People shift uncomfortably, then sensing the crisis has passed, quietly return to the business of shopping, as though nothing has happened. She wants to get away as fast as possible but she has two more stops to make.

She walks further into the old city streets of Spaccanapoli, where expensive jewellery and fine gift shops vie for attention. The bell jingles when she enters one. The shopkeeper recognizes her. 'Ah signorina, it is ready,' he says, handing her a small parcel.

'The shooting, what do you think it was?'

He shrugs in the way she has come to recognize as a Neapolitan art form. 'No idea. None of my business.'

Although not quite dark, yellow street lights cast a sheen over the cobblestones as the jewellery shops give way to small book and music emporiums. Frances collects another package from one of them and packs it into her basket.

As she hurries towards the station she catches a glimpse of a man's shadow, which seems to be following her. She turns around but can't see anyone. She continues through the market laneway where the shopkeepers are closing, glancing back now and then. Scores of people are waiting on the platform and her eyes dart back and forth. Perhaps she imagined it, but her anxiety is real. The funicular arrives and she drops gratefully into a seat as it moves up the hill towards Corso Vittorio Emanuele.

Peppe waves to her from the petrol station as she walks the last stretch home. 'See you later tonight,' she calls to him. Still unsettled, she looks over her shoulder, then slams the front door of the apartment building, for the first time double-checking it's locked behind her.

The sound of a cello greets her on the staircase. She pauses to listen to a melody she hasn't heard before, upbeat and cheerful. When she knocks on Pasquale's door, he stops playing immediately, opens the door and lets out a joyful shriek. He grabs her and hugs her tightly. She's about to tell him her feeling of being followed but doesn't want to break his mood.

'I have something to show you!' He's laughing as he pulls her inside. 'My beautiful cello!' He holds aloft the red-hued instrument she had seen in the music shop window.

'How on earth . . .?'

'It seems I have a mysterious patron, who paid off what I owed. I went to the shop convinced the cello was sold and Benedetto presented it to me.'

'He didn't give you any idea who it was?'

'He knows but he said he promised to protect their identity.' Pasquale strokes the cello like a favourite pet. 'And there's more good news, Frances. I passed my audition. I have a place in the orchestra from next year.'

'I'm so proud of you. But I didn't want to interrupt your practice. What are you playing?'

'Something for tonight's party, one of Schubert's Christmas carols.' Pasquale radiates joy as he begins to play; his distinctive green-blue eyes are shining jewels again and his slender body melds with the cello.

Frances quietly waves goodbye and climbs the last few steps to her apartment. Camilla. Maybe Camilla paid for it. She's a monster to everybody else but Pasquale seems to have hypnotized her, melting her stone heart into marshmallow. But why would she do that? Her key crunches in the lock and although Riccardo has barely left to catch the night ferry to Stromboli, the apartment already feels strangely empty. She drops her shopping basket and flops onto the sofa, almost squashing a package wrapped in Christmas paper. She removes a card attached to it and opens it.

Dearest Frances,

Have a wonderful Christmas. The silver package proves how much you mean to me. The boy will bring you good luck! See you in Stromboli.

Yours always, Ricky.

She wishes he was here as she unwraps the package to solve the riddle and finds two smaller parcels inside. One is covered in tin foil and she smiles when she finds two Tim Tam biscuits inside, immediately eats one and rewraps the other. Peeling the paper off the second parcel she discovers a tiny figurine of a young boy. She holds it up and can't believe what she is seeing. The boy's trousers are around his ankles and he is crouching and defecating.

Good luck indeed! She already misses his mischievous charm. His eye was nearly healed and his bruises and scratches were disappearing when she farewelled him, but his spirits were down and she worried about him. Her disquiet deepens when she remembers the shadows of the previous night.

Her letter from the university is still on the table. She picks it up to read again.

Dear Signorina Nelson,

It is my duty to inform you that owing to administrative changes at the highest levels of the university, it has been decided to suspend the activities of Progetto Vulcano for at least three months. While monitoring of Vesuvius and other areas will continue at the observatory, the team's work in Naples will cease until further notice. Regrettably, your colleague Signor Cocchia is no longer attached to the project. However, the university will honour your contract, and as such, we require you to install and test the new acoustic monitoring system on Stromboli. We have advised staff at the Stromboli Observatory to expect you in the New Year. In the meantime, on behalf of the director and myself, we wish you a Merry Christmas.

Professor Bartolo Caterno

She had gone into the university the next day but it became clear no one wanted to talk to her. She had sat outside Professor Corsi's office for more than an hour before giving up. When she spotted Professor Caterno at the end of a corridor and called out to him, he promptly turned his back and disappeared.

Monitoring at the observatory was still proceeding. She had checked all of the microphones she had placed on the flanks of the volcano and seismographic readouts for Campi Flegrei and Vesuvius and was comforted there were no signs of increasing volcanic activity. After gathering the equipment she would need for Stomboli, she had signed off.

When Frances opens the shutters in her lounge the day has already dissolved into night. She looks at her watch. Winter darkness comes early — it's barely six o'clock. The moon is starting to rise and there is promise of a clear evening as the dark shape of Vesuvius looms over the city. Even dormant, it remains stunningly vital.

Frances' mind wanders to another volcano on the other side of the world, also thought to be dormant on another Christmas Eve. Mt Ruapehu deceived its watchers in New Zealand in 1953, when Christmas Eve was also a clear night. Yet two hours before midnight, the crater lake burst without warning, engulfing the valley and a train carrying hundreds of people.

The nightmarish images of her baby sister sucked down into the icy waters of the river flash back; her parents desperately searching for her in the swirling sulphurous brine. Frances closes her eyes and wills the pain to go away. She has already put her sister's spirit to rest, along with the ghosts of the past.

The little Fogliano children talking, laughing and squabbling in their apartment below are like a balm to the wound of her lost family. She empties her basket on the table, lining up the gifts she will take to them later. One package she puts aside.

CHAPTER TWENTY-NINE

A Christmas wreath of holly and red and yellow forest berries welcomes Frances as she taps on the door to the Foglianos' apartment. Nonna Fabrizia ushers her inside, apologizing for her apron, brushing back her white hair and scurrying back into the kitchen. The twins rush her and try to wrest her basket from her.

'Stefano, Lorenzo, stop that!' Laura chides. She places Luciana on a cushion on the floor and the baby gurgles at her brothers. 'She's just at the good stage,' Laura says. 'She can sit up now but she can't move!'

Pasquale is on the floor, and the boys rejoin him, adjusting the figures in an enormous Christmas crib. It is an elaborate wooden stable extending along most of one of the walls.

'Careful!' Laura cries as Lorenzo picks up a weathered figure of Mary painted in dark colours. 'She's more than a hundred years old. Many of them are antiques, passed down in our families for generations.'

Frances hands a package to each of the boys. 'Here are some new ones.'

They tear off the wrapping and hold the reindeer and shepherd up to the light then whizz around the room with them as though they are aeroplanes.

Laura chases them. 'Madonna. If I can just get through tonight!'

The boys flop in front of the crib and place the figurines, switching their positions around, competing to be the closest to the baby Jesus. Frances unwraps the angel and holds it up to Luciana. She immediately grabs it, puts it in her mouth then starts crying and drops it.

Her brothers howl with laughter.

'Sorry, I'm not used to babies,' Frances apologizes, rescuing the angel and placing it in the crib.

'What do you think of this one?' Pasquale is sitting cross-legged on the floor looking like a boy himself. He passes her an intricately carved figure of a man playing a cello. She looks at it carefully. The musician is wearing a dark suit and his curly hair pokes out beneath a fedora.

'It's you!' Frances exclaims.

'Yes! One of my friends is training as a presepe artist. He made it.'

'What do you think of this one?' Frances takes the figurine of the boy out of her pocket. 'Ricky gave it to me and said it was good luck. Is he having me on?'

'No, it's true,' Laura interrupts. 'Cazzo, shit, it's a symbol of good luck.'

'Cacata! Cacata!' the boys echo each other, laughing and nudging each other. 'He's pooping!'

'Enough,' Laura growls. 'If you're not good, Father Christmas will leave coal in your stockings instead of sweets.'

The boys jump up and drag Frances to the fireplace where three long stockings are hanging from the mantle. They scrunch them and try to peek inside.

'Leave them!' Laura says. 'You can't look until tomorrow.'

The doorbell rings and before they can answer it, Peppe bursts in, Marcello in his wake. Frances notices both wear strained expressions but as soon as they see the children their faces relax.

Marcello puts his arms around Frances and she tastes the night chill as she kisses his cheek.

'There's been another killing,' he whispers to her. 'In the old city.'

She pulls him aside. 'I was there. I saw a man with a gun, he was short and had a grossly deformed ear.'

'The same one Pasquale saw, Basso Mezzanotte, Shorty Midnight, the dwarf. The police have put out messages on the radio saying they're hunting him. It seems they're the only people in Naples who haven't seen him!'

'I heard a shot . . . and there's something else.' Frances holds Marcello closer. 'I thought someone was following me tonight. I'm not sure but . . .'

Marcello nods. 'I hate to say it but that could be so. None of us is safe. Maybe it's a good thing you're going to Stromboli.'

The doorbell rings again and Laura opens it to Poppaea.

'Sorry I'm late. I've just finished making dessert.' Poppaea hands her a large white cardboard box.

'Now that we're all here, let's eat!' Peppe calls out, as Nonna Fabrizia emerges from the kitchen with a white tureen and places it in the centre of the table. Crowding around the table, the twins jostle to sit either side of Frances.

'Hey, I'm on that side,' Marcello says lifting Lorenzo out, who then rushes around to sit next to Poppaea. Peppe sits at one end of the table and Laura is at the other, with her mother beside her. 'Welcome to our home,' he says. 'Christmas for us is la famiglia, l'amore e il cibo, family, love and food. And we have plenty of that here tonight.'

He passes a bottle of white wine around the table. 'The wine of Vesuvius. Salute!' They all raise their glasses and sip the sweet wine.

Frances looks at the faces gathered together for one of the year's most special dinners; three generations of a family welcoming relative strangers into their midst. She has tasted the worst this city has to offer and now she savours the best. And it all becomes clear — no wonder you sit on the fence if the survival of your family is at risk. Why wouldn't you turn a blind eye when choosing sides could cost you everything that was dearest to your heart? In the outside world, Peppe is an employee of a small business. Here, he is the protector of his castle.

'Mangiamo! Let's eat!' Peppe speaks with the authority and assuredness of a man who acknowledges his fortune is his family. Frances sees how his eyes lock now and then with Laura, their love and loyalty binding and strengthening them.

Nonna Fabrizia fills plate after plate with piles of pasta and seafood from the tureen. 'Spaghetti alle vongole in bianco, clams in white wine sauce.'

They eat quickly, complimenting the pasta, cooked to perfection. Baby Luciana sits in a high chair, picking up strands of the spaghetti and chewing on them happily.

Nonna Fabrizia and Laura are on their feet again, returning with two huge covered silver platters.

'Yuk, eels!' Lorenzo says, as Peppe lifts one of the lids.

'I hate eels,' Stefano says. 'I want chicken.'

'We don't eat meat on Christmas Eve, just fish. And eels, capitone, they're a luxury. So don't be ungrateful,' Laura says, spooning pieces of the fried fish onto the plates.

Peppe lifts the second lid. Roasted red, yellow and green peppers sit alongside crispy potatoes dotted with rosemary.

'Yay! Potatoes!' Stefano shouts.

'And please take some pepperoni,' Nonna says, passing around the vegetables.

Frances picks at the eels, silently agreeing with the boys. She nibbles on a piece. Not bad, but she keeps picturing the eels she's seen under the sea and hides her portion under some pepper.

As they finish the meal, Pasquale stands up and summons the twins to follow him. His cello is resting against the side of the crib. He takes it and sits on a chair with a boy on either side. He starts to play and after a few bars nods at the boys to begin.

Poppaea has edged her way behind Pasquale. She bends down to kiss him and whispers in his ear.

He nods. 'A special request from my sister, and everyone has to sing.'

They all gather around him as he leads them into the carol Frances had heard him practising.

'*Mille cherubini in coro ti sorridono dal ciel. Una dolce canzone t'accarezza il crin.*

'*Una man ti guida lieve fra le nuvole d'or . . .*'

The boys' faces glow, and as they sing their open mouths reveal their front teeth have fallen out.

Marcello drapes his arm around her and hears his mellow baritone voice melding with the others. 'A choir of a thousand cherubs smiles on you from the sky. A sweet song caresses your brow. A hand is gently guiding you through the cloud of gold.'

Nonna Fabrizia has her arm around Laura. She sings in a tuneful soprano, her eyes glistening with tears.

'*Dormi, dormi, sogna, piccolo amor mio. Dormi, sogna, posa il capo sul mio cor.* Sleep, sleep, dream, my little love. Sleep, dream, lay your head on my heart. Thank you, Pasquale. That was my husband's favourite.' She comes over to Frances and Marcello. 'Be happy,' she says taking one of each of their hands. 'Life is so short. My husband Ugo and I had more than fifty wonderful years together, and then he was gone.'

Poppaea and Laura are fussing around the table and Peppe is bending over the fireplace. 'I almost forgot,' he says, setting it alight. A pile of paper and kindling wood bursts into flame. Soon, larger pieces of wood start to burn and he places a decorated log on top. 'Gather round.' He turns out the lights and Laura and Poppaea emerge with lighted candles and a large cake. The boys are giggling and shove each other aside to get to the front. They settle side by side. Nonna Fabrizia holds Luciana on one hip.

Peppe clears his throat. 'We have a saying that you can spend Easter with whomever you please but Christmas must be spent with family. You are part of our family. And I wish you all the happiest of Christmases.'

Frances hands him the bottle of limoncello and he fills a tray of small glasses with the yellow liqueur. The cake shimmers in the candlelight, encased in a bright red crust of almond paste. Poppaea slices into it and reveals its white interior of ricotta dotted with candied fruit. The boys pass around pieces of the cake and the glasses.

'Merry Christmas,' they toast each other.

Music floats up from the courtyard. 'Bagpipes! In Naples?' Frances says.

Pasquale laughs. 'It's true. The shepherds come down from the hill towns and play carols on their bagpipes.'

Laura throws open the shutters and they all gather to listen. Six men wearing felt hats and sheepskin vests have gathered in a circle. Each of them plays a set of bagpipes. Families from the surrounding streets have gathered around them.

'Can we go down, Mama?' Stefano asks.

'No, it is too cold. Stay up here with us.'

They play one carol after another but the wind chills them and Laura closes the shutters as the shepherds move away. By now Luciana has fallen asleep in her Nonna's arms and is put to bed. The boys collapse on cushions on the floor, finally quiet and struggling to keep their eyes open. The log crackles loudly in the fire.

'A good sign,' Peppe says. 'We burn the yule log every Christmas Eve. It purges the evils of the old year.'

Frances and Marcello exchange glances. 'Let's hope it works,' he whispers.

Frances yawns, hoping Marcello will take her cue. He nods at her and together they stand to say goodbye.

Church bells ring out the midnight hour as Frances and Marcello return to her apartment, where he hands her a tiny box tied in a blue satin ribbon. 'For you. Merry Christmas, Frances.'

She opens the box and nestling inside is a gold chain and a cameo pendant. The background is a deep blue and the white face is the Venus from under the sea. 'It's beautiful,' she says as he puts it around her neck.

'And for you.' She gives him her gift.

'Great minds.' He holds up a miniature engraved woodcut of Venus and Mars entwined.

The room glows in the reflected light of the moon and as he reaches for her, a deep longing floods her body. As they kiss, the fatigue, the fears and betrayals that have enveloped them in the past months are replaced by a powerful passion. They fall together on the sofa, hurriedly peeling away each other's clothes. At last there is only flesh between them and their desire for each other. Frances lowers herself to him and he rises to meet her, their lovemaking fuelled by a great energy. They move to her bed and sink into each other's arms.

The traditional Christmas bells mark each hour of the night. She hears one o'clock, two o'clock and still they explore each other's bodies. Tender and loving, they are finally spent.

The bells ring on through the night, but it's not until they sound nine o'clock that the lovers stir.

CHAPTER THIRTY

Marcello toots his horn as a large truck veers towards them at the entry to the ferry terminal. Frances grips the front seat but relaxes as the driver sees them and turns sharply away.

Dozens of people straggle along the wharves, dragging and carrying suitcases and crates of food and wine towards the ship that will sail through the night to the Aeolian Islands. A stream of taxis spill their passengers onto the roadside and a man struggles to extract an oversized bag from the back seat of one while his wife waits passively holding a wriggling young boy.

Marcello squeezes his four-wheel-drive between two vans and leaps out to remove Frances' luggage from the rear. She sits there for a moment, her feelings conflicted about this departure. She feels excited about the days ahead, yet her intimacy with Marcello has restored her; a joyful union she is loathe to leave. But New Year has come and gone and Frances has delayed her journey to Stromboli for as long as she can. And besides, Marcello has his own work waiting on an archaeological dig in the ancient city of Carthage, in Tunisia.

Frances slides out and he is there to help her down. Seagulls soar and dip around them, their shrill cries piercing the late afternoon sky. As he strokes her hair and cups her face in his hands, their eyes say more to each other than words ever could.

The ship's horn blasts loudly but they are silent as they join the other passengers on the long walk along the pier. They trudge slowly, dragging out this small final journey together, but find themselves beside the ship soon enough. 'Come back safely.' His voice is soft as he passes the suitcase to her. 'Spring will come quickly and we'll be together again.'

Resisting saying goodbye she smiles at him, drops her bag and they hug each other so tightly she can feel his heartbeat. The horn blasts again, three short sharp beeps, and clouds of black smoke rising from the ship's stack warn of the imminent departure.

Frances kisses his ear. 'Roll on spring,' she whispers and releases herself. She picks up the bag and walks away.

'Say hello to Riccardo, won't you?' he calls after her.

She turns, nods and pauses for a second, then walks on up the broad ramp to where two sailors are checking tickets. Twenty or so cars and several trucks are parked on the lowest level and hundreds of crates of wine, olive oil, bottled water and sacks of fruit and vegetables are stacked along the sides, like a floating marketplace. Frances edges her way around them to a narrow metal staircase.

The stairs lead her to a reception area where she joins a long queue waiting to collect keys to their cabins. Tourists among the passengers have settled together on reclining seats, preparing for a long night in the open area. Their backpacks marked with tiny flags of America, Australia, New Zealand and Germany reveal their origins. From the conversations around her, Frances learns most of the travellers are islanders, returning home from the mainland. They jest and tease each other, older men and women, faces weather-beaten from lives spent on the far-flung islands where the Mediterranean melds into the Tyrrhenian Sea.

'Cabin number thirty-three.' The purser passes Frances her key. 'Dinner is served as soon as we set sail but there's no need to book. It's the off season so it won't be very busy tonight.'

Frances carries her bags down one level and along a narrow corridor to her cabin. Two narrow bunks covered in thin red blankets are against one wall. She hurls her luggage onto the top bunk and sits on the bottom one. The room is tiny with one door leading to a shower and toilet cubicle. It smells of stale cigarette smoke, urine and diesel fumes. The lurching of the ship and the odours combine to make her feel nauseous. She remembers gratefully that Marcello had insisted she bring seasickness tablets. She retrieves a bottle of water from her backpack and swallows two.

The whirring engines of the ship vibrate through the cabin. She takes her wallet, locks the door behind her, and climbs two flights of stairs to the deck. Already, they are leaving Naples in their wake, but Vesuvius is still visible, rising out of a haze veiling much of the city. The sea churns below, great navy-blue swells of water washing up as the ship ploughs through. The sun has already gone and the cold rushing air soon sends her back inside, seeking shelter.

Passengers are gathering in the lounge room, snippets of conversations filling the void. Frances orders a brandy, swirling the spirit a few times around in the glass then sips it. Her stomach responds, settling down. She wanders past the food buffet but the pre-cooked tomato pasta and cold vegetables are unappealing.

A tourist video about the Aeolian Islands is playing on a large screen. She curls up on one of the high-backed seats with her brandy to watch. Flashes of eruptions, turquoise underwater scenes, mudbaths and stories of life on the islands of Lipari, Stomboli and the smaller islands of the volcanic archipelago hold her attention. There are older, frightening tales, of its mythological Greek origins. It was the home of Aeolus, God of the Winds, who swept through the islands and sent many a passing ship to the ocean floor. 'Please, not this one,' Frances thinks. She starts to yawn and although it's still early evening, heads back to her cabin, planning to be up at dawn to watch the sunrise.

The bunk is hard and cold and she struggles to settle. The ship rocks and rolls and she tries to relax her stomach to move in time with the sea, ignoring images in her mind of an angry sea god. Before long she feels herself drifting to sleep. She has no idea how long she has been asleep when a squeaking noise wakes her. She can't see anything in the darkness but can hear somebody trying to open her cabin door and lies still, her heart thudding. Then she reaches behind her and turns on the light. The handle stops turning.

'Who's there?' she calls out. There is no reply. She stays in her bed listening, afraid to move. The fluorescent light glares greenly in her eyes and casts a harsh lime aura over the cabin. She contemplates going to look outside in the corridor but decides that would be foolish. Perhaps someone made a mistake, confusing the numbers of the cabin? She goes to the door and turns the handle. It's still locked. She returns to bed and turns the light off again. Tossing and turning, sleep evades her. She tries to recall the faces of the other passengers. Was it one of them? Or a crew member? Or was it the unseen person who was following her in Naples?

Gradually she falls into an uneasy sleep, one made all the more uncomfortable as the rolling sea drums up her memories of that life-changing day on White Island.

∽o∽

Bob Masterton was lying crumpled on a rock shelf ten metres below them. Boiling water lapped over his head, which was still covered by the orange mask. Frances could see his body was motionless, one leg beneath him, the other sticking out at an odd angle.

'No!' She'd screamed and without thinking had started to climb over the rim.

'Don't!' Hamish had pulled her back. 'He's dead. We can't do anything.'

She had known in her heart he was right but it felt wrong not to try. 'We can't just leave him.'

'There's nothing we can do now.' Hamish had been firm, suddenly assuming the maturity of a much older man. 'I'll come back with a recovery team and we'll bring him out. But we have to go, Frances, it's not safe and I don't like these vibrations.'

Frances had let Hamish lead her back to the helicopter, feeling gutted but also guilty. Could she have prevented Bob's death? Had she put a hex on the whole operation by coming against Tori's warnings? 'I'm not thinking logically,' she had chided herself. Bob came here all the time. It's not my fault. And yet . . . The wind kept shifting and the roaring of the crater was unrelenting. As they emerged from the steam Frances had taken off her mask.

'I'll have to phone. To let them know.' She'd stopped to pull out her cellphone but couldn't find a signal.

Hamish stood with her, tears coursing down his unlined face. 'I'll call from the chopper.'

She had hugged him. 'I'm sorry. I know you and Bob were friends.'

They strapped themselves into the helicopter and were soon spiralling up above the island, circling the crater where they could see the orange dot of Bob's mask by the water.

Hamish had dialled air traffic control and in a faltering voice gave the flight path details. 'We have an emergency . . .' he said. 'A death on White Island.'

∽o∾

The direction of Frances' life had turned on a pin that day. She could scarcely bear to face Tori again but knew she must. It would be only a matter of time before he learnt about the death. After all, Bob Masterton was 'Mr Volcanoes'. She and Hamish had barely returned to base before news bulletins broadcast the events surrounding Bob's death throughout New Zealand. A stream of journalists wanted to interview her but Frances was in no state of mind to endure a media blitz and flicked the requests to her boss. She was mortified when she saw the photos in the next day's newspapers and on the Internet. Her office had released the happy snaps they had taken of each other shortly before he died; him raising his fingers and her in that ridiculous dance pose.

On a beautiful warm day when she knew he would be home, Frances drove to Tori's little timber house on the shores of Lake Taupo. He had welcomed her inside but the mutual reserve that characterized the early days of their relationship had returned — and they were guarded, self-protective, suspicious. Love, desire and passion were kept at bay.

They'd sat together on the small beach where the waters of the great lake lapped around their toes. She'd told him what had happened on White Island, the terror, the heartbreak when Bob was killed. Tori had said little, displaying none of the anger or disgust that she had ignored his warnings and concern for her safety she had expected from him. Nor did he criticize her for showing disdain for Maori belief that the island was tapu, a forbidden place. Instead, he took her hand and held it to his mouth, kissed it and smiled at her tenderly. But nevertheless, their love seemed fractured.

A car had arrived while they were sitting there. Tori's children, Moana and Hemi, piled out and ran to join them, lively, funny and happy. Frances wasn't surprised when his ex-wife, Cheryl, followed them and sat proprietarily on Tori's other side.

After a while, Frances made her excuses to leave, hoping Tori would ask her to stay, but he didn't. They had talked on the phone before she left for Italy, each time promising they would see each other again soon. It never happened.

CHAPTER THIRTY-ONE

The volcano ahead spits brown and white clouds out of its crater, staining the deep-blue morning sky. Frances blinks in the pale sunlight, the wind blowing her hair back as she leans against the ship's rail.

Stromboli rises sharply out of the sea and as they sail closer she can see how the volcano completely dominates the island. Massive, with a jagged peak, the swelling mountain is nearly a kilometre high. Yet, like a rocky iceberg, most of it is below the waves, anchored deep into the ocean floor. Excitement ripples through her, fuelled by the sight of another magnificent volcano ready to explore.

The cold competes for her attention and she sniffs, hoping she hasn't caught a cold in the draughty cabin, as she pulls her jacket tight. Although sleep seemed to evade her, she must have finally succumbed because she had missed the sunrise.

'Signorina!' She starts, the man is so close behind her she can feel his hot breath. 'Coffee is ready in the lounge!' She relaxes and thanks the crewman who has already moved on to the sprinkling of other passengers on the deck.

Uneasiness has followed her upstairs like an unwanted companion, and she wonders whether she dreamt someone was trying to enter her cabin during the night. She shrugs it away and escapes the wind for the comfort of the lounge. The coffee is undrinkable and she abandons the cup on a table.

As Stromboli is the ship's first port of call, she gathers her luggage, stacks it in the reception area and returns to the deck.

The island is now clearly visible and she can just make out rows of white buildings close to the shore. High above, the expulsion of the muddy clouds from the brown crater continues every few minutes or so, accompanied by loud, short pops.

A small wooden fishing boat sails to their starboard. Two men, their long grey hair blowing in the wind, are hauling in a net dotted with the morning catch. There's a sense of timelessness about the fishermen, as though they had trawled these waters since the days of the ancient mariners, thousands of years earlier.

The ship toots, jarring and raw in the early morning, and soon its engines are churning. It slows, spins around and reverses alongside a long jetty. Frances scans a small group gathered at the end of it but can't see Riccardo.

Few of the people from the night before are around and she guesses they are still sleeping, bound for other islands. She clambers down the stairs to the car deck with the handful who are disembarking. They wear hats and scarves to ward off the cold and she resists staring too hard, subconsciously searching for her phantom stalker.

Stepping afoot Stromboli for the first time, Frances is struck by its bleak beauty. The air is so fresh after dust-filled Naples it courses into her lungs. There's an eerie silence. No traffic. No highways. Ahead, she makes out one small road, not much wider than a footpath, leading away from the tiny port.

She traipses to the end of the wharf and her eyes travel instantly from the broken row of houses and shops in front of her straight up to the summit. The pop popping of another round of mini eruptions shatters the peace.

'Frankie!' The woman's voice is unmistakable, her North American accent at once familiar. Frances looks around excitedly. There's only one person in the world who calls her that. Olivia Jackson is bearing down on her in a golf buggy, with Riccardo beside her.

'Ollie!' Frances shouts back. The two scientists share a past working on the tumultuous slopes of Mt St Helens. They had met at the university in nearby Seattle after Olivia travelled north from San Francisco, where she had researched earthquake risk.

She races along the track to the pier, her tightly curled black hair impervious to the wind. As she beeps and skids to a stop, Frances drops her bag and the two women run towards each other. As they hug, Frances towers over her friend whose slightly tubby appearance belies her extreme fitness. Riccardo is close behind.

'I'm overwhelmed,' Frances says. 'My two wicked friends in the same place!'

'Chances of bumping into each other here were rather good. It's not exactly New York City,' Riccardo says.

'Population around five hundred and no prizes for guessing we met at the observatory,' Olivia giggles.

Riccardo picks up her suitcase and slips his other arm around Frances. 'Missed you.' He kisses her cheek. 'But I haven't missed Naples for a second. I've got a new contract with the observatory here and I'm also helping an American/German scientific team attached to the observatory, the same as Ollie.'

Frances can see the oppressive burden that had weighed down Riccardo has lifted. She runs a finger gently under his left eye. 'All healed. You're looking a lot better, Ricky.'

'I am. But how has it been for you? I want to do more to help, but I don't know if I can now that I've been garrotted. Any more trouble?'

'No, not really,' she hesitates, recalling the shooting and the stalker. 'We all got caught up in the Christmas spirit. And by the way, Marcello sends his regards.'

He grins at her. 'Do I detect some amore in your complexion?' He pinches her cheeks and they laugh together.

'What's the joke? What am I missing out on?' Olivia leans into her.

'Gossip, and I know how you hate that!'

'Sit up front with Ollie,' Riccardo urges her, putting her luggage in the back of the buggy and propping himself next to it. 'Then you can talk all you like.'

Olivia accelerates hard and the buggy jumps into action. She points it up a rise and they drive quickly away from the harbour.

'You're staying with me,' Olivia says. 'Rustic, but close to the observatory. Mind you, everything here's close to everything else. The whole island's just a speck in the ocean.'

'You'll be more comfortable there,' Riccardo says. 'I'm back living with my elderly uncle and it's a bit squashed.'

The track divides into three, one heading back to the sea where a beach is swathed in jet-black sand, the other two heading higher.

Olivia turns sharply left and they drive up towards the centre of a village. She navigates though a maze of lanes so narrow Frances could touch the walls of the attached houses on both sides. Suddenly, she stops dead and they all lurch forward and Riccardo drops off the back.

'My God, Ollie, you're such a petrol foot!' Riccardo says affectionately.

'I think you've found your match,' Frances laughs.

'This is my stop. Make yourself comfortable and I'll be up to fetch you soon and show you around.' He disappears down a flight of gnarled steps in a gap between the houses. Olivia drives higher, through a little town square and past a line of shops and cafés, not yet opened for business. The buildings peter out and soon they reach a white-washed cottage sitting in a field studded haphazardly with cacti and olive trees.

'Home, sweet home.' Olivia pulls up in front. 'It belongs to the observatory and it's mine for as long as I'm working here.'

Frances stretches her arms and drinks in the air.

'What a view!' she exclaims looking down through sparse yellow and green vegetation to the village and on across the ocean that seems to go on forever, navy water blending with an azure sky. Just below is a small white church, the contrasting towers on either side telling a completely different story; one is a bell tower, the other a transmitter with satellite dishes.

'The observatory's up there.' Olivia points to a circular orange building on the hill behind them. 'It might be remote here but we're plugged into the universe!'

She pushes open the door of the cottage and Frances follows her into a small living room furnished simply with a wooden table, some hard dining chairs and a worn, floral-covered sofa. 'Your room's there. I'm afraid you've got the nun's bed.'

Frances takes her bags into a small room with a narrow bed and a row of photos of Stromboli exploding in an array of colour across one wall. She peers out of the window and sees the real mountain, rising straight up.

Olivia is pouring tea when she joins her at the table. 'It's been way too long, Frankie.'

Frances smiles at her friend. 'You haven't changed at all, still wonderfully cheerful. Has life been treating you well?'

'All the better since I arrived here. It's strange, but I feel more at home on this mound in the Mediterranean than I have anywhere.'

'It wouldn't have anything to do with Ricky, would it?'

Olivia grins and says nothing.

'I thought as much.' Frances throws a cushion at her. 'He's a good man. I hope it works for you both.'

'Talking of which?' Olivia leans across the table towards her. 'Whatever happened to your man Tori in New Zealand?'

'Ah. Not a very happy ending, if it was an ending.'

Olivia stares at her questioningly.

'I thought he was the love of my life. Maybe he was. Or is . . . But we unravelled. My work came between us and his cultural beliefs.'

'You're kidding!'

'No. It sounds weird, I know. And I've thought about it a lot, trying to wind back the clock to when it first became an issue. To tell you the truth, maybe we were never meant to be. Our worlds are so different.'

'So it's over?'

Frances sips her tea and pauses for a few seconds. 'Truly, I don't know.'

'What do you want?'

Frances shrugs her shoulders.

'Ricky said there's someone else . . .'

Frances laughs. 'No secrets around here. He means Marcello, his good friend. And we have become close.'

Olivia throws the cushion back at her.

'Hey, stop looking at me like that!' Frances jumps up and they throw the cushion back and forth, finally flopping together on the sofa. 'A girl's gotta have a bit of fun,' she jokes.

Olivia laughs. 'Just like the song. I agree.'

There's a tap on the door and Riccardo walks in. 'Ready to explore?'

Olivia groans. 'You two go on, I want to catch up on some sleep. I hate these early morning starts.'

Riccardo's motorbike rests outside the cottage, dusty but familiar. 'Hello, old friend.' Frances taps the back and climbs on. They ride a few minutes and pull up outside the observatory, where Riccardo beckons her to follow.

Inside the building the buzz of banks of monitoring equipment fills a silence. A woman sits alone in front of the seismographs in one room. 'The nightshift.'

'Impressive!' Frances gazes at the mass of machinery.

'Stromboli is under extra scrutiny after the eruption last year. It blasted all of the equipment out of the crater without warning. And there've been some dramatic discoveries. Scientists have come from everywhere — the north, the south and the internationals.'

'Sounds like the United Nations.'

Riccardo grimaces. 'Almost as much politics too, though not as sinister as Naples.'

She follows him over to a large picture window where he points south, towards the horizon.

'Sicily is that way. And Mt Etna. Sometimes you can see it.'

Frances stares far out to sea, sun glaring in her eyes. She shakes her head. 'I can't, but I can see the other islands.'

'Yes, you can see how the rest of the Aeolian Islands curve in a giant arc. What the research teams here have discovered is the source of a large earthquake zone. It extends beneath the islands and deep under the Tyrrhenian Sea.'

'Like the Ring of Fire in the Pacific?'

'Exactly. The new data shows there's a mammoth magma lake beneath the earth's crust under Stromboli. It's making us change our thinking. We're trying to find out whether the lakes of magma in this part of the world are more connected than we thought.'

'So if Stromboli coughs, Vesuvius sneezes?'

'That sort of thing.'

Frances hears footsteps and turns to see a tall grey-haired man approaching them. 'Here comes the boss,' Riccardo whispers.

The man's brown eyes are friendly and welcoming and immediately he puts his hand out to Frances.

'You must be Frances Nelson. I've been expecting you. I'm Giuseppe Nocella,' he says, shaking her hand firmly. 'Welcome to the Stromboli Observatory. We've been looking forward to you installing the new acoustic microphone system.'

'Me too, there's nothing like a new challenge,' she smiles. 'Who will I be working with?'

'I understand there have been some problems with our friend here.' He pats Riccardo's shoulder. 'But that's Neapolitan politics and we don't have to bother about that here. So if it suits you, I am happy for you to work together.'

'That sounds just fine,' she smiles.

Riccardo revs his bike and they head further up the mountain, bumping along a mule track until they can go no futher. He stops where the scrubby vegetation ends, merging with dark craggy rock stretching to the summit.

'There are two important things to remember if you want to survive on Stromboli. If there's an eruption, head towards the sea. If there's a tsunami, head up the mountain!'

'You're teasing!'

'No. It's true.'

He scrambles up a rise and calls to her. 'Follow me and I'll prove it.'

They trek over rough steep terrain until they come to a great gash on the mountain, where a huge black scar marks the volcano, a curtain of rock dropping sharply all the way down into the crashing waves.

'Look over there. Sciara del Fuoco.'

'The Slope of Fire? Isn't that where the lava flows into the sea?'

'Yes. There've been huge eruptions and lava flows here for thousands of years so this whole side of the volcano collapsed. A few years ago, the Sciara del Fuoco gave way again and the landslide under the sea was so forceful it triggered a tsunami. The waves caused massive damage on the island.'

Frances shields her eyes and stares at the steep flank. Overhead, she hears another small explosion from the crater and shortly afterwards some small boulders thunder down the slope. The wild landscape and unpredictable volcano remind her of White Island, yet unlike that godforsaken place, people live here defying the odds and dancing with fate every day of their lives.

'This is one crazy place to call home!'

'Yes, as my Uncle Gaetano would say, Stromboli e magica!'

'Magic? I suppose it is. But it drove your family away.'

'Three generations of my family. They left after the huge eruption in 1930 and never came back. They lost their houses, their crops and they couldn't survive. And it wasn't just Stromboli. All the Aeolian Islands emptied and thousands went to Melbourne. I was born in a little Italy on the other side of the world.'

'So you're a reverse immigrant?'

Riccardo chuckles. 'That's right. And you know, Frances, the first time I came here I was hooked. Immediately. The volcano, the island and the people — I feel like I'm in no-man's-land in Australia and Naples. But here, in Stromboli —'

'E magica!' Frances is laughing as another eruption punctures the sky. 'When can I see some lava flowing?'

'You'll see plenty when we climb to the summit.'

Frances sighs. 'Great. But I don't feel up to that today.'

'Don't worry, plenty of time. We're going to spoil you with a feast at my uncle's house. Since my aunt died he loves company and he's looking forward to meeting you.'

When Frances returns to the cottage, Olivia is asleep. After a sleepless night, fatigue is catching up with her too. She unpacks her bag and lies on her bed, intending to take a quick nap.

But hours have passed and the sun is high in the sky when she awakes. The house is silent. She takes a shower and hears the front door slam as she dries herself.

'Ah, the sleeping princess is awake,' Riccardo calls.

'The royal buggy is ready to drive you to lunch,' Olivia adds.

Frances emerges from the bathroom, wrapped in a towel, hair dripping. 'Give me five,' she laughs. 'I'm starving after that boat trip so I'll be quick.'

The steps leading down to his uncle's home dissect small terraced gardens on one side and the walls of the houses on the other. Rows of grapevines and plots of vegetables are neatly cultivated. The gate squeaks when Riccardo pushes it and the three of them step into a courtyard crowded with potted plants and small statues.

On the veranda of the house, an elderly man is asleep in a cane chair, his white hair peeping out from beneath a straw hat.

Meow! A startled tabby cat jumps off his lap.

'Uncle, sorry to wake you.'

He looks around disoriented for a second then breaks into a wide smile, revealing large uneven teeth. He stands up, tall and nimble for a man in his nineties. 'Gaetano Cocchia,' he says to Frances, his voice resonant. 'Welcome to Stromboli.'

'You two sit and talk,' Riccardo says. 'We'll bring lunch out here in the sun.'

Gaetano sinks back into his chair. His weathered, lined face is broken up by a wiry moustache and blue eyes that sparkle. Frances sits on a chair next to him and he reaches over and pats her knee. 'Bellissima!' He leans over to her conspiratorially. 'Would you like to learn the secret of Stromboli? He is our father, Iddu, the volcano of love. He has magical powers.'

'What do you mean, magical?'

The old man is staring at her intently. 'If I was a young man like Riccardo I would take you there now to show you. If you kiss someone at the top it is a kiss you will never forget. It is the kiss of fire!'

'And can you prove it?'

Gaetano smiles. 'Many times. Of course, my dear wife, we kissed there. And . . . well, I might have persuaded a few other young ladies to accompany me up the mountain in my time.'

'So it's not just the one kiss then?'

'As many as you can get!'

The two are laughing together when Riccardo and Olivia carry platters to an outdoor table.

'Up to your old mischief, uncle?' Riccardo teases. 'You have to watch him Frances.'

'I can see. The Stromboli magic, apparently.'

The aroma of freshly baked bread and fish sharpen their appetites.

'Catch of the day. Everything here is fresh, fresh, fresh,' Olivia says with relish.

'Grilled octopus with garlic, swordfish with capers from Lipari, tomatoes with fresh oregano. Enjoy!' Riccardo adds.

'And don't forget the wine,' adds Gaetano. 'You must try some of my wine.' Riccardo winks at Frances and fills her glass from a bottle of deep yellow wine. The taste is sickly sweet.

'Fantastic,' she fibs, as she toasts the old man.

When they finish lunch, Gaetano insists on showing Frances his garden and she follows him through the gate across to the terraced gardens. He stoops to pull out a few weeds then sits on a bench. 'Sit. Sit with me,' he says gently. 'All of this,' he says sweeping his arm in front of him, 'all of this was lost when I was a boy. Iddu, he took it, and nearly all of my family. My uncles and aunties, my brothers and sisters — they left forever. They went to Australia.'

'Why did you stay?'

'My parents wouldn't go and I didn't want to go with the others. I was born here. This is my home, no matter what happens.'

'Can you remember the big eruption?'

'Like yesterday. It was on a warm September morning in, in . . . I forget when exactly, but a long time ago.' Gaetano mutters under his breath then picks up the story again, his eyes blazing. 'Suddenly, there were two huge explosions, loud roars that shook the whole island. I looked up and saw flames coming from the volcano. Lots of rocks were falling. Big ones were crashing into houses and little ones were raining down on us like hail. My grandmother grabbed me by the hand and pulled me inside her house and we hid under the beds.'

'It must have been terrifying.'

'I was very afraid. Everything went dark. The sun disappeared and for hours ash and rocks fell and the island was burning. We stayed there all night, too scared to move and not knowing where the rest of our family was. The next morning all was quiet. When we came outside, nearly everything was destroyed. All the crops, many houses, the fishing boats, and worst of all, six people lay dead.'

'And still you stayed?'

'My brother, Riccardo's grandfather, tried for years to persuade me to join him in Melbourne, but I wouldn't leave. No, I had to stay. There were hard times with very little to eat, then slowly the island started to recover and I could grow things again.'

The winter sun lights a healthy row of corn near his feet. He kicks the dirt with his foot and turns to her, his eyes moist.

'You can see, Frances. Iddu gives back. He gives us food. Everything is growing again. And he gave me back Riccardo.'

CHAPTER THIRTY-TWO

Strong winds had battered Stromboli for days, ruling out any ascent of the volcano. The foul weather is a respite for Frances; time to fine-tune the complex system of the new generation of microphones she will plant on the wild summit, and a chance to discover the rhythms of the island.

A blustering northeasterly buffets her as she strolls along the black beach. The fishermen are back with their catch, a measly collection of crustaceans and beady-eyed silver fish reluctantly given up by the churning sea.

She's watched from afar these strong men of the sea take their chances on the waves twice a day, every day. Their boats are wedged into the sand and they chatter quietly among themselves, clearing the fish from the nets and folding them for the return bout in the afternoon.

'Shit, what a whopper!' The accent is Australian.

Frances spins around. One of the men, his long brown hair and beard obscuring any facial features, is trying to detach a giant red crab clinging to his net. She walks over and stands there watching, the creature seeming to know its struggle is to the death. The man speaks in Italian and for a moment Frances thinks she must have been mistaken.

'Gidday,' he says a minute or so later, glancing at her and continuing to fold the net. 'Where're ya from?'

'All over — England, the States, New Zealand. I'm working at the observatory.'

He laughs. 'Trying to tame old Iddu?'

As if on cue, the volcano belches out a puff of brown smoke.

'If not tame, at least try to predict what he might do next,' she says, surprising herself that she's accepted the local belief that Stromboli is male. 'Been fishing here long?'

'Coupla years.'

'You're not from here?'

He's won his round with the crab and plops it into a bucket. 'Fitzroy, Melbourne, Australian, born and bred. But this is where I want to die.'

The volcano belches again and Frances laughs.

'You must be a betting man!'

'Could say that.' He grins, his mouth barely visible beneath strands of his curling beard. 'I miss the horses and dog races in Melbourne, but that's about it. This is the home of my ancestors and this is where I belong.'

'You must know Riccardo Cocchia?'

'Yeah. We're all related some way or other. But he's a mountain cousin. I'm a man of the sea.'

The wind drops and sun streaking through the dense white cloud bathes a tiny rocky island just offshore in a brilliant light. He sees her gazing at it.

'Strombolicchio, the volcano's cap — blown off the top of Iddu and resting in the sea.'

Frances smiles. She's heard the legend before about the rock that was a part of the formation of the volcano hundreds of thousands of years earlier.

'Ulysses is smiling on us today,' he continues. 'He's my namesake. Story has it he stopped over here on his way home after the Trojan War. Don't know why he didn't stay.'

The wind picks up again and Frances grips the boat to catch her balance. I have to keep going. See you again, Ulysses.'

Frances picks her way further along the beach. Winter is already half over and she wonders what pile of earth Marcello is examining on the archaeological dig in Carthage. She checks her phone. No new messages. She smiles to herself, imagining him retrieving another ancient skeleton or cooking pot.

A rogue wave sweeps in and washes over her boots, the cold water leaking through to her skin. She scrambles off the beach to the track where a couple of smart hotels and restaurants nestle against a hill. Trudging back to the village, she hitches a ride on a buggy with one of the chefs on a buying trip. He insists on taking her further up the hill to the observatory and she gratefully accepts.

Her feet squelch as she walks into her office. She pulls off her boots and drenched socks and puts on a pair of running shoes. Maps of the summit are strewn across the desk and she resumes the task of plotting exactly where she will place the new microphones. Remnants of the old system lie in a pile in the corner — pieces of burnt electrical cord and broken microphones, destroyed by lightning.

Opening the carton she's brought from Naples, she checks everything is there: ten microphones, coils of lightning-resistant fibre optic cable, foam packaging and ten small transparent resin boxes.

'Hey Frankie, got your treasure trove there?'

'Oh good, glad you're here. Can you lend me a hand?'

'Sure thing.'

Frances picks up the carton and joins Olivia in the corridor. 'Come to the lab with me. I need some help to adjust the microphones before we take them up to the top.'

They lay the small sensors in a line on a bench in the lab. Frances takes one in her hand and inserts it into a machine, sets a timer for one minute and turns it on. A small tingling is the only sound it makes.

'We have to increase their sensitivity so they can detect the infrasonic acoustic waves and vibrations coming out of the crater. These little beauties can work at much lower frequencies than the old ones, so they're much more effective.'

'That's cool.'

'Can you test they're all working after they've been through the transducer?'

Olivia and Frances work together until all of the microphones have passed the test. 'I'm going to plant five on the summit. The rest are reserves. Just one more thing, I need to check the recording centre.'

'No problem. Follow me.' Olivia leads her to an adjacent laboratory where a bank of monitoring equipment winds around two walls. 'Here it is. You can see it's picking up the signals from the microphones on the flanks of the volcano. Your system will link into this one.'

'Perfect. Now all we need is to get up there.'

'The weather's clearing. Hopefully we can make the climb tomorrow.'

'It can't come soon enough for me — I'm anxious to install these as soon as possible.'

Morning brings clear skies and light breezes.

'Wake up! Today's the day!' Frances taps her friend's shoulder as she sleeps. As she waits for Ollie to get ready, she sends a text to Riccardo and seconds later receives one back.

ON MY WAY. R.

The three of them pile onto the buggy and drive as far along the track as possible before it is too narrow to navigate.

They put on yellow helmets and backpacks and start climbing. Clusters of wild flowers brush their legs as they approach the Sciara del Fuoco. The ground around them shakes with an explosion and hot red rocks tumble down the abyss and splash, sizzling into the sea.

'You wanted lava, Frances, you're going to get it! Let's go!' Riccardo is ebullient and his mood infects Frances and Olivia. They double their pace to keep up with him on the long winding path across an ancient solidified lava field, the terrain gradually changing from hard rock into soft fields of ash. Their legs sink into the loose black ash like deep heavy sand, testing their muscles. From time to time, they hear a dull roar as the mountain expires.

At last they reach the top, puffing loudly. Frances can feel the heat of the earth through her boots, as they crunch on piles of shining crystals. Her throat is dry and she tosses back half a bottle of water.

Clouds of sulphur drift over and they quickly put on facemasks. The crater yawns beneath them and Frances recognizes the bumpy terrain from her maps; a terrace of rock where they will work and three vents, glowing red like a demon's eyes. She'd read that it was the eye of Cyclops, the inspiration for the ancient myths about a one-eyed man-eating monster. Other sources said no, it was the vents in Etna's crater. Whichever one it was, Frances is mesmerized and turns to Olivia. 'Is this what hell looks like?'

'It had that effect on me the first time too — scared shitless!'

Scared shitless is about how Frances is feeling herself. Flashes of White Island return — Bob, lying dead on the shelf next to the boiling cauldron.

'You OK?' Riccardo asks.

She nods. It's an odd thing, fear. She'd talked about it with an actor friend who said he would stand on the edge of the stage petrified about walking on. But he was driven and once out in front of the crowd, experienced the ultimate highs. That's what kept him doing it; the highs made up for the lows, the panic attacks.

Poking around in the innards of volcanoes — this was the job she had chosen. But the fear she must overcome every time she ventured inside a crater was more confronting than a hostile audience, more physical, more visceral. It was fear of the worst fury that nature could hurl at you. God knows there had been close calls . . . she remembers when she was knocked out on the top of Mt Ruapehu. Frances drops a mental veil on those memories, telling herself this is not the time as she steps down.

Riccardo pulls on her jacket. 'Stay here a minute, we should see an explosion from one of the vents soon.' Almost before he finishes the sentence, a fountain of red molten rock shoots in the air, then drops.

'Classic Strombolian,' Riccardo says. 'A whole lot of gas and a trickle of lava. It's been doing this for at least two thousand years.'

And far worse than this! Uncle Gaetano's terrifying tales ring in her ears. Frances stares in awe, her eyes travelling from one extraordinary sight to another; the terrifying hot centre of the crater to the bird's eye view over the ocean. Smoke is curling into the sky from another far-off island in the volcanic chain.

'Are you ready to go?' he asks.

She hesitates for a moment then punches the air. 'Let's do it!'

With magma puffing up from the earth's core pouring out of every orifice, the three of them had planned their assault on the dangerous landscape to the last detail.

Their target — to bury five microphones at one-hundred-metre intervals in an L-shaped pattern four hundred metres from the explosive vents. From there, they could transmit the source of the acoustic waves and vibrations back to the observatory. The new equipment was so accurate, once installed, it would then be possible to isolate precisely which vent was exploding at any given time.

Inside the crater they edge slowly towards the terrace, Riccardo taking the lead. The explosions are roughly fifteen minutes apart and each of them understands that the job will take much longer than that. They will be in a perilous position and had agreed on rule number one: don't turn your back on the vents.

They reach the first position and immediately start their allotted tasks. Riccardo removes some markers and a one-hundred-metre coil from his pack. He plants the first marker in the crumbly tephra and, compass in hand, moves away to mark the second spot.

Olivia takes out rolls of fibre optic cables, connectors and a trowel. She digs a shallow trench in the loose surface and starts to bury the first line of cable.

Frances removes five small boxes from her backpack. She has already wrapped the microphones in foam to protect them from wind, heat and humidity and placed them inside the protective containers. She digs a small hole at the first marker, buries the first box and connects it to the cable.

Riccardo has started digging a trench back from the second marker and meets Olivia at the halfway point. He drags the rest of the cable along to the second point where Frances is already burying the next microphone. Their teamwork is exacting. So too is the work of the volcano. Like clockwork, the explosions continue. With each blast, the scientists face the vents, always calculating where the rocks might fall, ever ready to dive out of the way.

An hour passes and Frances signals to the others to rest. Her throat is burning and her eyes sting. They climb back to the lip of the crater like a trio of yellow-headed ants and sink to the ground, exhausted. Sweat coats their faces. They remove their masks and drink more water. Olivia produces three oranges and they devour the juice-laden fruit. The wind has picked up but not enough to deter them and they welcome the icy blasts.

'Last leg to go. Let's get it over with.' Frances' voice sounds feeble. The sulphur clouds drift over again, hot and suffocating. They don their masks and together head back into the crater. Working side by side they lay the last section of cable.

'Moment of truth,' Frances thinks, crossing her fingers. She sends a text back to the director at the observatory.

MISSION ACCOMPLISHED. PLEASE TEST AND ADVISE. FRANCES

She's staring at her phone waiting for the response when a low rumble shakes the ground. When she looks around Olivia is on her knees smoothing an uneven part of the trench. Riccardo is further away looking at the vent. The crater explodes so loudly, her head reverberates.

A pile of hot boulders rockets out of the volcano. Frances watches them rise, plateau, then fall, a massive rock as big as a car hurtling towards them. Frances hears herself screaming and drops to the ground as she watches the fiery comet, seemingly moving in slow motion.

'Ollie, look out!' Riccardo's voice echoes around the crater.

The rock is heading straight for her friend. Olivia's scream ricochets from wall to wall of the crater. The rock smashes, rolls and come to a halt.

As Frances watches the rock steaming she can't see Olivia or

Riccardo and for a few seconds, she can't move. The eruption has stopped. She scrambles to her feet and sees something blue trapped beneath the rock has caught fire. Her heart misses a beat when she recognizes Olivia's backpack.

'Frankie! Frankie!' Beyond the rock she sees Olivia on her hands and knees, calling, at the same time Riccardo is running towards her.

Frances keeps running, dodging hot pieces of the broken rock strewn all around. The three of them see each other safe and intact at the same time. Panting, Frances slows and walks more carefully now towards the others.

Her phone beeps and she stops to read the message.

CONGRATULATIONS! ALL WORKING. WHAT WAS THAT EXPLOSION IN THE SOUTHWEST VENT?

Frances starts to laugh, her fingers shaking so much she can't reply. What the hell? If the rock had dropped a few degrees closer, she wouldn't have any fingers.

Ahead she sees Riccardo pulling Olivia to her feet. And then they kiss, a long, slow kiss, right there in the crater of Stromboli, the kiss of fire that lasts forever.

CHAPTER THIRTY-THREE

As Camilla counts the names on the guest list, her pen hovers uncertainly over the last two — the British Ambassador and guest. Brian? She has tired of his antics; her opinion of him soured after catching him groping a young African girl at a cocktail party the other night. Silly old goat! Still, let him come and see her presiding.

'Avanti! Come in!' she responds to a knock on her office door.

Maria leads two porters carrying her precious credenza. 'Over there, near the window,' Camilla tells them.

Although her appointment as chancellor has yet to be officially announced, she's already feeling at home in Alfonso's old office. Poor Alfonso, who'd have thought? On the verge of retirement, then another stroke. She had sent flowers to the hospital from the university but his wife had rung to say he had lost his short-term memory, so not to bother visiting. That was no hardship! Conveniently, Umberto had ensured Camilla would be acting in the position until her investiture.

'The university is fortunate to have a new chancellor of the calibre of Professor Corsi . . .'

Camilla inserts the words 'and talent' after 'calibre'. She wants to have the media release just right in time for the announcement in the coming week.

'Professor, is there anything else before I take my lunch?'

'Yes, Maria, arrange to have these hung on the wall.' Camilla hands her the framed certificate of her doctorate and her university gold medal. 'Oh, and could you get a carpet specialist over here to have the Persian rug cleaned? And I need a list of Naples' best portrait artists. Make sure it includes some abstract painters. I want to choose one to paint Professor Galbatti's portrait to hang in the corridor with the former chancellors. That will be most appropriate, especially as he is so fond of contemporary art. That will be all for now.'

Camilla flicks through her diary. A late lunch with Umberto — she grimaces — the price she must pay. Five o'clock, appointment with Professor Luigi Paoli. All things considered, Alfonso's nephew had taken her elevation with grace. A true pragmatist that one. Clever too, and attractive. She had considered making him her assistant chancellor, but only for a moment. No point having him sniffing around. No, he could stay running the chemistry faculty, at least for as long as it suited her. She'd string him along a little, and tell him her plans later that day, over a drink.

She picks up the morning newspaper and flicks through. On page eight there is the story, buried at the bottom. It was inevitable there would be something about it in the media, in spite of efforts to muzzle the journalists. Since Umberto's mammoth construction had started in the Red Zone, there had been local protests. But nothing would be done to stop it and a story so far back in the paper? Well, that would do little harm.

She checks the story again. Good, her name is not mentioned, nor is the Progetto Vulcano report, just a local gripe about proper planning processes being ignored. Camilla snorts derisively. Half of Naples would have to be demolished if those rules were applied!

A file on the desk is marked 'Urgent'. Something she will have to deal with, now that Rome was involved. She picks it up and reads the latest correspondence. Pressure was mounting to reinstate Progetto Vulcano, with a group of American vulcanologists making noises about Vesuvius being the world's most dangerous volcano and complaining about inaction by local authorities. Camilla could almost smell her team members' names on that one. Universities in Pisa and Bologna were also poking their noses in, going on about academic freedom. She looks at a handful of articles about the volcano in international magazines — they could live with that. No, it was the threatened intervention by Parliament that was causing the most grief. The Neapolitan politicians were nervous about it, and it certainly hadn't helped that the toxic waste issue had now spiralled out of control.

She knew she had no political option — she would have to kickstart the project and reform the team. Most were still spread around Naples. She would ask Bartolo Caterno to head it up this time, although she would control him. Frances Nelson would soon be returning from Stromboli. And Riccardo Cocchia? Perhaps he had learnt his lesson. Camilla had been furious when she heard he had been badly beaten and had let Umberto know, reminding him he had promised there would be no violence. He brushed it aside, excusing it as his son Fabio getting carried away with his work.

Damn Umberto and his family! Greed — that was the problem. How much money does one person need? Camilla liked the answer attributed to a New York banker. How much money is enough? Just a little bit more. And that was the Dragorra family's flaw. They always wanted more, a lot more. If they stuck to cement and construction it would be easier to smooth the way. But garbage! That was everyone's problem. Fabio was becoming the family problem: a few too many photos of him in the paper and on the television news, spotted near too many violent crime scenes as protests against the dumping of toxic waste escalated. His alibis were wearing thin.

The last crime shocked even battle-scarred Camilla. She didn't know if Fabio was involved but nothing would surprise her. Il Sistema was changing its time-honoured rule of not murdering women. But after the shooting last month, that taboo was well and truly broken. She reaches for the newspaper coverage of the murder. The photo shows a woman's body lying in the middle of a car park, her stockinged legs sticking out from under a blood-splattered blanket. Two bullets in the nape of her neck, her skull shattered. She recognizes those shoes; she'd nearly splurged on an identical pair. Expensive shoes. Camilla shudders. The woman was only thirty-five, the wife of one of Umberto's competitors in the waste disposal business, from a well-known family. Retribution wouldn't be far away.

The sun is rising higher and filters into her new office. She glances out of the window at Vesuvius across the bay. The winter snow has melted leaving the volcano fresh and bare. Spring isn't far off. She picks up the invitation to the concert and smiles. The helpful man in the music shop had made sure she received one.

You are invited to the Spring Gala Concert of the City Orchestra, at the Teatro San Carlo. The soloist is Naples' new classical sensation, cellist Pasquale Mazzone.

She reads the invitation over and over, savouring each and every word until the alarm rings on her watch. She sighs and puts the invitation to one side. Time for lunch with Umberto.

CHAPTER THIRTY-FOUR

As the ship glides the last few hundred metres into the port of Naples, it creates a poignant sense of homecoming. Frances stands among bleary-eyed passengers on the deck, shaking off a vague nausea from the rough overnight crossing, and gazes into the city. The contrast between the cobalt skies of the Aeolian Islands and the city is startling. Though early, a grimy film already covers the metropolis, from the imposing ancient fortress of Castel Sant'Elmo high above the city to the faded elegant facades of the buildings behind the wharves.

The ship slides the last metres to its berth. She searches for Marcello's face among a small crowd gathered below but sees no sign of him. Gathering her luggage she bumps down the stairs with the other travellers to the car deck, where her phone beeps and she reads the new message. ONLY 2 MINS AWAY. X M

Although the weeks had flown since she had left Naples, she had missed Marcello deeply. They had communicated as often as they could — texts, phone calls and emails. But it was unsatisfying; two people caught up by necessity in situations that demanded so much of each of them. Sometimes it seemed better to let things be for a while and resist an addiction to a daily dose of small talk from a far-flung shore.

But when his four-wheel-drive pulls up at the end of the wharf, she realizes how much she is looking forward to seeing him and hurries, dragging her suitcase. He is soon out of the car, running towards her. It is the sweetest reunion, their lips meeting, soft and pliant.

'You look wonderful.' Marcello caresses her cheek. 'That island has been good to you.'

Frances laughs, recalling her close call on Stromboli's summit. 'What doesn't kill you makes you stronger.'

She regards Marcello closely, comparing his darkly tanned hand to her pale one. The desert winter sun has etched his smile lines deeper and his brown eyes have lost the troubled expression he wore before Christmas. 'The break has been kind to you too.'

'Come on, I'll take you home.' He wraps his arm around her waist and helps her into his vehicle.

The city is still half asleep, allowing them to drive quickly through the streets up towards Corso Vittorio Emanuele. The building is quiet, her neighbours not yet stirring, and they hurry up the stairs. Frances turns the key and the apartment door swings open, knocking a pile of letters pushed under the door. She scoops them up, notices one is from the university, but puts them aside, unwilling for them to intrude just yet. Inside it is cold and dark, shrouded with the mustiness that creeps into a space when people leave. She throws open the shutters and the room instantly fills with warm spring sunshine.

She turns to Marcello, who is waiting for her. On Stromboli she had wondered whether their time apart would have dulled their passion, but their lovemaking is urgent — skin on skin, tingling with love and desire. They stay in each other's arms afterwards, still and warm.

Frances hears the twin boys talking below and baby Luciana calling out.

'It does feel like home,' Frances says as they lie together listening to the building waking. 'Familiar sounds and voices, yet it also seems so temporary, and so odd without Ricky.'

'Will he come back?'

She had kept Marcello up to date on Riccardo's progress on Stromboli, both at the observatory and with Olivia.

'I doubt it. He seems to have found peace on the world's most volatile island.'

Marcello chuckles. 'As you said, the kiss of fire. That must be awesome!'

Frances kisses him hard and falls back laughing. 'Sort of like that but with lots of flames threatening to kill you at any moment.'

Marcello lies back on the bed and pulls her close. 'We may have some of our own fiery moments ahead. You've heard Camilla Corsi is now the chancellor?'

'Mmm. The news made it to Stromboli faster than rocks fly out of the crater. Remarkable. And to think Ricky thought she was doing Alfonso Galbatti's bidding.'

Frances remembers the mail and slides out of bed. She shuffles through the letters, disregards all but two and returns to the bedroom. One letter bears the university's monogram, the other, in a rich cream envelope, is hand-addressed to her. She rips open the first and pulls out a single-page letter.

'The letter's from Camilla. Would you believe it, they're starting up Progetto Vulcano again and she wants to meet me as soon as possible?'

Marcello raises an eyebrow. 'I wouldn't trust her.'

'I don't. But at least on the inside there's a chance of making a difference.'

'I hope you're right.' Marcello is sitting up, his face serious again. 'Everything all right?'

'I hope so. Nonno phoned me the other day and he wants to see me, which in itself is unusual. He never calls; he's more frightened of the telephone than Vesuvius.'

'Did he say why?'

'No. Just said I might be able to help with a problem. I want to go out this afternoon. Are you up to it? I'd love you to come and I know Nonno would like to see you again.'

'Sure. Give me a few hours to catch up and come and pick me up later.'

After Marcello has gone, Frances carefully opens the second envelope. An invitation to a gala concert at the Teatro San Carlo is inside. She traces her finger over Pasquale's name on the bottom, her heart leaping when she sees he is the soloist. The date of the concert is the following night.

Frances bolts out of the door and down the stairs. She knocks on Pasquale's door but there is no answer. She dashes back to her apartment and returns with a note, slipping it under his door.

She had intended to take a short nap but within minutes of closing her eyes, the rocking of the ship returns and sleep claims her. The ringing phone jolts her awake. Four hours have passed and Marcello is on his way over.

Frances showers and dresses hurriedly, her hair still damp as she runs downstairs.

'Hey, welcome home,' Pasquale cries as she almost knocks his cello out of his hand. 'Did you swim back?'

'Ooops. Sorry, Pasquale.' She pulls up short. 'Yeah, straight across the Tyrrhenian Sea just in time for your concert, I hope.'

He kisses her on both cheeks. 'I've been crossing my fingers you'd be here in time. I have saved you two seats. You will be sitting with Poppaea and Satore and his friend Rufus. He seems to be a fixture these days,' he smiles.

Pasquale's face is pale and his luminous eyes ringed with dark shadows. Frances takes one of his hands and squeezes it. 'I'm so proud of you. You've made it!'

'Not quite. Still have to get through my baptism of fire.'

'Nervous?'

'Yes. But I've been practising around the clock with my secret weapon.' He taps the cello and shrugs his shoulders.

'Take it easy, Pasquale. You'll be brilliant. And you can always give them a burst of "Santa Lucia"!'

He laughs and unlocks his door. 'At least that is one I don't have to practise.'

∞◊∞

Clouds of dust blow over their faces. From the brow of the hill where Raphaele Vattani grows his grapes, they can see directly into an excavation site the size of two city blocks. The arms of two cranes rise above them like a giant stick insect, lifting heavy steel girders as though they are matchsticks and lowering them into the massive hole. Acres of fertile sandy soil that nourished orchards and vineyards have disappeared, concreted over in a dull grey patchwork. A small army of construction workers swarms over the area, digging, climbing, drilling, shouting. A continuous low-pitched drone punctuated with loud clangs fills the air and assaults their senses.

'Scandalous! Barbarians!' Raphaele hisses. 'Can't you stop them, Marcello?'

Marcello puts his arm around his grandfather's shoulders, which seemed to have stooped in the months since Frances first met him. His old suit is more creased than she remembers and he has neglected to polish his shoes.

'I'm sorry, Nonno. I am as shocked as you. When did this start?'

'It started just before Christmas, when everyone was too busy to notice. We weren't told anything. Everything was quietly moved into place and then in the New Year, after you went away, all hell broke loose.' Raphaele picks a bunch of his own grapes and squeezes the green, hard fruit. 'So much lost!' He shakes the vines and dust flies into the air. 'Concrete! They're poisoning my grapes and now they want my land!'

'What do you mean?'

Raphaele pulls a piece of paper out of his pocket and shoves it into Marcello's hands. 'I'm not the only one to get one of these.'

'I don't believe this,' Marcello splutters. 'The local council wants Nonno's land to build a road to give better access to the largest and most prestigious shopping centre in southern Italy.'

Vesuvius rises beyond them, the solidified river of lava shining on its slopes. Frances is stunned by its proximity to the construction site, which has already gouged the landscape and pillaged its beauty. 'This is madness!' she exclaims. 'The buildings will be directly in the path of the volcano.'

'They tell me at the café there's also going to be a high school and a hospital next to the shopping centre,' Raphaele says.

'My God, they would put even their own children in danger! Who owns the land, Nonno?'

'It belonged to one of the old families but they were forced out, offered money by the government to leave so there would be fewer people in danger from the volcano. That's what they were told, and that their land was worthless, because it was in the Red Zone and could never be developed. They sold it for a song and moved away to live in the north.'

'Who bought it?'

'I only know what I hear. They say a woman from the city bought it, a stranger. She said it would stay as farmland.'

The old man kicks a mound of soil. 'Marcello, can't something be done?'

Marcello takes his arm and guides him back down the hill towards his cottage.

'I'll try, Nonno, but I don't hold out too much hope. You know how things happen around here.'

Frances sees them exchange glances, cynical and resigned. She follows them inside where Raphaele sinks exhausted into an old armchair. Marcello brings him a glass of wine and he sips it half-heartedly.

She curls up next to him, not knowing what to say. He doesn't seem to notice her and as he stares at the photo of his wife on the wall he mumbles to himself.

Marcello interrupts him. 'We have to go, Nonno. I'll find out what I can and come back soon.'

He goes to stand up but Marcello insists that he rests. As they leave he calls after them, 'I'm only glad Teresa's not alive to see this!'

CHAPTER THIRTY-FIVE

'Be careful, Marcello, and don't forget the concert tonight.' Frances worries as she watches him drive away. They had spent much of the night before poring over documents about development on danger zones around Vesuvius until the trail had run cold.

Angry and frustrated, he had resolved to spend the next day investigating the sale of the land, the government approvals for the development and the people behind the push to seize his grandfather's land.

Her appointment with Professor Corsi is imminent. She quickens her step, pushing through hundreds of students lingering outside cafés and Internet shops near the university.

Her heels clicking loudly on the mosaic floors leading to the chancellor's office, Frances has the hapless feeling of a condemned woman walking to her own execution. Entering a grand hallway adorned with gilt-framed classical paintings, she realizes they are portraits of past chancellors, the oldest wearing wigs, the more recent ones with little hair at all. Their expressions are uniformly grim, as if they don't like what they're seeing. Frances finds herself tip-toeing as though one of them might stretch a hand out and smack her for disturbing their peace. She reaches the door to the office and is just about to knock when a glimpse of something out of place compels her to turn back. She walks over to the last portrait, clearly new. The frame is the same as the others but the brilliant-coloured paint and abstract style sets it apart. She stares at it for a minute or so, not recognizing the face. There's a familiarity about its form; a sort of cross between Modigliani with the elongated head and neck, and Picasso, with its layers of distorted eyes, nose and mouth. Her eyes travel down to a tiny gold plaque at the bottom of the frame: *Professor Alfonso Galbatti*.

Frances giggles. Nothing in the portrait resembles the squatly built chancellor she knew. She remembers him flattering Camilla while lording it over the Progetto Vulcano team, then kindly rescuing her when she dropped her champagne glass on the precious palace carpet. As she also recalls his dismissive comments about the modern art exhibition, it becomes suddenly clear that this is a legacy he would have loathed.

When Frances knocks on the door a woman opens it and ushers her inside. 'Wait here, Chancellor Corsi will see you soon.' Her expression is severe as she indicates a row of plushly upholstered chairs in the waiting room.

Frances picks up one of the magazines arranged tidily on an elegant coffee table. She is about to start reading when the woman returns. 'Please come this way, Signorina Nelson.'

She follows her into a capacious office, richly furnished with highly polished antiques. Chancellor Corsi is sitting behind a large desk. To one side of her, a vase of large red roses and silver-framed photos rest on a carved dresser. Behind her the large picture windows allow a perfect view of Vesuvius, glimmering beneath an unusually clear sky.

'Ah Frances, come and sit down. Welcome back to Naples.' Camilla beckons her over, her voice warmer than Frances had expected.

'Thank you, chancellor. Congratulations on your appointment.'

She waves her hand in a faint attempt at modesty then seems to reconsider. 'You would have enjoyed my investiture if you hadn't been so busy on Stromboli. All the city's most important people came. Have a look at the photos if you like. Over there.'

Frances feels obliged and walks over to the dresser. The largest photo shows Camilla wearing a plunging black dress partially covered by an ermine-edged purple velvet academic gown and a thick gold chain of medallions. In the other photographs she is posing with a variety of people, some of whom Frances recognizes: the British Ambassador, the President of Campania and Umberto Dragorra. A particularly handsome man is holding her arm in a photo placed in the middle.

'I'm sorry I missed it,' Frances says. 'Was Professor Galbatti there?'

'Sadly no, he is still recovering from a debilitating stroke, poor man. He was represented by his nephew, Professor Luigi Paoli. He's in one of the photos with me. I really miss Alfonso, but fortunately, I have a daily reminder of him now we have his official portrait in place. Did you happen to see it outside?'

'I did, it's very different to the others. Does he like it?' Frances strains to keep a straight face and has a vision of a portrait of Camilla hanging there in years to come. The Mona Lisa in a velvet cloak springs to mind, with that same unreadable expression.

Camilla clears her throat and sips a glass of water. 'He hasn't seen it. But I'm sure he would. He is a great connoisseur of avant-garde art.'

She shuffles some files on her desk and beckons Frances back as the woman returns with a tray. She places it on the desk. 'Coffee?'

'Oh, just pour it, Maria, then leave us.'

Camilla spoons some sugar into her coffee and stirs it vigorously. 'Have a pastry. Sfogliatella, fresh this morning from my favourite baker.'

Frances crunches into the seashell-shaped pastry and a rich, spicy ricotta cheese fills her mouth, aware that Camilla, eating daintily and frequently dabbing her chin with a linen serviette, is scrutinizing her. She's at pains not to drop a single crumb.

'Buono, yes?'

'Yes, very good,' she answers in a muffled voice.

'But now it is time to talk.' Camilla leans back in her enormous leather chair and swivels towards the window. The sun shines on her face, emphasizing a sleek new haircut and red highlights through her black hair. 'Vesuvius is so beautiful.' She swings back to look at Frances. 'But like everything beautiful there is a flipside, a dark side. And Vesuvius has the darkest side of all, as the people of Naples have learnt only too well over thousands of years.'

Frances is wondering where Camilla is leading her, what game she is playing.

She leans across the desk and stares directly at Frances. 'I want Progetto Vulcano back in business and I hope you will be part of it.'

Marcello's grandfather's devastated face flashes in her mind. 'It depends on what my role will be. I was very unhappy about the treatment of Riccardo Cocchia and I'm concerned that we scientists will not be able to work independently.'

An angry twitch contorts one side of Camilla's mouth. She says nothing for a few seconds then sips from her glass again. 'Of course you can be independent. And maybe Signor Cocchia can rejoin the team, although it might be mutually convenient if he makes his contribution from Stromboli. I understand he has expanded his personal interests there. Isn't that so?'

Frances nods, surprised by her knowledge.

'You might be right. But my concern is about the development going on around the Red Zone and along the coastline of Campi Flegrei. We believe it is madness . . .'

'Frances,' Camilla interrupts in a controlled voice. 'Vulcanology might be a science, but it is an inexact science. My responsibility is to find the middle ground between an extreme view that would see all commercial development and activity around this city cease and a more reasoned approach. While we clearly have to respect the unpredictability of Vesuvius and Campi Flegrei, we still have to accommodate the needs of the three million people who live here. It's the art of the possible, my dear.'

'But we wouldn't want another Pompeii.'

'Quite, but you must remember that it's very unwise to make too many waves in this city.' She stands and walks over to Frances, an invitation in her hand.

'Are you going to the spring gala concert tonight? I am looking forward to hearing your friend, Pasquale Mazzone, play again.'

'Yes, I am. And you know he has his new cello? An anonymous donor paid a considerable amount of money for it. He's very grateful.'

Camilla smiles. 'A very deserving young musician, don't you think?'

Pasquale has already left for the dress rehearsal at the theatre by the time Frances returns home but he has pushed an envelope with tickets under her door. She phones Marcello but there's no answer. As evening falls, she still hasn't heard from him and prepares to go to the concert alone, texting him a message to meet at the theatre. Her mood swings between anxiety and annoyance at his failure to call.

Frances chooses a well-cut female version of a black tuxedo with a silver top beneath, another buy she couldn't resist from Via Toledo. She brushes her hair up and twists it into a knot, fastening it with a silver clip. Her high stilettos squeeze her toes but she likes the look and decides the discomfort is worth it.

Her taxi pulls up behind a line of others outside the Teatro San Carlo. The building is spotlit and a red carpet spills down the steps and onto the pavement. A glamorous crowd of Neapolitans crams the entry, chatting and laughing. Frances climbs the stairs and searches for the box office.

'Frances! Darling, you look marvellous!' Satore rushes over, closely followed by Rufus and Poppaea.

'Thank you, Satore. You all look wonderful. Is that a new earring?'

'An emerald, darling, as real as your green eyes.'

Poppaea embraces her. Her face is glowing, her blonde hair strikingly curled and her eyes complemented by a deep-blue evening dress. For once, she looks relaxed and happy.

'I'm really quite nervous. I hope Pasquale does well,' she whispers to Frances.

A loud bell rings and ushers start to move the crowd from the foyer. Frances rings Marcello again but there is no answer. She represses a rising sense of panic and sends him another text, telling him his ticket will be in the box office. She leaves it there in an envelope marked with his name and joins the flow of people into the theatre.

In contrast with the rather austere exterior, the inside of theatre is so sumptuous it almost takes her breath away. Everything is red and gold, from the carpet, up the six levels of balconies, to the brilliant chandeliers.

The four of them find their seats a few rows from the front, where the orchestra's larger instruments — double basses, harps and percussion — are already placed around the stage. The theatre fills quickly and Frances looks around for Camilla. A few minutes later she walks down the aisle, arm in arm with the handsome man in the photo. She is wearing a white fur over a white floor-length dress and heads turn as she takes her seat in the front row.

The lights dim and the musicians file onto the stage, the men in tuxedos and the women in black evening dresses or pants. The four of them are straining to see Pasquale, who is one of the last to walk on, taller than the others, his eyes seeming to search the audience. They clap loudly and he appears to be looking right at them.

Satore squeezes Frances' arm. 'Not a bad debut for a boy from Caserta.'

The musicians start tuning their instruments then stop and stand as the conductor, a woman in her early thirties, walks to the podium and bows deeply to the audience. Frances notes she is wearing impossibly high stilettos. Pasquale had told Frances the conductor was a tough taskmaster and an up-and-coming star, specializing in Bach. But she had warmed to him and chose him to join the much more experienced soloists.

She flicks her long red hair, turns to the orchestra, raises her baton and the music starts. Two bars in and the audience erupts in wild applause and whistling. Frances nudges Satore. 'What's going on?'

'Neapolitans love Rossini. He composed many of his operas in this theatre, including *William Tell*. The overture is a favourite.'

The clapping subsides and Frances can hear Pasquale and four other cellists playing several slow passages, then the tempo suddenly quickens and the entire orchestra is playing furiously. The sound prompts more whistling and calling from the audience. There's another lull as the English horn comes to the fore, doleful and haunting. The conductor raises the baton again and brings in all the musicians for the finale, trumpets, horns and percussion filling every crevice of the theatre. As the last notes sound, the audience clap and shout and cheer.

'It's a nightmare when the audience hates the performance,' Poppaea says. 'Then they boo and hiss.'

Frances shrinks inside. Please don't let that happen to Pasquale.

Bach dominates the middle part of the programme and Frances recognizes the music Pasquale had played laboriously over many months in the apartment. Here it all comes alive, boosted by the opulence of the theatre, its pitch-perfect acoustics and a stageful of masterful musicians.

'Finally tonight, I would like to introduce you to a young man who is making his solo debut.' The conductor has turned to the audience and there's a hush in the crowd.

'He is a true son of Naples, with a brilliant future ahead of him. Please welcome cellist Pasquale Mazzone, who will be performing 'The Swan', the thirteenth movement of *The Carnival of the Animals* by Camille Saint-Saëns.'

Applause fills the theatre once more and as it fades, two pianos start playing the first few bars. Poppaea has linked her arm in Frances' and she can feel her breathing faster as the first notes of Pasquale's cello soar and swim through the theatre. No one makes a sound as Pasquale becomes one with his magnificent cello, its red hue shining under the stage lights.

Frances glances at Satore and sees his eyes are moist. She closes her eyes and remembers the first time she heard him playing 'The Swan' in the small apartment. The music sweeps her up, and again she pictures a perfect white swan, drifting in a flowing stream, and again she hears a tremendous sadness in the notes, a danger to the swan.

She opens her eyes again. Pasquale's eyes are glued to the instrument and he seems to be performing effortlessly. He plays the final notes and the last bars tinkle from the pianos.

For a few seconds, the auditorium is utterly silent. Then there is an explosion of applause, the audience on its feet, cheering. 'Bravo. Bravo, Pasquale!'

The conductor raises her hand and urges him to stand. He walks to the front of the stage and bows deeply. As he does, Frances sees he is sweating profusely and his face is wet and pale.

The clapping continues. Pasquale bows again. Then he collapses.

CHAPTER THIRTY-SIX

Pasquale wakes up in the dark and looks around, for a minute confused about where he is. His dreams had been vivid and stay with him as he sits up in the strange bed. He tries to grab on to them. He is a child again, running around his father with Poppaea chasing him. The images fade and he can't get them back again however hard he tries. His head is spinning and he is sweating. It's coming back. He's fallen asleep at Satore's place after hours and hours of practice. Too tired to go home, he accepted the invitation to stay for the last few hours until dawn.

Dawn. He walks to the window and pushes open the shutter. Not quite here yet. A shadowy pall covers the rows of terraced apartments opposite and a garbage truck drives by, its lights flashing.

So thirsty. He grips his throat and stumbles out of the bedroom into the tiny lounge where he finds the light and creeps past Satore's bedroom into the kitchen.

Blast! The tap creaks like an old brass bed as he fills a glass of water, echoing through the apartment. He swallows and almost gags, but at least it slakes his thirst, for now. He walks back into the lounge, turns the light off again and slumps into an armchair.

Tonight is his night of nights. Before the next dawn, it will all be over, the debut he has craved will be completed. How will the audience react? Please, not booing or slow clapping. That would kill him.

Why is he so exhausted? Months of tension and endless hours of playing in the build-up to this day could be the reason, but he feels constantly drained, scarely able to drag himself from one place to the next. And now he can't stomach food he once wolfed down. No one else seems to have noticed, so his playing must be all right. The conductor doesn't stand on ceremony — she would tell him if his performance was below par. He rubs the palms of his hands. They ache. So do his shoulders, knees, elbows. Shit, why now?

He returns to the bed to sleep again but the sheets are so tangled he has to shake them out and remake it before he can climb between them and close his eyes. But he cannot sleep. He starts to play each piece of the concert music note by note in his head. Rossini, Bach, Saint-Saëns. Over and over, until he feels giddy, then worse, then nothing.

He sits up again. Sun is streaming through the window. 'Hey, sleepy head. You're awake at last!'

Satore is standing there, a cup of coffee in his hand. If only he knew.

'Thanks,' he mumbles, sipping the sickly sweet brew.

'Come on, into the shower, now. You look as if you've been shipwrecked.'

Pasquale turns the tap on hard and waits until the water is as hot as he can stand it. It prickles his skin and soaks into his sore joints. He could stay here for hours. He stoops to wash his thick hair and lets the lather pour down his face.

Satore has brought him his best towel, large and white and fluffy.

He mops himself dry, cursing when he sees the deep bruising on his arms and legs, then wraps the towel around himself and walks into the lounge.

'Omelette and orange juice. I've made you some breakfast. You'll need to be strong for tonight.'

Pasquale dresses and sits with Satore at the table. He skipped dinner the night before, yet he is not hungry. He makes himself eat then stands to leave, cello at the ready.

'Don't worry about any more practising, you're already playing brilliantly. Rest up and I'll see you at the theatre later,' Satore says, embracing him.

The bus arrives and soon he is on Corso Vittorio Emanuele. Trailing wearily through the courtyard, he lifts his cello case and struggles up the stairs.

He hears her footsteps first then Frances Nelson flies down the stairs and nearly knocks him over. How he envies her! So well and fit! He's glad she's coming tonight.

Must rest. He sinks gratefully into his own bed and almost immediately falls into a deep, dreamless sleep.

The alarm on his phone wakes him at four. He showers again and dresses carefully. His suit is freshly cleaned and pressed and Poppaea has bought him a crisp new white shirt and bowtie. He adds his fedora for effect and looks in the mirror — then again, maybe not. He tosses it onto the sofa, picks up his cello and heads for the theatre. Sharing the backseat of a taxi with a cello is becoming something of a habit. He smiles, never believing a musical instrument would constitute his most regular date.

He decides to treat himself and wanders across to the Café Gambrinus, where he takes one of the favoured outdoor tables and orders a cappuccino and a cannolo. The late sun warms him and for the first time that day he relaxes. The waiter places the steaming hot coffee and tube-shaped pastry oozing mascarpone and pistachio nuts and he enjoys them both. Across the way he sees the Teatro San Carlo, where his dream is about to be realized. He can't help himself. He salutes the statue of the woman on the roof of the theatre. By now other musicians are streaming towards the stage door and he joins them, an insider, no longer knocking on an unanswered door.

The first concert of the season has all of them buzzing. Most of the musicians are permanently with the orchestra but he learns there are always a few ring-ins, visitors from Bologna or Barcelona or Basel or the like. The German conductor has imported a few from north of the border and yet she still gave him the tap on the shoulder. Heaven knows why! He just hopes he is worthy. It had happened so quickly. She had been listening to him practising the Bach suites and afterwards asked him what was his favourite piece.

'The Swan' was the first thing that came into his head. It was his lucky piece.

'Five minutes, everyone!' The last call has come quickly. He lines up at the back of the stage with the other cellists and suddenly the applause is starting and he's walking onto the stage. The lights glare in his eyes and he can't see the audience. He knows Poppaea and the others are out there. He thinks of his father for a few moments and sees his sad face, then thinks of his mother, but her face eludes him.

The conductor prompts them. *The William Tell Overture* is so fast, it's over in a flash. Then the Bach, one piece after another. And then . . .

He hears his name, the clapping, the shouting. Is that Satore? The pianos start. He grips the cello, ever supple and compliant, raises his bow, counts the bars and launches himself. The music flows. He gives everything, every ounce of his being. He maintains the intensity to the very last note, as if he is wringing his own soul.

The applause is deafening, louder than the loathsome experience of playing next to the percussion section in the orchestra pit. The conductor is calling him over. He walks towards her and faces the audience and bows. As he does he sees faces behind the footlights, smiling and cheering, and hands clapping. He feels hot and giddy, but he knows he must acknowledge them. He bows again and then everything goes black.

He feels himself falling into a hole. Has he gone blind? First he hears nothing. Then he has the strangest sensation. A woman is cradling him in her arms.

'This is my son. This is my son,' she says.

'Pasquale! Pasquale!' The woman is calling his name, her voice anguished.

He opens his eyes and looks into the face of a stranger.

A small crowd is gathered around him on the stage where he is lying. The conductor is there, some of the musicians, Poppaea, Frances and Satore.

And this woman in a white dress. She helps him to sit up and he sees the curtain has closed.

'It's OK, Pasquale,' Poppaea says. 'You fainted.'

He looks at the woman. She's talking to him but her words confound him. 'I am your mother. My name is Camilla Corsi.'

He cannot speak and dizziness overwhelms him again. The last thing he hears is a siren as he sinks into the woman's arms and into blackness.

CHAPTER THIRTY-SEVEN

Pasquale bows then keeps on falling until he is lying flat on the stage, motionless. As one, Frances, Poppae and Satore leap to their feet and struggle to get out of the middle of their row, past the crush of people.

The conductor and other cello players rush to help the fallen musician. Ahead, Frances sees Camilla bolting up the stairs, holding her gown high. She looks distraught, tears streaming down her perfectly made-up face. The curtain falls before they reach the stage and the manager emerges to thank the audience and bid them goodnight.

'Let us up! That's my brother!' Poppaea is screaming and Satore holds her arm as the manager lifts the curtain aside for them. She freezes when she sees Camilla holding Pasquale in her arms.

She's rocking him and weeping. 'My baby. My baby.'

'Who are you? What are you doing?' Poppaea stands beside her, stunned.

Camilla looks at her. 'I am his mother.'

'You're crazy. Let go of him, he's my brother!'

Poppaea has dropped to the floor and is stroking Pasquale's brow.

'I promise you, I am his mother.'

'We had the same mother and she is dead.'

'Pasquale was my baby. Your mother adopted him.'

Frances and Satore stand there, unsure whether to intervene. 'I'll check the ambulance is coming,' Satore says and dashes away.

Poppaea is shaking now, half in shock and half in anger.

Pasquale's hands move and he groans. He opens his eyes wide. Both women talk to him but he doesn't seem to hear. Seconds later he drops back into unconsciousness.

'Camilla,' Frances says softly. 'It's time to let his sister take over. Let him rest.'

Poppaea throws her a grateful glance. Camilla nods and eases his head onto a cushion and stands up. She spreads her white fur over him as Poppaea continues to stroke his brow.

Camilla is quivering and Frances puts her arm around her. She feels strange comforting a woman who, just a day earlier, seemed invincible.

'It was the eyes. I knew as soon as I saw him,' Camilla tells her. 'Someone else in my life had those cloudy green-blue eyes — his father. I was so young when I had him, I had to adopt Pasquale out when he was just a few days old. I have spent my life putting him out of my mind.' She grips Frances' hand. 'Now I want nothing more than to have my son back.'

'So it was you who paid for the cello?'

'Of course.'

Satore is back, leading three paramedics. They surround Pasquale, two men and a woman in blue uniforms and rubber gloves, checking his pulse and blood pressure and putting an oxygen mask on him. They remove the fur and put it on the floor. All colour has drained from his face, his damp hair is matted and, dressed in his evening suit, his thin, still body looks like a shop mannequin.

'Will he be all right?' Poppaea asks.

'We'll take him to hospital. It's too early to know what the problem is.'

They lift him onto a stretcher. Many of the musicians are lingering still, chatting together in concerned circles. They step aside as the paramedics wheel him across the stage.

'I'm going with him.' Poppaea moves after them.

'I want to come too,' Camilla adds.

'I'm afraid there is only room for one, so immediate family only,' one of the paramedics replies.

Frances pulls Camilla back. 'Not now. Let Poppaea go. You will be able to see him later.'

Camilla relents, slumping like a ragdoll. As Frances helps her put her fur coat on, the man she brought to the concert walks across the stage to them.

'Ah, Luigi. Can you take me home?'

Without a word, he takes her arm and escorts her away.

Frances walks back down into the rapidly emptying theatre, where the opulence now seems clownish and mocking. She looks around for Satore and Rufus but they have disappeared. A scattering of patrons are milling around the foyer, subdued after the unexpected finale. Outside, Frances hurries to a taxi rank. The night has cooled and she shivers as she waits on the kerb with a handful of others. For the twentieth time, she checks her phone but there is no message from Marcello. She punches his number and again it rings out.

Soon her taxi is whisking her home. Worry plagues her, Marcello's disappearance and Pasquale's illness vying for her attention. She pays the cab and alights on the pavement. The blonde-wigged prostitute is standing beneath the lamppost, cigarette glowing as usual. But as Frances walks the last few metres, the woman notices her and strides quickly away in the opposite direction.

Frances looks down the lane to the courtyard. The lights are on and everything is quiet. Her own footsteps sound to her like a banging drum as she heads to her apartment building and fumbles in her bag for her keys.

Suddenly, she feels herself pushed and pulled. Someone grabs her from behind, one arm around her neck, the other her waist. A second person gags her mouth. She chokes, staring ahead, unable to speak or see her assailants.

A cold steel instrument is digging into the nape of her neck. Terrified and helpless she doesn't struggle. She stares ahead towards the building, hoping and praying someone will come out.

'Signorina Nelson,' the man behind her hisses, his voice guttural and young. 'Don't go poking your nose where it's not wanted, or you'll end up like your boyfriend. This is your last warning, bitch.'

Another band is wrapped around her eyes and all is now darkness.

One of the men presses something into her hand and then releases her. She stands there shaking, not knowing if they are still there, the object falling from her frozen fingers. All is silent. Somehow she finds the courage to pull off her blindfold and spins around. Not a soul is there. She removes the gag and coughs and splutters, trying not to vomit as she stoops to pick up what she had dropped. The cream envelope is familiar. She turns it over and sees Marcello's name on it. Inside is the ticket she had left for him at the box office.

Frances unlocks the door and stumbles up the stairs. She taps on the Foglianos' door. Their apartment is in darkness. She taps again. A minute or so later she hears soft footsteps behind the door.

'Who is it?' Peppe asks quietly.

'Frances. I'm sorry. I need your help.'

The key turns in the lock and as he opens the door, he pulls her inside.

'Peppe, I've been attacked! And I think Marcello is kidnapped, or he may be dead.'

He takes her arm and leads her into the lounge room.

'What's wrong?' Wearing her dressing gown, Laura comes out of her bedroom, rubbing her eyes.

'Outside, just now, I was grabbed from behind and gagged. Two men threatened me. They've got Marcello.'

'Shall we call the police, Peppe?' Laura asks.

He shakes his head. Not long ago, such a reaction would have stunned Frances, but by now the Neapolitan way is all too familiar. Peppe is calm. He sits closely next to Frances on the sofa. 'What did they say?'

'They warned me not to poke my nose into things. I guess they mean about the developments we've been trying to stop around Vesuvius and Campi Flegrei. Marcello went looking for information today and . . .'

Laura passes her a glass of grappa. 'Here, cara, drink this.'

The strong liquor still tastes vile but calms her.

'You should stay here,' Peppe says. 'Try to sleep. There's nothing you can do tonight. Let me think about who I can ask for help.'

Frances sips the grappa and turns to them. 'There's something else. Pasquale.'

'I forgot, the concert. How was —' Laura interrupts but stops when she sees the distress on Frances' face.

'He was brilliant, but afterwards he collapsed on the stage. He's in hospital. No one knows what is wrong.'

Peppe is bringing blankets out to the sofa when Frances stops him. 'I'll be fine. I'd rather go home. But maybe you can come upstairs with me to check.'

Locked securely inside her apartment, Frances struggles to sleep. Morning seems an eternity away. She twists and turns, remembering the first warning, the drawing of a man hanging and imagines the worst.

She wakes to the sound of a revving engine. The grinding and accelerating rises from the courtyard, scraping on her nerves like chalk on a blackboard. She stays lying in bed, staring at the window. Her phone rings and she snatches it off the bedside table.

'Frances. It's Poppaea. I'm at the hospital. Can you come?' Her voice is girlish and frightened.

'Yes. Is Pasquale conscious?'

'No. He's drifting in and out of consciousness. I still don't know what's wrong with him. I've been here all night.'

'I'll be there as soon as I can.'

The owner of the car is still revving and a companion's head is under the bonnet when Frances runs down the stairs. As she climbs onto her motorbike the postman arrives waving a package at her. She takes it and sees her name written in Marcello's handwriting. She rips it open. Inside there are documents with a note scrawled on the front. '*Thought it best to post these. Dynamite! See you at the concert tonight. XXX M*'

She flips through the papers. Marcello has highlighted some pages and names. One is a map of a new plan for the Red Zone, one they had never seen. The land near his grandfather's has been rezoned as safe for development, even though it is closer to the volcano. At the bottom of the page is the date and a signature. *Camilla Corsi.*

The next page is a title deed. The new owner of the land is highlighted in pink: *Rosanna Dragorra*. The land sale went through a week before the rezoning, for one hundred thousand euro. Attached to it is a newspaper clipping: a photo and story in the local paper when the university appointed its new chairman. The caption reads: *Umberto Dragorra with his wife, Rosanna, at the swearing in of the new university board.* Beneath that is a development consent for the construction of the shopping centre and the school granted to Bon Accordo Constructions, naming its principals as Umberto and Fabio Dragorra. It is signed by Antonio Pane, the government minister spotted with Camilla and Dragorra at the British Ambassador's dinner, a week after the rezoning. The last page is a bank valuation of the land after the development consent. Two million euro.

Dynamite, all right! Frances climbs back off her bike and runs up to the Fogliano apartment. She shows the documents to Peppe and Laura.

Peppe lets out a long, slow whistle. He reads each page carefully, passes them to Laura and reads them again. He looks at Frances, his face serious.

'If anyone stands between Il Sistema and a pile of money, they are courting trouble. This amounts to a lot of money and a helluva lot of trouble.'

'Marcello?'

'I don't know. I just don't know. I'll ask around, see if anyone's heard anything.'

Frances nods slowly, unsure of where else to turn. 'Poppaea's asked me to go the hospital. Pasquale isn't fully conscious yet,' she says heading for the door. 'But at least we know he is alive.'

As Frances is pulling up outside the hospital, her phone rings inside her jacket. She stops her bike and grapples for it but misses the call.

She fumbles frantically with the phone. Riccardo's name appears and she calls his number.

'How was the concert?' He's cheerful, optimistic, stuck in yesterday.

'Ricky. Some bad things have happened.' Trying to say it out loud, Frances chokes on the words. She quickly tells him about Pasquale and Camilla Corsi's bombshell, then focuses on Marcello, describing his discoveries and his disappearance. 'I think he's been kidnapped, like you were. He's too close to the truth.'

'Have you been to the police?' Even before he's said the words he starts to retract. 'No. No point.' He's silent for a few seconds. 'Frances, maybe Camilla's the answer. She must know something. Pasquale is clearly her weak point, and she knows you're close to him. You might have to throw yourself on her mercy. But be careful, and don't go anywhere alone. Stay close to other people.'

An ambulance siren blares behind her and she pulls her motorbike quickly away. She follows it to the emergency entrance, guessing this is where Pasquale was admitted the previous night. She drives by and parks her bike near the main entrance.

Her boots squeak on the waxed floors of the hospital's reception area. An orderly chaos prevails as the sick are sorted and categorized and their families and visitors are tolerated. 'Mazzone? Are you related?' the woman at the front desk asks, looking at a computer screen.

'No. But his sister rang me and asked me to come. My name's Frances Nelson.'

She picks up a phone. 'Pasquale Mazzone. No visitors, right?' She pauses. 'I see. I see. OK.' She looks over her glasses to Frances. 'He's on the sixth floor, in room 56.'

Frances shares the elevator with two orderlies and a man on a trolley bed. His skin is taut and as grey as his hair. Blue veins snake through his arms, down through his hands. Frances looks away guiltily, like a voyeur, and concentrates on the lights marking each floor. When the man is wheeled out on the fourth, she catches her reflection in the mirror, grey and drawn with dark circles around her eyes. A small bell pings and she exits on the sixth floor. An antiseptic odour pervades. She's in no hurry, sensing there will be little good news waiting for her in room 56.

She finds the room easily, the number at the centre of a white door with a window, which she peeps through. Pasquale is the sole patient. He lies on a raised bed, his head bandaged, a mask over his mouth, tubes attached to both arms. Poppaea sits alongside, head bowed, still in her evening gown. When Frances opens the door she looks up, her hair messy and black eye make-up streaked. 'Stay there, Poppaea. Stay there.'

Frances finds a second chair, drags it next to her and gently takes her hand. 'Is there any news yet?'

Poppaea shakes her head. 'Soon. They've taken so many tests. The doctor will be here soon.'

The two women assume a vigil, watching Pasquale and the mesmerizing monitors above him, their red, green and pink lines measuring his vital signs of life.

'Signorina Mazzone?' The door opens and Frances instantly recognizes the woman standing there.

'I'm Doctor Fabbiana Masina, the hospital's chief oncologist. Can we talk about Pasquale?' The word oncologist rings like a warning bell. She leans against the rail at the end of the bed, clipboard in hand. Her face is lined and tired, kindly. She speaks quietly, a contrast to her rousing speech at the rally against the dumping of toxic waste. 'The news is not good, I'm afraid.' The doctor removes her glasses and lets them dangle around her neck with a stethoscope. She props herself on the end of the bed and touches one of Pasquale's feet.

Poppaea squeezes Frances' hand.

'Leukaemia,' she says looking up at them. 'Pasquale is suffering from acute leukaemia.'

'My God!' Poppaea exclaims. 'Is he going to die?'

The doctor pauses. 'The cancer is treatable. We're going to do everything possible to help Pasquale beat this.'

'But how did he get it?' Frances asks.

'The tests have shown high levels of dioxin in his blood. I note that he grew up in Caserta. Unfortunately there is an epidemic of cancer among people from this region. Dumping of toxic waste seems to be a factor. The poisons have got into the water table and the food chain, milk, cheese and so on.'

'Mozzarella!' Poppaea exclaims. 'Pasquale always loved it, he ate it by the tonne. Then, six months or so ago, he stopped, he said it gave him stomach ache.'

'His system was probably rejecting it.'

'But I am his sister. We grew up there together, we lived in the same apartment, we ate the same food and drank the same water.'

'I would recommend you also have your blood and bone marrow tested. But cancer is a strange, unpredictable disease. Some people are susceptible and others are not. We still don't understand the reasons for that; it may even be a genetic factor.'

Poppaea leans over her brother to kiss him on his cheek. 'What's going to happen to him?'

'We will be starting him on chemotherapy as soon as possible. He is suffering acute myeloid leukaemia, and many people are cured of this disease. We can only try.'

Dr Masina stands and puts her glasses back on. 'I'm very sorry about Pasquale. Unfortunately we have many similar cases here in the hospital. But he is young and we hope he can fight this.'

Poppaea sniffs and searches for a tissue. Frances hands her one and she dabs her eyes.

'Nothing will happen for a few hours. Maybe you should go home and rest,' the doctor says.

Frances pulls Poppaea to her feet. 'Come on. I'm calling a taxi for you. I'll wait here with Pasquale. Come back when you're rested.'

As Frances sits alone with Pasquale, an eerie silence descends on the room, and she feels as if she is sitting inside a bubble, protected from the clatter and noise of the hospital. His breathing is light and even the machines seem to be paying a quiet respect. She sits back in her chair, wondering if she will ever hear his cello again and trying to think of a way to find Marcello.

She slowly drifts into sleep, and an hour or so passes before she is woken by a light tapping on the door. Camilla opens it tentatively. She walks over to the bed, touches Pasquale's hand and sits quietly next to Frances.

'How is he?'

'Not well.'

Frances hesitates to tell Camilla the truth. Her face is stripped of make-up except for lipstick and she wears a tailored pair of black pants and a plain white blouse. But she's in the mood to talk.

'I was sixteen when he was born. He was a big baby, tall like his father,' she says. 'I thought I was going to die giving birth to him. I wanted to hate him but I couldn't. I held him in my arms just the once, then he was taken away from me. The nuns strapped my breasts when my milk came in. It was agonising.'

Her voice is deadpan and Frances senses that this is the first time she has told this story.

Camilla takes hold of one of Pasquale's hands. 'I put this boy out of my mind all these years. I told myself I didn't care and I didn't want to know about him. Now, I would gladly die for him. Gladly.'

A nurse walks into the room and checks the machines around Pasquale. She picks up his medical charts from a side table and studies them. 'You'll have to go,' she says. 'No more visitors until tonight. We have to start treatment for his leukaemia.'

Camilla swallows hard. She looks from the nurse to Pasquale and then to Frances, her eyes filled with dread. 'Leukaemia? He has cancer? But he's so young!'

'Camilla, let's have a coffee. I need to talk to you.'

The hospital café is busy with harrassed-looking staff in an array of medical uniforms, patients in dressing gowns with intravenous drips in their arms, attached to mobile drip stands, and visitors, bleary-eyed and uncomfortable.

As the two women sip espressos, Frances wonders how deeply Camilla is involved in the corrupt deals and Marcello's disappearance.

'I need a cigarette,' Camilla says, her voice unusually subdued. 'But I guess this is not the place.'

Frances shakes her head and decides to take her chances. 'I'm sorry about Pasquale, but someone else he cares about is in trouble and you may be able to help.'

Camilla looks at her curiously and shrugs her shoulders.

'Marcello. Remember Marcello?'

She nods.

'He's disappeared, just like Riccardo. You won't be surprised to know we are still opposed to the new development near Vesuvius. I know you have been involved with the rezoning and . . .'

'Before you go on, I have no idea where Marcello is and I've had nothing to do with him.'

Frances shifts in her seat. 'Umberto Dragorra. You know him well, don't you?'

Camilla doesn't react.

'You have to help me! I'm sure Dragorra's involved with his disappearance!'

Camilla drains her coffee and puts the cup back firmly on the saucer and looks at her watch. 'I have to go back to the university. I will make some enquiries for you. That's the best I can do.'

'Thank you. You have my phone number. Please call me if there is any news.'

CHAPTER THIRTY-EIGHT

'Take me to Santa Lucia. The Grand Hotel.'

Camilla sits back in the leather-lined seat of her chauffeured university car and sighs deeply. Is this what being a mother does to you? Having the baby when she was little more than a child herself did not wrench her like this. She had been so determined not to let the baby get the better of her, she didn't even give him a name! Pasquale — the name suits him. His adoptive mother chose well; though, poor woman, she never lived to see him grow. But then, she didn't see him suffer either.

How ironic! Nearly thirty years on and she finds her mothering genes at last. His beautiful face and his extraordinary music had penetrated the protective armoury she had worn since the day of his birth, as nothing else ever had.

'I'm sorry, chancellor, it's a slow trip, with all the traffic,' the chauffeur apologizes.

'It's not important,' she replies, for once not in a hurry.

They pass through Via Toledo, a galaxy of shopping treasures in every window. Meaningless. She can't even be bothered looking. Finally, she has arrived to where she has always wanted to be, and she can buy anything she wants, yet she feels stripped and naked.

∾⟡∾

It was such a long time ago; the village, with everyone caught up in the grape harvest, a balmy night . . . Lorenzo was much older, in his twenties and back visiting from his job in the city; tall, muscular and with those unforgettable eyes. She had been flattered by his attention over the previous few days. Camilla hadn't been used to it and was surprised when he stole a kiss behind the huge shed in the vineyard.

That night he joined her and her friends, who had been picking the grapes. He sat with them in the café and in the piazza. When she said it was time for her to leave, he insisted on driving her home. When he pulled over into a dark picnic area she had started to object, but he was funny and playful and when he started to kiss her, she had relented.

He had taken her quickly, so much so that she wasn't sure what had happened. It hadn't hurt and it wasn't until later when she found all the sticky stuff in her panties that she started to worry.

So naïve! He had left town the next day and she had waited for him to call, fantasizing that he must be in love with her and it was only a matter of time. He never called. It wasn't until a month later when her period didn't come that Camilla had become alarmed. The skinny girl tried to ignore her growing belly for another four months, until her mother caught her vomiting one morning and dragged her to the doctor.

The village had a tried and true way of dealing with such problems. Abortions were out of the question but a closed convent in the city hosted a procession of unfortunate girls like her.

By and large, the nuns were kind in the four months she was there, as long as she attended mass daily. The girls repaid their board by cleaning, cooking and gardening the large walled garden that was bursting with citrus trees, flowers and vegetables. Camilla had regarded her growing girth with disgust and loathing, and not a day went by without her cursing Lorenzo. He had no way of knowing she was bearing his child but she now understood he wouldn't have helped if he had.

The birth had been long and painful. One of the nuns was an experienced midwife but she had called a doctor to help with Camilla's delivery. They had strapped her legs in stirrups and many hours later, when she thought she could no longer bear any more pain, she was urged to push as hard as she could. Out came her baby, a perfectly healthy boy. His eyes were closed when he was nestled, warm and sticky, on Camilla's breast. She hadn't wanted to touch him, but they left him there for half an hour or so and then he was taken away.

The girls had seen eager couples coming to the convent, chatting to the nuns, and leaving with their little bundles. Camilla heard a rumour that her son had been adopted by a family with a daughter. The mother couldn't conceive another baby. She never knew the family's name and she never asked.

∽ o ∾

It was that night, at Capodimonte, Brian's dinner. That was the night when Camilla's past came thundering back. As soon as she saw Pasquale's eyes she recognized him, and a few discreet enquiries confirmed her suspicions. Or was it a mother's intuition?

Her car pulls up in the porte-cochere of the hotel behind a line of shiny limousines. 'Wait here. I won't be long,' she tells the driver.

For as long as she had known Umberto, he had frequented the health club in the hotel and then taken his coffee while he did his business. She walks through the foyer across polished parquet floors to the lift. She gets out at the roof garden and scans the terrace. Umberto, pink and pudgy after his massage, sits cross-legged on a large cane chair reading a folder on his lap.

'Ah, Umberto, what a surprise to see you here.' She falls into the chair next to his.

'Don't give me that bullshit. What do you want?'

'As gracious as ever, I see.'

She looks around for a waiter. 'Mineral water with lime.'

'You're looking pale. Are you sick?'

'No, not at all. Just been working too hard. How have you been?'

'Busy.'

'The land development. How is that going?'

He looks at her suspiciously and puts the folder on the table in front of him. 'Universities are your business. Construction and cement are mine.'

'Except when people from my university get mixed up in your business, Mr Chairman.'

'Meaning?'

Camilla laughs. 'You have something that belongs to me, I believe.'

'To you?'

'To my university and therefore to me. What have you done with him, Umberto?'

He gazes out across the Bay of Naples to Vesuvius. 'You said yourself, that volcano may not blow for a couple of hundred years. Why do you let your people run around poking their noses in and alarming everybody? You said you'd stop them.'

'And I also said that no one was to be harmed!' she hisses. 'Don't forget, Umberto, deals can be undone!'

'You're not threatening me, are you, chancellor?'

She doesn't reply. Her water arrives and she drinks it slowly. 'No, of course I'm not threatening you, Umberto,' she says soothingly. 'But a deal is a deal. And you always say you're a man of your word.'

Umberto laughs. 'Ah Camilla, charming as ever. Of course, I don't know whom you are talking about. But I'll have a word to my associates.'

'Thank you, Umberto. I knew I could rely on you.'

A young man is playing a piano in the corner of the garden restaurant. He smiles at her as she heads back towards the lift and she recognizes a jazzy version of 'Santa Lucia'. It jogs her memory of the first time she heard Pasquale playing, busking across the road from the hotel. As she travels down in the lift she tries to hold on to that image of him. But the more she tries, the more it fades away until she can no longer picture him at all.

CHAPTER THIRTY-NINE

Do you believe in miracles?' Poppaea whispers earnestly to Frances as they sit in a pew in front of a side altar of the vast cathedral of Chiesa del Gesù Nuovo in the ancient city. In front of them people queue to touch the outstretched hand of the statue of a bespectacled, middle-aged man, wearing a Nehru jacket. Vases of fresh roses and banks of candles light the shrine of Doctor Giuseppe Moscati, canonized for miracles he was said to have performed for the sick and the poor of the city one hundred and fifty years earlier. The casket of the saint is embedded beneath the altar, a frieze of his body with hands clasped adorning its side.

Frances witnesses the raw faith of the worshippers of 'the Saint of Naples'. A teenage boy kisses the bronze hand, discoloured from countless thousands of other human contacts, then moves on. An elderly woman on a walking frame shuffles painfully into his place. She pauses, clutches the hand, and screws her eyes tightly shut. The procession continues; young, old, healthy, infirm, each praying for a personal miracle. A group stands to one side reciting the rosary quietly in unison, beads swinging in closed hands.

'That's the nature of miracles,' Frances says, 'the inexplicable. I truly hope they exist.'

Poppaea had insisted she come to the cathedral and after the gruelling weeks they had endured, she was happy to oblige. Spring is melting into summer and already the baking southern sun is taking a toll on all of their energies. The cool of the cathedral is a respite from the hot city streets and the suffocating hours spent in the hospital.

For a while, Frances began to feel she was living between two medical wards, constantly moving back and forth between Pasquale and Marcello.

After Marcello had been dumped in a dark alley like an abandoned animal, he had needed surgery on a broken arm and dislocated shoulder and treatment for a range of infected scratches and bruises. The break had occurred when his captors threw him out of the moving car. His other wounds had come from a week of rough treatment in the basement of a foul waterfront warehouse somewhere in the port. He told her he could hear the sea lapping against a wharf outside and the chatter of Chinese and Italian workers. He'd stopped crying out for help after one of the young hoods had punched his mouth and then gagged him. He had lost track of the time he was imprisoned but thought he had slept on and off for seven days and nights. One day he was blindfolded and led into a car. They had threatened to kill him, then, inexplicably, he was released, albeit violently.

It was nearly a week after Frances had spoken to Camilla that Marcello had phoned her. Maybe that's when she started to believe miracles were possible. She had been sick with worry and had felt utterly powerless. Peppe had tried all his networks but came up with nothing. Riccardo had phoned many times a day but they had agreed there was no point him coming to Naples.

Marcello's voice had sounded fractured and weak. After he was dumped, he had torn off his blindfold, stumbled to the end of the alley and recognized he was in the Spanish Quarter. He was ringing from the bar where he and Pasquale had sought information on Riccardo. Frances had just returned home from the observatory in the early evening. She had taken a taxi to the bar, where she found him filthy and in pain. When she got him to the hospital he was immediately put on a drip for hydration. But while Marcello was out of hospital and his body and spirit were healing, Pasquale's were deteriorating.

The doctors could no longer conceal their concern. He had endured the maximum levels of chemotherapy, his body now wasted and his beautiful hair fallen out clump after clump until none was left. Poppaea had hidden her tears well. She had brought his black fedora and lovingly placed it on his head while he was awake, and it sat on the bedrail when he slept.

Poppaea edges past Frances, eyes glowing as brightly as the candles, jaw determined. She had been checked and cleared of the disease herself. The cancer had bypassed her and stolen into her brother.

Frances watches her join the queue. She has brought a bunch of red and white roses, symbolizing the blood cells that were fighting a losing battle in Pasquale's body. When she reaches the head of the line, Poppaea kneels. She lays the flowers at the foot of the statue. Then she stands and stretches her arms, one hand grasping the statue, the other touching the hands on the casket. She stares into the face of the saint and then silently moves away.

CHAPTER FORTY

Pasquale knows he is dying. As he hovers in and out of consciousness he dreams, strange vivid dreams, like fairytales. Yesterday he dreamt he was in a jungle, swinging from vine to vine like Tarzan, skimming over wild beasts snapping at his heels below. He wasn't frightened; on the contrary, he felt masterful, in control. The nurses had warned him the drugs could give him hallucinations. He was never sure if the dreams were drug-induced or simply his subconscious at work. It didn't really matter either way. He liked the jungle dream; he'd always intended going to Africa and this had seemed so real it felt as if he had made the journey after all.

Now he is awake. There is no one else in his room, and he likes it that way, some space to think, without a fuss. Everyone has been so kind. Beloved Poppaea was there every day, for hours at a time, pretending to be cheerful when he could see she was always so sad. She had always put him first. It wasn't fair on her — since she was a tiny child she had been responsible for him, and now she also had to deal with the fact that they weren't even related.

His 'new' mother had been there, spinning him out and making it hard for Poppaea as well. Camilla Corsi had concentrated three decades of motherhood into three months, just in time to catch his swansong. He liked that thought. 'The Swan' was his swansong; his first and last major public performance. Still, she was trying. And she read to him in her husky voice, quite entertaining in her own way. Stories he had never heard before of ancient Roman and Greek mythology. She had been reading Homer's *The Odyssey* this week. He really liked that one, its poetic tales of the hero Ulysses blending with his dreams. There was no one to read him bedtime stories when he was small; his adoptive mother dead, his father always working and

Poppaea too young. Life's like that. You don't always get to experience ordinary things in the usual order, if at all.

His eyes travel around the room. It's large and his bed is more like one in a smart hotel than one in a hospital, with soft, white cotton sheets and large feather pillows. And there's room for his things. His cello is propped in one corner, his books on a shelf in another. Camilla had organized it for him — there was no way he or Poppaea could have afforded such luxury. He was moved from the main hospital a couple of weeks earlier to the hospice, an elegant villa located high above the city in Vomera with views to die for. He liked that idea too — views to die for. Odd how so many words for death and dying had crept into use and yet it wasn't until you were dying that you noticed. His eyesight wasn't as sharp any more, but propped up in bed, he can see the deep blue of the sea and the lighter blue of the sky. He leans forward to drink it in.

He was glad when they stopped the chemotherapy; his veins were collapsing and he couldn't take it any more. There had no longer been any point: his immune system was shot, his body was no longer responding and the leukaemia was unstoppable. It was spreading to his brain. The pain had been unbearable, and the nausea and headaches made him wretched. But here, in this place, it was all OK; they kept the morphine coming, just enough to erase the pain but not so much that he didn't know what was going on.

He runs his hand over his head, where a soft stubble is growing back. Will it have time to grow before . . . before what? The thought keeps coming back. Before he dies and goes . . . where?

Frances had been there earlier. She told him she'd gone to the cathedral to pray with Poppaea for a miracle. Imagine! He wakes the next day and the leukaemia is gone without trace. He's back with the orchestra, centre stage once more. No, he can't believe that for a second, but if it comforts Poppaea he's not going to say anything.

He loves the music soaring around his room — his mother had bought the best digital sound system on offer and it's like having a band in your room. Mother? He can say the word now quite naturally.

She had loaded all his favourites and he has the remote control right on the bed. Funny how he'd gone off Bach completely and if he had to hear 'The Swan' one more time, well, he would vomit. He had discovered jazz. Satore and Rufus had helped him choose: Miles Davis, Cleo Laine, Aretha Franklin and Count Basie. They had a lot of modern stuff too but he favoured the old greats. And then there was Chick Corea, in a class of his own. This one — Corea's string trio — fills his head. He wants to play it himself. He stares at his cello. They could do this together. He's memorized his part in his head, without actually playing one note. Satore would play violin and Rufus viola. What could they call themselves? Triple Caserta? No, sounds like an ice cream. The Toxic Trio? Sounds too much like his disintegrating body. Three Strings to a Bow? Yes, that works. So there's the name, now they will have to practise. He just needs to find the strength.

He can hear footsteps. He wonders who it might be. Probably Poppaea coming back. He'll run the name of the trio by her and see what she thinks. He wants so much to stay awake, but he feels so very, very tired.

The sea is looking bluer and bluer. He would love to swim in it, or sail across it like Ulysses. Oh, how strong he was to resist the Sirens and their beautiful songs, luring him to their island. That ancient trio — what were they called? The Slaying Sirens? They promised Ulysses, and all who sailed by their paradise, wisdom and life, but to succumb to their temptation was fatal.

Pasquale needs to sleep. He closes his eyes and a feeling of bliss envelops him; so restful, like floating in a warm bath with no pain. When he hears it, the most beautiful music he has ever heard in his life, he doesn't want to resist.

CHAPTER FORTY-ONE

The summer heat is stoking the city's rage. Throughout the metropolis and into rural Campania, people are lighting fires, trying to burn the disgusting mountains of garbage choking their streets and destroying their health.

Frances can smell the anger, as potent as the stink rising from the trash. She is losing sight of Marcello and Satore. She edges around a pile of wrecked fridges, turned on their sides and sprouting bags of foul-smelling rubbish. She glimpses the tops of the men's heads, marching ahead, shoulder to shoulder in a solid line of protesters. She tries to catch them but a crush of new protesters blocks her way.

Slipping sideways out of the pull of the crowd she rests against a wall. Dark is falling but the glow of the fires light the cobblestone streets. Sirens blare, dogs bark and she fears what the night will bring.

'Frances!' Poppaea is waving at her from across a sea of marchers as she steps into the melange of Naples humanity, unusually united against the lawlessness of Il Sistema, her blonde head bobbing towards her. Frances reaches out and pulls her to safety.

Since the funeral, the two had been swept up in a campaign fuelled by Pasquale's death. The brilliant young musician had become a cause célèbre, a victim of all that was rotten in a society where greed ruled and the lives of ordinary people counted for nothing.

The city rallied. Students, musicians, academics, doctors and lawyers joined the inhabitants of Naples, Campi Flegrei and towns around Vesuvius and beyond to raise their voices. No one wanted the talented young man from Caserta to have died in vain. Against the odds, he had risen out of poverty and achieved his dream. Struck down on the cusp of greatness, he was like the martyrs of old whose images filled every church and art gallery. But Pasquale was murdered with a weapon far more pervasive than a single spear, an axe or a gun. The weapon his assailants used was deadlier: poisons dumped in his backyard by soldiers of greed led by corrupt generals. His cancer was one of thousands attributed to toxic waste — men, women and children were riddled with tumours at rates unseen before, spreading through the population like a modern plague.

∾o∾

On the day of Pasquale's death, Frances had gone to visit him at the hospice twice. In the morning he had been lucid, cheerful and somewhat amused when she told him she had been praying for a miracle with Poppaea at the cathedral.

After a few hours' work at the observatory, she had felt an urge to see him again. The day had been particularly clear and still when she had ridden her motorbike up to the villa. She had stopped on the way to buy him some flowers, a bunch of chianti-coloured calla lilies, long-stemmed beauties that somehow reminded her of him.

She had heard the music coming from his room as she walked along the polished wooden floors of the corridor, classical jazz played louder than usual. She recognized it as one of his new favourites and had heard it many times in the previous weeks. It wasn't to her taste and she missed the classical music he had abandoned.

As she approached his room, she saw Pasquale was alone, propped up in his bed on cushions. When she called to him he hadn't looked up. Her heart skipped a beat and she hoped he was sleeping, but as soon as she saw his face, she knew he was gone. His eyes were closed and his head was drooping. He was smiling, and held an open copy of *The Odyssey* in his hand. She rested the flowers on his bedside table and had turned to look out through the open doors to where he would have been looking. The beckoning sea was bluer than she had ever seen it — vast, sparkling and azure.

She had turned back to him and touched his hand. It was still warm. She wanted to scoop him up, tell him everything would be fine. Instead, she lightly kissed his cheek, then ran out of the room to seek assistance, knowing he was beyond all help.

The cathedral was full for Pasquale's funeral. The university emptied, staff and students packing the pews. Outside the church, grief had collided with anger. Some had brought banners with painted images of Pasquale as a medieval saint, wrapped in a loincloth with cans of poisons strapped to his bare torso with barbed wire.

They had carried banners: 'Enough is Enough', 'Never Again' and 'Stop Killing Our Children'.

Frances had sat up the front with Poppaea, Satore and Rufus. Behind them was the Fogliano family, Luciana on Laura's lap, and the twins silent and still.

Camilla had arrived alone, erect, her face covered dramatically with a black mantilla. She had slid in next to Frances and spent most of the service staring at the casket in front of the altar. At the end, she had walked over to it, bent and kissed it. When a group of cellists started playing 'The Swan', Frances noticed Camilla had slipped away, leaving the church ahead of the pallbearers.

The music had soared through the barrel-shaped interior of the sixteenth-century church. Frances had looked upwards at the ceiling, richly decorated with frescoes of the communion of saints. Perhaps Poppaea was right. They might well be waiting for him.

∽o∾

The marchers are now a block ahead, heading towards the Parliament, the sound of a mass of moving feet and shouting echoing through the streets. 'I know a short cut,' Poppaea tells Frances. 'We'll be able to catch them up.'

They hurry through a labyrinth of lanes until they overtake the protesters. Ahead there is a line of police with batons and raised transparent shields spreading across the entry to the Parliament. She looks back and sees the marchers coming towards them. 'Poppaea! We can't stay here. We'll get crushed!'

The women step back into a lane as the sea of people flows by.

'There's Marcello!' Frances and Poppaea run forward and fall in step with him.

They all stop abruptly. A loud, distorted voice fills the air. They can't see her but Doctor Masina is addressing the protest. She calls for calm, tells them they can go no further, then begins to describe Pasquale's courageous struggle, urging that his legacy should be an end to the dumping of toxic waste.

'We will not take this any longer.' A new voice, male, rings out. 'Pasquale Mazzone was my friend. He never hurt anyone in his life.'

Marcello takes her arm and pulls her close. 'Satore. He's been getting ready to speak,' he whispers to her.

'Pasquale represented everything that is good in Campania. He had a big heart, a beautiful spirit and a love of art and music.' Satore sounds strong and sure and he holds the crowd. 'My friend wanted to trust in democracy, but he was betrayed. We are all being betrayed! Our leaders have forgotten what it is to be human. They are putting money ahead of our people. They are allowing our land, air and water to be poisoned and they don't even care when our children die.'

Loud applause and cheering greet his speech.

More speakers follow, calling for a general strike that would bring Campania to a halt unless the politicians pledged to end the dumping. As the last speaker finishes, a ripple of restlessness runs through the crowd. It starts to break up and Satore pushes through to them, his face flushed, sweat beading his forehead.

Suddenly, a loud roaring rises behind them.

'Look!' Poppaea screams. Fire is ripping through four buses spread across the road. The flames take hold quickly and people start pushing and shoving.

'Quick, let's get out of here!' Marcello grabs the women's hands and, with Satore, they run back into the lanes, sirens already blaring behind them. They criss-cross several city blocks but their way is blocked again. Large skips of garbage have been dragged onto the road and set alight. People linger in groups, their expressions wary and angry.

Acrid smoke floats around them and sparks crack and splinter the night air. As the four of them sidle past, Frances sees something strange dangling out of one of the smouldering skips. She stops, stunned. An arm, glowing white, hangs out from the garbage. On the middle finger is a gold signet ring. 'There's someone in there!' Frances points to the arm.

They follow her gaze. Satore goes up to one of the men watching nearby and speaks to him, then comes back to tell them, 'Fabio Dragorra. They got him at last.'

'We have to get some help.' Frances says. 'We have to get him out!'

'It's too late. He was dead when they put him there,' Satore says. 'He lived like a hyena, let him die like a hyena. He and his scum, they killed Pasquale.'

They are only metres from the arm. Frances can see an eagle's head engraved on the ring, identical to one she had seen on his father's hand.

'Marcello, what can we do? If we do nothing, we're as bad as them.'

He shakes his head. 'I'm sorry, but there's nothing we can do. That's how it is here. You live by the sword, you die by the sword.'

CHAPTER FORTY-TWO

Camilla is feeling particularly pleased. It is her forty-fifth birthday and Luigi is more attentive than ever. When she woke this morning she found a beautiful crystal vase full of roses he'd left before he had gone home to his wife, sometime after midnight.

Her appointment as Italy's youngest university chancellor is beginning to bring rewards; invitations to join the board of the city orchestra and to international symposia as well as speaking engagements at prestigious conferences on volcano research. Interest in the monitoring of Mt Vesuvius was escalating and who better than she to take this knowledge to the world?

She pads across the Persian rug to the credenza and picks up a silver-framed photo. Pasquale poses in a tuxedo, cello in hand. She kisses it, a daily habit formed not long after his funeral. How fortunate the orchestra had arranged a photo shoot before his debut. Her beautiful son — his whimsical smile offsets his wonderful eyes. They had so little time together. Yet, in spite of his declining health, she will always treasure those weeks.

The experience had changed her irrevocably. She believed that passionately. She wanted to be a better person, like him, to put her double life behind her. Well, almost all of it. Occasional exceptions in her love life didn't count, surely!

The newspaper is spread across her desk. She chuckles when she reads the headlines for the fifth or sixth time that morning.

IL SISTEMA CHIEF DRAGORRA ARRESTED IN DAWN RAID.

A photo shows two policemen escorting him into the police station, handcuffed, his face hard and defiant. Since the mass protest following Pasquale's death, the Parliament had passed new laws, cracking down on toxic waste dumping and illegal developments. The situation had become an international embarrassment and Rome's rulers were breathing down the necks of Naples' jittery politicians.

Camilla had rightly guessed that it would be only a matter of time before Umberto Dragorra's time would be up and had moved to distance herself. Now he was in the city jail, arrested on charges of dumping waste in building sites and mixing toxic waste with cement.

When unfortunate questions were raised by the Minister's office about her report on the Red Zone, she had invited the Minister to dinner and over a glass or two of the best red wine successfully persuaded him that it was all a terrible mistake. The report had been a draft copy and was awaiting public input; it was never intended to be the basis on which consent had been granted to Dragorra for his shopping centre and school. There had been an appalling bureaucratic blunder. Work on the development had ground to a halt.

'Chancellor, excuse me for interrupting.'

Her new assistant taps lightly on the door and walks in. Romeo is still in his twenties but had shown immediate promise.

'The news is about to start. You wanted me to remind you . . .'

'Thank you, Romeo. Please, go ahead.'

Picking up a remote control, he turns on a large new plasma screen attached to a wall in the office.

'There, it's just starting.' He smiles at her as the music for the noon bulletin starts.

'Perfect. Thank you.' She watches his svelte body leave her office and thanks the stars she had given the annoying Maria her marching orders. She settles back into her large chair.

Umberto's arrest is leading the bulletin. The newsreader says his lawyer is about to make a statement and throws to a reporter on the steps of the police station who introduces a bald, bespectacled man.

'My client is completely innocent of these charges,' he says. 'He will fight them to the end.'

As he finishes, a woman with curly blonde hair steps into the frame, her heavily made-up face and impossibly long eyelashes filling the screen. 'I wish to say something.' Her voice reveals heavy traces of a Sicilian accent and her large breasts are well-displayed by a plunging neckline.

'Umberto Dragorra is a good man. I know he is innocent. I have known him for more than six months and I am bearing his child. He has promised to leave his wife and I trust he will do the right thing by me, as I will do the right thing by him. I love you, Umberto!' She blows a kiss into the camera lens.

Camilla can't stop smiling. She even feels a little sorry for Umberto. They had enjoyed some good times. And she was about to have many more!

There had been news too of old Alfonso. He had survived his stroke and was in a rehabilitation hospital. His wife had taken the opportunity of escaping for a few months' holiday with some family at Lake Como. Rumour was that she might not return.

All in all it is shaping up to be a wonderful day. She is feeling magnanimous towards her Progetto Vulcano team, even that pest, Riccardo Cocchia, on Stromboli. She had opened the coffers of the university wider to give them the resources they needed and today is the day to give them the good news. Maybe she'll surprise them after lunch.

She opens a small wardrobe in the corner of her office and pulls out the clothes she once wore when she worked in the field. When she lays them on the sofa they look a tad old-fashioned but they were expensive classics and she hasn't put on a centimetre so they will fit her still. Removing her shoes and suit and silk blouse and hanging them carefully in the wardrobe, she slides into a pair of tailored jeans, a fitted white shirt and a navy jacket. She considers the suede trekking boots but quickly dismisses the idea and puts on her high-heeled shoes again. She regards herself in the full-length mirror attached to the inside of the wardrobe door.

Not quite to her taste but at the observatory she would fit in just fine.

'I'm going to the observatory for a few hours, Romeo. I'll drive my own car,' she tells her assistant as she leaves, smiling with some satisfaction as she notices him furtively looking her up and down. Camilla strolls, relaxed and happy, out of the university and crosses the road towards the car park. She stops on the other side of the road and turns around. *Ad Scientiarvm Havsvm Et Seminarivm Doctrinarvm.*

The engraved ancient mission statement is burning down at her from its position above the entrance. She feels as if she's been struck by Neptune's fork. This is what she was destined for, and how she will honour the memory of her son, who had brought such unexpected joy into her life. She would revere the pledge.

In the past she had been guilty of omission, but beneath it all she was still a scientist, born to honour research and the truth. Her journey to the top had meant sacrifices and short cuts but there was plenty of time to remedy matters. No more nepotism, no more political favours. Chancellor Camilla Corsi would be remembered in the history of Naples as The Reformer.

CHAPTER FORTY-THREE

Frances can't believe her eyes. The microphones she planted on the summit of Stromboli are sending in the strongest vibrations she has ever seen from a volcano. The message is clear: the main vent is exploding.

She grabs her mobile and punches in Riccardo's number. There's no reply. She tries Olivia. No answer. She rings the switchboard at the island's observatory. The call rings out.

Her eyes flit across the other monitors filling the nerve centre of the Naples Observatory. The seismographs recording movement on Stromboli are going crazy, the zig-zag lines leaping up and down the screens.

Out of the corner of her eye she glimpses the water in her drinking glass washing from one side to the other. The glass starts to rattle on the desk then falls off, smashing on the floor.

'When Stromboli coughs, Vesuvius sneezes.' Riccardo's words ring in her ears. Like a chain reaction, the monitors from one end of the room to the other start convulsing in concert, the jerking lines on each revealing a swarm of earthquakes stretching from deep in the Tyrrhenian Sea through to Campi Flegrei, the Campanian Ignimbrite and on through to Vesuvius.

As Frances reaches to push a red alarm button, the room starts to shake and plunges into darkness. She pushes the button but there is no sound. Dropping to the floor she crawls around the room, fumbling until she finds her backpack propped against a wall. Putting it across her shoulders, she moves on all fours to the space beneath the doorway and stops to listen. Voices, crying and shouting echo around her. People are running in the distance and a low rumble makes her tremble. But she can't see a thing. Her stomach heaves as the building sways and she feels as if she's in the hull of a ship as it rides a huge wave.

Her phone rings and she prises it out of her pocket. 'Frances, thank God. Are you all right?'

She sits against the door-jamb, hugging her knees, shaking. Beads of sweat slide down her face and she wipes them with her sleeve. 'Marcello!' Her voice sounds hollow, shrill. 'I'm at the observatory. The whole place is shaking but I'm OK. Where are you?' She bites her lip as she listens, trying not to alarm him but wanting to reach through the phone and hold him.

'On the tangenziale, going to see Nonno. But the earthquake — the whole road is shaking and cracking. I've abandoned my car. Everyone has. People are running. I'm going to try to walk cross-country to my grandfather's house.'

'Be careful, Marcello. I'll try to get there.'

'Frances, I . . .'

'I can't hear you. Marcello?'

The phone has died and Frances feels utterly alone. The building has stopped shaking and all is quiet. She stands and pulls off her backpack, groping inside for a torch and a water bottle. When she shines the light up and down the empty corridor it flickers on wall posters and closed doors. Nothing seems damaged. She flicks a light switch but the power is off. Her watch says one thirty-five — everyone must have left the building for lunch. She walks slowly along until she reaches a water cooler. She drinks all of her own water then refills the bottle. Three empty bottles have been discarded in a bin so she fills them and stuffs them into her bag.

Hearing voices nearby she turns into the hall leading to the entrance, where she sees a dozen or so people crammed beneath the doorway. She wriggles between them, out into the full glare of the summer sun. At first she struggles to see anything, then notices more people standing in groups outside the observatory, strangely quiet.

'Signorina, it's not safe!' a man shouts to her.

She waves at him but continues walking to the car park at the rear of the building. A pile of rubble blocks her way. The back half of the observatory has crumbled. Desks and chairs dangle precariously in offices smashed and open to the air like a doll's house. Satellite dishes have fallen from the rooftop to the ground, broken amid a tangled mess of wires. Frances clambers over the wreckage, avoiding large jagged pieces of glass. Many cars are buried beneath her, flashes of red, silver and blue revealing their presence. She searches at the far end of the car park until she finds her motorbike, lying on its side among the surviving vehicles.

She starts to run, ignoring the sirens screaming all around. Picking up the bike she guns the throttle and it bursts into life. A thick pall of dust hovers in the air. Her helmet is back in the building but she retrieves sunglasses and a large handkerchief from her bag. With the checked cloth tied around her face, she drives cautiously through a rear gateway.

The streets are like obstacle courses, cracked and blocked in places by piles of rocks and debris. As she passes the pizzaria she glimpses her work colleagues sheltering in the entry, and feels a pang of guilt for leaving. But Marcello needs her more right now. And she needs him.

She heads towards the tangenziale, weaving in and out of the mounds and cracks. There is little traffic as the roads are almost impassable, with only a few earthmovers clearing the way for rescue crews.

Smoke rises from an apartment building ahead where children's cries greet her and she slows. Families are crowded out the front, watching helplessly as their homes collapse before their eyes, raining concrete, glass and iron. Somehow, an ambulance has forced its way through and paramedics are treating people lying on the ground, their faces and arms cut and bloodied.

Frances is torn but knows she can do little here. She drives on, passing lines of people, staring dazed at one damaged building after another like survivors of a bombing raid. They seem in shock and don't look back as her motorbike breaks an eerie silence. No birds sing. No dogs bark.

When she reaches the highway she stops abruptly. The road is a car park. As far as she can see in both directions, cars have stopped and people are walking and running along the road. Forced to slow to almost walking pace, she ventures on slowly, at times having to edge between narrow gaps separating cars and trucks.

She gasps when she sees the road ahead — buckled and twisted like a leather belt. Cars have been tossed off the edge and lie upside down. Fire is sweeping through grass and trees and a petrol tanker lying on its side appears to have exploded and ignited several cars. At every turn, she sees people wandering confused and lost.

A large military helicopter flies overhead. It circles then descends, landing close to the tanker. A dozen or so soldiers jump from the chopper and spread around the burning cars, searching for survivors.

Frances eases her bike off the road onto a siding as far away as possible from the fire. She drives over rough terrain, dodging rocks and broken glass, until the road ahead of her is intact. She rides the tangenziale again, curious as to why this section is empty of vehicles. In the distance she sees trucks and cars stopped and can't work out why, speeding now, the wind gusting through her hair and pushing the handkerchief tight against her face.

All of a sudden she sees a huge chasm ahead has split the highway in half making it impassable. People are lined up on the edge of the far side. She screeches to a halt metres from the massive hole and hops off her bike, fixing it on its stand. The only one on this side, she is facing a small crowd on the other, some twenty metres or so away, all peering into the abyss.

She follows their gaze and, for a moment, thinks she must be dreaming. A woman in jeans and a shirt is standing on top of a crushed silver Smart car and calling for help. When Frances hears the voice she knows she is fully awake. 'Camilla?' Frances shouts down.

The woman looks up at her. 'Frances! Thank goodness! Tell them to get me out of this hellhole! Quickly!' Her husky voice echoes, as strong and commanding as ever and apparently unscathed by her brush with death. 'I rang the Minister directly and asked for help. But the phone went dead so I don't know what's happening!'

Before Frances has time to answer, another helicopter hovers noisily overhead. A soldier in army greens and a helmet drops down on a rope onto the bonnet of the car. He clips a harness around Camilla and holds her tightly as the helicopter rises again.

As the two of them float above her, something drops back into the chasm. 'My shoes! I've dropped my best shoes,' Camilla bellows. The crowd cheers and whistles as Camilla, her feet bare and wriggling, and the beaming soldier are winched into the chopper. It circles one more time then flies swiftly away. 'So much for our team leader,' Frances thinks. 'Probably heading to the nearest hairdresser.'

But she has more to worry about. The road has collapsed and she must get to the other side. She stands there, perplexed, trying to see a route through and decides there is only one option. Mustering all her strength, she manoeuvres the bike down the shoulders of the highway. Her feet skid and slip on loose gravel and she pulls hard to stop the bike tumbling away from her. Step by step she edges around the chasm to the other side. She reaches another mound of debris, bitumen and rocks compressed together. Dropping onto it, exhausted and sweating, she guzzles a bottle of water.

The ground suddenly moves beneath her. Another earthquake, this one small and quick, ripples around her. Above, people on the road cry out.

She tries to phone Riccardo again but there is no signal and she wonders if Stromboli is still erupting. She rests a few minutes longer, fearing more aftershocks that could cause even greater havoc and knows she has to keep going. She drags herself up and starts the hard ascent with the bike to the road. As she nears the top, she sees cars and trucks stretching into the distance. Most of them have been abandoned. Those who have stayed look tired and anxious yet appear to have banded together.

'The army is coming to get us out. I just heard on the radio,' a truck driver calls out. 'Hey, let me help you!' the driver says spotting her. He slides down to her and heaves the bike up easily and leans it against his truck.

'Thanks. Thanks so much.'

'Where on earth are you going?' The man stands, square and stocky, dirt stained hands on hips, appraising her.

'Got to help a friend, he's stranded in one of the villages.'

'We're all stranded,' he laughs. 'But I'm not leaving my rig. We've got food.' He indicates a bucket of oranges on the ground, 'and some water. I'm staying here for as long as it takes for them to clear the road. I'll go backwards or forwards. It doesn't matter.'

'Maybe if there's another big shake, you'll be going up there,' another driver points to the sky, 'or down there, to Hades.'

'Whatever will be, will be. *Carpe diem.*'

He lifts the flap on the back of his truck and brings out another bucket of oranges.

'Take some,' he says. 'From my cousin's farm in Sorrento. Buono! Beautiful! I was taking them to Rome, but now?'

She takes two and he grabs a third. He peels it quickly and puts the soft fruit into her hand. She bites into it, the sweet juice quenching her thirst and soothing her dry throat. The driver passes the bucket to the others gathered on the road. 'Eat some more! Come on, my friends. Eat while you have the chance.'

'Madonna, it might be the last piece of fruit we ever eat in our lives!' the other driver exclaims.

'Well, at least you will die knowing you have tasted the nectar of the gods, the sweetest oranges in the world.'

'I have to get going,' Frances says. 'Does anyone need a lift out?'

They shake their heads. 'No, we're staying with our cars, we don't want them to be looted. But do you have any spare water?'

She removes her second last bottle from her bag and hands it to him.

'Grazie, thank you. Travel safely, signorina.'

Frances drives easily now, travelling around the edges of the banked-up cars and sometimes switching to the middle of the road. Soon she reaches the exit ramp leading to Nonno's village. It is clogged with cars and people walking in the opposite direction, towards Naples. She remembers the footsteps of the Bronze Age people captured in the ash. How little things change! And do we know any more than they did? The breeze has picked up and she recalls the wind report, predicting the direction of pyroclastic flows from the volcano.

She stops to stare at the mountain, brooding and stark before her. What if? She dismisses the danger and drives on. Every road is jammed with cars. She wonders if the Civil Defence has started to evacuate the villages. If it has, the result will be disastrous. If Vesuvius does erupt . . . She puts the idea out of her head.

The farms and houses on the outskirts of Nonno's village appear untouched by the earthquake and she is relieved to find his cottage undamaged when she pulls up outside. The door is open but she taps on it lightly anyway and pokes her head in.

Marcello is sitting cross-legged on the floor and looks up startled.

'Frances!' He leaps up and holds her tightly. She hugs him close and when she kisses his cheek she tastes his tears.

'What's wrong?'

He says nothing but takes her by the hand inside. 'It's Nonno. He's gone.'

'Gone?'

'Dead. I just found him.' He inclines his head towards the bedroom.

Frances walks to the doorway. Nonno is lying on his bed, dressed in his worn suit with the photo of Teresa in his hands. She pauses to look at the body of the old man whose life had been so rich and full and yet one he had been ready to leave behind. So different to Pasquale, his young life so brutally snatched away. The colour has drained from Raphaele's face, leaving it pale but serene.

Marcello moves past her and pulls a blanket over him. 'Poor Nonno. He never recovered from my grandmother's death.'

'I'm so sorry, Marcello.'

'I think he died peacefully. I've called the doctor but with the earthquake, I'm not holding my breath that he will be here soon.'

A loud cracking and crashing noise interrupts them.

'It's coming from Dragorra's development.'

Marcello locks the door of Nonno's cottage and they run through the vineyard to the top of the rise. Below them the massive concrete slab has broken in two as though someone had thrust a giant knife through it.

'The earthquake. It must have been built across a faultline.'

'Or divine retribution perhaps?' Marcello says.

As they stand together, hands linked, another aftershock ripples around them. The half-built walls of the shopping centre crumble and fall with a terrific roar.

CHAPTER FORTY-FOUR

*T*wo thousand nine hundred dead, ten thousand injured and three hundred thousand homeless.

Camilla reads aloud a summary of the earthquake's impact like a shopping list.

The first jolt measured 7.2 on the Richter scale and there were ninety aftershocks. Two villages in Campania almost completely destroyed, including a medieval church. Dozens of buildings in Naples collapsed including four apartment buildings. Pozzuoli lost three apartment buildings. Two hotels on the coast of Campi Flegrei fell into the sea.

She paces the room in her now familiar casual garb, her finger stabbing the air as she addresses the members of the Progetto Vulcano team. 'That was on the mainland. Signor Cocchia, what was the damage on Stromboli?'

'Two killed from rockfalls after the first eruption — tourists climbing near the summit. Three fishermen died when an avalanche of hot tephra rushed down to the sea and engulfed their boat. Severe damage to the Stromboli Observatory and twelve houses destroyed, including my granduncle's. Ash infiltration was extreme, covering the village, but the islanders are getting on with the clean-up with great optimism.'

Riccardo talks on the conference phone, his Italo-Australian accent filling the meeting room of the temporarily relocated Naples Observatory. His voice is warm and familiar and Frances remembers how grateful she was to hear it when she had finally managed to contact him, a full day after the earthquake. Stromboli had erupted continuously for twenty hours and communications with the island had been impossible. It wasn't until the Civil Defence helicopters had flown in that she was able to talk to him on their satellite phones.

Riccardo and Olivia had been eating lunch with Gaetano when the volcano had violently exploded and they had run outside to see a volley of massive rocks and fire shooting out of the crater. They had sheltered beneath the doorways until a huge fiery rock had crashed onto the roof, setting the old house alight. With the rest of the village they had fled to the beach, staying there until the explosions stopped, many hours later.

Riccardo's humour had survived while the house had not. He told her how the three had celebrated their survival with his new invention, a Tim Tam Sambuca Slam, made from a few of his precious chocolate biscuits and some shots of the aniseed liqueur. He had hollowed out the biscuits with a knife and they used them like straws to suck the liqueur, devouring the alcohol-softened biscuits afterwards. Frances loved his knack of turning adversity to advantage.

Back in Naples, it had been the darkest of days, as death hung in many doorways and lurked along the roadsides. Her own apartment building had escaped unscathed and the Fogliano family was unharmed. Evidence was emerging that the newer constructions had fared the worst, raising the spectre of unsafe and illegal building practices.

Thousands of people fleeing in cars were trapped, caught in columns of traffic, unable to move. Forty had died from heart attacks and it had taken two weeks for the emergency services to clear the roadways.

✤

The vulcanologists worked around the clock, restoring damaged monitors around the region and closely watching the impact of every tremor. On Vesuvius, the earthquake appeared to have had little impact. The rocky plug blocking the volcano's vent was intact. Some of the fumaroles had been pumping out more gas than usual, but all the vulcanologists could do was watch and wait. As far as they could tell, the magma lake below the region was stable, though no one was game to give guarantees.

'If there's any upside at all, it's that we have discovered the weaknesses in our evacuation planning,' Camilla continues. 'As well as running the university, I will be keeping a personal eye on a complete restructure of the Civil Defence organization and a tightening up on building in the Red Zone.'

Frances looks closely at Camilla, ever the chameleon. Strangely, her newly acquired zeal for serving the public good suited her. 'It is vital that we have a new emergency plan so if Vesuvius erupts, we can evacuate people as quickly as possible.'

She turns her attention to Frances, flashing her a rare smile. 'Signorina Nelson. Frances. I would like to thank you for your contribution to Progetto Vulcano by improving all of our early warning systems. I understand you will be leaving at the end of your contract. I hope you will come back to us soon.'

CHAPTER FORTY-FIVE

The bubbles swirl around her, hot streams of them popping out from the seabed just below. Marcello pulls her arm and she swims after him, kicking her flippers hard to keep up. There has been movement since their last dive here. Aftershocks from the massive earthquake had rippled through the town of Baia and split a huge cliff face supporting a new hotel complex. It had all slid into the sea. Below the waves, the debris had piled up, nudging against the ruins of the Roman Empire's pleasure palaces.

They had been searching for half an hour, their sentimental quest made more difficult by the rock shifts and swirling currents. She had begun to doubt that they would ever find the portrait again.

She catches Marcello as he slows and runs his hands over the bottom. He turns, excited, and beckons her down. Her face gazes at them through the turquoise water. Venus, the goddess of love has survived yet another earthly cataclysm. Her mysterious smile configured from the tiny mosaic tiles is intact, her almond-shaped eyes unblinking. Seagrass has sprouted through the yellow chips that form her golden neck chain. Marcello plucks them out. He removes a roll of thick blue plastic attached to the weight belt around his waist and spreads it across the mosaics, securing it firmly into the rock with sharp metal pegs. He was adamant that they wouldn't risk losing the submerged treasure a second time and intended to return and remove it so it could be preserved for all time.

Many weeks had passed since the earthquake and as the time came closer for Frances to leave, both of them had thought often of the woman at the bottom of the sea and wondered if she had continued to realize her immortality. Frances is happy that she has, feeling her survival might prolong her connection to Marcello.

She was leaving Italy with mixed emotions. Her contract was up and she was being called to another wild volcano, where her skills were needed on the increasingly unpredictable slopes.

Marcello points up, signalling an end to the dive. She follows him slowly, pinching her nose and feeling her ears pop as they swim to the surface. They remove their respirators and use their snorkels to swim to shore.

The water along the beach is warmed by the volcanic activity and people float in it, laughing, gossiping and seemingly unworried by the continuous threat to the entire coastline.

The weight of the air tanks pulls on her as Frances wades out of the water. She flicks off her weight belt and Marcello helps her remove her tanks. They strip off their wetsuits and carry their equipment to the dive shop above the beach where they shower and change.

The hot afternoon sun bears down as they stroll hand in hand through the town of Baia, along the narrow street of shops behind the harbour front, past cafés where couples eat gelati and sip coffee.

Rising in front of them are the golden brick ruins of an ancient Roman building.

'The Temple of Venus,' Marcello says. 'Except it wasn't really a temple at all but a huge Roman bathhouse.' Octagonal with huge arched windows, the edifice has defied yet another searingly destructive earthquake. Modern buildings around it haven't fared as well — cracks streak through their walls like jagged bolts of lightning.

Marcello guides her around the ruins to a plaque embedded into one wall.

Frances reads the inscription aloud. '*Anima feli vivas*. What does it mean?'

'Live happily.' He smiles at her and kisses her lips.

'That's beautiful. I don't think anyone could wish for more.'

'And I don't know if I can be happy if you leave, Frances.'

She puts her arms around his neck and meets his eyes.

'Nor me,' she whispers.

They walk to the edge of the town, content in each other's company, neither speaking, neither wanting to break the spell of Venus. The road rises steeply and they climb to the top where it bends sharply.

They scramble through a low wooden fence to a clearing, where a white marble statue of a child stands in the centre of a well-tended garden, surrounded by a low clipped hedge. The voluminous folds of the girl's dress are intricately sculpted around her slim form. Her air is melancholy and in one hand extended into the air she holds a butterfly.

Frances moves closer but reels back when she sees her eyes. 'They're the same as Pasquale's — not the colour but the expression. Eyes of infinity.' She runs her fingers over the girl's hand.

'She was the daughter of the Emperor Claudius, struck down by illness,' Marcello tells her. 'This portrays her at the moment of her death, when life departs. The butterfly represents her soul, released by her body as she accepts her death.'

Frances remembers the serene expression she saw on her friend's face after he died. 'Just like Pasquale.'

They walk through the clearing to a park bench overlooking a steep limestone cliff across the Gulf of Naples to Vesuvius, and sit side by side, gazing at the volcano.

'This is near where Pliny watched Vesuvius erupt,' he says. 'It was seventeen years after a major earthquake had devastated Pompeii.'

'Was that earthquake our warning? Is that what lies ahead?'

He squeezes her hand but does not reply.

Frances closes her eyes and soaks in the warmth of the sun. A year has passed since she had come to this ancient land where people lived just as uneasily with the forces of nature as their ancestors had thousands of years earlier.

She starts as something runs across her foot and glances down to see a tiny green lizard, the same species that had thrived here for millennia, sliding away into a thicket of trees.

As she looks again towards the volcano, the sun blinds her.

Through the glare, she imagines a massive mushroom-shaped cloud rising above Vesuvius. But in a moment, the illusion fades along with the sun. An umbrella pine on the cliff edge is silhouetted against the sky, its branches spreading like tendrils across the land of fire.

THE END